The beginning of [illegible]

A virgin landmass is ‘extruded [illegible] a solar-tidal magmatic pulse. Waiting to claim the emerging island are 80 people in a flotilla of trussed up barges with supplies to last a year.

Who are these accidental tourists?

How did they know the island would be surfacing?

And what do they plan to do with it *if* their claim to sovereignty is accepted by the world community?

Racy and thought-provoking, The O.D. paints a picture of how humanity’s rush to self-destruction could be halted, given the global will to take a colossal leap… *backwards.*

ISBN-13:978-1499158465
ISBN-10:1499158467

Cover by TJ Miles.

The O.D.

Chris James

For my brother, Wyatt

The world is undergoing immense changes. Never before have the conditions of life changed so swiftly and enormously as they have changed for mankind in the last fifty years. We have been carried along - with no means of measuring the increasing swiftness in the succession of events. We are only now beginning to realize the force and strength of the storm of change that has come upon us.

– H. G. Wells, The Open Conspiracy, 1928

PART ONE

I

May Day. Penwith, Cornwall. Black sky afternoon. A lone jackdaw battled the wind overhead, while a lanky figure on a bicycle did the same under Rosewall Hill.

Neither bike nor rider was well put together. The cycle jangled over the road's rough surface like a tambourine in a tumble dryer. The long body of the rider was stooped at the spine and punctuated at the head by a prominent nose. With the wind hitting him from the side, it was all the cyclist could do to stay upright.

Lonnie Pilot, twenty-five years old and prematurely grey, had just spent three hours in the library reading *The History of Human Migration.* Every day, he would take to the hills to digest his morning's intake and burn off nervous energy.

As Pilot pedalled south towards Nancledra, a grey 4 x 4 joined him at Cold Harbour and fell in behind. He moved to his left to allow the vehicle to pass, but as it came alongside, it slowed. Pilot looked over at the driver, then wobbled as his front wheel hit a stone. He dismounted. The car stopped and an electric window whirred down. "Lonnie Pilot." The wind almost blew away the driver's words. He held out a business card. Pilot squinted to read it.

IGP

Forrest Vaalon

Director

Institute for Geophysical Projections

"Your grandfather and I were friends and work colleagues and I need to talk to you. Please get in the car. It's a job offer, Lonnie. Put your bike in the back and I'll explain."

Pilot peered in at the driver as he weighed the man's words. It was the reference to his grandfather, not the employment bone he had been thrown, that caught his interest. He didn't remember much about his paternal grandfather, only that he had been an oceanographer at the Hydrographic Office in Bath. Pilot had come across the IGP more than once in his studies, and the fact that his grandfather and the man in the car once worked together was good enough for him. He lifted his bike into the boot as invited, got in the car, and sized up his host. The way the man was folded into his seat with knees sticking up at an acute angle said *tall.* The parchment skin and snow-white hair said *old.* The accent said *American.* Forrest Vaalon put the car in gear and drove off at a speed Pilot thought inappropriate for Cornish back roads.

"Before he got sick, " Vaalon began, "during his last year at the Hydrographic Office, your grandfather helped us research a particular theory we were developing. In our downtime, we'd talk about our families. What he said about *you* stayed with me. But it wasn't until eight years ago that something happened to bring you back into the frame. I've been keeping tabs on you ever since."

Pilot wondered what had been so interesting to have required ongoing espionage. "You've been spying on me since I was *seventeen*?"

Vaalon reduced speed. "I never thought of it as *spying*," he said. "More like monitoring – with a view to mentoring. I'll explain when we stop." Pilot watched the stone walls and Butcher's Broom flying past his window, then glanced again at the driver, trying to make sense of the strange scenario in which he found himself.

"What can you tell me about solar tides?" Vaalon asked.

Pilot drew a blank. "Solar *tides*? I know solar winds and solar flares, but *tides*?" Pilot closed his eyes and sat in silence around two bends in the road, rifling through his stored memory before recovering the answer. "About two years ago *Science* magazine published an article by the IGP on solar magnetics."

"And?"

Travelling in a strange person's car was not conducive to easy recall for Lonnie Pilot. "The gist of their… *your* theory will come to me in a minute."

Vaalon smiled, but gave no prompts. Soon, pieces of the article came out of the shadows into Pilot's working memory. "The title of your thesis was *Solar Tides and Magma Displacement*," he said.

"*Solar Tides and Magmatic Attraction.* Near enough."

"You believe that the Sun has a heartbeat – a regular pulse of magnetism capable of moving the Earth's magma."

"Well retrieved, Lonnie. Sixteen years ago your grandfather researched the properties of the Earth's crust as a sub-strand to our main premise. But it was another fourteen years before the final pieces came together and we were able to publish." Pilot's eyes widened at this piece of family history that had been unknown to him. "Next pub, we'll stop."

When they parked up at The Engine Inn, Vaalon took a briefcase from the back seat and led Pilot into the pub. "Mine's an orange juice," he said, pressing a ten pound note into Pilot's hand. "Have whatever you want, Lonnie."

"What's this job offer of yours, Mr. Vaalon?" Pilot asked, setting the drinks on the table a few minutes later.

"Call me Forrest. I'll come to the job in a minute. Explain the Sun to me first."

"*Explain* the Sun?"

"Yes. The way you'd explain it to one of your pupils."

Pilot felt uncomfortable being put on the spot by a man with such lofty scientific credentials, but rose to the challenge. "Okay. It's mostly hydrogen… some helium. Hot plasma interwoven with magnetic fields. It radiates charged particles across the Solar System – solar wind. The Sun rotates faster at its equator than at its poles and this causes the Sun's magnetic field lines to twist together, creating magnetic field loops that erupt from the Sun's surface. Solar flares and sunspots are caused by the Sun's strong magnetic field, which –"

"Do you know what the Thompson spiral is?" Vaalon asked.

"The *Thompson* spiral? No. Is it like the Parker spiral?"

"Similar. But this one occurs when the sun's rotation twists the magnetic field of the heliospheric sheet into overlapping knots of nuclear ferment – the Thompson spiral, named after the man who discovered it. Edgar Thompson used to work for me. And towards the end of his life, his work led him from the heliosphere down into the very core of the Sun itself, and to his theory of Solar Tides." Pilot sat frozen like a gundog. "Thompson hypothesized that this solar pulse, or heartbeat as you described it, occurs at regular intervals every 5,000 years or so. So powerful is each event, that the magnetic *explosion* it creates is capable of exerting a magnetic pull on the iron component of the Earth's magma – similar to the way the Moon's gravitational pull moves the oceans. He called this phenomenon the Solar Tide, or *magmatic pulse*. It was only a theory, of course, and Thompson died before we were able to prove it."

"You've *proved* it? I don't remember *that* in the article."

Vaalon's expression changed from conversational to conspiratorial. "I had my reasons for keeping the proof *out* and leaving it as just a theory," he said. "Before the end of today, you'll know why."

The two men sipped their respective drinks, their eyes locked together like magnets. Vaalon picked up a beer mat in his left hand. "This is the Earth's crust. And this," he said, placing the knuckles of his right hand under the mat, "is the magma. Thompson propounded that, where the Earth's crust is at its thinnest, under the sea, the pull of the solar tide on the magma is capable of lifting it in specific areas by hundreds of metres relative to mean sea level – like this…" He rotated his right hand until the knuckle of his middle finger caused the mat to rise.

"And the proof?"

"In the back of my car."

Vaalon set his briefcase on the table and opened it. "The *magmatic pulse* has never been witnessed by current humanity," he said, "but Thompson's premise was that magmatic pulses have been occurring at regular intervals since the Earth was formed." He shuffled through some files and extracted a photograph of a machine that looked like a dental X-ray gun, but twenty times larger, hanging from a gantry over a ship's side. "Do you know what this does?"

Pilot studied the picture, then hazarded a guess. "It measures the thickness of the Earth's crust."

"Precisely. To develop it cost a small fortune, which I could spare. Excuse me a minute. Enlarged prostate." Vaalon rose and headed off to the gents. While he was away, Pilot sat swirling his cider, wondering if *he*, and not the strange American with, it seemed, limitless wealth, were the lunatic. Five minutes later, Vaalon was back.

"So, what did your *crust caliper* divulge?" Pilot asked.

"During its 30,000 mile voyage, it identified twenty sites of interest – sections of continental shelves worldwide under which the Earth's crust is thin or weak. To prove the magmatic pulse theory, we had to prove that those sections of continental shelf had been above water at the 5,000 year increments Thompson theorized."

"How did you do that?"

"I'll show you. Let's go."

Out at the car, Vaalon raised the rear hatch and pointed to something on the floor of the boot next to Pilot's bike. It was a cylindrical, cement-like pole about four feet long and three inches in diameter, with tags attached at regular points along its length.

"Bore sample?" Pilot asked, running his finger along the surface.

"We bored eight of the twenty sites, but this one from the European continental shelf off Brest was always the most promising, due to its unique geological profile. This length represents the past 25,000 years only. I can show you photographs of deeper sections going back

200,000 years, but this one contains all you need to know. Read the tags."

Pilot ran his hand down the rough surface of the sample to the first discoloured ring. It was tagged *S.T. XXIX* and showed two B.C.E. dates spanning around 400 years. Ten inches further along was another discoloured ring, tagged *S.T. XXX*, with more dates, then two more tags – *S.T. XXXI* and *S.T. XXXII*.

"S.T.... *Solar Tide*?" Pilot asked. "And the two dates... the period of time the shelf spent out of the water?"

"An approximation, yes. We have readings going back to 187,462 B.C.E.. The first date on each tag is the important one – when the shelf came up, not when it went down again." Pilot did some quick mental calculations, subtracting the second date from the first, the third from the second and the fourth from the third. The answer to all three was 5,857 years.

"What do you think, Lonnie?"

"What do *I* think? It's incredible. Has anybody else seen this outside of the IGP?"

A faint smile appeared at the corners of Vaalon's mouth. "Not yet. We will publish when we're ready."

Pilot stared at the tags and numbers for a few seconds before it hit him. "S.T. 33 is happening *this year*."

"This August," Vaalon said. "Stay with that supposition, Lonnie. I'll expand over dinner."

Small talk wasn't one of Pilot's gifts, but on the drive back to Penzance he made an effort. "Where are you from, Forrest?"

Vaalon slowed the car to a conversational speed. "I was born in New Mexico. My father had dropped out there in the twenties while waiting to inherit – a pre-hippy by forty years. When I was eight, his father died and we moved to New York. I have a house there and homes in London, Geneva and Dubrovnik. I'm building a retirement ranch in New Mexico. That landscape from my formative years is in my blood."

"When do you plan to retire?"

"Never."

"Are you married, Forrest?"

"Fifty-two years. To Ruth." Pilot noticed a grimace pass over the man's face. "Due to a severe trauma when she was young, Ruth was never able to have children, so we threw ourselves into other things. My *child* was earth sciences and Ruth's was Scholasticorps, the educational charity."

"That's hers?" Pilot was impressed.

"She founded it in 1962 when she learned she'd never have children of her own. Her other interest was matchmaking, which she turned into a science." Vaalon chuckled. "Part of her Jewish heritage. I'll tell you about that another time. This next bit is important. In addition to our separate pursuits, we had one common one. An intense and passionate desire to save the world. To most people that sounds trite."

"No. I'm with you *there*."

"I know. That's why I'm with you *here*." Vaalon concentrated on some tricky manoeuvring for the next three minutes, his over-wide vehicle brushing both hedgerows in some places. "Getting back to the *Vaalon Plan*," he said when the road had straightened and widened, "the physical health of the planet was my area and Ruth concentrated on its social maladies. I set up the Institute for Geophysical Projections the same year Ruth founded Scholasticorps. Since then, we've also funded over a hundred think tanks, social action projects, scientific research programmes and environmental groups." There had been a gradual change in Pilot's affect, which Vaalon must have noticed. "What is it, Lonnie?" he asked.

"I'm sorry to interrupt, but… the job offer? Is it in research?"

"No, not research. More along the lines of *head of state*. That's the only way I can describe it at the moment."

"Head of state…" Pilot peered at Vaalon's profile, trying to read between the lines of his face.

"You have no idea what I'm talking about, do you, Lonnie?"

"Not a clue." Pilot was consternated. "Can I ask you a question, Forrest? Why is someone like *you* talking to someone like *me* in the backwaters of Cornwall? I can't figure out why you're here."

"Your isolation at the toe-end of Britain actually works in your, *our*, favour. You're isolated in the physical sense, yet you've been to all the important places – vicariously." Vaalon's expression softened. "I've spent the last eight years trying to get inside your head. Through my observers I know every book or journal you've read or looked at, including our article in *Science*. And when you'd log off the library computer, we'd check your browsing history, too."

Pilot gulped, trying to remember all the questionable websites he'd visited growing up. Vaalon responded to his protégé's obvious embarrassment with a shrug. "Don't sweat it, Lonnie. Curiosity is a highly rated human trait. It was the breadth and depth of your studies that impressed me most. People are formed by what they experience and what they read and are taught. Your reading history over the years gave us a snapshot of what's up there." Vaalon pointed to Pilot's head. "For example, the fifty-plus biographies of world leaders you took out – provided you actually read them – will have imparted some insight as to what makes a good leader and what makes a bad one. Through osmosis, you can't help but have picked up an understanding of the leader's mindset."

"I read them."

"I'm relieved. The variety and depth of your other readings are a model of self-education. There's something else I can tell you, Lonnie, about Ruth's penchant for matchmaking. The children of three of our best friends are still enjoying near perfect marriages arranged by Ruth over thirty years ago. I decided to set her another matchmaking project – to apply the same process to finding a partner for our island-to-be. We worked hard defining our prerequisites. Independence; intelligence; that rare mix of humble self-confidence; passion; charisma; incorruptibility. The candidate had to have an understanding of politics, but no direct participation in it – an uncut diamond with the potential to be a consummate leader. They had to work well with others, be excellent orators and have an element of ruthlessness about them."

"Ruthlessness?" Pilot had never considered himself to be a ruthless person.

"You're a mongoose among cobras. I could give you examples. In the pursuit of something just or right, nothing stops you. Of our six candidates, you scored second overall."

"Second?"

"I'll be honest with you, Lonnie. Six months ago, our first choice was killed in a drive-by shooting in Philadelphia – innocent bystander caught in the cross-fire. That you and I are here together right now is a gift of fate. A *must happen* transition."

Pilot smiled with his eyes. "I'll have to take your word for it, Forrest. Your people are very good, by the way. I never noticed anybody watching me, ever."

"That's because you saw no reason why anybody would *want* to. We see things when we're wary – miss them when we're not. If I put one of my people on you tomorrow, you'd spot them immediately."

As they approached Penzance, Pilot gazed at the endless parked cars that had taken the place of the trees. "Is Mrs. Vaalon here with you?" he asked.

"No. She's in Flushing, New York. Mount Hebron Cemetery. She died seven months ago."

Pilot noted an emptiness in the man's voice. "I'm sorry, Forrest. I didn't – "

"It's okay, Lonnie. She's cheering us on from the sidelines now."

Half an hour later they were eating fish pie at the Tolcarne Inn. "So, Forrest, let me get this straight," Pilot said. "You want to hire me to become governor of a strip of rock in the Bay of Biscay."

"Correct." Vaalon rotated his chair forty-five degrees and crossed his long legs in preparation for a monologue. He leaned forward and lowered his voice so as not to be overheard by the adjacent tables. "There's a simple scale at play in the world today, Lonnie. On one side you have the accepted order of the human presence. Let's call it the old oak tree. It's well established, with roots that go deep and a canopy that throws its shade over everything. To many, it's a beautiful and magnificent tree. Others know it's dying because it has extracted all but the tiniest remainder of nourishment from the soil. It's grown too big. On the other side, we have this," he said, picking up the nearest beer mat, his chosen prop of the day.

"An acorn."

"Most definitely *not* an acorn, Lonnie. That's the whole problem. Acorns only grow up to be other oak trees. It's cyclical." Vaalon turned the beer mat over. "The world needs to be turned upside down, inside out and back to front just to get it back to where it should be. And to do that, we need a base. Not one within an existing country, but a virgin land free of history, tradition, religious and political dogma and the other barnacles of so-called civilization. But where do we find this place? In Africa somewhere? The South Pole? Lapland? All used up. There's nowhere on earth that isn't already in the hands of the opposition, apart from the bottom of the sea." Vaalon paused to let his words settle across the table. "Lonnie, it's my job to give you that base and your job to use it – to establish a state which, by its very nature, calls into question the entire validity of the existing order. If all goes to plan, you'll have it. It's simply a matter of being in the right place at the right time and then stepping ashore and claiming it. Believe me, your nation will be far more than a strip of cold, wet rock in the Bay of Biscay."

Vaalon stopped talking and Pilot stopped eating to allow the man time to catch up. "For the first few years you'll be playing under the world's rules," Vaalon continued when their plates were equal, "using its resources and financial institutions, sheltering under its international laws and so on. You've got to be clever, though, and not build lines of exchange that can't be severed if necessary. Here –" Vaalon reached into his briefcase, withdrew a thick hardback book and handed it to Pilot. "This is to supplement your previous studies. Read, digest, memorize and then, from August, *live* the contents of this book."

Pilot looked at the title and smiled. *The Psychology of Leadership.*

"Back to our island, the first part of the process shouldn't last more than five or ten years," Vaalon continued. "By then, your land should be self-sufficient. It'll occupy a strategic location in the world, yet be free from the world's grip. At this point you'll be in a position to develop your model more effectively. But before we carry on this conversation, there's something else I'd like us to do over a hot cup of something."

When Pilot's coffee and Vaalon's mint tea came, along with two brandies, the old man stood up, lifted his snifter and beckoned his guest to do the same. "To Ruth," he toasted.

Pilot was watching the scene as if he were a one man audience at a one man play. He did not yet buy the pretense. "To Ruth."

"We needed to wet our whistles for this next exercise," Vaalon said. "Word and phrase association. I say something and you pass the thread back to me with whatever comes into your head – no hesitation allowed from either side. We go back and forth like this, sewing our word garment until one of us falters. Are you ready?"

"Ready…"

V: "The forgotten old."

P: "The betrayed young."

V: "The death of the buffalo."

P: "The death of the American Indian."

V: "Deforestation."

P: "Rape."

V: "The Dodo."

P: "The Maldives."

V: "Skylines."

P: "Bread lines."

V: "Wine lakes."

P: "Butter mountains."
V: "Gross National Product."
P: "Gross National Paradox."
V: "Sinking coastlines."
P: "Sinking morals."
V: "Organized crime."
P: "Organized religion."

They played verbal ping-pong for two minutes – batting back and forth over a hundred different 'passwords', each one a door into its own vast debating room beyond. They stopped only because Vaalon had to urinate again.

On his return, Pilot said, "It was like a mantra, that thing we just did."

"A litany against life's dark side," Vaalon replied. "By the way, you'll be pleased to know that you passed the interview. What I need to know now is whether you'll accept this position. I've already told you too much."

Pilot pretended to weigh up the offer, but found it hard to keep a straight face. "Your secret's safe with me, Forrest," he said through his thawing skepticism. "I accept." At the same time, he was wondering what the hell he was getting himself into.

Vaalon took out his wallet, withdrew a gold credit card and handed it over. "This is yours. Sign it on the back. You'll need spending money between now and August." He slipped Pilot a small piece of paper. "This is the pin number. There's a £50,000 credit limit. The statements will come to me and I'll pay them off each month. If you need more than your £50,000 limit for anything, my man in Zurich, Franz Barta, can release any amount for you, but I'd appreciate it if you ran it past me first. One last piece of weaponry," Vaalon said, reaching into his briefcase and taking out a smart phone and charger. "Press star-one for speed dial direct to me." He took the napkin off his lap and tossed it on the table. I don't know about you, Lonnie, but I'm exhausted."

"Ditto."

"In that case, let's call it a day. We've made good progress and we can start fresh in the morning – there's still a lot of ground to cover. I'm staying at the Abbey Hotel and I suggest we meet somewhere nearby after breakfast. Any suggestions?"

Pilot thought for a minute. "Morrab Library. It opens at ten. You'll like it."

New mobile in pocket, and carrying an over-stimulated brain, Lonnie Pilot walked his bike the short distance to his net-shed-cum-flat as if on air. He had begun the day like a prospector awaiting a map. Forrest Vaalon had given him the map and Pilot was ending his day within touching distance of the mother lode.

Just before going to bed, he decided to google *Forrest Vaalon*, borrowing the faint, non-secured broadband signal from the holiday cottage next door. It took a while to crack the navigation on his new phone, but when the search results eventually came up, he clicked the top link to bring up a page from Wikipedia and began skim reading.

'*Forrest Arnold Vaalon is an American geophysicist, environmentalist, investor and philanthropist best known as the founder of The Insitute of Geophysical Projections, which predicted the earthquake responsible for the Oregon-California Tsunami. After years of derision by the scientific community –*' Pilot skipped to *Early life and career.*

'*Forrest Vaalon was born in Taos, New Mexico, to unmarried parents. His father, Hunter Vaalon, was the son of wealthy east coast industrialist, Bertram Vaalon. His mother, Annemarie Frey, was a Swiss artist. Together they had one child. On inheriting the Vaalon fortune, Hunter took his family back to*

New York and enrolled his previously home-schooled eight year old son in The Taft School, Watertown, Connecticut. At the age of fourteen, Forrest Vaalon was sent to Lake Forest Academy in Illinois – '

Pilot scrolled further down the page, looking for a reference to Ruth, and soon found it.

'*…and later that year married Holocaust survivor Ruth Belkin, who went on to found the international educational charity, Scholasticorps.* Pilot remembered what Vaalon had said about Ruth's inability to have children as the result of a trauma endured when she was younger. *Holocaust survivor.* A cold chill ran up Pilot's spine. He went back to his search results and clicked on one at random, which landed him half way down a page on the Forbes website.

36. Forrest Vaalon. 'Thirty-sixth what?' Pilot scrolled to the top of the page. *The Forbes 400. The Richest People in America.* He clicked a link to another Forbes page, *The World's Billionaires*, and there, in black and white at number 97, was Forrest Vaalon.

II

"You won't determine the shape of this island by walking around its coastline," Vaalon said to Pilot across a first floor table at Morrab Library the next morning. "I'll give you a brief flyover now and over the next three months you'll have time to read all the support files and background studies in detail.

"On the first of August a launch will take you from Falmouth to an ocean-going barge anchored offshore. She'll then be set on a southwesterly course, and, two days later, will rendezvous with the other barges about here." In the atlas open before him, Vaalon pointed to an area west of Brest in the Bay of Biscay. "We calculate that the island will crest some time between August fourth and August eighth." Vaalon opened his laptop and switched it on.

"I read that Ruth was a Holocaust survivor," Pilot said as they waited for the computer to boot up. Vaalon looked up with a pained expression. "How old was she when she got out, Forrest?"

"Twelve." A vein in Vaalon's forehead had grown larger. "But she survived, and threw their hideous crimes back in their faces with what she achieved over her lifetime. She's a silent partner now, sitting here with us as we dot the i's and cross the t's of what is, to a large extent, *her* vision. I couldn't have done this without Ruth."

Vaalon typed in a password and the screen lit up the old oak tabletop. He clicked *Documents*, then the folder *Flotilla*, then the document *Configuration*, positioning the laptop so that Pilot could see the screen. Although it was just past ten thirty, Pilot had been up since five, too overstimulated to sleep. His eyes felt grainy and the bright light of the screen made him squint. Vaalon scrolled down a page of text and stopped on a series of images.

"Fourteen other barges will be converging on your position on August third." Pilot looked at a diagram showing three rows of five barges each, all tightly bunched in a rectangle. Vaalon returned to the Flotilla folder to give Pilot a glimpse of its other files: *Mooring Procedure*; *Deployment of Barrage*; *Deckside Preparations*. "You'll have plenty of time to absorb what's in here. Moving on, once the flotilla is lashed together, the fifteen barge masters will be removed to the mainland. Then, it's just a matter of waiting. Before I forget, I need you to fill this out." Vaalon pulled a form from his briefcase and pushed it across the table. "Passport application. You can get photos done at the Post Office. Use your credit card to pay the fee."

"I need a passport to get on the island?" Pilot joked.

"Dublin." Vaalon pulled an envelope out of his case and handed it over. "This is your plane ticket. On June 2nd you'll be meeting three of your *crew*, for lack of a better word. It's easier for one person to travel to Dublin than for three to come to Penzance. Macushla Mara is chief speechwriter for the Prime Minister of Ireland, and her communication skills will be an important asset down the line. Jane Lavery has agreed to head up food production, and Josiah Billy will be your island's master builder. Out of the 86 who have signed up to the project, only you four and two others, who you'll meet later, know the true destination. Background details, photos etcetera for all your crew are in here."

"Where do the other eighty think we're going?"

"I told them they'll be taking part in a unique social experiment with other like-minded people; that they'll be travelling to a remote part of the world; that they might be in for a rough landing; that it'll be subsistence living to start with; but that all the hardship could be worth it at the end. None seemed to have a problem with that."

Pilot thought for a minute. "About that *rough landing*, Forrest, is there any chance the island could kill us on its way up? If so, don't you have a moral responsibility to tell us?"

"I exaggerated the dangers and even told them there was an outside chance that they could die. There would have been a hundred of you if fourteen had decided to accept the risk like the others. Let me just say that your landing module has been designed to absorb g-forces in excess of what the physics tells us will be the maximum collision speed. "

"Landing module?"

"Positioned above the central barge on hydraulic pillars. If there were any possibility of fatalities, Lonnie, I wouldn't be here. You'll be fine."

Vaalon scanned his document headings and stopped at 'Rendezvous'. "As soon as the barge captains have left for the mainland and everyone is aboard *Ptolemy*, you'll inform your crew of their true destination. They know you are the designated leader, but most of them will have never met you. So, before you tell them about the island, you have to instill confidence in you as leader. They need to know that the person leading them into the unknown is trustworthy and investable."

Vaalon looked back at his document headings. 'Post Landing… As soon as possible after landfall, and to ensure that the whole experiment doesn't fall apart, you and your cohorts will devise an administrative structure for your island. You've read enough books on governance to know the need for mechanisms and processes through which your people can articulate their interests, exercise their personal rights, meet their obligations, and mediate their differences."

"And I've observed enough Cornwall Council Planning meetings to understand the pitfalls," Pilot said. "It should be an interesting process." He worried a loose button on his shirt which had been threatening to fall off for a month. "Can I ask you a question, Forrest? This still bothers me – the fact that you picked *me* to lead this enterprise. Why not one of the other candidates you mentioned?"

"Up until eight years ago, we still had insufficient data to predict the next solar tide," Vaalon said. "We had no idea it could happen in our lifetime. Back then, it was just science to us. And theory. The breakthrough came with the development of our 'crust caliper' as you call it, which allowed us for the first time to identify soft spots in the Earth's skin. Other hardware crucial to predicting solar tides and measuring magmatic activity came quickly on its heels. Two years ago, we built the world's first Solarmagnetrometer and placed it on the Chinese satellite, *Joyous Harvest.* When we'd analysed all the new data, put it into our computer model and set it against the bore samples I showed you, we realized that an event unprecedented in recorded history was about to occur. To our astonishment – and horror – we now had a time, *approximately*, and a place, *roughly*, for a magmatic pulse capable of pushing the continental shelf out of the sea."

"Why horror?"

"Because the dream of a new Utopia Ruth and I had so much fun toying with when we were younger was now a looming reality. *But we were too old to do anything about it.* We had been looking into successors, albeit without urgency, but now we had to find one fast." Vaalon ran a liver-spotted hand through his hair. "I've told you about our six candidates and the untimely death of our first choice."

Pilot laughed. "I'll tell you one thing. I feel a lot more comfortable knowing that I was only your second choice."

"I'm glad," Vaalon said. "Back in the sixties, Avis were second to Hertz in the car rental business, but they turned that to their advantage with one of the most brilliant advertising slogans of all time. *Because we're number two, we try harder.*"

"Challenge accepted. Where are the other four candidates?"

"In your crew, but I don't think it would help if you knew their identities. Excuse me, Lonnie, I'll be right back." Vaalon stood up and left the room for his third bathroom break since breakfast.

Pilot ran his finger along the edge of France's western continental shelf and allowed himself a bemused smile. This is mad, he thought. Science fiction. He still had one foot in the mud of Penwith and was far from convinced that this unexpected meeting with a rich American scientist-fantasist was going anywhere.

Vaalon returned and opened another file. "For this colony of yours to work we can't leave any holes, so, among your crew you will find a dentist, two doctors, a nurse practitioner, a gynecologist, a topographer, and an IT/communications expert. The others are making the trip on the strength of their intelligence, creativity, awareness and drive. To help you get established, I've also employed five specialists – an arborist, a stonemason, a marine engineer, an amateur geologist friend of mine and an agronomist/nutritionist to help Jane. They'll be joining you several days after landing. Their contracts run from one to three years, depending on their field. To preserve secrecy, I've told them they're going to work on a development in Dubai. I don't think they care whether they go to Dubai or Santa's workshop just as long as it's not where they came from. And since I can say that none has been to where you're going, there should not be a problem."

An elderly man in shorts and sandals came into the room and began looking through the biography shelf, his failing eyes a mere four inches from the book spines. Vaalon closed the laptop, arose and beckoned Pilot to follow him out. They walked downstairs and through the reading room towards the exit, tracked as they went by half a dozen curious retirees, already seated for a morning lecture on 'The Bells of St. Mary's'.

In Morrab Gardens they found an empty bench near the bandstand and sat down. Over by the bushes, a young couple lay sunning themselves. Three old ladies on the adjacent bench sat stony still, as if dead. Vaalon raised his face to the sun and closed his eyes. "Mmmm, that feels so good," he said.

They sunned themselves in silence for fifteen minutes, then Vaalon opened his eyes and turned to Pilot. "Back to the real world, Lonnie. You'll be relieved to hear that your island won't be born poor. To ensure your fiscal strength, I've put aside a fifth of one percent of the world's gold reserves and two percent of its silver in the name of your country, whatever that name will be." He took two business cards from his pocket and handed one to Pilot. "Think of a name for the island and phone it over to this man in Brussels. He'll do the rest. Once you're established and self-sufficient – which could take years – then you can sever the financial umbilical cord managed by *this* man." He handed Pilot the second card. "Franz Barta. I mentioned him earlier."

"One of the barges will be carrying cash to the value of five million dollars in a number of currencies – spending money for anyone needing to leave the island for medical reasons or to see family. Dispense the cash as you see fit for their travel and other expenses. There's a box of false passports that can be personalized as well." Pilot stole a quick look at his watch. "Do you have to be somewhere, Lonnie?"

"Uhh, well, I didn't know all this was going to happen, Forrest. I'm sorry, but I've arranged to meet a friend for lunch."

The old man smiled. "A friend?"

Pilot's face went crimson. "Well, Jenny's more than a friend, but it won't be a problem come August. It's just a fling. I can finish it at any time. I'll cancel lunch if you want."

"Not necessary." Vaalon stood up and Pilot followed like a tall echo. "I have a dozen emails that need answering, Lonnie. Come by The Abbey at around two thirty and we'll pick up from there." Vaalon turned to go, then stopped. "Enjoy your lunch."

Twenty minutes later, Lonnie Pilot was at Archie Brown's sitting across the table from a strikingly beautiful, chronically destitute painter seven years his senior. He looked over at the Specials board, then took a menu out of its holder. "Have you decided what you want, Jen?" Pilot said.

"The usual. Shall I order yours, too?" As two people on the breadline, the couple always had the cheapest meal possible – soup for the main course and water to drink. While Jenny was at the counter, Pilot went through his options: One – finish their relationship there and then; Two – tell her he was leaving Penzance in August, but that they should carry on seeing each other until then; or Three – ask Vaalon if she could come with him to the Bay of Biscay.

Jenny returned to the table with soup spoons, napkins and tap water, sat down and stared into her glass as if it were a crystal ball. Pilot had first been attracted to her by her sexually alluring, hypnotic eyes, framed by a mop of burnt umber curls. When she looked him in the eye, he still went weak at the knees, but it seemed to him now that she was avoiding eye contact. The sexual charge, though, was palpable and he was inclining more and more towards Option Two.

"It's been a weird morning, Jen."

The painter looked up at last. "How so?" Pilot sensed something disengaging in her voice.

"Are you feeling okay, Jenny?"

"Fine. What's been weird?"

"I met someone who used to work with my grandfather. It made me realize how little I know about him."

"I never knew mine, either. Life's full of holes, love." She was staring into her water again.

They ate their soup in silence. Then, Jenny smiled, reached over and took Pilot's hands in hers. He wallowed in that same sultry look she would throw him from down between his legs, gazing up with her mouth full. Option Three – taking her with him in August – was now a strong contender.

"Lonnie," she said, "My exhibition opens in July and I have eight unfinished paintings in my studio. I haven't put paint to canvas since our first date. I'm sorry, love, but this just isn't working."

Before his appointment at the Abbey Hotel, Pilot went back to Morrab Library to finish filling out his passport application. He'd had plenty of time after his short lunch with Jenny to have his passport photos taken. He asked the librarian to witness his signature, sealed the envelope, then went back to the post office to mail it. While waiting in the queue, he thought about what Jenny had said. Her words had taken him by surprise, and he should have asked her she meant by them. *This just isn't working* could mean one of four things: One, it wasn't working sexually – impossible; Two, it wasn't working romantically; Three, once she finished her paintings it could work again – maybe; or, Four, she was dumping him. He had been ready to take their relationship to another level, that much he recognized, but to have been preemptively sacked by the woman cut him deeply. His life seemed to be slipping out of his control on all fronts and he didn't like the feeling.

"Is Mr. Vaalon available," he asked the hotel receptionist at 2.30 on the dot.

"I'm here, Lonnie," the tall American said, emerging from the lounge. "Let's go for a drive while the sun's shining."

Pilot took him to the Tremenheere Sculpture Garden. Their stroll through the Woodland Area was Vaalon's cue for the starting point of their afternoon session. "Trees are crucial, Lonnie. You'll need plenty, because your land will be barren. You'll be taking several thousand saplings, suckers and cuttings covering a variety of fast growing trees. You'll need them as windbreaks against the equinoctial gales, which will start within a few months of your arrival."

"How do you plant a tree on bare rock?" Pilot asked.

"In the Flotilla file, you'll note that the four heaviest barges, positioned at each corner of the configuration for stability, will be carrying nothing but topsoil and compost – several thousand tons of it. Over 75% will be used for tree-planting. The rest will be needed for cultivation. You'll be carrying provisions to last for a year and a bit, and that will have to suffice until your first harvest. Three hundred tons of topsoil should be more than enough to get your grasses and winter crops in. You'll need more later for your spring planting. There's a man in Cork, Liam O'Penny, with access to all the earth you need should you run short. O'Penny is no businessman and should be treated fairly by us. Whatever price he mentions, double it.

"As for water, there's ten thousand gallons divided between three of your barges, so even if only one gets through, you'll have adequate water to meet your immediate needs. It won't take that long to build your cisterns and there will be plenty of rain to fill them, believe me."

"Will we be taking animals?"

"It'll be a long time before you have enough grass to support livestock, but there's a rare breed of sheep from Orkney, the North Ronaldsay, that lives almost entirely on seaweed. Six of these hearty ungulates will be joining you after your landing, and there will be plenty of seaweed washing ashore to feed them. Their milk tastes like spinach juice, but you'll get used to it."

They found a bench in the Swampy Bog and sat down.

At that very same moment, in similar surroundings three miles south of Rumangabo in the Democratic Republic of the Congo, a young mother barely into her teens rocked rhythmically in her hiding place, her dead child clutched to her breast. The voices were getting closer, the pain in her abdomen, sharper. Removing one hand from her son's body, she explored her own wound with her fingers, trying to stop the bleeding. The hole in the side of her son's skull had hardly bled at all. She had heard the sound of gunshots before and they had always led to deaths in the family. Then, a sudden flash of sunlight from the blade of a machete caught her eye as it thrashed at the undergrowth in the distance. The excited chattering stopped. She froze. Her laboured breaths were the loudest noise around. Painful seconds passed.

The bullet reached her ear before the sound of the shot that fired it – if she had been alive to hear it. With a single 300-grain projectile in her brain, the last Western Lowland Gorilla remaining in the wild was dead.

"I'm not that worried about being able to survive on the rock in the physical sense," Pilot said, "but how are we going to be able to lay claim to it politically and legally?"

"That's the most important question of all, Lonnie. It has to be a fait accompli in the first hour. At the exact moment you're making your landfall, representations will be made by our advocates in Westminster, Dublin, Paris, Madrid, Lisbon and, most importantly, the United Nations. Their intercessions should leave no legal doubts as to your just and proper claim to sovereignty over the new land. Without solid diplomatic moorings in the world you'll just sit exposed, isolated and vulnerable to the outside. You'll run the risk of being treated as pirates, renegades or accidental tourists instead of an independent, legally bona fide member state of the world community. As I mentioned to you yesterday, you'll be playing by the world's rules to begin with. And that means following accepted procedures and protocols to ensure you're rooted from the first hour. To accomplish that credibly you need advocates on the outside. You can read about them in the file by that name.

"Another thing. All 86 of you will renounce your respective citizenships and burn your passports before sailing so that you're technically stateless on landing."

Pilot picked up an alien-looking seed pod and twiddled with it while constructing his next question. "What's to stop us from being overrun and removed from the island?"

"If your land has something the others want – oil, minerals, territory – then it'll be in their interests to take it. Just look at what my country did to the Native Americans when gold was discovered on the land we'd *allowed* them to keep. We just tore up the treaty, moved in and started digging. In your situation, the positive thing about being vulnerable is that people will hate to see you get hurt. Unscrupulous parties might try to harm you, but world opinion won't let them get away with it. The fact that you'll be forever underdogs is your strongest defense, stronger even than international law."

Vaalon shifted position on the bench, eager for another bathroom break. "Research and preparation can never be said to be 100% complete, but I've unearthed nothing so far to suggest that our plans aren't feasible, both in the physical and the political sense. I've put links to a number of IGP studies on the laptop and I advise you to read them all. We also have computer models at the Institute that I can show you in London. No-one can say what short or long term changes might occur as a result of the upheaval, or even how long you'll be above water. We'll just have to wait and see."

The two men ambled to the visitors centre to relieve themselves and have tea in the café.

"Any questions so far?" Vaalon asked.

"The initial goal is to get established and become self-sufficient," Pilot said. "I understand that. But then what? You said there'd be a second phase."

Vaalon adopted an apologetic air. "My work here is almost finished," he said. "After landing, you and your cohorts will take over the reins and plan Phase Two during Phase One. There will be many variables, and any plans will have to be molded around the shapes they make, without forgetting what the object of the game is."

"I've got a strong feeling that we both agree on what that object is," Pilot said.

"I wouldn't have asked you to take the position if we didn't, Lonnie. I have every confidence in you. Your ends will justify your means, provided the ends themselves are justified." Vaalon took a last sip and removed a tea leaf from the tip of his tongue. "I'm going back to the hotel for a nap. Come by at seven if you can. I'm looking forward to sampling some genuine Cornish street food."

Pilot scratched his head. "Do you like saveloys?"

The houses in the backstreets of Penzance exhibited all the qualities of a person in a coma. At close quarters they appeared stone dead, but deep within, behind their locked doors and curtained windows, a strange life pulsed imperceptibly on. A life of pinging microwaves, reality TV, heavy metal on illegal file-sharing, the next dose of calcium and iron supplement or the next heroin fix.

The only visible sign of life this sultry May evening was at the local pie shop several doors down from Pilot's aunts' seashell emporium. Formerly a fish and chip shop, the too-late moratorium on commercial fishing had forced its owner to turn to 'meat' pies a vegetarian could eat without guilt. Outside, gangs of alienated youths stood gobbling oily chips and throwing empty soft drink cans at one another. Pieces of paper impregnated with suet and gravy blew down the street like tumbleweeds through a ghost town.

In the doorway between *The Pen Sans Seashell Emporium* and *Morwenna's Tattoo Parlour*, Lonnie Pilot and Forrest Vaalon sat eating their saveloys, the computer case acting as a makeshift table between them. When they'd finished, Vaalon took out the laptop and switched it on.

"Do you mind if we don't use that tonight?" Pilot asked. "I have a headache." Vaalon waited for the laptop to spring to life, then put it back into hibernation. The slamming of a door at the back of the building was followed a moment later by the coughing of an engine. "That'll be Sally and Hilda," Pilot said. "My great-aunts. This is their shop. They have a seashell stall at the St. Neot Flower Festival starting tomorrow. They were supposed to set off this afternoon, and they're both night-blind, so I may never see them again. Come on in, I've got a key." Pilot unlocked the door, switched on the lights and ushered his guest inside. "When did you say you were leaving Cornwall, Forrest?"

"Late tomorrow morning. I have to be back in London in time for dinner. Life goes on. My other life, I mean. That's a beautiful conch. Not from local waters, is it?"

Pilot picked up the shell and read the tiny writing on the label. "Sri Lanka."

They spent the next hour and a half looking at Penwith's finest shell collection and talking about coral reefs, sea turtles and dodos. "I need to wrap up a few more things with you in the morning before I go," Vaalon said. "Then I'll leave you to prepare for the rest of your life."

It was past midnight, two hours after he'd fallen exhausted onto his bed, but through a combination of cerebral overstimulation and sexual frustration, Pilot was finding it impossible to sleep. He was just about to take matters into his own hands when he thought of a better alternative.

"Who is it?" Jenny asked, answering the light rap on her studio door.

"It's me. I didn't get a chance to say goodbye to you properly. Can I come in?"

III

Lonnie Pilot, an only child, had been twelve when his father died, leaving his mother in dire financial straits, compounded by the negative equity of the marital home and her inability to keep up with the mortgage payments. Out of desperation – in an attempt to save herself, her son and her home – she surrendered to the advances of a travelling computer software salesman, who had sold her a program of empty promises and bogus claims to great prospects. However, even at his young age, Pilot was a good judge of bad character and his toxic dislike for the man had been so overtly expressed, and was so threatening to her 'rescue' that Phyllis Pilot decided to place physical distance between her son and Mr. Stoker. Before moving to Essex with her new partner she had lodged Lonnie with her two larky-legged spinster aunts, Sally and Hilda Tink. 'I love you, Lonnie,' she had told him, 'but I need this man. The two of you can't live in the same house together, so Les and I are leaving Cornwall. I hope you understand. I'll send money.'

Pilot *didn't* understand. The evaporation of his parents from his life, and the bank's repossession of the only home he had ever known, threw him into an early-teens crisis. As for sending money, at the beginning of every month until his sixteenth birthday, he would receive a crisp five pound note with words like, 'Don't spend it all at once,' and 'Buy yourself a warm scarf.'

ADHD - Inattentive Sub-Type had been the label given to Lonnie Pilot by the school psychologist. Whether or not the teachers had felt threatened by his eerie precocity or thought him a disruptive influence on the other students, the result was the same. Within six months of his mother's departure, he had left the Humphry Davy School to follow his own course of full-time higher education, the school system being unable to teach him things fast enough; the National Curriculum being too circumscribed for his expanding brain.

In the first floor reference section of the Penzance Public Library, at the farthest corner table, there was a chair acknowledged by all but strangers as being 'Lonnie's Chair'. The chewing gum screwed under that corner of the table was ninety per cent his. There, the autodidact had sat for days, weeks and years, systematically digesting everything the library had on its shelves and in its computers. Some afternoons, for extra quiet, he'd go to the antiquated private library in Morrab Gardens, where he had volunteered to dust shelves every Thursday in lieu of paying the annual subscription.

Pilot's aunts had never crossed him, because his insolent wit was more than they could deal with. Although they clothed and fed him with a clumsy virtuosity unique to elderly childless females, they moved mountains to avoid spending the time of day with him. They didn't understand the first thing about him. For his own part, Pilot was fond of them, but so disinterested he could barely tell the two apart.

At the age of eighteen, Lonnie Pilot's life changed again. For several years he had been making weekly visits to his great-uncle, Marrek Tink, who lived in a converted net shed in Newlyn. Of the four Tink siblings, Sally, Hilda, Marrek and Merryn, only Merryn, Pilot's grandmother, had reproduced, and Phyllis herself was an only child. With no brothers or sisters and no cousins in the locale, Pilot threw everything into his relationship with Marrek. They walked, went sailing, but mostly they talked, or rather, Marrek did. During his half century in the merchant navy, Marrek Tink had garnered the kind of knowledge not found in books, and Pilot had made the most of it until death parted them. In his will, Marrek Tink left the net shed to his great-nephew.

Living independently was one thing, but Pilot was penniless and had refused to sign on for benefits. To make ends meet, he tutored the children of local fishermen and farmers for cash, fish and dairy products. Subsistence living, Cornish style.

At 8.00am, Pilot peeled himself off Jenny's warm body and began getting dressed in the early morning light. She stirred, but remained deep in sleep. He thought how beautiful she looked and how much he would miss her. If she could get a few paintings done quickly, perhaps they could get back on track. Not wishing to wake her, he opened the door as quietly as he could, but was stopped by Jenny's sleep-soaked, sultry voice. "Lonnie," she said. "Don't do that again." Pretending he hadn't heard her, Pilot let himself out and began walking towards Penzance for his meeting with Forrest Vaalon.

On the stretch to Jubilee Pool and Battery Rocks, he saw no-one and heard only the occasional car or seagull. Seaweed and pebbles from the night's strong seas decorated The Promenade, but Pilot was too distracted by his early morning love-making and the pain of Jenny's admonition to avoid the flotsam and jetsum and he stumbled several times. He'd arranged to meet Vaalon on Battery Road at 8.30 and, true to the man's word, there he was, with a bag of Abbey Hotel croissants, two cups and a flask of coffee. They exchanged pleasantries and sat down on a bench to have breakfast.

"It'll have to be black," Vaalon said, unscrewing the thermos. It was a beautiful, windless spring morning, yet not even the blue skies and mild temperature could breathe life into the boarded up former guest house across the street.

"The town's seen better days, as you can see," Pilot said to his companion.

"That's one thing you will not be able to say when you plant your flag in August," Vaalon answered. "Your new land will be one of the few places in the world *not* to have seen better days – at least, not in the past 5,000 years."

Pilot thought for a while, then looked Vaalon square in the eye. "Forrest, we have the *theory* of an island coming up in the Bay of Biscay. No problems with that. And we have the *concept* of establishing a model nation capable of changing the world. No problem there, either, apart from actually doing it. There's that bore sample, but nothing else tangible to work with. We're just two men sitting on a bench at the end of England. How confident are you that the two things will ever happen? Out of ten. Be honest."

Vaalon answered without hesitation. "I'll give the theory a nine, but as to whether the island won't kill 86 people on its way up, I'll have to give that a five. The concept is an obvious ten. The odds on it ever being realized are for you to work out. I think anything between seven and ten is workable. Happy?"

For the next two hours, without opening his laptop, Vaalon expanded on the science of solar tides and magmatic attraction, Pilot's crew, the specialists, the advocates, and wrapped up the meeting with a colourful description of the house he was building near Taos.

"Lonnie, I'm so confident this island's going to appear on time that I'm betting the farm on it. If the island doesn't come up as predicted, my ranch is yours."

Pilot laughed. "And if it does, you'll own my net shed." They shook hands on it. "One more question, Forrest. Jenny's exhibition is being hung at the end of July and then she'll be free of all her commitments. I haven't said anything to her about this, but I think she could be an asset to us. I'd like to take her with me if that's okay."

A look of disappointment flashed across Vaalon's face. "That's the mongoose in you talking, Lonnie. You told me she'd severed the relationship. What makes you think she'd unsever it? It's all academic, though. Jenny is *not* part of the plan. She's not the one."

Pilot felt his stomach drop at Vaalon's answer and the firmness with which it had been delivered. The door Jenny had semi-closed had now been locked and bolted by Forrest Vaalon. There was nothing Pilot could say that would open it, and he knew better than to try.

"Jenny's just a familiar face… a sexual dalliance," Vaalon said, softening. "I don't mean to be harsh, but your future's with another. Trust me. Is there anything more you'd like to ask me?"

"Yes. What was my grandfather's nickname?"

Vaalon gave an open mouth smile, his white teeth set off nicely by his rich man's tan. "Would my ability to answer that question make all this credible to you, Lonnie? Is that the one word you need me to say before you can commit unconditionally to this enterprise?"

"Yes."

"Well I have bad news for you. I didn't know he even *had* a nickname."

Pilot's head sank in mock resignation. Then he looked up and laughed. "You pass, Forrest. He hadn't."

They meandered along the Promenade to Vaalon's car, savouring the aroma of seaweed as they walked. After belting up, the man consulted a list written in his expensive leather notebook. "Credit card, passport application, airline ticket, phone, laptop, chargers, business cards – that's everything, I think. I'll see you soon, Lonnie. In the meantime, call me if you need anything. This has been good." He reached out his hand and Pilot shook it firmly.

Pilot followed the car with his eyes to the South Pier. As it disappeared around the corner, the feeling of emptiness arising from his mentor's departure was washed away by a growing sense of his own destiny.

For ten minutes he stood there, his inherited laptop cradled like a baby in his arms, and gazed vacantly at the sparkling, fishless waters of Mounts Bay before jogging back to the net shed.

Monday, May 4th, began with the sort of rain Pilot hated. He delighted in thunderstorms where the raindrops sound like gravel being off-loaded from a dumper truck, but drizzle depressed him. Loath to leave his warm bed, he tried to reconnect with his thoughts of the previous three days. Foremost in his head was a vision of the barge flotilla, floating serenely in the Bay of Biscay, and a rock the size of Wales speeding towards it from below at a hundred miles an hour. Pre-coffined for a more convenient burial, he thought.

He arrived at the library just as they were unlocking the doors and was soon enthroned in his chair with three oversized tomes on the table in front of him. He wanted to get a better understanding of the physical nature of the continental shelf – anything to make it feel more real. He opened *The Atlas of The Oceans* to a map of the sea bed of the Bay of Biscay. Based on National Institute of

Oceanography soundings, it was about as informative of the true nature of what lay at the bottom of the Bay as a man's photograph is of his personality.

He noted that the continental shelf, from a point about forty miles off the elbow where Spain and France meet, progressed at a forty-five degree angle northwest. The edge extended farther and farther from the coast of France until by forty-eight degrees north, at the latitude of Brest, the shelf edge was at its greatest distance from land. The drop from the continental slope to the Biscay abyssal plain also got steeper and deeper as one moved northwest. On the floor of the abyssal plain there was the odd seamount, but the mountainous areas didn't begin until it was no longer the Bay of Biscay, or the Celtic Sea, but the open Atlantic. Pilot squinted at the map, hoping that an obvious island shape would leap out of the page, but none did.

He photocopied the map, then began shading in a sliver of the edge of the continental shelf in a shape one hundred miles from north to south and fifteen miles east to west. The dimensions were arbitrary, but would give him a starting point. The volume of water between the shelf and the surface was vast and, when displaced, would have to go somewhere. France and southwest England would take the brunt of the tsunamis, he reckoned. A lot depended on the speed of ascent, a figure he hoped the IGP computer simulations would provide. Pilot reasoned that if the shelf rose at, say, ten feet per second, it wouldn't be fast enough to kill them, but the barges would in all likelihood break up, unless they came up in a bed of soft, oozy sediment. How deep *was* the sediment on the sea floor? He opened *Submarine Topography* and thumbed through the pages until he found the answer.

Over millions of years the deposit of sediment on the seabed has produced a carpet in some places half a mile thick. This sediment covering consists of clay, shell particles, sand and dust, volcanic ash and cosmic spherules.

He couldn't begin to guess the consistency of this particular mixture, but feared the worst – sediment rising past them at 30 miles an hour, leaving them buried in hundreds of feet of mud. The sooner he went to London to view the computer models the better. First and foremost, he wanted to know if the flotilla could withstand the landing. The other worry was the threat the inevitable tsunamis posed to coastal populations. If his island killed even a single person and there had been no forewarning, he and Vaalon would be dead in the water – branded as mass murderers.

Pilot then turned his mind to political issues, beginning with how far out to sea a country could claim sovereignty. He found himself a computer, logged on and typed 'territorial waters' in the search box. He clicked on the most promising-looking result and began skim-reading.

A state's territorial sea extends up to 12 nautical miles (22 km) from its mean low water mark baseline.

So far, so good.

The contiguous zone is a band of water extending from the outer edge of the territorial sea to up to 24 nautical miles (44 km) from the baseline. Within this area a state can exert limited control for the purpose of preventing or punishing 'infringement of its customs, fiscal, immigration or sanitary laws and regulations within its territory or territorial sea'…

Depends on how far we are from France, Pilot thought.

An exclusive economic zone (EEZ) extends from the outer limit of the territorial sea to a maximum of 200 nautical miles (370.4 km) from the territorial sea baseline. A coastal nation has control of all economic resources within its exclusive economic zone, including fishing, mining, oil exploration, and any pollution of those resources. However, it cannot prohibit passage or loitering above, on, or under the surface of the sea within that portion of its exclusive economic zone beyond its territorial sea.

Pilot read this last sentence three times to make sure he understood it before moving on.

Before 1982, coastal nations arbitrarily extended their territorial waters in an effort to control activities which are now regulated by the exclusive economic zone. These include offshore oil exploration and fishing rights (see Cod War). Indeed, the exclusive economic zone is still popularly, though erroneously, called a coastal nation's territorial waters…

Using his ruler, Pilot calculated that the edge of Europe's continental shelf at its farthest from land was about 100 miles west of Brest – outside France's territorial waters and contiguous zone, but well within her EEZ. He felt his stomach drop, then continued looking for something positive.

Under the United Nations Convention on the Law of the Sea, the name 'continental shelf' was given a legal definition as 'the stretch of the seabed adjacent to the shores of a particular country to which it belongs'. The relatively accessible continental shelf is the best understood part of the ocean floor. Most commercial exploitation from the sea, such as metallic-ore, non-metallic ore, and hydrocarbon extraction, takes place on the continental shelf. Sovereign rights over their continental shelves up to 350 nautical miles from the coast were claimed by the marine nations that signed the Convention in 1958. This was partly superseded by the 1982 United Nations Convention on the Law of the Sea…

The more he read, the more Pilot's heart sank, and it got worse.

Rights Over the Continental Shelf
Articles 77 to 81 define the rights of a country over its continental shelf.
A coastal nation has control of all resources on or under its continental shelf, living or not, but no control over any living organisms above the shelf that are beyond its exclusive economic zone. This gives it the right to conduct petroleum drilling works and lay submarine cables or pipelines in its continental shelf…

Pilot was getting worried, because *wherever* they landed on the shelf, they'd still be within the French EEZ and thereby under French control. He went back to his original search and clicked a link to an article in *Interpreter* Magazine. It was a piece written in 2010 about France's attempts to extend the EEZs of her foreign possessions – specifically, the oil rich area west of New Caledonia. Pilot skimmed the first four paragraphs, but read the fifth and sixth in their entirety.

Many nations are trying to extend control over the undersea continental shelf. Under Article 76 of the UN Convention on the Law of the Sea, countries can ask the UN

Commission on the Limits of the Continental Shelf *to make a ruling on the outer limits of the shelf. The commission can only make recommendations to coastal states and has no authority to determine the legitimacy of territorial claims.*

France has an active program of undersea mapping and oceanographic studies to document its underwater continental shelf and show that it is a natural extension of the land.

Pilot gleaned from the article that the UN Commission on the Limits of the Continental Shelf could be an important ally for them, even though they had no authority. He made a note to ask Vaalon if this were a provision of his plan for the UN.

Pilot stood up and walked over to the window to think his way out of the problem they faced. When international waters overlap a country's continental shelf and the shelf then surfaces within them, what happens? Does it stop being a continental shelf and become something else? The change from 'continental shelf' to 'island' has no precedent. We'll be in uncharted territory. He began to feel more hopeful. If his advocates were as good as Vaalon claimed they were, they might be able to *spin* their way to sovereignty.

He took his photocopy of the Bay of Biscay and began placing dots in a line twelve miles off the French coastline from the latitude of Brest down to the latitude of Bordeaux. He connected the dots, then shaded France's Territorial Waters pink with a highlighter pen. He drew another line of dots along the edge of the Contiguous Zone 24 miles off the coastline and shaded that area yellow. The final line of dots denoted the edge of the Exclusive Economic Zone 200 miles from the coast. These waters he coloured green. In the end, he had a pretty pattern, but no answers.

At half past twelve, Sally and Hilda came upstairs from the shop for their lunch break. Pilot had called them from the library to ask if he could use their kitchen, as he often did, having only a small camping stove at the net shed. Hilda, out of curiosity, walked up to him and leaned over the pot to sniff the concoction he was creating and make some empty comment about how delicious it smelled. Instead, she couldn't help herself recoiling at the sight that met her eyes. A sodden pancake floated on what looked like porridge. On the pancake, well over to one side, rested a slice of spam and on the spam there was a saucer piled high with sugar.

Pilot noted Hilda's puzzlement and began to explain. "The porridge is the mantle, the pancake is the oceanic crust, the spam is the continental shelf, and the saucer is France." The woman nodded her head without a word or a smile and walked away.

The porridge was reaching boiling point and Pilot waited impatiently for the first bubble. Soon the pancake began to rise near the side of the pot opposite the spam, then subsided. The second bubble was nearer and the third was right on target. As it pushed up the pancake, the pancake in turn lifted the spam at its edge where it wasn't weighed down by the saucer – just the tiniest fraction of an inch, but hundreds of metres when scaled up to the Bay of Biscay. The bubble popped, the pancake dropped and the spam flopped. Pilot turned off the gas and sat down at the table with his notepad.

He tried to picture the moment of impact – not on France, but on his barges. He thought of his rectangle of barges ballasted at four corners by the weighty earth carriers and tried to picture the effect a rising mass of land would have on it. An image came to mind from a nature film of a whale breaking the surface of the sea at a very narrow angle and then disappearing like an escalator at the top of its run. He wondered what would happen if a small boat were over the whale as it surfaced. Would it be carried along on its back, or would the upward pressure capsize it? He drew some pictures, then decided there were too many variables: whether or not the surface of the land was coming up parallel to the surface of the sea; its speed of ascent; and the physical features of the terrain rising to meet the bellies of the barges. He could only imagine what the scene would be and concluded that if all the factors were in their favour – flat terrain, parallel planes, slow ascent – it *would* be possible for them to make a safe landfall. Possible or not, an inner voice told him he was wasting his time speculating about Vaalon's fantastic geological phenomenon. Whatever it was to be, it would be, regardless of what Pilot conjectured. The only thing that was in his power – the only thing that should concern him from now on – was what happened *after* the event.

Once again he felt a need to get out of the flat and into the fresh air. The aunts heard the door slam and went into the kitchen to tut at their great-nephew's culinary experimentation.

"Push, dear. Push." Diminishing amounts of sweat from a labour now in its fifteenth hour were being squeezed from the girl's body. "Breathe," her mother said, willing her fifth grandchild to appear. "You have to relax, Rosa. You're too tight."

"I'm thirsty, Mum," the girl gasped. "I need water. ANYTHING. A lager for fuck's sake." Truth be told, in this particular corner of Queensland, lager was nearly more plentiful than water.

After thinking about it for a while, the woman went out to the kitchen, where her husband and son-in-law were nursing warm beers by the broken fridge. "We need one of them," she said, grabbing an unopened can and racing back to the bedroom.

It may have been the world's first lager-assisted birth, but with things the way they were in these parched parts, it probably wasn't. When the eight-billionth nail in the Earth's coffin was extruded ten minutes later, nobody was counting.

Pilot spent the early part of the afternoon walking to Marazion, back to the train station for a cup of tea, over to the post office, into the police station for a look at the noticeboard and up Causewayhead to people-watch. He was observing something he never could understand – human life and all its working parts, functioning or not to a design he felt to be wrongly conceived from the beginning. He saw people over the years sell their lives and the souls of their children to their places of work without question or remorse. He saw the whole framework of humanity as a large animal coming to the end of a fat kill – unbeknown to it, the last of the game. To Pilot's way of thinking, a mass of human beings could no more exercise restraint than a thousand soldier ants happening across a juicy rodent. Anyone falling outside the scale on the side of sense or awareness would be left on the shoulder while the main column marched on, painting over any road sign that suggested it was traveling the wrong route.

Just then, one of the town's homeless walked by. Pilot had often found the man sleeping in the doorway of his aunts' shop and had made a practice of inviting him in, but the vagrant had always declined. As Pilot looked at the stubbled and grimy face, he saw a laughter and contentedness in this outcast's eyes, as if he alone knew that it was warmer outside than in.

When Pilot got back to the flat to wash up, his saucepan was still there, exactly as he, and subsequently his aunts, had left it. But the sugar-weighted saucer had pushed the spam down to a level where it was flush with the surface of the pancake. He poked it with his forefinger and forced a thin circular band of porridge up through the space between the pancake and the side of the saucepan. Then he pushed France all the way down to the bottom of the pot and watched the porridge wash thickly over her from all sides.

IV

Two days later, Pilot was on the phone to Brussels. He had based his initial ideas for the island's name on variations of Atlantis – *Atlantis Minor*, *New Atlantis*, *Atlantis Novus*. Then he moved on to anagrams of Atlantis. The island would comprise the edge of the continental shelf, pushed up wedge-like at a slant – *Atislant*, *Atslanti*, *At-Slanti*, *Slanttia*. Great anagrams, but ridiculous names. Same with *Listtaan*. 'Listing' in the ocean. Not an impressive picture. The other problem he was having was that all the names were based on English words and he felt it should be more international.

He liked the anagram *Nilstaat*, from the Latin root 'nihil', nothing, nil, and the German word for nation, 'Staat'. *Nilstaat* fit the concept of a nonaligned, unaffiliated state, but it sounded too German.

By lunchtime Pilot knew it had to be a made-up name – something *non*-lingual, like *Häagen Dazs*, dreamchild of an advertising copywriter. Of the fifty names he invented, he whittled it down to ten and then went to bed. By the morning, nine had evaporated. He'd based the tenth, *Eydos*, on the Greek word *eîdos*, meaning 'the distinctive expression of the cognitive or intellectual character of a culture or a social group.'

"I won't be processing any of the paperwork until the end of July," the soft-spoken Scottish voice at the other end of the line said, winding up their short conversation. "How do you pronounce it again?"

"Eye-doss, A-doss, Eee-dose, Ay-doze, Eye-doze, Eye-dose," Pilot replied. "It's non-lingual."

His next call was to his mentor to arrange a time to view the IGP's computer models. "As soon as you can get here," Vaalon said.

In the morning, Pilot arrived at Penzance station half an hour before departure time to ensure getting a table in the unreserved coach. The journey lasted five and a half hours, most of which he spent reading files on the laptop. Vaalon's vision was solidifying in Pilot's mind and things were beginning to seem less fantastical than at first.

The IGP building was just off Exhibition Road behind the Natural History Museum and Pilot found it easily. His anticipation and excitement when Vaalon greeted him at reception was impossible to hide. "Follow me, Lonnie," the man said without preamble. He ushered Pilot into a large room on the third floor housing a number of computers, sat down at one and signaled Pilot to pull over another chair.

The screen came to life and Vaalon began to play the keyboard like Chopin. One diagram after another – in 2-D and 3-D, black and white, multicoloured – danced across the monitor. "Bear with me, Lonnie. I'll start with 'pc-R00018', the pyrocoagulum we've been following for two years."

"What's a pyrocoagulum?"

"It's a lump of magma – a knot of greater viscosity than the material around it. By charting its movement, we can guage the pull of the magnetic field created by the solar tide."

Vaalon settled on an image Pilot guessed was a cross-section of the Bay of Biscay and began pointing out the various layers. "Mainland France, seawater, continental shelf, crust, mantle and this swirl here is pc-R00018. This is its position as we speak." Vaalon flicked the right arrow on his keyboard a few times, moving the magma lump deeper into the mantle. "And this was its position when we first identified and measured it." He tapped back and forth between the two images to give Pilot an animated rendition of magma in motion. "Now, look what happens when I advance it 13 weeks."

Pilot put his face closer to the screen and focused on the continental shelf and pc-R00018's increased proximity to it. The movement was so imperceptible that he almost missed it. Vaalon zoomed in and ran the sequence again. This time, the line of the continental shelf could be seen converging on the surface of the sea. One further click of the left arrow and part of the line rose *above* sea level. Vaalon traced the section that was out of the water with his fingertip. "From here to here is about 150 miles. Let's look at it from a different angle."

He rotated the aspect 90 degrees clockwise, giving a southeast to northwest view, and ran the sequence again. This time, the cresting of the continental shelf was much more graphic, appearing as a narrow angled wedge pointing towards the mainland. Vaalon ran his finger horizontally from the fat end of the wedge to where it disappeared under the sea to the east. "From there to there is around 20 miles. And this figure – " he pointed to the western elevation " – is between 300 and a thousand feet."

Something was niggling Pilot. "In that sequence you showed me just now, between your discovery of our magma lump and its position today, it hardly moved at all. How fast is it rising?"

"Approximately one foot every ten years," Vaalon said. "Slower than a glacier."

"Then how can it cause the island to surface so quickly? Logic says it would take three or four hundred years for that stretch of shelf to crest."

"In this case, logic is trumped by the harmonics of solar magnetics, tectonics, lithospherics and isostatics. Together they create the jolt necessary to trigger the pulse I described earlier. The equilibrium that keeps landmasses stable – isostasy – refluxes, or *hiccups*. A volcano will be many years in the making, but it only takes an instant to erupt. On the geophysical clock, the birth of your island will be a mere nanosecond event. On the human clock, it'll take anything from five to ten hours. Babies can be born quicker than Eydos, but I guarantee you it's not going to take 400 years."

Pilot sat baffled and mute in front of the computer.

"Lonnie, you'll just have to put your trust in the quality of knowledge and the accuracy of data used to program our software. The computer models all predict that your island's going to surface this August… stabilize… dry out for a few centuries… then sink again just as suddenly. It will – "

"Why doesn't the island keep on rising during the centuries it's above water?" As soon as he'd asked the question, Pilot had guessed the answer, remembering how, in his porridge-pancake-spam-saucer experiment, the weight of France had prevented the spam from rising any higher over its bubble.

"The solar tide holds the shelf in stasis until it ebbs. It can't rise higher because of the weight of the mainland and the magmatic pulse itself lasts at least four hundred years," Vaalon said. "So, Lonnie. How are you feeling now?"

"Hungry."

Over dinner at the Casa da Comina, Pilot brought up the politics of sovereignty. "I need to know if there's a plan, Forrest, and what influence, if any, our advocates have."

Vaalon's eyes locked onto Pilot's. "On June 23rd you're flying to New York with me to meet Fridrik Geirsson, Iceland's ambassador to the United Nations. I can understand your concern about this aspect of the operation, but a meeting with Geirsson will dispel your fears. He and his father before him have *owned* the UN Commision on Maritime Law for the past forty years."

Over the ensuing three weeks while he was waiting for his passport to arrive, Pilot meandered through Vaalon's hard drive as though through a spring meadow. He noted facts, figures, weights, measures, cargoes and personnel with the same part of his mind that fed on beautiful countryside, magnificent trees and poetic skies. This wasn't work. It was pleasure.

In preparation for his trip to Dublin, he read the files of his three Irish crew several times until he knew them as well as one can, short of actually meeting them in the flesh. Jane Lavery was in charge of the settler's vegetable-growing programme. A gardener for the Earl of Dungarvan, she had been an environmental activist since her late teens and had even spent six days in jail for handcuffing herself to the Minister for Agriculture, Food and the Marine during a demonstration against the genetic modification of potatoes. Now, at the age of twenty-seven, her protesting had taken a more mellow turn. The keyboard had replaced the sword, her popular blog having gained over a thousand subscribers in just six months. Pilot clicked the link to her blog site, read her latest entry – a well-documented case linking southern India's escalating birth defects to genetically modified rice – then went back to her photograph. *Frecklebound* was the only word to describe her. He'd never seen so many on one human face. He found her colouring of olive skin, rust-coloured hair, brown eyes and freckles unusual and very attractive.

The expedition's master-carpenter and builder, Josiah Billy, had been born in Australia. Orphaned while still crawling, Billy had learned to walk in a succession of foster homes before sprinting out on his own at fifteen. His paternal grandfather was Aborigine. The other three grandparents were Irish. A gifted club rugby player, but unable to make it into the Australian national team, Billy had been invited to play for Ireland, based on his Irish lineage. With few family ties in Australia, he took the first flight out. Josiah Billy had won fifteen caps as a loose forward in the Ireland national rugby team, but sin-bin offences in successive games had put an end to his international career. Vaalon's notes described 'a hefty, thirty-two-year-old joiner, wood carver and poet'. Pilot looked at the photograph, but couldn't see the poet. He thought Josiah Billy looked dangerously alpha and wondered if he'd be able to work with him.

He closed Billy's file, opened Macushla Mara's and went straight to her photo. Her thick black hair, prominent eyebrows and dark lashes could have washed ashore from the Spanish Armada; the green eyes were Irish; the nose and mouth Pre-Raphaelite. Governmental speechwriter Mara, a Trinity College classics graduate with a PhD, would soon be working for Lonnie Pilot, a Cornish tutor of seven-to-twelve-year-olds, as his 'press secretary'. With a sickening dip in confidence, he closed out the file. If he were able to pass himself off as a convincing leader to these people, no-one would be more surprised than Lonnie Pilot.

Three days before his flight, Pilot's passport arrived. He thought it a waste of money, because, in just over two months, he'd be throwing it, along with his past, into the English Channel. He re-read the postcard he'd received from Macushla Mara. Its calligraphy was exquisite.

Dear Lonnie Pilot,

Mr. Vaalon has booked us rooms at the Central Hotel, Exchequer Street. See you in the hotel bar at around seven? Looking forward to meeting you and the others.

– M. Mara

Pilot was relieved that he wouldn't be the only stranger in the group.

Maroon, moss green and peat brown were the predominant colours of the first floor Central Hotel bar. Four underpowered wall lights added little to the dingy atmosphere of a space more akin to a waiting room than a watering hole. An emaciated, acned youth in black trousers, white shirt and black tie hung loosely behind his bar, Pilot's Guinness being the only drink he had poured in half an hour. In the far corner, a young woman in an orange coat, already confirmed by Pilot as being neither Jane Lavery nor Macushla Mara, sat nursing a long-cold coffee and looking at her watch every two minutes. It was 6.45. Plenty of time to drown his nerves, which were still on edge. His flight from Exeter had been both frightening and exciting, as it was the first time Pilot had been on a plane. The bus ride into the city centre, consisting of road works topped by rush hour, was worse.

At seven o'clock, a large man entered the bar and began scanning the room. In the gloom, Pilot couldn't tell if he were Josiah Billy or not. The answer came when the orange coat leapt from her seat, skipped over to the fellow and threw her arms around him.

Five minutes later, Pilot's peripheral vision picked up another figure coming through the door. He turned his head, recognized Jane Lavery, and raised his hand. Lavery smiled and sauntered over to his table. She was tall and slim, and far more striking than her photograph had suggested.

"Glad to meet you, Mr. Pilot," she said, extending her hand. "How was your trip?"

"Uneventful." Pilot had decided not to mention the fact he'd never flown before. Heads of state *flew*. "Call me Lonnie."

Lavery pointed to his glass. "Would you like another drink, Lonnie?"

Pilot's natural reaction would have been to offer to get the drinks himself, but he decided to stay in character. "Guinness", he said. "Thank you, Jane."

As the barman was waiting for the head to settle on Pilot's drink, Josiah Billy walked in and went straight to the bar. "I'll have what she's having," he said, turning to face Lavery. "Jane Lavery – I recognize the freckles. I'm Josiah Billy."

"Hello, Josiah." She shook Billy's hand with unfeminine gusto. "By the way, the Guinness is Lonnie Pilot's."

"He's here?"

"Over at that corner table."

Billy looked over his shoulder. "Grey hair. I thought Pilot was in his twenties."

"He's younger than he looks. Go introduce yourself. I'll bring the drinks."

A few minutes later, Lavery took her seat and added to the awkwardness of strangers meeting for the first time. Pilot felt it was his job to break the ice, but Lavery beat him to it. "After thinking long and hard about this," she said, "I'm going to give Mr. Vaalon the benefit of the doubt… with a big *but.* No disrespect intended to you, Lonnie, but it's a ludicrously fantastical proposal by my way of thinking."

Before Pilot could respond, Macushla Mara appeared from the shadows and sat next to Lavery.

"You haven't missed anything, Macushla," Pilot said. "We've only just started. I'm Lonnie Pilot, this is Jane Lavery, and this is Josiah Billy." Polite greetings were exchanged and Pilot signalled Lavery to continue where she had left off.

"Don't get me wrong, Lonnie. We all turned up, including me. Now *that's* something."

Pilot laughed. "The fact that I'm not sitting here on my own is a miracle," he said, squirming in his chair. "But our proposal is neither ludicrous nor fantastical, Jane. What exactly did Mr. Vaalon tell you about what's going to happen?"

Lavery took a sip of wine, then gave a shorter version of the story Vaalon had given Pilot, but with her own twist. "A group of international idealists, led by a Cornish teacher, strap themselves to some barges, land on an emerging land mass in the Bay of Biscay and create Utopia. When *Vaalon* described it, it sounded believable," Lavery said. "When I describe it, it's the most outlandish fiction that's ever been imagined."

Pilot turned to Mara. "Macushla?"

"It's the basic premise of landing on an earthquake that perplexes me," she said. "The entire scenario is implausible, unbelievable, farfetched, unlikely and plain dangerous."

"Then why are you here?" Pilot took Mara's words as a challenge. He locked eyes with the woman, determined not to be the first to look away, but failed. The strength in her stare made it difficult for him to focus. "I had my doubts too, at first," he said, softening.

"But I've seen the computer models. It's a huge leap of faith we're asking of you, I admit that."

"Bizarre is what it is," Billy said. "I've made some big leaps in my life, but this is a leap too far."

"Then I think you should leave. I don't –"

"Hold on, man," Billy interrupted. "I know of an empty house just a mile from here. We could start building our Utopia there tomorrow. But on an island in the Bay of Biscay that isn't even here yet?"

Pilot's look stunned Billy to silence. It was an expression he had recently placed in his armoury as a weapon against anyone trying to usurp his authority. In combination with the right words, it was lethal. "Don't interrupt me again," he said, turning his stare up a notch while trying not to blink. He could almost feel the testosterone surging through his veins. This time, it was Billy the poet who looked away first.

If they'd all blindly believed in the island, and in him as its leader, Pilot would have been worried. Both were tall orders. But, as Lavery said, they had all turned up for this meeting, and that in itself was positive. Pilot decided to ignore the first hurdle of plausibility and concentrate on laying out his own credentials. He believed that if you can converse on a subject the listener knows little about, and can do so with confidence and conviction, they will unconsciously elevate you. So, he began summarizing the theory of the Solar Tide, the magnetic pull it exerts on the magma and the effect this has on the Earth's crust. Ten minutes into his oration, he could sense that they were beginning at least to believe the science.

"That's what's happening *below* us," Pilot said. "Now consider what's happening on the surface. Where other people see blue, cloudless skies, all I see is red. For me, there's no escape from the mass suffering taking place on our over-populated planet."

Pilot could sense Lavery and Mara warming to him.

"The Earth is sinking," he continued on his wave. "Humanity has tried any number of pumps over past millennia to clear the water from the hold, but none – Christian, Communist, New Age, you name it – has had the depth or the bore required to do the job. We're losing the battle. The more people who come aboard the ship, the more bilgewater that's created and the closer to sinking we get.

"With the raising of this island, we're being given the opportunity, unique in world history, to build a different kind of pump. Not one based on make-believe deities, or flakey philosophy, but on nuts and bolts. To make this pump work – to make it a credible force – it has to be seen as being *outside* the existing order."

"Anarchistic." Mara said.

"Literally speaking, the label fits us. We're trying to overturn the accepted order. But what happens if the accepted order is unacceptable? This same anarchist then becomes someone who is trying to overturn 'disorder'. What's important is being outside the existing chaos. Geographically, we *will be*. Conceptually, we *are*, assuming you feel the same way I do." Pilot looked at each in turn. "The priests have had their day. It's time to bring in the plumbers."

"*The priests have had their day. It's time to bring in the plumbers*," Mara repeated. "I like that."

Bulls eye, Pilot thought. "Your house down the road isn't up to the task, Josiah," he said to Billy. "The entire world, and every country, city and town in it, is a dystopia. That's why we need this virgin territory in the Bay of Biscay. No-one can touch us there."

"That's bull, man. They'll be on us like flies on shit."

"Not necessarily. Let's take it one day at a time, Josiah. Right now, we should be worrying about what clothes we're going to pack."

"We should be worrying about what's going to happen when we get there, surely," Lavery said. "What's the plan, Lonnie?"

"It's in there," Pilot said, pointing to Lavery's head. And in the minds of everyone else who will be landing in August. All we're taking to the island is the raw material for this experiment, not the finished product. We've set ourselves a basic survival agenda to begin with – food production, shelter, drinking water, medical. We've identified potential obstacles and devised ways of dealing with them. An astronaut-scientist can't get down to any meaningful work until he's in orbit. Once *we're* in orbit, we can start ours."

Mara laughed. "Dizzy answer."

"To a confounding question. The world population hit eight billion last month. Drug abuse has permeated up to the highest levels of government and business. The northern right whale became extinct last year, the Sumatran Rhino in April. And martial law has been declared in Hungary. We won't be taking the solution to these problems with us to the island. But maybe, after five, ten, or twenty years, we'll have created one."

"The precedents aren't good," Lavery said. "Take America's Founding Fathers. A group of spiritually aware, gutsy people flee the religious persecution and dogmas of the Old World to a new, virgin land – an entire continent no less. Ignoring the people already there, I might add. And what do they do with it? Within a blink of the Earth's eye they turn it into a bigger, brasher and more destructive version of what they'd left behind. What chance have *we* got out there in the cold Atlantic?"

Pilot's passion and frustration were boiling over. "Put 86 pessimistic optimists together on a slab of rock in the middle of the ocean and... Look, for the sake of a shorter and more constructive meeting, let's assume everything's going to happen just as Vaalon said it would. We make landfall, get up next morning... then what?"

"Make breakfast," Billy said.

For Pilot, returning to Penzance was an anti-climax. After his years of isolation, the energy generated through interacting with the others in Dublin was new and exhilarating. After dinner, the four of them had talked in Pilot's room until three in the morning, gradually molding themselves into a team fit for purpose. The skepticism of earlier had been superceded by guarded optimism, largely due to a power of persuasion Pilot never knew he had – because he'd never had anyone to persuade until now.

Jane Lavery stayed on after the others had left. Pilot had wanted to know more about the hydroponic growing system she'd written about on one of her blogs, and she was more than happy to expand.

"Hydroponics – suspending plants in water without soil – is perfect for where we're going and will complement the conventional growing methods we'll also be using. Pumping the nutrient solution from a reservoir requires electricity we may not have, so we'll be using *passive* hydroponics, where the nutrient solution is simply drawn up through the plants' root system. I've persuaded Mr. Vaalon to bankroll thirty hydroponic growing tanks, most of which I plan to use to cultivate Moringas."

"The world's most generous tree."

"You know the Moringa leaf. I'm impressed."

"Five times more iron than spinach."

"*Twenty*-five times more, Lonnie. And four times more protein than eggs; ten times more vitamin A than carrots; fifteen times more potassium than bananas. I've been testing a solution of nutrients specially developed for growing Moringas – manganese, copper, potassium phosphate, calcium nitrate, zinc, boron… the results are astounding."

For another half hour they had talked about the challenges of food production that would soon be facing them, until tiredness overcame both. As he showed her out the door, Pilot had surprised Lavery, and himself even more, by kissing her lightly on the lips.

Like a battery losing power, Pilot's high had begun to descend the moment his plane landed in Exeter. Now, in the cold light of his net shed, doubts were beginning to muddy his longer sight. On paper, Vaalon's vision seemed so perfect – a world of harmony, purpose, energy and life. But the reality from August would be nothing more than grim subsistence living on a naked shelf of rock – the first landfall in three thousand miles for the fearsome North Atlantic seas and freezing dagger winds.

Pilot's experience in Dublin with Lavery, Mara and Billy had underlined the need for unity and commitment among the crew. The remaining 82 recruits were still an unknown quantity, but Pilot decided that Vaalon's selection and screening skills had been passable so far, Josiah Billy being the only question mark, and that it was pointless worrying. He had three weeks to kill before his trip to New York and decided that the best remedy for toxic rumination was activity.

Two days later, Lonnie Pilot was boarding the Plymouth-Roscoff night ferry. He'd surrendered to a pressing need to see the waters of the Bay of Biscay for himself, feeling that in some way he might then be able to bridge the gap between possibility and probability; fiction and fact; blue printers ink and real seawater.

From Roscoff he took a train to Brest, then a bus to Le Conquet, where, at two on the afternoon of June 5th, Lonnie Pilot set eyes on the Bay of Biscay for the first time. A heat haze smudged the horizon, making it difficult to tell where the sea ended and the sky began. He was just able to make out the islands of Beniguet, Litiri, Ledenes and Molène, stringing out to the northwest towards the larger island of Ouessant, beyond which, somewhere on the floor of the Bay, he would soon be living. As he stood at the end of the pier looking out to sea he experienced a sensation similar, he thought, to what medieval seafarers felt when the Earth was still believed to be flat – a strange mixture of fear and wonderment at what lay over the edge of the world. He tried to imagine standing in this same spot in three months time watching a wall of water as wide as the eye could see, charging towards him.

Pilot walked to a small, sandy cove nearby and took out the crab sticks and cidre he'd bought at the Super 8. When he'd finished eating, he opened his notebook to the entries he had made at the IGP. According to the computer models, the wave would hit La Rochelle and Saint Nazaire first, whiplash up the coast to the furthest northwest tip of Brittany and Ushant and then carry on to Cornwall and County Cork. And it would be a killer. There had been nothing in Vaalon's files about any provision to warn the authorities and coastal populations of the impending catastrophe, and this bothered Pilot. He tried to divert his thoughts from the tsunami, but was only engulfed by another – a wave of invaders overrunning their island within hours of its emergence like Josiah Billy's flies on shit. With the beginnings of a migraine, Pilot took out his phone and began texting.

As he waited for a reply, serious doubts were growing as to his own suitability as chief novitiate of this extraordinary colonisation. He had every intention of resigning when his phone sang and vibrated three times. The message from Vaalon acted like the antidote to a snake bite.

The system's in place. It's foolproof and failsafe and took several years to organize. There'll be no shipping anywhere near the path of the waves at the time in question. Nor will there be a living creature within range of any tsunami anywhere in western Europe from Biarritz to Bantry Bay… IF people heed the warnings. Human nature will create its own victims, but we can't be held responsible.

Vaalon's text message was enough to close the subject for the time being. Pilot had no idea how the entire coastal populations of three countries could be successfully relocated, but if anyone had the resources to do it, it was the world's 97th richest man. He pulled himself to his feet and marched towards the road, leaving his headache buried in the sand.

V

Vaalon's idea of a limo was a two-seater Smart car, which met Pilot at Paddington station and took him to his mentor's London home in Douro Place, South Kensington. The following morning, Forrest Vaalon and Lonnie Pilot would be flying to New York for a meeting Pilot saw as being pivotal. Much as he wanted to, he could not see their claim of sovereignty succeeding and was impatient to hear Ambassador Geirsson's plan.

The first thing that met Pilot's eyes outside the arrivals hall at JFK was the elongated, charcoal-grey, chauffeur-driven Lincoln Continental with tinted windows waiting at the curb. Vaalon stopped at the back door of the limo. "These are as common as black cabs in London," he said. "An inconspicuous way to travel around Manhattan." He pointed to the car behind – a Nissan – and began walking towards it. "That's ours. Even more discreet."

The driver – black-haired, stocky and a lot shorter than Pilot – Vaalon introduced as Aaron Serman, one of Pilot's American crew. "Sit in front, Lonnie. I'll go in the back."

Vaalon's brownstone in the Upper West Side was as understated as his car – on the outside. The antique furniture, sculptures, carpets and paintings inside confirmed Forrest Vaalon as a man of taste and appreciation. Serman, who'd been working as the man's

New York assistant for three years and had a room on the top floor, showed Pilot to the guest suite and handed him seven take-out menus ranging from Armenian to Vietnamese. "I'll come back for your order in half an hour," he said, glancing at his Piaget. "Help yourself to a beer. They're downstairs in the fridge."

When Serman had gone, Pilot began touring his suite as if in an art gallery. An original Peter Lanyon hung over the sofa, with two Henri Rousseaus either side of a gold leaf sunburst mirror. A six foot tall by seven inch wide Giacometti sculpture stood guard between the two windows. On the wall opposite was a photo portrait by Robert Frank of a beautiful, coal-eyed young woman whose identity Pilot guessed, and confirmed on checking the back of the frame. *Ruth Belkin Vaalon, 1952.* He walked into the bedroom, where two more photos of Ruth, one by Man Ray, the other by Lee Miller, continued Vaalon's tribute to the love of his life. The en-suite bathroom was the largest Pilot had ever seen. He ran himself a bath, then lay down on the bed for twenty minutes while the water cooled, imagining what it would be like to drown.

Later, over enchiladas and refried beans, Pilot and Serman began to get acquainted, Vaalon having deliberately accepted a dinner invitation on the other side of town to facilitate the two men's bonding.

"How long have you worked for Mr. Vaalon?" Pilot asked.

Serman, dressed in loafers, white socks, navy blue corduroys and button-down Brooks Brothers shirt, crossed his legs and prepared to impress the man he considered to be his line manager. "After graduating from Columbia, I taught at Deerfield Academy for a semester. Thought it would be safer teaching in a prep school than trying to control fifty heavily armed high school students in Brooklyn. Boy, was I wrong. I couldn't cut it. So I answered an ad in the New York Times for a personal assistant/driver. Mr. Vaalon's only here maybe fifteen days a month and I spend the rest of the time at night school – computer technology."

"What did you study at Columbia?"

"Statistics and Japanese."

"Wouldn't that have qualified you for something grander than this?"

"I tried," Serman said with a smile. "Tried to *conform*, that is. Couldn't."

"In your dossier Forrest describes you as being a logistical genius."

"I most probably am."

Having been told by Vaalon that Aaron Serman was privy to the island's imminent arrival, Pilot had no problem asking his next question. "Statistically speaking, Aaron, what are the chances the island will be coming up as predicted?"

Serman thought for a moment. "Well, there *are* no statistics on this, so we have to resort to the racecourse. I've studied the form – the science and the computer models – and I think the odds on it happening as predicted are very good. Is that what you wanted to hear?"

"Yes, it is. Thanks, Aaron."

Serman rose to leave. "Sleep as long as you want in the morning, Lonnie. Your meeting isn't until two o'clock."

At six foot three, Lonnie Pilot was taller than most people he met, apart from Forrest Vaalon, but when Fridrik Geirsson greeted them at the door of his apartment, Pilot found himself looking *up* at the underside of a grey-blond fringe. At six foot eight,

Geirsson was a big man at the UN, both physically and influentially. Pilot guessed that he was in his early forties at most.

"Glad to meet you at last, Lonnie," Geirsson said, extending a wide hand. "Forrest, you look tired. Come in and sit down."

He led the two men down the hall and into his study, whispering something to his secretary on the way. In the centre of the coffee table was a ring binder. He offered Vaalon a comfortable armchair, motioned Pilot to a sofa and took a chair opposite him. He leaned across the table and positioned the binder in front of Pilot. "Mr. Vaalon has already seen this," he said. "It's a 200-page draft, substantiating and documenting your case for sovereignty over the island. Forrest told me this was a particular worry to you. We have had to be very creative in constructing our arguments."

Geirsson opened the binder and folded his hands on the top page. "It is all built on definitions and precedents, or rather on the *lack* of precedents," he said, drawing his forefinger back and forth under his nose as if it had been soaked in a liquid aid to concentration. "The crux of our argument is this: The moment a portion of the continental shelf breaks the surface of the sea, it ceases to be a continental shelf, under the current definition of such, and becomes an *island.* If this island surfaces *within* a country's territorial waters, the law declares that they have outright sovereignty. This is logical. Second scenario: It surfaces *beyond* the country's territorial sea, but still within its contiguous zone. In this case, ownership becomes less clear, but is still weighted heavily in favour of France."

Geirsson's secretary placed a coffee tray on the table and began pouring.

"Now, this is where it begins to get complicated," Geirsson continued when they were alone again. "Eydos will be surfacing between 80 and a hundred miles off the French coast – well outside her territorial sea and contiguous zone, but still within her EEZ." He pushed the binder towards Pilot while rotating it 180 degrees.

"You are welcome to read this from cover to cover, Lonnie, but it cannot leave the apartment. There is a guest room if you need to stay over."

"I wouldn't mind a quick read, but I'm happy with your summary."

"Good. It might help to define the different *types* of island, because they have relevance. And the reason they have relevance is that they are *irrelevant* to your claim. Unlike all these other islands, Eydos has no precedent in modern human experience, and this is the basis of our argument. The proof is in what is *extant*, held against what is to come – or rather what, on a certain day and time in August in the Bay of Biscay, will have occurred."

Geirsson swung the binder back to face him, located the relevant section and began paraphrasing.

"Oceanic islands are islands that do not sit on continental shelves. Most are volcanic in origin. The Mariana Islands, the Aleutian Islands and most of Tonga were formed by volcanoes arising from the subduction of one plate under another. Eydos will *not* be one of those.

"Where an oceanic rift reaches the surface, another type of volcanic oceanic island occurs – Iceland, for example, and Jan Mayen. Eydos will not be one of *those.*

"There are some non-volcanic oceanic islands that are tectonic in origin and arise where plate movements have pushed the deep ocean floor above the surface. For Eydos, we have to note the distinction between *deep ocean floor* and *continental shelf*. It is all covered in here.

"A third type of volcanic oceanic island is formed over volcanic hotspots. A hotspot is more or less stationary relative to the moving tectonic plate above it, so a chain of islands is *extruded* as the plate drifts, like the Hawaiian Islands and the Tuamotu Archipelago. Tristan da Cunha is an example of a hotspot volcano in the Atlantic Ocean, another one being my country's own island of Surtsey, formed in 1963. Eydos will not be one of *those*, either."

Unable to extend his long legs under the coffee table, Geirsson stood up and stretched. "Now we come to continental islands," he said, walking around the room. "These are bodies of land that lie on the continental shelf of a *continent*, as opposed to a particular country. Great Britain, Ireland and Sicily are all islands on the European continental shelf. There are similar examples to be found all over the world." He resumed his seat and turned a few pages until he found what he was looking for. "Sable Island off Nova Scotia is believed to have been formed by a terminal moraine deposited on the continental shelf near the end of the last Ice Age. Again, Eydos cannot be placed in this category of island. Nor is Eydos an atoll, a microcontinental island, a seamount, an islet, a skerry, a bar or a cay. Eydos is *nothing* until it is defined. And who better to define it than the UN Commission on Maritime Law?"

Fridrik Geirsson and Forrest Vaalon both looked at Pilot with broad grins of satisfaction. Lonnie Pilot returned their smiles with interest.

"Possession is nine-tenths of the law in terms of proving ownership," Geirsson continued. "If we are successful in establishing to the entire world your lawful claim to possession in that first hour, then we will have only the other one-tenth to contend with."

Geirsson withdrew a single sheet of paper from the back of the binder and handed it to Pilot. "This is an outline for a declaration to be transmitted to the world the instant you make landfall."

Pilot aimed a questioning glance at Vaalon, who took the floor.

"Both the transponder broadcasting your exact position, and the transmitter sending out your declaration, will be automatically activated on contact with the rising island," Vaalon explained. "As a failsafe, as soon as you're able to do so, confirm the position of your landfall by radio. Either way, within seconds and minutes, the entire world will know you're there."

Lonnie Pilot left Geirsson's apartment a happy man. He hadn't had the patience to read through the entire document – the tall Icelander's summary had been sufficient.

The following morning, with an entire day to fill before his evening flight, Pilot decided to take up Serman's offer of a city tour on foot. They started walking east at a purposeful gait, counting down the avenues as they went and, half an hour later, stood peering up at the sleek, slim, silvery monolith of the U.N. building as it toppled over on them, a trick of the scudding clouds behind it.

They were frisked going in and took the first available guided tour. Inside the General Assembly, Pilot tried to imagine the scene as their claim was made. As had happened at Le Conquet, his confidence was being eroded by his proximity to the actual stage in the coming play. It was not a comfortable feeling and he was relieved when the tour was over.

They left the building, turned left and began following the river down to South Street, stopping at the sight of the top third of a four-masted clipper ship visible over the wharves and warehouses. "Theme park," Serman said. "The theme being Nineteenth Century New York Maritime." They strolled around for half an hour then walked out to the end of the pier and sat on a bollard.

Pilot had often wondered why it was that eras, environments, ways of life, even everyday objects, were never appreciated until after their time had passed. Why, for instance, should an ordinary 19th century commode have appreciated in value a hundred fold since it was last sat upon, and today enjoy pride of place as a valuable antique in someone's best room – never again to be used for the purpose it was created? Had nostalgia always been as strong, or was this just a symptom of civilization coming as far as it could and looking longingly back at the paths it would never again tread?

With no consideration for Serman's understanding, Pilot launched straight from thought to expression. "It would make much more sense," he said, "if we could live the second half of our lives backwards."

"...*What*?"

"Then we'd be able to appreciate, through reverse nostalgia, the things that had passed us by in our past – now our future – redress the wrongs we had done and repair the people we had hurt."

Even at the age of twenty-five, there was a lot of material in Pilot's life that he would like to have a second go at. Like the way he had treated his mother when she said she was leaving with the man he called 'the snake with a snakeskin briefcase'. He had made her cry, but in the intervening years had learned that the desires that move people to do such things are much more powerful forces than basic loyalties, principles and ties to their children. They could rationalize *any* behavior and could no more help themselves than could rutting deer. He should have been more understanding.

The adenoidal hoot of an unseen tugboat closed this particular thought tangent and brought Pilot back to his current position. Serman was still looking at him as if he were ill. "Sorry, Aaron. Where to next?"

"You can't leave without visiting the The Freedom Tower."

The elevator to the 100th floor observation deck didn't feel as if it were even in motion, but when it stopped and the two emerged, there, spread out below them, was the whole of greater New York semi-obscured by a layer of smog, the roof of which must have been five hundred feet below them. His legs were like rubber and the urge to jump barely resistible. The half-inch-thick plate glass, although insuring his body stayed in the building, did nothing to arrest his imagined fall. He sat down on the floor as far away from the window as he could, dreading what the future held in store for them.

"Tomorrow morning I'm flying to Madrid to brief your advocate there," Vaalon said later. "As for you, Lonnie, you need to relax. With E-Day approaching, you can't afford a nervous breakdown. When you get back to England, think of a diversion and *do it*."

Pilot was glad he'd seen New York, because for him, that city – and he was thinking Wall Street, not Harlem or The Bronx – represented the advance camp in civilization's relentless march to the edge of the precipice. The rest of the world was fast catching up, and then, like the last pieces of garbage completing the landfill, it would all be over. The destruction of the World Trade Center and the Statue of Liberty by outside forces, and self-inflicted wounds by the bankers, fiscal conservatives, survivalists and the growing army of anarchistic, unemployed youth throughout the States had been mere surface symptoms of the deadly canker growing deep below the skin of the corporate global body.

As he was dropping Pilot at Departures, Serman began laughing.

"What's funny, Aaron?" Pilot asked.

"Just something I read in the flotilla manifest yesterday."

"What was that?"

"Five thousand condoms."

VI

Pilot discovered the diversion he needed in a banner ad on a hot air ballooning website. He pulled out his phone and pressed speed dial 1. "It's a week's course in theoretical and practical instruction," he explained to Vaalon. "Do you mind if I put the cost on the credit card?"

There was silence at the other end of the connection, and Pilot was ready to retract his request when Vaalon answered. "For this one, phone Franz Barta. You'll have to introduce yourself some time, so it might as well be now. He can pay them direct. Let me have a word with him first and you call him in the morning. It sounds like good medicine to me. Just don't fall out of the basket."

The next day, Pilot gave Barta the banking details of the Bath Balloon Club, thanked him and hung up. Then he headed for Newlyn harbour to read up on hot air ballooning in the 'plein air'.

"I can envisage an entire fleet of them, with flights to Spain, France, England, Ireland and maybe even Iceland, depending on which way the wind's blowing," Pilot said to his aunts on his return from Bath.

"Lonnie, what on earth are you talking about?" Sally asked.

"Blimps," Hilda said. "He's talking about blimps."

"Not blimps, Hilda, hot air balloons. Blimps use hydrogen or helium and have rudders and propellers. With mine, you heat the air in the canopy with a gas burner underneath and up you go. As the air cools, down you come ... slowly. The only thing you haven't got control of is your direction."

The two sisters raised four eyebrows. "What good is it then, if you can't go where you want to go?" Hilda asked.

"Having control of our direction only takes us to bad places," Pilot answered. "Human nature can't help but steer towards them. Like Icarus." His aunts looked at each other blankly. "By the way, I'm leaving the country for good on August first."

A piece of toast, which had adhered to Hilda's lower lip when her jaw dropped, fell off onto her plate. "Leaving the country? Whatever for?"

"You can't," Sally added. "It would break your mother's heart. We'd miss you too."

A rare feeling of affection welled up in Pilot. "I'll miss you, too. It's time I moved on all the same."

"Where are you going, Lonnie?"

"I was thinking Australia."

"In a balloon?"

The weather during the middle two weeks of July had been strange all over the world. In Penzance there had been neither sun, nor rain, nor wind – only a damp-looking, yellow-grey blanket spread from horizon to horizon. The air below was hot and heavy, like the people who walked through it, gamely trying to accomplish their daily tasks with the good humour expected in mid-summer. Not even Lonnie Pilot could motivate himself to a level deserving of his impending big day.

As if on cue, Eydos sent Pilot a message care of the BBC News website. He almost missed it, so lax had his concentration become, but the familiar detonation in his chest told him that what he was half reading was, in fact, news of their own first labour pains. He went back to the beginning of the item and shut out everything in the world but the text rising up his screen.

Earth Tremors Recorded in Bay of Biscay

AP– Geologists in France, Britain and Spain last night recorded a series of mild tremors centred in an area of the Bay of Biscay 150 miles southwest of Brest. At their most severe, the tremors registered 2.5 on the Richter Scale.

Dr. Philip Graff of the Royal Seismographic Observatory said, 'What we recorded was something called a harmonic tremor, which is caused by a continuous release of seismic energy typically associated with the underground movement of magma. Under land, this magnitude of activity would have caused tea cups to rattle in their saucers, but, occurring at sea at a depth of over 5,000 metres, the tremors were felt by no one.'

Dr. Graff also stated that, although there are no records of previous seismic activity in this area, the people of Western Europe have nothing to fear from the event. 'It is unusual, but unthreatening.'

According to RSO readings, eighteen separate tremors, lasting a total of two hours and twenty-five minutes, ended shortly after 0200 hrs GMT.

Any lingering doubts Pilot may have had regarding Vaalon's prediction no longer held water. Two point five on the Richter Scale was all it took to shake him out of his lethargy.

"There's another of your crew I'd like you to meet before E-Day," Forrest Vaalon said in a phone call to Pilot the next morning. "His name is Henry Bradingbrooke. We can meet you half-way, and I was thinking the day after tomorrow in Bristol." After they'd arranged a time and a place to meet, Pilot went straight to the laptop, opened Bradingbrooke's file and began reading.

Thinking it an apt venue, Vaalon had chosen a restaurant with a view of Bristol's floating harbour for their meeting. Pilot arrived first, was led to the table Vaalon had reserved, ordered a jug of water and got out his newspaper to finish reading a piece about the latest US crop failures. When he'd finished, he tore out the article, put it in his shoulder bag and ran his eyes across Bristol harbour. Cary Grant was born here, he thought, dredging up another piece of useless information from his vast well of ephemera.

When Vaalon and Bradingbrooke entered the restaurant, Pilot stood up, shook Vaalon's hand, pulled out his chair for him and was about to do the same for Bradingbrooke when he remembered his place in the pecking order. He sat down and let Henry Bradingbrooke, a baronet, pull out his own chair. Pilot had never been impressed with titles, especially inherited ones. But he *was* impressed by Bradingbrooke's qualifications. Henry Charles Finucane Bradingbrooke, Bart., held a PhD in meteorology and had been working at the IGP for two years. Over several days, Pilot had been harbouring a nagging suspicion that the man now sitting next to him was Vaalon's 'Number Three', and it wasn't a comfortable feeling.

"Glad to meet you, Henry," Pilot said, extending his hand.

"And you, Pilot." Bradingbrooke used the public school practice of addressing cohorts by their surnames.

"Henry's been running studies on the ramifications of solar tides on the world's weather patterns," Vaalon said. "Henry?"

"The solar tide exerts an imperceptible drag on the jetstream," Bradingbrooke explained. "Although barely measurable, it causes anomalies in our weather patterns, such as those we're experiencing at the moment. So far, they're working in our favour. When it comes time to bring the barges together and secure the flotilla, we just hope the seas are as flat as they are now. From what I can tell, it looks as if they will be."

"The calm before the storm," Pilot said.

"Indeed. What I'm also trying to ascertain is what sort of weather we'll have in the weeks *after* the storm. What we don't want are gales or torrential rains when we're trying to get a toehold."

"What's the forecast?"

For the first time in the meeting, Bradingbrooke smiled. "Easterly, gale-force French, followed by heavy British from the north. Joking aside, I think it will be mild and dry throughout August, with winds gradually building up velocity in September. Then, Pilot, all hell will break loose."

After dinner, the meeting took a more casual turn. Vaalon told them about his childhood in New Mexico and how the geology bug had bitten him at the age of seven. Henry Bradingbrooke attributed his interest in the weather to many months spent sailing with his late father in the Solent. Pilot wanted to know more about what lay below Bradingbrooke's education. "Are you married, Henry?" he asked, knowing full well the man wasn't.

"I very easily could have been – three years ago. But my head was in the clouds, *literally*, and I missed my chance. She married a banker."

"Not a good investment on her part. You're in a position to travel then."

Bradingbrooke laughed again. "I can't wait to shuffle off this mortal coil."

As he walked back to the station, Pilot reflected on his meeting with Vaalon and Bradingbrooke. He liked Henry. More importantly, he had at no point felt inferior to him. Whether that was through growing self confidence or Bradingbrooke's seeming acceptance of the leadership hierarchy remained to be seen.

Pilot spent the next few days saying goodbye to his old life and his old haunts. For all its lack of pulse, his neighbourhood had something he knew he was going to miss. He would never again enjoy the comfort to be found in being insignificant and living in an insignificant place. Ahead of him lay the prospect of a future on centre stage, forever a public person, and this frightened and enticed him at the same time.

He decided to take a last walk, and as he was passing Humphry Davy's statue, he came across a group of teenage girls, one of whom he had in the past privately referred to as *Botticelli's Cornish Venus.* He barely recognized her now, though, so dissolute and hardened had she become through three years on crack cocaine and two abortions. He railed at the cruel defacement inflicted on her and at his present impotence in the matter. He averted his eyes with sadness, gave them all a wide berth and began walking to Newlyn.

When a figure crossed his field of vision at Wherrytown, he recognized the walk as belonging to the vagrant with the special light in his eyes. On an impulse, closely followed by an idea, Pilot ran and caught up with him. "I'm leaving here for good in a few days," he said to the man, "and I'd like to give you something. Come for a drink at my place and I'll show you."

The sharp eyes blazed and Pilot feared the man was deranged. Then the face morphed into a grimy smile and answered, "So long as you're buyin', son..."

The hot spell had broken that day and it was just beginning to rain. Had Bradingbrooke got it wrong, Pilot wondered, or was this just a temporary anomaly? He bought a flagon of scrumpy from Lidl's and led his new friend through the downpour to his net shed.

The odd couple sat around the paraffin heater drying out and sharing their life experiences. When the cider ran out, the man dug deep in his overcoat and brought out a bottle of cheap, gut-rotting rum. Pilot reciprocated by bringing out the key to his net shed and holding it up to the man. "You'll like it here, Llewellyn," he said. "You can move in on Saturday. I'll leave the key behind the drainpipe."

The next day, Friday, Pilot was fighting a hangover. Despite the feeling of being three hundred feet underwater, he decided to cook his aunts a special farewell dinner of fresh squid from Trelawney's, spinach, sautéed potatoes and apple crumble.

Later that evening the aunts announced that they'd never had such an enjoyable meal, which Pilot thought a dishonest statement considering they hadn't touched the squid. They had resigned themselves to their great-nephew's leaving, but were still no wiser as to where he was going. "Do you at least have a forwarding address?" Hilda had asked.

"Not yet."

"If I were you, I'd let out the net shed for some extra income," Sally had suggested.

"Can't. It's not mine any more. The new owner's moving in tomorrow."

In the morning, the two women were travelling to yet another out of town fête and this was 'goodbye' forever. He would miss Sally and Hilda. They'd been good to him and, now that he was leaving, he wished he'd been a better ward. If I could reverse time, I would be, he thought.

On entering his new home the next afternoon, Llewellyn Martin found a seven word note from his young benefactor on the table.

THE BEGINNING OF THE WORLD IS NIGH.

VII

Pilot's train journey to Falmouth, which had started on a note of high excitement, soon became infected by an equivalent measure of loneliness, brought on by the knowledge that from now on everyone, bar the five crew he'd already met, would be a stranger. Every emotion took it in turn to share the carriage with him: exhilaration; regret; fear; excitement; wonder; and disbelief. Materially, he had managed to fit everything he needed into a single medium sized rolling suitcase, and this he propped up on the seat next to him – two travelling companions heading for a destination no man or suitcase had ever set foot or wheel on before. He had gone round to Jenny's studio to apologise for missing her Private View the previous week and to say goodbye. They had hugged wordlessly for five minutes. "Enjoy Australia," she had said at the door. "And write to me."

In his hotel that night, Pilot's final reverie before falling asleep was an image of Llewellyn Martin darning his socks by candlelight in his new home.

Pilot had asked to be woken at six, but this wasn't necessary. At five-thirty he was already dressed and pacing his room waiting for a reasonable hour to check out. He likened himself to a sixties astronaut, carrying one of those small silver suitcases to the lauchpad for his flight into the unknown.

Pilot reached the marina at quarter to eight. It felt as if his heart were trying to fight its way out of his ribcage and he thought neither the heart nor the cage would last another hour. There were over a hundred boats moored up and it took him ten minutes to locate the *Polcrebo*, resting at the furthest quay. She must have been sixty years old if she were a day and looked only just seaworthy.

A few minutes later two figures appeared from the wheelhouse and called over to Pilot. From his files, he recognized them as Jack Highbell and Jason Budd. Both had studied social psychology at the London School of Economics, but had dropped out after two years. They had also been recent cell mates in Dartmoor Prison, having served an eighteen month sentence for arson. The owner of the boat they'd set fire to in Brixham harbor was a cocaine dealer who Highbell maintained was responsible for the ruin of his sister. Through lack of solid evidence, English law had been unable to touch him, so 'Devonian law' had been invoked.

The two men were typical of the majority of Pilot's crew – apostates and militants, not by inclination, but through necessity. It was wise heads, not chips, they had on their shoulders. The mysterious but inspiring Forrest Vaalon had had little trouble signing up Highbell and Budd for the voyage. They, and 78 of their crewmates, had no idea of their true destination, only that they were answerable to Lonnie Pilot, who was to be in charge of the experiment. They helped him onto the confined deck, where nine other crew stood compressed, shoulder to shoulder. Macushla Mara, Jane Lavery and Josiah Billy squeezed forward and greeted Pilot with hugs and hand shakes.

It was crowded on the old boat, but at least there was no baggage to accommodate. Everything but hand luggage had already been sent to Hull and stowed away on *Ptolemy* before her run down to Falmouth. Three miles offshore, the ocean-going barge carrying 24 further crew awaited *Polcrebo's* arrival. The others would be joining them at the Bay of Biscay rendezvous.

Pilot made his way to the launch's stern and watched the white, foamy ribbon between the marina and *Polcrebo's* churning propellors lengthen. The weather was warm and there was a heat haze, so it wasn't long before Pendennis Point and Cornwall and Britain and Pilot's whole life up to this hour had dissolved from view.

He looked around to see what the others were doing. Highbell was glued to the compass in the wheelhouse. Budd stood on top of the cabin roof combing the horizon with a pair of binoculars, while another man kept his ear to an engine which wasn't sounding at all healthy. Josiah Billy caught Pilot's eye and made a grimace.

"I hope you brought your tools, Josiah," Pilot said.

"A bottle opener's all I need, mate. I don't do engines."

"There she is," Budd shouted some time later. It took a while for 'her' to come within the scope of the naked eye and the first thing Pilot saw was a white dot on the horizon reflecting sunlight through the haze. As they got nearer, a dark smudge appeared underneath the white one. Then the entire image resolved itself into the identifiable shapes of ocean-going barge below jumbo jet.

"What the fuck?" someone said.

Although most of the passengers remained slack-jawed at the sight before them, when they reached *Ptolemy*, they knew exactly what to do. Ropes were being passed between *Polcrebo* and the barge by busy hands and soon the two vessels – one small, wooden and rotten, the other huge, steel and refurbished – were being pulled together. Aaron Serman, who had been aboard *Ptolemy* for two weeks, threw down a rope ladder.

As Pilot crested the rail, he got a clearer picture of the barge's strange appendage. It wasn't a whole jumbo jet, merely the front quarter of the fuselage, attached to the deck of the barge by eight hydraulic suspension columns. He walked around the plugged rear of the plane to a fixed ladder leading up to a small platform at the plane's forward door. "Come on up," Serman said. Pilot followed him up the ladder into the interior of the jumbo where a dozen rows of seats spanned two aisles. "There's secure seating for 56 here and 30 upstairs."

They climbed a narrow spiral staircase to the plane's second deck where the bulkheads had been removed all the way to the cockpit. "The generator is in the cargo hold and feeds the aircon, lighting etcetera," Serman continued. "There are four digicams – one in the nose, two either side and one mounted at the back." They stepped into what used to be the jumbo's lounge. A single chair was positioned in front of a bank of monitors and other instruments. "The cameras are controlled from here."

"Toilets?"

"At the back. Both decks."

They finished their tour of the fuselage and entered the body of the barge, where Pilot was shown storerooms, cabins, toilets, shower rooms and a state-of-the-art galley adjoining a spacious messroom. Everywhere, the smell of fresh paint and yacht varnish hung thick in the air.

The sea was as flat as a snooker table and the transfer of personnel to the barge proceeded without incident. Just before leaving the launch, Budd walked over to Pilot. "Do you think she'll fly, Lonnie?" he joked.

Pilot gazed up at the massive white fuselage of the jumbo – majestic, yet ludicrous – and at the contrastingly un-aerodynamic barge below it. "Looks sound enough to me."

Only Highbell remained on the launch. Pilot watched him go below, return a moment later and climb the rope ladder to join him. "How long will it take?" Pilot asked.

"Less than ten minutes."

The entire complement watched in silence as the scuttled *Polcrebo* was slowly pulled into the sea to finally disappear, leaving only oily rainbows and floating debris in the space she'd once occupied.

"This feels the same as when I left Sydney," Josiah Billy said to Mara.

"Not Dublin?"

"No. Australia is my real home. Never felt that until now. There's no going back, I guess. You going to miss Ireland, Macushla?"

Mara thought for minute. "Like you said, there's no going back."

Pilot sized up the chaotic scene around him and noted that order was being restored by some of the crew who seemed to know what they were doing. Leaving them to it, and taking one last glance at the nebulous coast in the distance, he followed Serman down the companionway into *Ptolemy's* belly to his cabin. It was spartan, but five star compared to his net shed.

An hour later, Serman took Pilot to the bridge to meet the barge master. "Captain Turner, we're ready for takeoff," Pilot said.

Turner laughed. "Let's see if we can get this plane of yours to fly." By this time, everyone knew that the jumbo jokes were running a bit thin, and Turner's was the last of them. Soon, there was a noticeable feeling of forward movement as *Ptolemy* began to plod through the water.

The lookout came running in with news of a visitor just before they heard it for themselves. A helicopter was flying about fifty feet above the water on a line directly towards them, and as it passed overhead Pilot could make out the Coastguard insignia on its fuselage. He could also see a pair of sunglasses peering down from the cockpit as the twenty tons of metal hurdled them.

The helicopter began a steep turn ahead prior to making another pass. This time it carried on past *Ptolemy* towards a small boat following them at a distance before disappearing from view. "*That's* the visitor I meant, not the Sikorsky," the lookout said to Pilot. "It's an RHIB. Rigid-hulled inflatable boat – the Coastguard uses them."

A frightening thought occurred to Pilot – that they would be shadowed all the way to their landing site by the French and British navies, which would then get beached alongside the flotilla and thereby have every right to plant the Tricolor and Union Jack on Eydos alongside their own. It was a scenario that had never entered his head.

He was relieved when, an hour later, the lookout reported that the RHIB had u-turned and was heading home. Pilot was only half pleased with this news. The Coastguard might lose interest once they had left UK territorial waters, but *Ptolemy* was now heading straight for France, a nation Pilot viewed as the bigger threat of the two.

"There should be nothing to draw undue attention to ourselves when we enter French waters," Turner said, "apart from the jumbo on our deck. As far as they're concerned, our destination is Lisbon."

Pilot scanned the horizon. Behind and to either side of them the sea was empty, but ahead it was a different story. It was as if they were driving down a small country lane approaching a motorway at right angles, because as far as the eye could see, vessel upon vessel plied one of the busiest sea lanes in the world. It took them just under an hour to cross the road. Later, at a point level with Ushant, Turner picked up an urgent shipping warning being broadcast on at least five different frequencies. Pilot settled down to listen.

'...make for the nearest haven immediately. Severe wave activity can be expected if the tremors continue. The epicenter of this latest disturbance is the Bay of Biscay at latitude Ferrol, longitude Nantes. All shipping in sea areas FitzRoy, Biscay, Sole, Plymouth, Shannon, Fastnet and Lundy are advised to make for the nearest safe haven. Ports on the French west coast, Spanish north coast, and the south coasts of England and Ireland are considered to be at risk. Shipping now on course for the danger zone should remain outside the sea areas mentioned until further notice. We repeat this urgent warning to all shipping. Severe seismic activity in the Bay of Biscay is pushing up seas potentially hazardous to shipping in sea areas FitzRoy, Biscay ... '

The first plane, an old turbo prop, appeared at dawn and circled overhead for around twenty minutes before disappearing northwards. The shipping warning was still being broadcast. The tremors had increased in severity and the first mini tsunamis were washing up against the coasts of France and Spain. They had caused no damage, but the experts were alarmed by their increasing frequency and magnitude. Pilot could feel his body bristle with excitement at this further emphatic evidence of the waking of their island.

A hundred miles west of Brest, cracks began appearing in the ice floe sky. Shafts of light rained down on the sea to form an S-shaped curtain of sunbeams which *Ptolemy* now parted.

Pilot pulled up his collar and left the bridge. There was nothing in the instructions that forbade use of the jumbo before the landing window opened, so he invited the entire complement to climb aboard the jet and enjoy the view and the improving weather from higher up.

From their seats it looked as if they were flying very low over the sea, but unlike a transatlantic flight where half the passengers are asleep and the other half are watching the film, every eye was pressed to a window.

Up in the cockpit, the two camera operators were familiarizing themselves with the video equipment while Pilot stared ahead at the horizon. It wasn't visible from his viewpoint in the pilot's seat, nor could he feel it, but from a thousand feet, the pattern was obvious. When *Ptolemy* had cleared Ushant and changed course southwest towards the epicenter of the current disturbances, she had sailed straight onto a washboard – thousands of wave lines, escalating across the surface of the sea from horizon to horizon. At first they'd been small and far between, but had increased in height and frequency to five feet from trough to peak and twenty metres apart.

When the call came for dinner there was little enthusiasm for going below for first servings. Half the passengers had already begun to feel seasick.

Shortly after dinner, Turner altered course due south to take him to the designated coordinates. This had the effect of changing their angle into the waves from a straight ninety degrees, to forty-five degrees, with the result that, not only were they rocking front to back, but side to side as well. Only half the crew returned to the jumbo, the others deciding instead to take to their bunks within easy proximity of a toilet.

"JESUS. LOOK AT THOSE," someone shouted. Everyone felt the new, higher band of waves at the same time as their arrival was announced. Row upon row, they passed under the barge. Just before she threw up in her sick bag, Jane Lavery likened it to traveling over a liquid cattle grid.

Fifteen other people lost their dinner. Pilot hoped they wouldn't lose their nerve.

At three-twenty in the morning, sensing in his sleep that Ptolemy's engines had stopped, Pilot got out of bed, hurried topside and found Serman, Mara and Bradingbrooke already in the wheelhouse.

Turner was trying to keep *Ptolemy's* nose into the waves, which Pilot couldn't see in the darkness, but which felt enormous. They were striking every seven seconds now.

"Don't want to get ourselves broadside to *those*," Turner said. "Not enough ballast under the water line. I saw a light to the northeast earlier. Could be one of the other barges."

"We're to signal every fifteen minutes," Serman said, leading the others out of the wheelhouse and placing a flare in its firing tube. With a thump and a whoosh it cut through the night, its magenta light hanging in the sky for nearly a minute before dropping. Pilot followed it down to extinction and for half a second, before the light died, he could see a barge three or four miles away. Almost immediately, the blackness was split by the rising trail of an answering flare.

"We have company," Mara said.

By dawn, three barges were standing just off *Ptolemy*, with a further seven in sight. What Pilot also noticed when he came on deck after breakfast was the placidity of the sea. He wondered how the waves could have died so fast.

Not more than fifty yards away, the barge *Julius* was resting on the upturned image of herself. Pilot could feel his body tingle with the input of extra adrenalin the scene triggered. Not far behind *Julius* were *Fort Lowell* and *Douro*, the latter painted green from stem to stern.

The entire scene was softly lit by a low, orange sun on the horizon and covered by a fine muslin mist. The sun hadn't been up for long and Pilot guessed it would burn through the mist as the morning went on. A few degrees off the line of the sun, seven dark specks marked what was otherwise a clean horizon.

An inflatable dinghy, with Highbell and Budd aboard, had been put in the water earlier and they were now directing the positioning of the barges in preparation for the trussing up operation scheduled for later.

Pilot went below, gathered his instruction sheets, inserted them into his plastic pocket necklace, and returned topside. He'd been wrong to think that the sun would burn away the mist. Instead of dissolving, it was thickening and rising, and by 0730 the sun was obscured. Already, the day was taking on that same oppressive yellow-grey emptiness that had beset England for most of July. In light of the close maneuvering they would soon be undertaking, Pilot was glad of the flat seas, but not so the stale, bell jar atmosphere, which he found sinister and portentous.

Josiah Billy, taking his turn as look-out, shouted down that he could make out three more barges on the horizon. That made fourteen in all, including themselves. One short.

There was plenty of preparation work to get on with and Pilot went through each procedure with as much calm as he could muster to mask his growing nervousness. It was Serman's job to attend to the details and Pilot's to direct the overall operation.

Bulldozer tyre fenders were manhandled over the sides of each barge – five crew to a tyre, such was their weight – and soon *Ptolemy* was ready to begin drawing the other barges in around her.

The vessel which hadn't yet made the rendezvous was *Shenandoah*, one of the water carriers. As all the vessels in the central row were present, Pilot called them into position in readiness for the mooring operation.

First, *Bimbo's Kraal*, which would temporarily stable the sheep when they arrived, and *Chiswick Eyot*, a floating supermarket warehouse of canned goods, were pulled in on his port and starboard sides. When they were both in line, all three barges exchanged steel cables and winched themselves together as tightly as the fenders would allow. The incoming crew and the two barge masters used the fenders as stepping stones to board *Ptolemy* from either side.

Westcliff and *King Solomon*, carrying building materials and pre-fab sections respectively, followed and within an hour all five barges of the centre row were snugly laced.

A French Air Force reconnaissance plane from a base near Nantes – the first of many aircraft to pass over them that day – appeared and made three low passes before taking its leave, having been unable to raise so much as a wave from anyone on the fourteen barges. Item 18 of Pilot's instructions read, 'Under no circumstances communicate with any outside presence after arriving at the rendezvous.'

The shipping warning was still in force, but had been modified to say that although no serious seismic activity had occurred for over fifteen hours, shipping was to remain outside the danger zone until the experts agreed it was safe. These 'experts' had not yet done so, thanks to some erroneous readings being supplied by the IGP research vessel *Pima Verde*, which was observing events five hundred miles west of Brest. Pilot hoped that the only interference they would get now would be from the air.

The mooring operation was slow, which was understandable considering it had never been practiced. After a few hours, all fourteen vessels were snugly laced, effectively relieving the barge masters of their commands. Their job done, they were gathering aboard one of the outer barges in readiness for their collection and return to the mainland. They watched the scene with a mixture of bafflement and wonder until the launch from St. Helier arrived and began taking them aboard. Within minutes, they were on their way to the Channel Islands.

The rubber barrage, in 25 parts, was hauled up from Douro's hold and each section fed out into the water, with only their inflation tubes still on deck. The man whose job it was to work the air compressor was explaining how the machine worked to three assistants.

An hour later, twelve long red snakes floated on the sea, joined together by adjustable cable which would be cranked in when the time came to form a tight rubber collar round the convoy. Further cables would then lock the ring to the outer walls of the flotilla, which was still one barge short.

"How long before we have to lock the ring, Aaron?" Pilot asked.

Serman consulted one of his lists. "We still have two hours before the window opens and the door shuts," he said. "It's your call, Lonnie."

Pilot had already decided to wait until the last possible moment to lock the rubber barrage in case *Shenandoah* appeared. Her captain and the remaining five crew members were potentially in great peril, and for the first time Pilot admitted the possibility of there being fatalities. He saw no point in dwelling on the subject, but at the same time wanted to know how to place it within the framework of the whole idea should the unthinkable happen and six people perish in defiance of a well broadcast shipping warning. It didn't seem right to think of it in these terms, but Pilot believed that the ultimate success of the venture was far more important than the human lives within it. His own coldness shocked him, but he knew that sentimentality could be as destructive and deadly in its own way as cold-blooded murder. Is callousness a prerequisite to being an effective leader? he asked himself. Does a leader need to dress in delusions of grandeur before he can block out matters of conscience and decent humanity? More importantly, am *I* now deluded? It reminded him of the admonition Vaalon had given him in London about the dangers of self-aggrandisement. "You're only 25, Lonnie," he had said. "The temptation towards self-elevation is stronger the younger we are, and the line between delusion and reality is thinner. Having said that, to be an effective leader, you often have to act out of character. Your responsibility is to make sure the character you're acting is true to the play and not a 'prima divus' reading from a different script."

The sound of another plane brought Pilot racing up on deck. This one was an antique Royal Air Force reconnaissance aircraft. He went to the wheelhouse and watched as Jim McConie, his radio operator, tried to make sense of the scrambled communications taking place between the plane and the mainland. It made one final pass, then flew north. "Did you catch any of that, Jim?" Pilot asked.

"Not a word."

At 1230 hours, two more French Air Force planes flew over the floating seed that would soon germinate the new island. The French had been demanding explanations from the United Kingdom as to the purpose of the strange convoy of British barges congregating off the Brittany coast. Whitehall had denied all knowledge and France had accepted, but not believed a word of it.

Do they know something we don't know? they were asking in Paris. Already, the ocean research vessel *Largesse* had left Cherbourg for the Bay of Biscay to investigate.

In London, the mystery of the barge-cum-jumbo jet was deepening. The Royal Navy had been requested by both MI5 and MI6 to dispatch a seaplane to investigate, and this arrived just as Pilot was giving the order to lock the barrage, *Shenandoah* or no *Shenandoah*.

With some annoyance, Pilot watched the RM20 Seahopper land in the water some thousand metres away and it soon became a race to see which dinghy crew could finish their task first – those drawing together the head and tail of the red rubber snake, or the naval ratings from the seaplane. The former finished first and were hoisted aboard *Earthmover IV* with the aid of rope ladders just as the navy Lieutenant touched the collar at the far side. Without the cooperation of those on the barges, there was no method by which the sailors could scale the fourteen-foot rubber wall. They looked for a way through, but the joins were too tight. In two places the lengths overlapped, owing to the extra space afforded by being one barge short.

"AHOY THERE," the Lieutenant hailed in true naval fashion. "I REPRESENT THE ROYAL NAVY. WILL YOU SPEAK?" He was greeted with nothing but the slapping of his own dinghy on the flat water. "PLEASE ACKNOWLEDGE."

On board *Ptolemy*, Pilot asked McConie to find Radio Three and feed it through the P.A. system at full volume. The British Lieutenant didn't listen to Mahler's Sixth for long. Access to the barges was impossible, and cooperation unforthcoming from those within their rubber-walled fortress, so he took his bad humour back with him to the Seahopper.

It was 1345, just a quarter of an hour before the opening of the IGP's 'landing window' and the order to retire to the jumbo, so Pilot and Serman ran through the final checklist. Apart from the missing barge, everything was in place. Pilot took a deep breath and was happy to notice that the air once again contained an adequate amount of oxygen. He'd been too busy to notice the change in the sky that had been taking place since noon. The low, featureless, monotone roof had risen. The yellow tinge of malady had disappeared to be replaced by the most magnificent vaulted ceiling of grey, white and black sculpted cloud. What was unusual about this cloud layer was its extreme altitude. It was the kind of cloud that normally lived at between one and three thousand feet, but was in fact hanging at around three miles, engendering a feeling of infinite space.

There was still no wind, but the air had cooled by twenty degrees. "I don't understand how cold air can replace hot air so quickly without so much as creating a breeze," Bradingbrooke said to no-one in particular.

"Looks mighty windy over there, Henry," Jane Lavery said, directing Bradingbrooke to a point just short of the horizon where a magnificent water spout a thousand feet high marked the white wedding of warm front to cold front.

From his position in the front seat of the cockpit area, Pilot scanned as much of the horizon as he could, hoping *Shenandoah* would not appear. Perhaps she had never left Southampton, he thought. But if that were the case they would have received a message. Pilot looked at his watch. It was time. He picked up the PA mic and, through loudspeakers mounted on the barge stanchions, called everyone into the plane.

Aaron Serman positioned himself at the door and began checking people aboard. "Wait in the main cabin," he told each of them. "Lonnie wants to say a few words." When the last name was ticked, Serman closed the door and sat down on the first step of the spiral staircase. To his right, towards the nose of the fuselage, the full complement of crew sat, or stood in the aisles, waiting to hear what the man in charge had to say. Pilot bounded down the stairs past Serman and found a central location where everyone could see him and he could see them. He was holding a long white tube in his right hand and something small and black in his left – yin and yang, positive and negative. In a slow, measured tone, he began to speak.

"When Mr. Vaalon first recruited you for this ground-breaking social experiment, he told you that we'd be travelling to a remote part of the world… that we might be in for a rough landing… that there was an outside chance some or all of us could die." He looked around at the assembled faces and caught Jane Lavery's eye. She already knew what was coming, so he found an ignorant crew member at whom to aim his words. "Before I continue… if, after what I'm going say, any of you want to bail out, I just have to activate this." He held up the device in his left hand. "It will signal Saint Helier aerodrome. When the helicopter gets here, you'll be winched aboard and returned to terra firma. There, you will be guests in a mansion on Jersey until it's safe for us to release you."

"Prisoners?" someone asked.

"No. Prisoners are allowed to make phone calls and have visitors. You won't. During your stay you'll be incommunicado, but very comfortable. If the science is correct, you'll be free to go home after no more than six days. Don't make your decision until I've told you our final destination." Pilot unrolled the chart he had taken from Captain Turner and held it up. It showed the northern half of the Bay of Biscay with the Brittany peninsula filling the top right quarter. To the far left, in the empty waters of the Bay, a large red X had been drawn. "This is where we are *now*," he said, pointing to the X. He lowered his arm, then immediately raised it and pointed to the X again. "And this where we're *going*." He looked over at his 'sounding board'. She was looking bewildered. "Sometime in the next five days, the western edge of the European continental shelf will be surfacing underneath us. It will impact with some force and carry us with it. How hard it hits us falls within a range we've already computed. The hydraulic columns we're sitting on have been designed to absorb a maximum collision speed far in excess of what the physics tells us it could be."

"And we're the crash test dummies," someone said. "How high will we be lifted?"

"We don't know what our final altitude will be," Pilot said. "The computer model suggests a few hundred metres, give or take." By the look on their faces, his audience was far from converted. It was Dublin all over again, but this time he actually believed in what he was saying. "Let me tell you about Solar Tides…"

For ten minutes, in the same manner he used to give his geography lessons in Newlyn, Pilot delivered an exposition on the geophysical phenomenon that was primed to deliver them to their new home within the next 144 hours. To his relief, there were no more snide comments or doubting asides from the listeners, who were riveted to his every word. When he'd finished the lesson, he held up the transmitter and placed his right finger on the button. The moment of truth had come. His heart was pounding. "Does anyone want to leave?"

Macushla Mara looked around the room with 'don't you dare' eyes while the crew merely looked at each other. For half a minute the question spun on its edge and Pilot's arms were beginning ache.

"Put it away, Lonnie," Mara said.

Pilot made a final scan of the faces, then placed the pager in his pocket. "Below us, a virgin land is waiting to be deflowered," he said, deciding to use an analogy he had at first rejected, but now retrieved. "We can impregnate her with more of the same out there..." he waved his hand at a window, "or with a seed of change." When he'd written down 'seed of change' two months earlier in his net shed, it had seemed clichéd, but, when articulated in the confines of an aged 747 riding an ocean-going barge, it worked.

"You renounced your citizenships for a reason. We can no longer be party to a world hell-bent on self-destruction. But we can't just run away from it, either. By coming here, we're not escaping *or* retreating. We're *regrouping*." Pilot made a quick calculation in his head – 86 minus five. "Eighty-one people on a strip of barren rock in the Bay of Biscay... what can we possibly do to change things in the world we left behind? First, we have to understand the history of the problem, which begins at the Industrial Revolution. Two hundred and fifty years ago, mankind left the *real* world behind and embarked on a journey which –"

"BARGE." The shout came from a port side window seat. Pilot immediately squeezed his way through the packed aisle to the stairs, which he took two at a time to the higher vantage point of the top deck. He sprinted down the aisle to the cockpit area with Serman hard on his heels and peered out the portside window. Serman followed his gaze to a small dark speck just discernible under the horizon.

Then, as suddenly as the waves had stopped earlier, they reappeared from nowhere, accompanied by a distinct sensation of vibration underfoot. But this time, the waves were angrier, and topped with churning white caps. Pilot looked at *Shenandoah* again as she began to rise and fall on the boiling sea. Worse deaths have been exacted during the march of the human race, he thought. His eyes remained firmly on the script, and the rubber barrage remained closed.

Fifteen minutes later, the crew were all seated and belted up. Pilot looked behind him to the lounge, where the camera operators were tending the bank of digital video equipment and trying to get *Shenandoah* in picture. Every seat had a video screen, so, whatever the cameras saw, everyone else saw, too. Pilot drew a deep breath and waited. 1415 passed, then 1430 and 1440 with still the only sign of life on the water that of the approaching barge. He watched with growing anxiety as it closed on them, remembering that, apart from her human cargo, *Shenandoah* carried two hundred thousand gallons of fresh water, plus half the pumps, pipes and other equipment they would need in the construction of their cisterns and the distribution of their water.

Shenandoah was only 400 metres from the outer barrage now and he could make out figures scurrying about on deck. The smoke billowing from the barge's funnel looked unhealthy, the result of a do or die effort to reach the flotilla in time.

"They're in trouble," Billy said, looking over Pilot's shoulder.

A breathless silence had replaced the raucous excitement of earlier and Pilot could read fear on some of the faces around him. Then, at five minutes to three on that strange Monday afternoon, the world turned over.

The full 360 degrees of the horizon fell away as the tethered flotilla began to rise up on what would be described more accurately as a vast plateau of water rather than a wave. Internal organs followed muscle, bone and skin by a millisecond, but long enough to cause severe discomfort as the eighty-one passengers were thrust upwards at five feet per second. Protesting squeals of rubber against rubber tore through the air as the fenders were crushed and pressed between the barges. A second later the din was augmented by a series of ear-shattering cracks as the barge hulls below the waterline slammed together and tried to grind each other to shards. There were a few expletives and some vomit, but everyone remained, on the surface at least, calm.

The upward acceleration lasted for twenty seconds. Pilot's stomach told him when they'd reached the top of the ride and told him again, a few seconds later, that the plateau was collapsing beneath them and that they were now dropping at a frightening speed, seemingly without support, straight down. The fear which filled the jumbo wasn't vocal. It dwelt far deeper. With strange detachment, Pilot noticed that the white-knuckled hands gripping the armrests along the aisle looked like tiny snowcapped mountains. For a brief moment, he glimpsed *Shenandoah* following them down and feared she'd be flipped over on top of them.

It took half a minute to reach the bottom of the valley, at which point Pilot found himself looking *up* at the horizon. Straight ahead, there was no sky visible at all, just grey-blue jumping water.

They'd barely had time to collect their thoughts, or indeed to think at all, when the valley floor began rising again with a surge that left everyone fighting for breath. Thirty-five seconds later, they found themselves once again atop the vast watery plateau. Vaalon had had enough foresight to provision each seat with extra sick bags and these were being used by the bucket load.

"They're listing badly," someone shouted. Pilot could just make out the foundering vessel, now less than 300 metres away. Above it, a human figure was dangling in the air. Through the rattles and crashes of the barges, a helicopter's rotors could just be heard, but owing to the rotation of the flotilla, the rescue attempt was soon lost to view.

"Are you picking anything up on the stern camera?" Pilot asked.

"Nothing," a voice behind him replied. "Yes. Yes. There she is."

Pilot switched on his own video screen. The picture was split into four quarters, one for each camera. In the stern image, he could see that *Shenandoah* was still with them, but noticeably lower in the water. Then he saw a dinghy emerge from behind the foundering barge. Pilot counted six figures. Seven, if you included the figure dangling on a wire above them. He asked the camera operator to follow the line upwards, and seconds later a Sea King helicopter filled the screen. There were no military markings on the machine, so Pilot deduced it was a 'private hire' Vaalon had organized.

Only fifty feet separated peak from trough now, but even so, it would require skillful flying to lift six people out of a rubber dinghy that was travelling up and down like a yo-yo.

The figure underneath the helicopter was winched down to a point where the dinghy had, a moment before, been at the top of the swell. As the dinghy descended, the man on the winch remained dangling in his fixed position, like a worm on a fishhook. The flotilla's rotation soon brought the rescue operation back into normal vision, and those who could see it from their seats lent commentary to those who could not. There were audible sighs on board as the first attempt failed.

The dinghy, the sinking *Shenandoah* and the fourteen-barge flotilla dropped down once more, leaving the helicopter pilot to work out what he'd done wrong. Whatever it was, he compensated for on the next run, for, when the dinghy peaked again he was able to drop his man into the water just an arm's length from the inflatable. Within seconds he was harnessing the first person to the wire. On board the helicopter the line was fed out as fast as the dinghy was descending. When their man signaled that the harness was secure, the brakes were applied slowly to the winch and two bodies were left suspended in the air as the dinghy carried on falling.

A huge cheer broke out on *Ptolemy* as the first survivor was winched aboard the helicopter. Ten minutes later the scene was repeated with a second successful rescue, but that was it. They lost visibility of the dinghy and the Sea King, both actual and via the four cameras.

Inside the jumbo, the braver occupants felt they were beginning to get the measure of the ride and started talking and laughing nervously. The surges they were experiencing now were no worse than the first and may even have been easing off.

Pilot tried to imagine what was happening around them, but the scale was so vast, he could only guess. Their vertical movement and even keel suggested that whatever was happening under the earth's crust, was happening directly below them. It was like being in the eye of a hurricane while all around them the most horrendous seas were radiating outwards. He wondered how long it would take the first ones to hit mainland Europe and tried to calculate the height of the tsunamis by estimating the speed and duration of the next descent. As a guide he used the pressure his stomach exerted on the underside of his diaphragm, but in the end he gave up.

By three o'clock it was obvious the seas were diminishing and half an hour later, trough to peak measured less than ten metres.

Fifteen hours of welcome calm ensued…

By first light, things had taken on the atmosphere of just another transatlantic jumbo crossing – with turbulence. Croissants and coffee were being dispensed to those who were awake and Pilot was beginning to wonder if the solar tide had failed to exert sufficient pull on the magma to deliver Eydos. He imagined the scene at the IGP – Vaalon and his team monitoring the situation on their computer screens with worried looks on their faces, like NASA mission controllers hearing Lovell's portentous transmission, 'Houston, we have a problem'.

Forrest could have got this wrong, Pilot thought, picturing the barge masters returning in the morning to take them all home.

Just fifty miles to the east, the French ocean research vessel *Largesse*, which had miraculously ridden the waves, was almost upon what from the air looked like a small islet, wrapped by Christo in red rubber, bobbing about in the Bay of Biscay.

Pilot decided that if one person had to remain positive in this flotilla, it was he. Attributing the calmer seas to a natural 'stutter' in the movement of the magma, he began to re-read Items 56-79 under the heading Making Landfall. He was just beginning the instruction on *disembarkation* when Josiah Billy tapped him on the shoulder and pointed out of the window. Everyone on the port side was craning to get a glimpse of the horizon. It had a strange bow in it to the southwest that was difficult at first to process until Dubravka 'Dubi' Horvat, the daughter of Vaalon's Dubrovnik housekeeper, calmly announced, "I think it is tidal wave."

A wall of water stretching a full quarter of the compass appeared to be running in their direction. Pilot could see it swallowing up the smaller waves that were still echoing from the upsurge of the previous day. In the main cabin all conversation stopped, replaced by a swooning sound and expletives of the terrified as opposed to the angry kind.

Pilot raised his binoculars to his eyes and fastened his gaze on a smudge of foam on the surface just in front of the wave. He followed it up the wall to the top and watched it disappear over the other side. Then the swell took them down again and he could see no more.

"When do you think it'll hit us?" A voice asked no one in particular. There was no answer. Everyone was thinking the same thoughts anyway. Pilot hurried downstairs and stood at the head of the aisle. "CRASH POSITIONS." He returned to his seat and attempted to gauge the wave's size and speed as it rolled inexorably closer. It had probably been ten to fifteen miles away when it was first noticed, and was now nearly upon them. It could be traveling at anything from twenty to thirty knots, with a height that was impossible to judge. He was more worried about the steepness of its leading face. If the angle weren't too extreme they could conceiveably ride it, whatever the height. But if it were –

When the jumbo rose up on the next swell and the scene unfolded outside the windows, Pilot saw nothing but water curving upwards and away as far as the eye could see. The wave was so close now that it blanketed half the sky and he only just got his head down and between his knees when it hit.

First, the rubber barrage and three outer portside barges were tilted up forty-five degrees to the rest of the convoy. The three vessels inside them followed a split second later and so on across the pack. The pressure on the bulldozer tyres was enormous, but they absorbed it as effectively as the cartilage between the vertebrae of a gymnast doing a forward roll.

Because the flotilla was meeting the wave sideways on, less pressure was placed on the spines of the barges. A hit forward would surely, in Pilot's opinion, have cracked their backs. When the wave hit them, it swept them up from zero to twenty-five knots in little more than a second. This sudden acceleration, coupled with the boat's extreme list, was as dramatic as it was traumatic. The interior of the jumbo was a jumble of minds, spirits, bodies, and personal effects. There wasn't an honest soul on board who did not think they were about to die.

The rubber barrage had prevented the mammoth wave from inundating the portside barges, but in doing so had sent up thousands of gallons of water in the form of spray which was hitting the windows of the jumbo with the force of hail and blotting out the entire scene from view. For the people inside, it seemed as if they'd capsized. Pilot shuddered at the carnage the wave would deliver when it hit the mainland. As it carried them forward at speed, the flotilla was slowly climbing up the wall, like the foam Pilot had witnessed earlier, though of course he was seeing nothing now. After a minute of excruciating fear and physical discomfort, the occupants of the plane found themselves 'above the clouds' and in daylight once again. The acceleration had dropped, along with their stomachs, and they'd leveled off, too.

"We made it," someone shouted. "We're on top of the wave."

No sooner had the words been uttered than the outer barges fell away down the back slope of the mountain. As they did so, their hulls, far below the water line, crashed into those of the barges inside them. In quick succession this happened all along the line to the far side of the flotilla. *Ptolemy* took a blow on her port side from *Bimbo's Kraal* so hard that the shock wave dislocated Dubi Horvat's shoulder. She'd been placing too much weight on her elbow in an attempt to get a view out of the window.

The wave reminded Pilot of the first surges they'd experienced, and he knew there'd be another hurdle right behind the one they'd just straddled. As had been the case earlier, the second strike didn't seem to be as bad as the first, only because they were prepared and knew what to expect. In truth, the second wave was higher than its predecessor.

There were those on board in whom panic killed all forms of logic and detached observation. With faces buried between knees and forearms, they were unaware when the flotilla hurdled the second wave successfully. However, as they dropped down the other side, the barges swung around so that they faced the oncoming third wave head on.

From Pilot's position in the cockpit, the distance to the bow of the leading barge was ninety metres. Twenty metres above that point was the awesome peak of the third wave over which the entire surface of the sea was rolling, separate and detached from the mass of water beneath.

As Pilot braced himself for the impact, he didn't feel in the least confident that his convoy would survive this hit. Whatever modifications Vaalon had devised to reinforce the hulls of the barges, the approaching leviathan would be their ultimate test. And so it was.

With an impact equivalent to a car crash at twenty-five miles an hour, the flotilla hammered into the wall of water and was pitched upwards and thrust backwards at the same time. The four leading barges were lifted fifty degrees, shredding seven fenders at their sterns, before being followed up the watery wall a split second later by the second row of barges, with *Ptolemy* in the middle, and then the third. When the spray hit the windows, all visual reference to what was happening to them was lost. The noise from outside and within assaulted the senses with an intensity and a menace no one could afterwards describe.

Pilot had been convinced that the leading hulls, at least, would have been snapped in half by the impact, but despite the severe shuddering and the painful sound of rivets and plates screaming to part company, all appeared intact.

The fourth wave was much less powerful than its predecessor, and when it rolled away behind them, audible sighs of relief were expelled. Pilot unbuckled and put his face to the window to get a better view of the seas ahead. There was another wave coming, but it was the runt of the litter. Then he noticed something strange about *Earthmover II* at the starboard corner of the formation. "Josiah, look," he said, pointing. Billy unbuckled and joined Pilot at the window. "Looks like she's shipping water." The foundering barge, with her heavy cargo of Irish topsoil, was two metres lower in the water than *Ocean Queen* on her port side.

The two resumed their seats and buckled up in preparation for the fifth wave. When it was successfully ridden and behind them, it was clear that the worst was over. Apart from a few bloodied noses and cut lips and tongues, where faces had collided with knees, everyone seemed shipshape. Not so, the flotilla.

Pilot and Billy returned to their viewpoint and were horrified by the sight before them. Not only was *Earthmover II* submerged, with just her wheelhouse and a few cranes and masts visible, but she had also begun to pull *Ocean Queen* down with her. "Jesus Christ, Lonnie," Billy said.

Pilot calmed himself and began sizing up the situation. The chains attaching *Earthmover II* to the barrage were holding, unbelievably. Although *King Solomon* at the barge's stern was being pulled down at the bow, her extra buoyancy through having a light cargo was aiding in keeping *Earthmover II* afloat. *Ocean Queen* was not faring so well. The water level was beginning to crest her deck and she was listing badly to starboard. Pilot could see nothing but dominoes before his eyes. "*Titanic* sank because five of her sixteen watertight compartments had been breached," he said. "Two of our fourteen barges are sinking."

"I was thinking the exact same thing," Billy replied.

They watched in stunned silence as the sea began to wash over *Ocean Queen's* decks and she, in turn, began to pull down *Baltimore*, the barge directly in front of them.

"It's a race between us and the shelf now," Pilot said with a calmness that surprised him. "Will Eydos get here before we sink, or will we be making our landfall half a mile underwater?" Part of his stoicism was due to a gut feeling that the shelf did not have far to come now. He reasoned that, as the volume of water between the surface and the rising shelf lessened, so too would the waves. The sea would flatten out first and the water would fall off in whichever direction the tilt of the shelf sent it – in this case probably northeast, at right angles to the edge of the shelf and towards the mainland – the same direction the waves were traveling now. On the other hand, the wave sequence might be the result of this very run-off, the shelf already having broken the surface somewhere up ahead.

As Pilot wrestled with the mental aspects of the experience and the visual evidence that his flotilla was sinking under his feet, his companions were grappling with their own inner turmoils. Riding the waves without personal injury had been each person's primary concern, but the moment they pulled themselves up on the ropes, they'd been knocked down again. With grim apprehension, they remained in their crash positions waiting for the other shoe to drop. If they could have seen what Pilot was now watching – *Ptolemy's* bow now being pulled down by the three barges in front of her – they would have taken to the lifeboats without a second's thought. Only, there were no lifeboats to take to.

"SHIT, MAN," Billy shouted seconds after the shock waves from an explosion almost blew the cockpit's windows out.

"One of the barrages just popped," Pilot said, assessing the situation in seconds. "We're wide open to starboard."

The waves, which earlier had been broken by the barrage ring, were now inundating the three sinking barges of the front row. Only their radio masts remained above water. Pilot knew it was only a matter of time before *Earthmover I*, *King Solomon* and *Chiswick Eyot* were also submerged and wondered when the crucial sinking point would come. The remaining barges couldn't keep the others afloat forever. There was a section in Pilot's instructions headed 'Abandoning Ship', and he reluctantly began to read it.

Ten minutes later, with five of his fourteen barges now underwater, Pilot was seriously contemplating throwing the switch that would turn their landing module into a lifeboat. Vaalon had assured him that the jumbo would stay afloat indefinitely once jettisoned. Before he could act, something changed beneath him. Severe vibrations began to all but shake the flotilla to pieces. They were not being caused by the rough seas, but were the physical manifestation of shockwaves being transmitted from the seabed, through the intervening water and into the body of the convoy. Nobody on board had ever experienced an earthquake at sea.

'It can't be far away now,' Pilot thought, glancing at his watch as a way of summoning their salvation. But so violently was he being shaken, he had great difficulty reading the time. He held the tarnished old timepiece once worn by his grandfather up to his ear, but what with the noise from protesting bulkheads, spray pelting against the windows and the general uproar in the cabin, he couldn't tell if his watch were ticking or not.

Whatever the actual time, he knew it was only a matter of minutes before the transponder in the nose cone would be activated and Geirsson and the others would stake their common claim. From then on the eyes of the entire world would fall forever on this unlikely band of colonisers – aground in the Bay of Biscay on fourteen trussed up barges and half a jumbo in a rubber ring.

'Possession is nine-tenths of the law ...'

With a jolt Pilot realised he was getting ahead of himself and that the only thing they were in possession of at that moment was a floating barge cemetery that was fast sinking. So intense were the vibrations that Pilot had lost track of his observations of the wave pattern. When the next one washed over the front row of the flotilla, he knew that the worst of their ordeal was over. This assessment was confirmed over the next few minutes as consecutive waves shed power at a rate that could only, by Pilot's reasoning, be explained by there being a sudden and massive loss of water volume beneath them.

The shockwaves had also taken on a different expression – not so frenetic and brain-rattling now. It was more like feeling and hearing an underground train through five feet of earth. All around them the sea was a jumping mass of whipped up foam. A snow-white circular wake was spreading out from the convoy as if churned up by a thousand propellers set all round them. Beyond this wake and all the way to the horizon it was as if a billion tuna were thrashing their lives to extinction in two feet of water.

"HERE IT COMES." Pilot shouted. "CRASH POSITIONS."

He tore his eyes from the drama outside and clamped his head in the vice of his knees and hands.

Amidst the noise, the vibration and his own almost boundless excitement, he noticed that the entire flotilla was rotating, and he couldn't resist the temptation to look out the window for a sign.

When he lifted his face, there were the 'thrashing tuna' as before, but as the jumbo rotated, the random display of white water began to take on a definite ripple pattern. Thousands of tiny whitecaps were marching in close formation as if breaking across a very shallow sea.

As the plane continued its pirouette, the next vision to assault Pilot's eyes nearly stopped his heart. In the fading light, his immediate reaction was that it was another giant wave. But, as the setting sun broke through the cloud canopy at last, it wasn't water that Pilot saw before him, but land.

A trick of the eye made it seem as if they were flying low over the sea towards an island runway – an illusion of speed and direction caused by a shoreline moving towards *them* at fifty miles an hour as the continental shelf rose majestically from the sea at an angle of two degrees and the emerging island reached across to take the flotilla ashore.

PART TWO

VIII

Earthmover II, *Ocean Queen* and *Baltimore* were unrecognizable as sea-going vessels. They had taken the brunt of the collision, being lower in the water on impact, and had come apart at the seams. Their cargoes had been shed in a strangely appropriate christening of the new land, with six hundred tons of hard core, gravel, sand and topsoil-turned-mud from *Earthmover II* lying in random piles across the solid rock as if in preparation for laying down. Next to them, *Ocean Queen's* tinned goods, rehydratable 'space meals' and freeze-dried foodstuffs had formally taken possession of the island in the name of 21st Century convenience. Three panels of the all-green *Douro* in the back row had also split, allowing forty-seven saplings the distinction of being the first living things ashore.

The shelf had hit the underbelly of the convoy at twelve miles an hour, or twenty feet per second – a hundred times faster than Pilot had estimated.

Two things had saved them from catastrophe. First, due to the angle at which the land was rising, the leading barges had made contact first and soaked up at least some of the impact. Second, the eight crumple areas between the jumbo's collars and *Ptolemy's* deck had performed to specification, absorbing 90% of the collision energy.

On board the old Boeing, minds, bodies and spirits were slowly being reassembled after the impact shock and the twenty minutes of violent tremors that followed. The only serious casualty had been Dubravka Horvat. Having dislocated her shoulder earlier during their roller coaster ride over the waves, for the landing, she thought she'd be safer sitting on the floor between seats. As a result, she now had a hairline fracture of the coccyx to augment the pain in her shoulder.

Pilot got word of Horvat's condition after the tremors had subsided to a comfortable level and went down to see her. She was in a lot of pain, but one of the doctors was attending to her. Pilot squeezed her forearm gently and offered some words of commiseration, apology and encouragement. By way of reply, she ran her free hand up the back of his leg and forced a smile. "Hvala," she said. "Thank you. Was my fault, not yours."

The sun had set quickly behind a distant weather front that evening of August 4th and what light remained was insufficient to clarify the scene outside. A strong wind was whipping the water on the windows into fine tendrils whose progress across the glass distorted the scene outside. Very little of the features of their landing place was discernible. The sea was nowhere to be seen, that much they could tell, but they had no idea how far away the nearest coast now was. Nor was their current altitude known. At least it wasn't snowing and the air didn't seem any thinner than before. More important questions awaited their attention.

Four hundred and fifty miles away, in the Wapping offices of *The Morning Journal*, Thursday night's read-in man, Len Wenlight, sat po-faced in front of his computer screen alerting his back bench to the evening's running stories.

Most of the news coming in that afternoon had concerned the tremors in the Bay of Biscay and the tsunamis that had begun hitting Europe's western seaboard, but there'd been a lull from that quarter for nearly an hour.

"SRI LANKA TRAIN CRASH," Wenlight called out.

"Got it," came the back bench reply.

"CHANCELLOR CHEATS ON WIFE."

Reg Fuller, the night editor, stopped what he was doing for a second. "Cheats on wife? Who's our magpie?"

"Veronica."

"I might have known," Fuller answered. "I think the Chancellor's got enough problems—"

"SCILLY ISLES EVACUATION UPDATE," Wenlight interrupted.

"Time?"

"It's running now. Started 1930 hours."

"O.K. I'll read it."

Wenlight didn't bother calling out the next catch line. *The Morning Journal* had never carried Hollywood gossip of a sexual nature and never would. For a further five minutes the bantam-weight journalist, who hated this job but willingly took his turn with the rest of the writers, fished his directory for usable copy. Eventually, he hooked a big one, or so it seemed at first glance.

"BISCAY ISLAND LANDING, Reg."

From Fuller: "Biscay what?"

"ISLAND LANDING." He spoke the words with inflections of urgency and puzzlement.

"Who's the corr?"

Wenlight didn't hear the question. He was reading the copy.

"WHO SENT IT, LEN?"

"It's unattributed. I think you should have a look, though."

Anything from the Bay of Biscay was news that night, so Fuller swiveled round to inspect the fish for himself on his own computer screen.

Wenlight read the first few lines of the release, then looked across at Fuller in disbelief. "There was nothing about an island before I came on, was there?"

But Fuller was too engrossed in the text marching up his screen to answer.

On impact with Eydos, the transmitter in the jumbo's nose cone had automatically sent Geirsson's declaration, largely rewritten by Pilot, to the iPatch News21 system, a satellite facility used by journalists to file stories anywhere in the world to any number of locations simultaneously. Vaalon's 'redilist', comprised the codes for every broadcast, print and internet news source in the world. Through the magic of technology, BISCAY ISLAND LANDING was worldwide in minutes.

Bay of Biscay. 46° 42'N., 6° 04' W. 4/8. Filed 2003 GMT.

150 words. 20 screen lines.

BISCAY ISLAND LANDING.

PRESS RELEASE AND DECLARATION.

At the exact time coded above, the outer edge of the continental shelf of Europe surfaced in international waters in the Bay of Biscay. As numerous sources will verify in the coming days, simultaneous with our landing on the aforementioned land mass, representations were made by our agents in London, Paris, Madrid, Dublin and the United

Nations presenting our legal and indisputable claim on this island, which, as of this moment, will be known as Eydos.

We have displaced no indigenous population to get here. Nor have we relocated from an existing political, sociological, ideological or religious base. We have left everything behind, and our baggage contains only clothes. We appeal to the international community to respect our claim on this island. And we invite the support of friendly nations in upholding it.

Our geographical position is as logged above.
-- L. Pilot

"Who the hell's L. Pilot?" Fuller asked no one in particular. "Run a check on the name, Tony. Alan, call the BBC, SKY and the Foreign Office. See if they have anything on an island. And New York... Paris. COME ON. Get the calls out." Fuller seemed to be talking to everyone at once. "AND CHARTER A PLANE."

Behind his small, wire-rimmed spectacles, Wenlight's pupils were like sharpened pencil points. "I reckon it's a hoax, Reg," he cautioned. "Look. The corr is unidentified. Plus, the story was filed at 8.03, and yet it claims this island came up at 8.03. How would they have had time to both write and file in one second? The whole country knows about the tremors and this is just some jokester journalist or hacker having a punt, but screwing up his timings."

Fuller weighed the evidence.

"You're probably right, Len, but let's get the calls out all the same."

Satisfied with his detective work, Wenlight removed the hook from this strange fish and threw it back into a sea frothing with the fact, fiction, innuendo, gossip, half-truths and scoops being poured into it by sources on every shore.

Ten minutes later, two 'snaps' came on screen in quick succession that made Len Wenlight forget all about jokes and hackers: EARTHQUAKE ISLAND U.N. CLAIM, and immediately below it, LANDMASS SURFACING BISCAY m.f.

"This thing gets curiouser and curiouser, Len," Fuller said over his colleague's shoulder.

Back on *Ptolemy*, Lonnie Pilot sat listening to Serman's damage report. It seemed as if every joint in the barge had been dislocated by the impact. There wasn't a right angle to be found anywhere. Yet, for all that, everything still functioned: the galley was operational; water came out of the taps and the lights worked.

The messroom of the barge was turned into a makeshift infirmary and the dozen most severe cases of shock had been taken down to be treated. Quite a few of the crew were making their way to their cabins to recover privately from the impact, while those who remained in the jumbo were experiencing a different form of shock.

The tremors had ceased at last and after four days at sea, culminating in the earthquake, the sudden calm – signifying as it did a return to solid ground – was disturbing in itself. Less than an hour before, the coordinates 46° 42'N, 6° 04'W had been 190 metres under water. It wasn't surprising that the distinguished American billionaire had taken on new stature with his passengers, none moreso than Lonnie Pilot, Henry Bradingbrooke, Aaron Serman, Jane Lavery, Josiah Billy and Macushla Mara. Someone appeared at the door with a tray of mugs partly obscured by the steam from the hot tea, an instant reminder that no one had taken any food or liquid for eight hours.

The features of the barges around them were clearly visible in the fading evening light but all horizons were hidden from view. Those who remained in the jumbo shared the unspoken desire to disembark to look at, stand on and take in the world's only current virgin territory. When Henry Bradingbrooke began toying with his torch, Pilot uncoiled himself from his seat. "We're not going to sleep until we've seen it, are we?" he said.

They decided to disembark aft, not yet aware of the easier descent forward from the damaged barges. Using a trestle table brought up from the messroom as a bridge, they crossed over to *Fort Lowell* and then to *Earthmover IV* where they secured one end of a nylon rope. Pilot tested the knot, then, taking the free end, walked over the trestle table to the top of the rubber barrage which bounced him up and down like a trampoline. With great ceremony he gathered up the slack, threw the rope to the ground and began abseiling down. On the way, he tried to think of something Neil-Armstrong-like to say to the others when he set foot on the surface for the first time.

Lonnie Pilot's desert boot met with solid rock, smooth as polished granite and still wet and slippery from its long, underwater sleep. "ONE BALD BABY'S ASS FOR A MAN. ONE CLEAN SLATE FOR MANKIND," he pronounced.

"That's terrible," someone called down.

"One innocent child for a man. One ripe virgin for mankind," Bradingbrooke said, joining Pilot on the ground.

Jane Lavery was the next one down. "One empty vessel for a man. One shiny new toilet bowl for mankind."

Pilot could make out in the moonlight the disappointment on Jane's and everyone else's faces. There were no pebbles, no rocks, no sand, no sediment. The entire landscape had been scoured clean of its skin by billions of tons of seawater dragging over it during its ascent. "I can't believe how pessimistic you all are," he said. "This place is beautiful. Use your imaginations. It might not look great now, but we've inherited nobody's mess to clean up and nobody's bad planning."

The others just looked at their feet.

Macushla Mara parted her dark tresses and said, "A unique opportunity, to be sure."

Fatigue, hunger and cold soon got the better of them and, as the exhausted, bedraggled party made its way up the rope in front of him, Pilot bent down, ran his palm over the smooth, clammy rock and rapped it lightly with his knuckles, as if testing its solidity. Then he grabbed the rope and hauled himself up the rubbery slope of their fortress wall.

In the messroom later, with everyone fed and watered, Pilot appeared with half a dozen bottles of liqueur. "Kruskovac. Pear brandy from Croatia, courtesy of Mr. Vaalon," he announced. "Pass it around."

Pilot was still finding sleep elusive at 4am when he heard the unmistakable sound of rotor blades threshing the air to the east. He rushed up on deck and was joined by at least fifty of his crew. No one needed the moonlight to see what was happening. Searchlights from half a dozen or more helicopters zig-zagged over the glistening surface of the island looking for suitable landing spots. Pilot watched with growing anxiety as eight troop-carrying Chinooks with French markings set down next to the convoy and disgorged nearly two hundred of that country's elite fighting men. The French commandoes were well-oiled, sliding out of their helicopters and encircling the convoy in under five minutes.

Those on board *Ptolemy* waited to see what their visitors would do next. The all-too-visible firearms cradled in the soldiers' arms like malevolent babies struck fear into the watchers' hearts. Some ran below to their rooms and locked themselves in. Others just braced themselves for the worst, frozen to the deck, hearts pounding.

An hour of stand-off passed. While lookouts were sent to the four corners of the flotilla, Serman suggested that everyone else take it in shifts to go below for an early breakfast in case they didn't get a chance later.

Lonnie Pilot, who had fallen asleep from exhaustion just twenty minutes before first light, was wakened by a gentle hand on his shoulder. "It's like an air show out there, Lonnie," Jane Lavery said. "You'd better come up." Eydos was ten hours old and the news of her birth was reverberating around the world.

They climbed the ladder onto the wheelhouse roof where Aaron Serman was counting planes. "Where do you think that one's from?" Pilot asked as a plane sliced the air overhead.

"This is its second pass. Royal Navy, I think. Two French planes were just here and waggled their wings at our friends over there before leaving." Pilot glanced across at the French commandoes and could see the smoke from their camp stoves. There was an aroma of coffee on the breeze. Another plane appeared from the south and buzzed the convoy at just a hundred metres. Its red and yellow roundel declared it to be Spanish.

Someone appeared with a tray of steaming coffee mugs and a plate of toast – no butter. Seven more planes came and went by the time the three had finished their breakfast. Pilot wiped the crumbs from his mouth and began to take in the scene around him. Beyond the ominous French encirclement, the view confirmed his fears that the whole of Eydos was nothing but rock – undulating but otherwise formless, apart from the cloud shadows that rolled over its bald surface. They would have their work cut out planting one blade of grass, let alone themselves.

He scribbled a note to Vaalon. 'One injury, not serious,' it read. 'One no-show – *Shenandoah*, as I think you already know. We're surrounded by French troops, but they haven't made contact with us yet. Looks like they're just flexing their muscles for now. We're nine-tenths in possession and we'll see what today brings. ~Pilot.'

The previous evening, he had set a rota of volunteers to monitor the airwaves and he was eager to find out what they'd heard. Entering the radio room with the note, Pilot recognized the sole New Zealander in his crew, Kerry Jackson, sitting next to McConie. In his file photograph, Jackson looked like a fair-haired version of Lonnie Pilot. In the flesh, the resemblance was uncanny. He was wearing headphones and typing into a kPad. Pilot gave the note to McConie for encrypting, then addressed Jackson. "What've we got so far, Kerry?"

Jackson scrolled to the beginning of the log and handed Pilot the tablet. The first mention had come at 2230 GMT and as he read through the entries, Pilot was able to piece together the jigsaw of what had been happening in the outside world since the Bay of Biscay had exploded the previous day.

The first major waves had hit the Pilat Dunes in southwest France at 1630 and had reached St. Nazaire by 1700. The tsunamis had not abated until 2130. In spite of repeated warnings, and a deliberate exaggeration supplied by the IGP of the projected height of the waves, many people had ignored the order to evacuate to higher ground and had paid for their intransigence with their lives. Although the exact number of French dead was not yet known (and wouldn't be for several months) it was estimated at between 3,000 and 5,000. Only a handful of casualties had been reported from the Channel Islands in what the Bailiffs of Jersey and Guernsey were calling the most successful evacuation before the jaws of death in history. In fact, the islands had been largely shielded by the Brittany peninsula, which had taken the brunt of the seas. The more exposed Isles of Scilly had been scoured by 20-30 foot waves, but not before every living soul, bar nine St. Agnes dairy cows, had been evacuated in what the British Prime Minister had described as 'the most comprehensive relocation of an island population since Tristan da Cunha'.

[In Penzance, two elderly women, having sandbagged the entrance to their shop earlier, had only minimal flood damage to clear up.]

An American seismologist noted that, unlike the Japanese and California-Oregon tsunamis, the seas thrown up by the island's rising had been lower, due to the slow surfacing of the continental shelf. Even so, the damage they caused was already running into tens of millions of Neuros. [Derived from the German word *neu*, the new currency that had replaced the collapsed Euro had an unintentional similarity to *neurosis* – unintentional but perfectly appropriate. The entire global financial foundation was more unstable now than it had been since the minting of the first coin.]

Pilot read through the remaining entries quickly but found no reference to his five advocates, the press release or anything at all suggesting that the risen land had already been settled and christened. They were merely updates on wave damage, terrible loss of life and remarkable rescues and evacuations, but no mention at all of Eydos or its mysterious flotilla of barges. Until the satellite dish could be erected, they were unable to check what the world wide web was carrying.

The early morning BBC news bulletin was just about to begin, so Pilot made himself as comfortable as he could, given his growing agitation, to listen. Again, no reference to them was made beyond a physical account of the new island. Aerial radar reconnaissance during the night had confirmed it to be a 155-mile ribbon of bare rock running from northwest to southeast parallel to the French coast from Brest down to Nantes. At its widest, the island was only 23 miles. The average width was 17 miles and the shortest distance to the French coast was 62 miles. The BBC's Science Correspondent confirmed that the island was, in fact, the edge of the European continental shelf. Pilot noticed that it wasn't referred to as the *French* continental shelf.

'This accounts,' the report continued, 'for the island's peculiar topography, in which the entire west coast consists of cliffs rising in some places to over three hundred metres, whereas in the east the land rises at such a narrow angle that even two miles inland it is still only a few feet above sea level.'

The last item in the bulletin made Pilot choke on his coffee. 'Political commentators are already predicting a major diplomatic wrangle between Britain and France as to who has legitimate claim over the new island. Another solution being promoted is that it be declared an international protectorate, similar to Antarctica.'

Pilot summoned Odile Bartoli, a French woman from Aix, to the radio room. When she arrived, he asked McConie to find a French radio broadcast for Bartoli to translate.

Seconds later, a torrent of French burst from the speakers. "They are talking about it. Shhhh," Bartoli cautioned. When the newscast finished, she looked at Pilot in disbelief. "They say all about the wave damages and that there are many dead. Then they say about the island ... where it is… how big. There is no mention of us. Then they say its name – *Ile de Bonne Fortune*."

Pilot could feel his heart sinking. He never thought it would be easy, but neither did he suspect the French would stonewall so blatantly. Someone, somewhere must have received their declaration.

"Incoming message from London," McConie said. Pilot watched as line after line of indecipherable gibberish rolled up the monitor. When it stopped, McConie pushed a button and the letters relocated into English. Pilot squatted down and began reading Forrest Vaalon's first communication in weeks.

> *You made it. Five didn't. Rebecca Schein only survivor of Shenandoah. French vessel* Largesse *also lost with all hands. Declarations made UN, Dublin, London, Madrid. Not in Paris. Good and bad news. I read your declaration. Wouldn't have said it like that myself, but there's no mistaking your presence. Well done.*

The *Shenandoah* deaths hit Pilot like a sledgehammer and he was composing a reply to Vaalon when a noise outside caught his attention. He stepped out on deck with McConie to investigate what sounded like a helicopter close by. In fact, it was coming in to land just outside the French cordon.

He watched the heavy machine descend with a mixture of dread and hope – hope that it was carrying his North Ronaldsay sheep and not more troops. He was relieved to see that it wasn't a military helicopter, but a private charter of some kind. The second it touched down, swarms of newsmen leapt to the rock like D-day troops at Juno Beach. They were halted by the French commandoes, and Pilot could make out the officer in charge being harangued by reporters. The standoff lasted five minutes before the French opened their human wall and let the reporters through.

In *The Psychology of Leadership* Pilot had read that, in a situation such as this, the leader leaves it to his lieutenants to make the initial contact. So he sent his press secretary and Eydos' deputy leader to meet the media.

Mara and Bradingbrooke crossed over to the wreck of *Earthmover II*, descended the aluminium ladder that had been placed at her bow, met the newcomers ten metres from the convoy and were quickly engulfed. The reporters were all talking and shouting at once, swishing their microphones and cameras through the air like butterfly nets.

"HOW DID YOU KNOW THIS PLACE WAS COMING UP?" "ARE THERE ANY CASUALTIES?" "WHICH ONE OF YOU IS L. PILOT?" "WHAT ARE YOU DOING HERE?" "DO YOU SERIOUSLY THINK YOU CAN LAY CLAIM TO THIS ISLAND?"

Macushla Mara stepped forward to silence the mob, which was becoming unruly. "We'll speak to *one* of you only," she said, fishing the sea of faces before her. Pilot had briefed her earlier about the tactic President Reagan had employed when dealing with a White House press corps that had grown competitively obnoxious during Jimmy Carter's more laid back presidency. "The tall man over there with the white hair and the safari suit. Austin Palmer. Does anyone object if he acts as your spokesman?" Mara had seen the man fronting television documentaries and knew him to be impartial, honest and well-respected. No one objected to the choice, so Palmer stepped forward.

"L. Pilot, I presume," he said, extending his hand.

"I'm Macushla Mara, Pilot's Press Secretary. And this is our Deputy Leader, Henry Bradingbrooke. We never thought you people would beat the Royal Marines to our island."

"Neither did we, "Palmer said, "and I'm surprised, given the presence of the French troops here. The Government knows about you, but have their reasons for not admitting to it."

"You got our press release, "Mara said. "*Everyone* must know we're here."

"We got it, but we needed physical confirmation."

"I can understand that, Austin. Well, here we are. Will you publish now?"

"I gave the go-ahead the second I saw your convoy from the helicopter window. By the way, your declaration's all over the internet, but only one broadsheet ran it. *The Morning Journal* went ahead and printed your statement in their early edition and by the look of things here, they've stolen a march on all of us. Give them a copy, Len."

A small man in his thirties stepped forward with a rolled up newspaper, which Mara and Bradingbrooke retired into a huddle to read. The press release/declaration was printed in full below half a page of reports on the amazing happenings in the Bay of Biscay. The speech by the MP from Falmouth in support of Eydos had also been printed. The gist of Len Wenlight's account was as follows: With the British Parliament on holiday, and the summer recess not due to finish for another month, a handful of sour cabinet ministers had been rounded up to handle the necessary business of government in the wake of the tsunamis devastating the southwest coast of England. Sixty-eight-year-old Hugo Gramercy, the soon-to-retire MP for

Falmouth, had arrived at Westminster at 7pm, purportedly to represent his constituents' needs in the disaster. [*Not* in Wenlight's report was the fact that shortly after 8pm the MP's pager, activated by a signal from The Bay of Biscay, had gone off in his pocket.] To the bafflement of everyone present, Gramercy had begun making a speech supporting a claim of sovereignty on behalf of L. Pilot and his followers over a new land mass which was at that moment breaking the surface of the sea in the Bay of Biscay. For an hour the man had been humoured by his parliamentary colleagues, who thought him quite mad, until first reports of the emergence of the island reached Westminster at 9pm.

Further down the page, another headline caught Mara's eye:

CORNISH MP'S STORY BOLSTERED BY UN CLAIM

The article stated that, during a debate in the United Nations General Assembly on Third World Labour Exploitation, the Ambassador for Iceland, Fridrik Geirsson, had interrupted proceedings to deliver a statement echoing that of Gramercy. Addressing the assembly in his capacity as an expert in maritime law, Geirsson advised that if reports of a landing proved to be true, then the colonisers could indeed have a legal right to sovereignty over the island.

'There is no denying,' the paper concluded, *'that, simultaneous with the raising of this new island in the Bay of Biscay and Geirsson's statement at the United Nations, claims to it on behalf of L. Pilot and his or her followers were also being made by their representatives in Britian and Ireland. Improbable and impossible as it sounds, the new land may already have secured its independence under international law. It only remains to be seen*

whether the settlers' physical presence on the island is a reality or merely an elaborate hoax.'

"Did you write this?" Bradingbrooke asked Wenlight.

"Yes."

"Thank you. Elaborate hoax we are not. Nor is L. Pilot a her."

"Can we talk to him?" Palmer asked, pointing to the convoy.

"No."

Palmer turned to look at his fellow journalists, then asked Bradingbrooke, "You seem very well prepared – as if you knew in advance that this island would be surfacing. This was *not* an accident. Can you explain?"

"I used to work at the IGP in London as a meteorologist," Bradingbrooke began. Although he had rehearsed the story many times with Vaalon, he had never done so in front of ninety journalists and his discomfort was noticeable to all. "For several years we had been researching and measuring the movement of pyrocoagula in the Earth's magma –"

"Pyro what?" a voice asked.

Bradingbrooke spelt the word and went on to explain in laymans' terms the science behind magmatic pulses, the new measurement methods developed by the IGP, the theory of Solar Tides, and how their computer model had predicted the ascension of the island.

"So, the IGP knew all along that this was going to happen?" Palmer said with a note of pique in his voice.

"Yes and no," Bradingbrooke replied. "We know that this spot was last above water 5,000 years ago. The Director also knew it was due to resurface about a year from now. He was going to make a formal announcement this coming January. He was not aware that I had gone into the data the previous month and added a year to the predicted date of the event. The IGP is not the culprit in this. *I* am." The pack of newshounds began to yelp and Mara raised her hand to silence them. "The only thing I doctored was the date of the island's emergence," Bradingbrooke said. "The fact that there has been minimal loss of life during this event is primarily due to the information and warnings the IGP began issuing back in May, long before the first tremors began." Bradingbrooke looked beyond Palmer into the eyes of the other reporters and lied. "No one but I had prior knowledge that the island would be surfacing *this* year." [Vaalon, Pilot and Bradingbrooke had agreed during their meeting in Bristol that this was to be the only untruth ever voiced in the name of Eydos.]

"THAT, I cannot believe," Palmer said. "L. Pilot's declaration was time coded 2003 GMT, the exact minute your flotilla made landfall. How do you expla –"

Palmer's last few words were drowned out by the sound of another helicopter approaching from the east. Thirty French newsmen and women exited the hot machine, passed easily through the wall of their military compatriots and took their place next to the British contingency. Mara signaled Odile Bartoli over from the convoy to translate and asked the French to nominate a spokesman. There was much arguing and gesticulating, but no decision, so she asked a tall, middle-aged man with no shoulders and a face like a bloodhound to step forward. After fifteen minutes of conversation with him, it was clear to Bartoli that the situation in France was no better than that in Britain. Those few papers and radio and TV news services not attached to French government strings had given fair coverage and printed a translation of the press release. On the other side, those with the national interest at their throats and a lot more influence in the country, were already labeling it a conspiracy and a hoax. They went further, stating that if, indeed, there were already non-French nationals on the island, then they were trespassers on what was obviously and unquestionably French sovereign territory – part of France's natural continental shelf. The journalist added that as far as he was aware, no representation had been made at a high level in Paris, as had happened in London, New York and Dublin. The French military presence, he explained, was natural, as this was French territory.

Mara sensed that it was time to wrap up the meeting and report back to Pilot. "We have work to do," she said to the reporters. "You're welcome to stay here and film from a distance, but the talking is over for now."

As she and Bradingbrooke turned to walk back to the convoy, Mara called over her shoulder, "All of us on Eydos thank you for coming here to document our presence."

Pilot greeted them in Ptolemy's wheelhouse and debriefed them. "It's not a perfect situation, but it's not a disaster either," he said. "We've got allies in the media of both countries, the story is public and the timings of Gramercy's, Geirsson's and the others' speeches are on the record. The evidence, if nothing else, is on our side. Let's just let those for us and those against us thrash it out for a week or two in the open. Public opinion will come down on our side in the end."

He almost convinced himself.

By ten o'clock the media circus had set themselves up in little encampments around the convoy, their telephoto lenses aimed like siege guns at the flotilla. As a result, they were perfectly positioned to record every minute of the action when the French commandoes stormed the convoy at noon.

IX

The rough tactics used to round up and manhandle everyone into the barge's messroom were uncalled for. People were arm-locked, pushed and shoved, rifle barrels pressed into their spines. "CECI N'EST PAS ADMISSIBLE," Odile Bartoli called out. "OÙ EST VOTRE COMMANDANT?" The reply was a slap around her ear and a shove to the floor.

The convoy's camera operator, meanwhile, hearing the troops entering the jumbo, quickly switched off her equipment, removed the memory card on which she'd just recorded the invasion and concealed it in her panties just as the first commando appeared at the top of the steps. Two soldiers stayed behind to examine the video equipment and search the lounge and cockpit while half a dozen others frog-marched their prisoner down to the barge. Three females were rousted out of *Bimbo's Kraal*, where they had been preparing the stalls for the sheep's arrival, and two further crew members were plucked from their hiding place behind a rubber barrage.

The round-up took a full hour, the colonel in charge demanding that every barge be thoroughly searched and all fugitives netted before ordering the next stage of the operation. When he was satisfied that no further 'trespassers' would be found, he said in English, "You will now be escorted to your cabins to retrieve your passports or identity papers, if you do not already have them on your person." He shouted a command and the captives were hustled away, each accompanied by two commandoes.

Twenty minutes later, all 81 crew were back in the messroom empty-handed. With no way of identifying his captives, the Colonel had no choice but to resort to Plan B. He barked an order to an aide who relayed it another step down the rung of command to a soldier who produced an indelible marker pen. Another soldier placed himself before a laptop at one of the tables.

"You will come up here to be logged in," the Colonel instructed. "You will give your name and nationality, be photographed and given an identification number on your forearm, which you must display at all times." When a queue began to form in front of the registration desk, Pilot imagined a young Ruth Belkin taking her place in a similar queue.

In his place near the back of the line with Jackson and Bradingbrooke, Pilot whispered an instruction that was passed down to the front of the queue just as registration commenced.

One by one, the captives were processed and photographed. All but one gave a false, but believable, name. Aaron Serman was Ron Mann and Macushla Mara was Mary Cushing. For *nationality*, everyone said *Eydosian.* The atmosphere in the messroom was tense, but it reached boiling point at detainee number 57. "EMBARQUEZ LE," the Colonel shouted. The crew looked on impotently as their compatriot was spirited out of the messroom and up the companionway by four commandoes.

Several minutes later, the swishing of rotor blades announced the departure of a lone helicopter. "Tout va bien," the Colonel said, "Monsieur Pilot will be asked some questions in Paris this evening and you will be our guests here on French soil until I receive further orders.

Ne quittez pas le vaisseau, s'il vous plait. Do not leave this vessel." With two hundred guns trained on them, they couldn't have left if they tried.

As the helicopter crested the escarpment above Nillin to begin its run to Paris, Kerry Jackson, unable to contain himself any longer, began to laugh, much to the puzzlement of his two guards.

At the register, Lonnie Pilot gave his name and nationality – Ollie Bolling, Eydosian – and was photographed. The number 60 was then written on his forearm. He had always felt certain numbers to be special or significant, but couldn't attach any meaning to this one. He sat down at the furthest table he could find from the French guards and, through some gravitational force of sexuality, locked eyes with Dubi Horvat, who was sitting at the far side of the messroom. She gave him a loaded smile. He gave one back. His tension immediately began to be replaced with a feeling of familiar helplessness. He recognized the signs – that tipping point when innocent eye contact between two people morphs into something more auspicious. But that something would have to wait. They were going nowhere.

He studied the faces of their guards – some tense, some relaxed, some fearful, some bold. It was easy to separate the men from the boys. Then he turned to Jane Lavery, who had taken the seat next to him.

"What do *you* think of the situation here, Mrs. Normal?" he asked.

"Mrs. *Who*?"

"Get in character, Jane. You're *Mrs. Normal* from *Normalton, Normalshire*. You represent the status quo. I want to know what you think. Does France have the right to invade and occupy Eydos?"

"Let me ask *Average Joe*," Lavery said. "Get in character, Lonnie."

Pilot smiled. "Touché. It's not our job to give an opinion, Norma. It's to follow the lead of others."

"You're right, Joe. The rights and wrongs of this invasion will be determined by our leaders, not by us."

"That's the problem, Jane. A billion Mrs. Normals and Average Joes sitting on the fence, waiting to see which way the wind blows."

"So, here we are then," Lavery said, removing her mask. "Becalmed in a sea of indecision and indifference."

Those were the last words Lonnie Pilot heard. In the confined space of the metal-walled messroom, the two gunshots that cracked the air ten feet from Pilot's head caused instant deafness. Thinking they were about to be massacred, crew members began flinging themselves under tables and behind chairs. Others rushed for the exits, but were stopped by their captors. In the far corner, four French soldiers were holding a fifth one flat out and face down on the floor in a full nelson. One soldier had his knees in the assailant's back, and two others were attempting to smother his flailing legs with their arms. Nearby, a body lay motionless in a pool of blood.

"Lonnie," Lavery screamed. But there was no response. "LONNIE."

Pilot could see her mouth moving, but he pointed to his ears and shook his head to indicate he couldn't hear. Then he rushed over to the body on the floor and saw immediately that Ali Jeckyll was dead.

Alistair Bremner Jeckyll had grown up in the Gorbals of Glasgow and seemed dim to those unwilling to look deeper. Rather, he was just verbally challenged. Ruth Vaalon and the Director of the Glasgow chapter of Scholasticorps had recognised Jeckyll's hidden depths and latent brilliance when the boy was 15. Had Mr. and Mrs. Vaalon not plucked him from the stairwells of the Languthrie Estate, circumstances would eventually have suffocated the man. Conversely, had the Vaalons not plucked him from the stairwells of the Languthrie Estate, Ali Jeckyll could still be alive.

Jack Highbell and several of the others were hurling abuse at their guards in the far corner of the messroom. One of the shepherdesses snatched from *Bimbo's Kraal* was wailing beside Jeckyll's body, and Macushla Mara was kneeling at his head, tears running down her cheeks. Pilot bent down between the two women and lowered the lids on the man's dead eyes.

"Leave this to me, Lonnie," Bradingbrooke mouthed slowly as he pulled Pilot away. He faced Mara, whose hearing was beginning to return. "Take him away, Macushla. Lonnie Pilot is supposed to be on his way to Paris, so we need to keep this one out of sight." Calm was beginning to replace distress, but it was the calm of shock, not respite. A French medic appeared, squatted by the body and realized there was nothing to be done.

Bradingbrooke, meanwhile, had found the commanding officer and was looking him square in the face. "Quoi est arrivé?" he demanded.

The Colonel shrugged. "Je ne sais pas," he said. "We are very sorry for this."

"Pourquoi votre soldat tiré?"

"En auto-défense."

"SELF DEFENCE? BASTARDS."

"Asseyez vous. SIT DOWN." With that, the Colonel turned on his heel and directed his men to remove the body.

Outside in the journalists' colony, there was much speculation about the gunfire. Although no more shots had been heard, an explanation was being demanded of the soldiers posted at the entrance to the convoy, but they refused to be drawn.

Inside, Pilot, Bradingbrooke, Lavery, Mara and Josiah Billy were holding a post mortem. Billy had been sitting across from Jeckyll when he was shot.

"What happened, Josiah?" Pilot asked, hearing his own words as if through water.

"It's the way Ali was looking at him," Billy said. "I can't explain it. It was like some primeval animal stare… burning… accusing… threatening. He didn't divert his eyes from the soldier for a second, and I could see the guy begin to squirm and the red mist fall across his face. There's no excuse for what happened, but even *I* felt uncomfortable. This went on for five minutes. I never even saw Ali blink. If I'd known the soldier was going to crack, I'd have done something."

"It's not your fault, Josiah," Mara said. Pilot remained silent, composing a statement to be issued the moment they escaped their current predicament. For the moment, they could only sit and sweat it out.

In the outside world, information had been scarce until the ever-thickening layers of reporting, mostly internet-driven, forced the British and French governments to admit to the settlers' presence on the island. The snowball in favour of Lonnie Pilot's Eydos was rolling, but there was still the chance it would melt in the heat. There were many behind-the-scenes goings-on that were not yet, and probably never would be, public knowledge. The British Prime Minister had ordered an expeditionary force onto the island within two hours of its appearance. However, in light of the claims made at the United Nations, at Westminster by Gramercy and in Dublin, the PM had been advised to postpone the landing.

On learning that the French had occupied the island, Britain reacted strongly. Exhibiting the hypocrisy of all governments, they called it a 'unilateral, imperialist act' tantamount to 'piracy on the high seas'. They demanded immediate French withdrawal until the matter of sovereignty could be resolved multilaterally. The British Ambassador to the United Nations called for a special meeting of the General Assembly to condemn France's hasty and heavy-handed occupation, unaware that the Icelandic Ambassador had already done so.

Before this meeting convened, however, the French Government made a fatal miscalculation. News of the killing of one of the prisoners had just reached them, although it had not yet been made public. Panicking under this, and the realisation that perhaps they *were* acting unlawfully, their top tactical brains decided to pressure their prisoner, Lonnie Pilot, into making a statement admitting that the landing had been a fortuitous accident which had then been manipulated by the castaways themselves. A video press conference to that end was convened in which Jackson played the role of proud resistance followed by reluctant acquiescence. His 'confession' was shown throughout the world, but of course it only required one look at the photograph of the real Lonnie Pilot, on file at the Passport Office, to show that, although there was a clear resemblance, the man in French custody was in fact an imposter. A government-sanctioned 'leak' from London ensured that the photograph of the real Lonnie Pilot was worldwide within hours. Condemnation of France was global; her embarrassment acute. 'Where did law, justice and liberty originate from, if not from La Belle France?' one British paper proclaimed. In another fatal error, the French Prime Minister ordered that news of the killing be kept secret until their international standing had improved.

The healthiest climate for Eydos was in the Republic of Ireland. A prominent Irish intellectual had staked their claim in the Dáil, the members of which had shown much interest. The entire event had appealed enormously to the Irish national character. There was no love lost between Dublin and her near neighbours in London and Paris, although in the highest circles this fact wasn't often admitted. Eire was therefore committed from the outset to keeping both Britain's and France's hands off Eydos.

Pilot's advocate in Spain, a descendant of Cervantes and a personal friend of the Spanish Prime Minister, had timed his intervention to perfection, although luck played an important role. He had invited the Prime Minister to his home for dinner, along with three high-ranking ministers and a Cardinal, on the evening Eydos had surfaced. In the middle of cocktails his pager went off, much to his surprise and relief. He had immediately raised his glass in a toast to the settlers of the newly risen island of Eydos and proceeded to make the speech prepared for him by his friend Forrest Vaalon, but with a few embellishments of his own. His stunned guests had thought him mad and quixotic of course.

The following morning, with the first official reports from Spanish television of the island's emergence, at least a small measure of credence was being shown by his guests of the previous evening, none more so than Cardinal Peña. Noticing the Godless tone of Pilot's declaration, which was now public, the Cardinal had already begun formulating plans to send one of his deputies on a mission to export Roman Catholicism to the colony.

Vaalon's appointee in Paris had failed them at the last moment, fearful that support of Lonnie Pilot against the interests of France would poison his reputation – a reputation already dead as far as Forrest Vaalon was concerned.

Three and a half thousand miles away in New York City, the emergency session of the UN was just coming to order. The French Ambassador, whose tour of duty had so far been routine and undemanding, suddenly found himself centre stage with his trousers down and had been up since midnight trying to think of a way of maintaining French honour in the affair. The Kerry Jackson incident had multiplied his problems a hundred-fold. He couldn't believe that the incompetence of his colleagues back in Paris could have risen to such damaging heights.

As Eydos had no seat at the UN, Iceland demanded that the French forces retire at once and that diplomatic relations be established with the settlers. The French Ambassador thought this provocative, not to mention impudent, implying as it did that the settlers had a valid claim on the island. He would have done better to agree, though, because his reply was greeted with derision and disgust by all but France's closest allies.

Under pressure, he had agreed to move the troops a thousand metres away from what he called the 'alien settlement', but under no circumstances would they leave Ile de Bonne Fortune. He added that his government was prepared to grant temporary resident status to the settlers until their removal. The island was a natural extension of France, he insisted, and its fate could not be decided on the accidental presence over the surfacing shelf of a fleet of 'Gypsy barges'. France's official policy towards 'travelers' wasn't unfair, he went on, digging himself even deeper into his hole, and the so-called settlers would be removed to the destination of their choice at the government's expense as soon as it was convenient. In conclusion, he explained that the impersonation of Lonnie Pilot had been a ruse of the trespassers and *not* of the French government, which had only been trying to clarify matters.

The question was then passed to the member nations to decide. As one of the five members of the Security Council, it was France's right to veto any resolution passed by the General Assembly. When the latter duly called for France's *complete* withdrawal from the island until the matter could be resolved by the international community as a whole, France invoked her veto.

Back on board *Ptolemy*, the French forces were preparing for their third night in occupation. They had been unable to set up their tents the previous two nights, owing to the fact that tent pegs weren't designed to penetrate solid rock, so they had slept fitfully in their helicopters instead. Pilot and his crew had been forced to sleep under guard in the messroom, access to their cabins having been forbidden. Every chair, table-top and available stretch of floor had a body on it.

At 10pm that night, however, as the same process was about to be repeated, the French Colonel received a general order from Paris to withdraw immediately to a line one thousand metres from the convoy in compliance with their agreed undertaking.

As the last commando grudgingly left *Ptolemy* shortly before midnight, Pilot noted that it was exactly 60 hours since they had first stormed the convoy. Exhausted and relieved, he pulled his sleeve down over his #60 and followed the others to their cabins.

X

Pilot's statement on the shooting of Ali Jeckyll reached the iPatch satellite just two hours after the 1,000 metre withdrawal of the 'Commandos Marine'. It was short and to the point:

> *From the barge, Ptolemy. Eydos. 0210 hrs. 8/8*
>
> *On August 5th at 1530 hrs, one of our people was shot dead by a trooper of the French platoon occupying our flotilla. Alistair Jeckyll was 33 and from Glasgow. He was unarmed, as are we all.*
> *We understand that the perpetrator had mental issues and that the French command was not complicit in the killing. Through their swift action in restraining the gunman, they may have prevented further deaths and for that, we thank them. However, the French Commander's claim that the soldier fired in self-defense after being attacked is a fabrication – a gross defamation of a good and gentle man's character. Such dishonesty pollutes the integrity of this island and will not be tolerated. We demand the* total *withdrawal of French forces from Eydos forthwith.*

Within minutes, the statement had travelled from the iPatch satellite into the dishes of the world's hungry news media, and from there back into space and down to a dozen smart phones in the news village outside the convoy. The Ali Jeckyll killing played out exactly as Pilot thought it would: The journalists had beaten a path to the French commander's helicopter, demanding either confirmation or denial of Pilot's claim and reminding him that the shots they heard had occurred at the exact time of Jeckyll's alleged killing. The French Colonel had played dumb until international pressure had forced his superiors in Paris to issue their own statement three hours later, which Pilot pulled up online.

Oui, il y a eu une fusillade sur l'Ile de Bonne Fortune. Un de nos soldats a été attaqué par les intrus et a tire en auto-defense. Notre revendication était juste et vraie. L'ordre a été rétabli et nous faisons le nécessaire pour la répatriation du corps du défunt et le retour a la famille.

"What does it say, Odile?"

"That one of their soldiers was attacked by the interlopers and discharged his firearm in self defense. That their claim of self-defense was not a lie. That order has now been restored and arrangements being made to repatriate the corpse of the deceased to his family."

Whether the world would ever learn the truth, Pilot doubted, but he had planted enough of a seed of veracity to keep France firmly in the hot seat of suspicion.

"Should we invent something new, or use an existing model?" Pilot said, opening the discussion on devising a system of government for the island. There was an air of excitement and apprehension in the messroom. No one knew where this was going to go.

"Why reinvent the wheel?" Jane Lavery said.

"Because the wheel has fallen off the wagon."

"Not *our* wagon," said Mara. "We've never had a wheel before. There's nothing to say that Marxism or some other system wouldn't work here."

Pilot stood up. "Does everybody agree with Macushla? That we construct a wheel using all the broken pieces out there?"

"Just as long as it gets us where we want to go, that's good enough," Lavery said.

"Okay. As a starting point, who thinks Eydos should be Marxist? Show of hands. Let's make this quick." Pilot looked around the room and counted just three raised hands. Mara's wasn't one of them.

"Who thinks we should be a democracy?"

"Majoritarian or Consensual?" Aaron Serman said. "Who do we want to rule us, the majority of the people or as many people as possible?"

"Everyone on this island should have a say in how it's run and how our political agenda is determined," Pilot said without hesitation. "Our government needs to be equitable, transparent and accountable."

The pros and cons of democracy were discussed for half an hour, with several alternative systems suggested, voted on and rejected. In the end, they settled on consensual democracy, with 80% consensus required to carry a motion. The vote itself had been 100% in favour.

"Right, then. Nominations for leader," Pilot said, proceeding to the next item on the agenda.

"Vaalon told us *you* were in charge," someone said.

"For the moment. We needed a leader at the beginning and he chose me. But his work is done and he's out of the picture now. It's one thing to have Forrest Vaalon's backing, but I need the support of all of you if I'm to carry on as head."

"Then I nominate Lonnie Pilot," Serman said.

"Seconded," a number of voices echoed around the room.

Pilot scanned the assembly twice. "Come on. Doesn't anybody else want to run?"

"I nominate Jane Lavery," Mara said. "It wouldn't be an election otherwise."

"Seconded."

"Can I nominate myself?" Bradingbrooke asked. Everyone laughed.

Pilot thought for a minute. "We don't have a rule yet that says you can't. I'll second you."

As there were no further takers, a polling booth consisting of a table and chair surrounded by curtains made of sheets was constructed. Aaron Serman, the island's resident IT expert, placed a laptop containing the Fingerprint Voting Program on the table and booted up. He'd been looking forward to using FVP and explained to the crew how it worked. "First of all, we register our prints. Place your left thumb in the box on screen, press Scan and, when prompted, type your information in the required fields. Once everyone is registered, I'll enter the three candidates into the program. Each will have a box below their name. Place your left thumb in the box of your choice and press Enter. It's simple, fast and tamper proof."

"What percentage of support is required for a candidate to be elected leader?" someone asked. "I suggest the standard consensus of 80%."

"All in favour?" Pilot said. Seventy-nine hands went up.

After the prints were registered, voting commenced. When the last thumb was cast, Serman sat down at the laptop and clicked Result. No one was holding their breath. "Lonnie Pilot has been duly elected Leader of Eydos. Seventy-six in favour, zero against." The three candidates had all abstained.

"What about checks and balances?" Bradingbrooke asked.

"Because of our size, checks and balances won't be a problem," Pilot said. "A group of four or five elected people under the leader could provide the first level. The remainder of the population, with the power to vote a leader out, would provide a second."

"How would that work?" Mara asked.

"Every four or five years, or at any time a consensus demands it, a vote of confidence in the leader could be taken. If they lose, then an election for a new leader should be held."

Everyone seemed happy with that, so an election was held for the five members of 'The Pentad', a name suggested by Macushla Mara for Eydos' first level of checks on the leader. From the twelve candidates, Bradingbrooke, Serman, Mara, Lavery and Josiah Billy were elected. A natural hierarchy had already begun to establish itself on the island. The rest of the day and half the next was spent defining the powers and responsibilities of the Leader and The Pentad, structuring their consensual democracy and writing a constitution that included 10% minority veto power and the right of anyone to call for a referendum on any issue at any time.

Just before the lunch break, the question of what to do with those who didn't follow the 'Eydos line' was discussed. It was decided that no-one would ever be forced to support ideas they didn't believe in. Nor would they be forced to stay on the island. They called it the 'There's the Door' option.

The first item on the agenda after lunch was the Eydos Bill of Rights. The laptop was switched on and the crew invited to enter their suggestions in their own password-protected file. They were given the rest of the day to do so, and when Serman clicked Harvest late that afternoon, 256 proposed rights were extracted from the 81 files onto a single list. When duplication was taken into account, the actual number of unique rights boiled down to just 13, ranging from 'the right to leave the island at any time without ostracism or hindrance' to 'the right to petition.' Under a proposal by Serman, if eight or more people objected to any proposed right, it would be stricken from the list. Of the 13 proposed rights, only one failed to make the cut: 'The right to bear arms'. Pilot had thrown that one in as a test and it had been rejected by 81 votes to zero.

Dan Heiberg pulled the last tent peg from the ground and threw it on the pile with the others. "Bag 'em up, Johnny," he said to his son. "Looks like weather coming." After three baking hot days in Elk City State Park, Kansas, the heatwave had broken, and the blue skies were being painted over from the southwest by a growing mass of grey-black cloud.

"Dan, come here," Heiberg's wife called from the front seat of the car. "They're playing our song." Heiberg settled into the driver's seat and smiled as You're the Reason God Made Oklahoma *rattled the speakers. Halfway through the song, the music was interrupted by the station's engineer.*

'Sorry to break in folks, but I just got a call from my cousin about a twister that's touched down near Enid. Said it's headed for Blackwell and Ponca City. As soon as we have any more information, we'll let you know.'

Their song came back on again, but Heiberg's smile had disappeared. He checked the map, then looked at his wife in alarm. He reached over and pressed SCAN on the radio, searching for more news. Oldies… Country… Top 40… more Country… When they picked up the public radio station out of Ketchum, the announcer was breathlessly reporting on the tornado… and what he was saying was unbelievable.

'Enid has been wiped off the map, according to storm chaser Jared Tillott who just got off the line with us. We have no confirmation of this but…' There was a click, followed by 10 seconds of silence. Then there was another click and the voice was back. 'We've just been told to shut down the station and find shelter. The tornado is travelling due east, and we're right in its track. As soon as we get the all clear, we'll resume broadcasting, if we can, but meantime, if you live anywhere on or near the line Ponca City-Bartlesville-Ketchum-Springfield we advise you to take to the nearest shelter immediately. This is KOSN Public Radio. We'll be back on air momentarily.'

Dan and Debbie Heiberg looked out at their three children playing in the sunshine, then exchanged a glance which said far more than words ever could. Their own storm shelter was over ninety miles away at home in Bixby. To reach it, they'd have to cross the route of the tornado. Not an option. With a gentle squeeze of his wife's forearm, Heiberg leapt out and gathered up the last bits and pieces of camping gear. "GET IN THE CAR, GUYS," he said jovially to the children in an attempt not to scare them. "WE'RE OUTTA HERE."

As his family was belting up, Heiberg opened the map again to check their options. If the tornado stayed on its line 50 miles to the south and continued to move east, they'd be okay. To be extra sure, he decided to drive west.

On leaving the park, they had no choice but to drive towards the tornado for a mile until they reached the junction with Highway 160. In front of them, as far as the eye could see, lay the heavy blackness of the weather front, somewhere inside of which the tornado was wreaking havoc and death to all in its path.

When they reached the highway and turned west, the skies were meaner than ever and it had started to rain heavily. The wipers could barely keep the road visible and the radio was broadcasting nothing but intermittent hissing.

"Daddy, I'm scared," their youngest daughter said, pressing Jumble, her favourite soft toy dog, to her cheek.

"We'll be fine, honey. Tell Jumble everything's going to be okay. It's just rain." Dan Heiberg's confident reassurances put everyone at ease for the moment.

Unbeknown to the family, the four-mile-wide swathe of the tornado had veered north-northeast, after removing half the city of Pawhuska from the Earth, and was now heading straight towards their SUV at 90 miles an hour.

"LOOK, THERE'S A STRIP OF WHITE SKY UNDER THE BLACK," Johnny shouted. "AND ANOTHER ONE OVER THERE. IT'S CLEARING UP." But the area in between remained black as night and had begun taking on a distinct funnel shape unlike anything they had ever seen before on YouTube.

"I thought it was supposed to be moving away *from us, Dan," his wife said softly so the children wouldn't hear the fear in her voice.*

"Is that a tornado, Dad?" Johnny asked, pointing at the funnel that now filled 45 degrees of the horizon. His father, a ball of knotted concentration, didn't respond. Dan Heiberg's knuckles gleamed white on the steering wheel as he tried to outrun the storm.

"Daddy. I'm scared." the small voice behind Jumble said again after a gust of wind had nearly blown the SUV into a ditch. With forward visibility all but gone, Heiberg was forced to stop the car.

"What are you doing, Dan?"

"Come up here with Mom and Dad, QUICK," he said to the children. He reached over the back of his seat and lifted their youngest into his lap. The other two hoisted themselves over and were immediately enveloped in a desperate circle of love and fear. "Merciful Lord in your heavenly – "

Their bodies were never recovered – at least, not in their entirety. DNA extracted from a partial human foot found near Emporia, 83 miles north of their estimated take-off point, was matched to a sample given by Dan Heiberg's brother. It was sufficient for closure.

The family were just five souls in a death toll in excess of 19,000. It was the deadliest tornado in America since 695 people lost their lives in the Tri-State Tornado of 1925.

In this part of the Bible Belt, more people than not were calling it an Act of God. Wiser heads were calling the world's first F6 tornado, with wind speeds in excess of 320mph, an Act of Man.

"I'd like to put a motion to the vote," Pilot said after breakfast the next day. "*Two* motions. One, that there be no populating of the island until we have a population policy. And two, that we wait five years before we even *discuss* a population policy. We have enough work ahead of us not to have it slowed down by offspring. We should wait."

"I second both motions," Mara said.

"As do I," Bradingbrooke added.

One by one, every person in the messroom seconded Pilot's motions.

"Unanimously seconded. No vote needed," Serman said.

Early the following morning, the helicopter carrying the specialists arrived. Pilot and the rest of the crew welcomed each of them aboard *Ptolemy* with a handshake and the last of their Cornish pasties. By this time, news of Jeckyll's shooting was worldwide and Pilot noticed some fearful glances being cast by the new arrivals towards the French soldiers encamped in the distance.

The first man Pilot spoke to was Harvey Giles, the 50-year-old arborist/forester from Montana. "Welcome to Eydos, Harvey," Pilot said, recognizing the bolo tie from the man's file picture. "It's not Dubai, but I promise you it'll be a lot more interesting."

Giles looked out across the bleak, grey landscape through his thick glasses. "I thought planting trees in sand was going to be hard. But… bare rock?"

"Mr. Vaalon's got it covered. After dinner I'll hand out the briefing files."

Before the newcomers sat down to a meal of pesto pasta and canned peas, Pilot apologized to them for the deception. "Although it may not look like it to you," he assured them, "you're now part of one of the most exciting experiments in human history." He almost believed it himself. But one man in particular did not buy it.

"I don't do experiments," the Venetian marine engineer said. "Please arrange transport from this island as soon as possible." Pilot took the man aside and began using every form of cajolery he could think of to change his mind, but he seemed dug in. In frustration, Pilot pulled the man's contract from an attache case and threatened to tear it up. The loss of $30,000 a month was more than Sergio Carpecchio could entertain and he grudgingly acquiesced.

Within the steel walls of the city, Vaalon's delayed plans were being put into operation. The priority was to select sites for a harbour and a farm. A general survey of their surroundings was required in order to bring potential harbour sites and possible cultivation areas as close to each other, and to the barges, as possible. Five parties were formed – two to explore the Atlantic coastline, two to survey the interior, and one to walk the mainland-side coast. The crews' topographer and agronomist briefed the explorers on how to evaluate the terrain, determine drainage lines, measure tides and so on. Much of the island could be ruled out just by applying commonsense, they said. Each group was provisioned and equipped for two weeks on the rock and by one o'clock they were ready to move.

"There are two more things to look for," Pilot said just before they left. "The French ship we saw just before our landfall, *Largesse*, sank with *Shenandoah*. We need to look out for both wrecks, but most importantly that of the *Largesse*. If it's on the island, we have to find it before the French do. If they beat us to it, it'll blow our sovereignty claim out of the water, especially if there are any dead French nationals aboard." Pilot was hoping that the mass of moving water would have swept the French ship off the shelf and into the Bay to the east, but there was a possibility it might not have.

As the five teams trudged off in different directions over the sunlit, windswept landscape – each followed by a detachment from the French encampment – Pilot headed for the communications room. Jim McConie was on duty and smiled when he entered. "We're an internet sensation, Lonnie," he said. "Our clip of the French invasion has had 700 million hits. 'Lonnie Pilot' is up to number three in search topics, 'Eydos' is at number seven, and half a million people have signed the online Book of Condolence for Ali on the Scholasticorps website."

"If they find the *Largesse* it won't matter how many people sign it, Jim." Pilot thanked him and exited to observe proceedings outside. The component parts of the trolleys and wagons were being brought up from *Westcliff's* hold and arranged on the rock in preparation for assembly. A crewman from Rome was orchestrating this little operation with Toscanini-like precision.

The cargoes of the three disemboweled barges had been removed for sorting, and work was in progress on the other side of the convoy, lifting out the prefabricated sections of the portable building systems from *King*

Solomon's belly. The sections of rubber barrage not shredded on landing were now being deflated.

Rather than pitch in with the others, Pilot felt a need to get away from the noise and activity of the convoy. Getting himself a notepad, pen and collapsible stool, he turned his back on the barges and strode southwest across the endless expanse of denuded rock, turning around every few minutes to wave at the two French soldiers shadowing him.

Thursday's sun came up behind a dome of rain clouds half a mile thick and wasn't seen for the entire day. The rain was relentless. Worried that it would wash away their spilled topsoil, Serman directed that the portable buildings be loosely assembled over the exposed piles, and this rain-drenched operation took most of the morning.

Everyone felt refreshed after having had a proper night's rest in the comfort of their own beds and relieved not to have the French soldiers on their backs, although the legionnaires could still be seen less than a mile away, constructing the pre-fab barracks that had been airlifted in at first light.

McConie and his team of listeners were logging the exploration parties' radio reports and keeping track of what was happening in the wider world beyond. The UN resolution, although ineffective, had given everyone heart. Britain's attitude, gleaned from the news reports of government statements, Pilot translated as being, 'If we can't have it, no one can.' They were more interested in getting the French off the shelf than in removing Lonnie Pilot and his cohorts, although they were not too happy about the settlers' growing stature.

McConie opened a file on his kPad and handed the tablet to Pilot. "Coastal casualty and damage reports," he said. Pilot sat down and began skim reading. The naval dockyards at Plymouth had taken a major hammering, as had those at Portsmouth. Several warships had been swamped and sunk by the waves. A preemptive strike by Eydos, he thought. The tidal surge up the Thames had been less discriminating. Although the death toll had been in the tens, not hundreds, the cost of the damage was being expressed in figures he could barely comprehend. Similar devastation had visited the Low Countries, not surprisingly. Government ministers of all the affected nations were blaming the deceased for their own deaths, claiming that all necessary measures had been taken to remove them from harm's way. That morning, Pilot had gone onto the *thisiscornwall* website for news. Although Penzance had received a severe soaking, no-one had died in the flooding.

Other worries played on his mind and these he tried to deal with rationally one by one. Kerry Jackson was in no danger from the French, he reasoned, because he was too much in the public eye now – a media hero. The fact that Jackson's father was the Prime Minister of New Zealand was also helpful, even though his son was no longer a New Zealander.

Four hundred and fifty miles east of the beached convoy, Kerry Jackson was released penniless onto the streets of Paris. Almost immediately, and out of the jaws of the newsmen about to devour him, he was bundled into a black Citroen and taken to a hotel near Paris Beauvais Airport. There, he was introduced to Rebecca Schein, who had been there for a week.

"Glad to see you, Rebecca" Jackson said. "Watched you being winched up. We saw the next rescue, too, but then lost sight of the chopper. I'm really sorry about your mates. What happened out there?"

Schein winced. "Hard to describe, Kerry. Fear, helplessness and hopelessness as we were being whipped and tossed around by the waves. Then, relief when they attached the winch to my waist. Then, elation as they pulled me aboard. Then, joy when they got Mary in. Then, despair when their CPR on her failed. Then, when I knew that was it – that all the others were dead, too… I've never felt an emotion like it." Schein forced a smile. "Life goes on, Kerry. We're both flying to the island in the morning in the same helicopter that rescued me."

When Pilot emerged from his cabin, it was raining harder than ever and all work outside had stopped. He sat down with Serman to try to clear the fog in his brain and organize some indoor work, but it was obvious that he didn't want to work and neither did anyone else.

The remainder of that wet Thursday Pilot spent trying to get to know the advisers. Of particular interest was stonemason and jack-of-all-trades, Mirko Soldo. Soldo had worked all over the world in a variety of occupations, from car assembly worker to masseur. For Pilot, his attraction was a seemingly inexhaustible knowledge of all subjects from dowsing to smoking ham. He struck Pilot as being the vocational version of Forrest Vaalon. Normal lifespan and normal brain capacity ruled out the ideal – to know everything about everything – but Pilot's white-maned mentor and the bearded Soldo came pretty close in their different ways. "Do you know the history of cement, Lonnie?" Soldo said, launching a monologue that captivated Pilot for over an hour.

Dr. Leidar Dahl, coming from the highest latitudes of Norway, hated to waste sunlight, so it was only natural that he was always the first one up in the morning. But when he entered the messroom to fix himself breakfast, three people were already there. Billy, Bradingbrooke and Nirpal Banda, the crew's only Indian, had been so close to the convoy the previous evening that it seemed crazy to spend another night on the rock. So, under a bright moon, they'd walked back through the night and were exhausted. What they had found, they wanted to deliver in person, rather than by radio. While the three finished their coffee, Dr. Dahl left to wake up Pilot.

A few minutes later, Pilot entered the messroom and sat down at their table. "Make my day," Pilot said, digging the sleep from his eyes.

Billy slapped his notebook on the table and flipped a few pages. "We set off in a southwesterly direction, which we thought would be the shortest route to the coast," he said. "After two hours we reckoned we'd covered ten miles, but even from that distance we could still see the convoy. Not a lot of woodland out there to get in the way. Nothing but slick, grey-black rock as far as the eye can see."

"It smells like salt and dried snake skin," Banda said.

"All we could hear was the wind in our ears and we might as well have been the last people on the planet," Billy continued. "We carried on walking for another three miles, expecting to fall off the edge at any minute. Over to you, Henry." Billy went to refill his cup, leaving Bradingbrooke to continue the story.

"Because the view in front was always uphill, we never saw a horizon, and when we finally did come to the edge, it caught us by surprise. Below us was a fog bank. It was impossible to gauge how far down it was. We followed the cliff edge northwest and after a while saw a gap in the white-out below. Waves were crashing against the base of the cliff about two hundred metres down. The elevation began lowering from there, and after four hours of walking, we'd dropped to about two hundred feet above the sea. It was nearly five o'clock by then and we were tired, so we stuck our tents to the rock and went to bed. In the morning we carried on northwest and came to the mouth of a kind of loch or fjord."

Or a turbidity canyon, Pilot thought.

"It was only a few hundred yards across at the entrance. We followed the inlet eastward for a mile, descending all the time, then the loch turned south and started narrowing. We followed it for another half a mile before it ended with gentle waves lapping against the rock. It was too steep to get down from our bit of the cliff so we carried on south. Where the water stopped, a basin continued, surrounded on three sides by escarpments."

"How big was the basin?" Pilot asked.

"At a guess, half a square mile. At the head of the basin, ravines drop down from the high ground – not steeply, but too narrow to get our wagons down. Further around, though, there's a wider and much gentler slope that we could easily handle." Bradingbrooke passed the floor back to Billy.

"We climbed down into the basin and as soon as we dropped below the rim, the wind, which had been blowing a gale, stopped. Five minutes later we were sweating like suet puddings. Show him what we found, Nirpal."

Banda reached into his rucksack, pulled out a plastic bag containing a browny-grey substance and handed it to Pilot. "The entire floor of the basin is pockmarked with large pits, and inside the pits are tons of that shit," Billy said. "It smells like peat and feels good and mulchy. We ought to get it analysed. I might be wrong, but I reckon we've found our farm. And there's a built-in harbour with it. *And* it's only five hours from here." The arrival of a hot breakfast of porridge, scrambled eggs and the last of the black pudding formally brought the debriefing to an end.

Up on deck afterwards, with the early morning sun at last beginning to make its warmth felt, Pilot, Billy, Bradingbrooke and Banda stared out southwestwards where, only thirteen miles away, the crooked loch and pitted basin were beginning their fifth day out of water.

"What should we call it?" Billy asked.

"That's the job of the discoverers," Pilot said.

Bradingbrooke pulled out his phone and opened 'Notes'. "We've written a few names down."

Pilot took the phone and began to read. "*Avalon. Ys?*"

"The Welsh and Cornish Celts called it Avalon," Bradingbrooke said, "and the Bretons called it Ys – the Valhalla of the Celtic Heroes. It sank into the Western Sea."

"What does this one mean?"

"Ah," said Billy. "*Gurigay* is from the Bundjalung indigenous language and means *the meeting of the waters*. Coraki, a corruption of Gurigay, is where my grandfather was born."

Pilot pondered the name. "*Gurigay's* not doing it for me, Josiah. Sorry. What's the thinking behind this one?"

"When you told us about coming up with a name for the island, one of the possibles was *Nilstaat*," Bradingbrooke said. "You said it sounded too German. though. So, what about dropping the 'staat' and just calling it *Nil*. Latin root. Pretty universal. Nil describes what we are – nothing. Neither one thing nor the other. Write it in reverse and join the two and, in line with your idea of living the second half of our lives backwards, you get *Nillin*."

"I've always wanted to live in a palindrome," Billy said.

"Then you will." Pilot liked the name. "*Nillin.* Full circle back to zero, where we can start over. I'm just going to check something."

In the communication room, Pilot looked up nihilism in the online dictionary. Nihilism; from the Latin *nihil*, nothing. The two definitions he felt did NOT miss the mark were: 1) rejection of all distinctions in moral or religious value and a willingness to repudiate all previous theories of morality or religious belief; and 2) the belief that destruction of existing political or social institutions is necessary for future improvement...

XI

In the world of normal men and women, reaction to the events in the Bay of Biscay was slow to crystallise into hard opinion. The emergence of the island was as yet of no more significance than a solar eclipse would have been. The political wrangling over its sovereignty was lost on the majority, who were more interested in cricket, the price of petrol or how to make the most of what remained of their summer holidays.

The fringe world of the astrological, the three-dimensional, the quasi-religious and the just slightly off-centre, however, was humming like the national grid over the apparent supernatural aspects of the settlers' landing on Eydos – their foreknowledge of events; their seeming second sight. The IGP's role was conveniently ignored. Already, an obscure religious sect based in Idaho calling themselves the Disciples of the Seraphic Prodigy was arranging means of transportation to the island – money no obstacle. Lonnie Pilot was The First Cause, The Second Coming, The Third Side of the Coin, The Fourth Wise Man or The Fifth Rider of the Apocalypse, depending on which cult you subscribed to. It didn't end there. Every organised minority in the world saw Eydos as a potential new homeland on which to cultivate and strengthen its hatred of belonging. There were individuals, too, who saw in Lonnie Pilot the mirror image of themselves, although they had never seen him and knew not the first thing about him. These lost souls were sitting down in their hundreds, composing letters to Pilot on *why* they should join him, *how* they should join him and *when* they should join him. The only communion these misfits would share with each other was inside the mail sacks which began to arrive on Eydos from the end of September (word having gotten out that personal mail to the settlers was routed through the aerodrome at Saint Helier), and on the forty fake Eydos accounts that had sprung up on Facebook and Twitter.

On a diplomatic level, Britain's attempt to turn the island into a United Nations Protectorate had been defeated. Standing against it had been the increasing number of allies Geirsson was helping to win over, particularly Canada, Russia and the Scandinavian countries. More importantly, America had been throwing her weight behind Eydos, seeing the island's strategic location as being worth every manner of cajolery. Indeed, it was the USA that took the islanders' claim and showed it to be unassailable in law as a bona fide statement of ownership and possession – a possession, what's more, that had been verified by the remarkable videos taken of the landing from the flotilla itself. These had been given to Austin Palmer by Pilot on the newsman's second visit and Palmer had ensured their widest possible exposure, including 1.2 billion YouTube hits. The initial stages of the French invasion, filmed by the settlers themselves, had also been shown in an attempt to shame that nation into leaving the island. But it had the effect of making France only dig in deeper.

Although wreckage from *Shenandoah* had been found by one of the east coast exploration parties, there was no evidence, so far, of the *Largesse* to scupper Pilot's claim.

When the Spanish Cardinal's representative arrived on Eydos carrying the word of God, Pilot had told him politely that Christianity was founded on events that had taken place, or been composed, over two millennia earlier. As Catholicism had not sought to move with the times since then, there was no meeting point between the Church and Eydos. "We're sorry you've come all this way for nothing," Pilot had said. "We could have told you this in a letter." The chastened priest had been quick to leave the island. Pilot's ambassador in Madrid, meanwhile, had asked the Spanish government to make a formal representation to France to relinquish its illegal foothold on the island. This, Spain had done, but only after it had become clear to them that the wind was in favour of an independent Eydos.

The British tabloids had been having a field day with headlines like:

> **Sir Henry Bradingbrooke, the Knight who stole an Island**
> and
> **L. Pilot – el Capitan of the good ship Eydos**
> and
> **The Pirate of Penzance gets stuck in**

More serious investigations were being made into the settlers themselves and the people behind them. The fact that the ocean going barges were part of a fleet owned by the American billionaire Forrest Vaalon, who also happened to be the Director of the IGP, was a coincidence too far. Also, Alistair Jeckyll and three of the other settlers had been products of Scholasticorps, the charity founded by Ruth Vaalon. Very little information was available on the mysterious tutor from Cornwall, Lonnie Pilot, who was already being called 'Vaalon's Puppet'. The Puppetmaster himself had gone to ground in New Mexico.

On the Wikipedia entry for Eydos, there was a link to the 86 settlers, which included the five deceased, and biographical information was being added all the time. The point was made that half of the islanders came from well respected families; at least ten of them had criminal pasts; the group spanned eight nationalities; and their ages ranged from 23 to 34.

As for the island's enigmatic leader, those people who read the more respected titles with any understanding saw 'a subject of interest' through the contradiction, obscurity and riddles. Others were beginning to get nervous. The policy-makers of the world found Pilot's manner provocative, simply through its lack of definition. His declaration on the day of landing had sounded ludicrous and fanciful at first, but as time had passed, and Eydos' credibility increased, it had become a source of worry to many. Like the sniper in the trees who can't be seen, Lonnie Pilot, each feared, would start taking pot shots at them the moment they strayed within his sights.

More worrying to the islanders, if they had known, was that a group of lawyers in the Hague had already begun drawing up papers to bring Henry Bradingbrooke before the International Court to face charges of 'negligent genocide'.

Progress on the island had been good. Three weeks after landfall, the thirteen mile route from the beached barges to Nillin, marked out initially by bits of wreckage, but now delineated by wheel marks and the extra shininess of the rock, was constantly busy as the haulage of materials and goods went into full swing.

None of the wagons they were using was motorised, but rather drawn husky-style by ten or more crew depending on the weight of the load. From the barges, although the uphill gradient was very slight, it was enough of a pull to make a difference to calf muscles, with loads often in excess of one ton. Nobody was asked to make more than one trip a day, so on average eight tons only was shipped every 24 hours. It was a slow process and the bags of cement alone required twenty trips.

Mirko Soldo's first responsibility was to build the cisterns. He and two crew were testing the depth of the sediment pits by pushing long metal rods into the forgiving earth until they hit rock. "This one is deep enough," he said to his companions after they'd measured the fifth pit. "Why waste time and dynamite to make the holes when we have shovels and spoons?" The pit he chose was located at the base of the western cliff wall and offered a capacity far in excess of their needs. By redirecting the rivulets in the cliff face into the cistern, a more than sufficient supply of rainwater from the adjacent high ground would find its way into the reservoir. Gathering a digging crew of twenty, Soldo set to work clearing the pit.

The theory proved to be far easier than the practice, and just removing the sediment from the pit and scouring its walls clean took two weeks. Cement and stone pillars were then raised to support a roof of reinforced concrete six inches thick into which two access hatches and two manual pumps were incorporated. A separate compartment housing the filter bed was made at the point the water was to enter, and the entire construction was covered over by the sediment as part insulation, part camouflage. The rain channels would take longer to fashion, but in the meantime, there was all the water from *Fort Lowell*, *Chiswick Eyot*, and *Bimbo's Kraal* to transfer. The water wagon, with a capacity of four thousand gallons, was used half-empty for each trip, as the manpower required to pull a full load couldn't be spared.

In these early days, everyone was camping in the sediment beds which had dried quite hard, but not so hard as to make tent pegs unusable. The only problem with the rubber suckers was that they tended to come unstuck from the rock in high winds, so the pegs-in-sediment option had won through in the end. The weather was mild and the wind only felt when it came from the north or south. Harvey Giles hoped to cure this over a period of years by planting rows of poplars, which could grow six to eight feet a year. Cottonwoods could guarantee windbreaks and firewood in four years, pulp timber in eight years and lumber in less than 20.

When another prolonged rainstorm came on September 15th, Soldo's rainwater collection system was ready for it. At the deluge's end three days later, the cistern, previously only three or four percent full, was at 45% capacity. Despite this success, a second, smaller cistern was begun as a back-up, in case the main one was accidentally or deliberately contaminated.

To help keep morale high, Pilot allowed everyone two nights a week back at the convoy to use Ptolemy's hot showers and to rest in comparative luxury. Everyone was aware, however, that this style of living was limited to how long the fuel for the barge's generators lasted. Energy would then have to be provided by solar panels and wind turbines, but these were not scheduled to be installed at Nillin until December. Not wanting to be away from the action, Pilot stayed at the embryonic settlement and made do with cold washes.

The results of the sediment analysis had been cause for genuine celebration, for it was found to be rich in nitrates and minerals. In the agronomist's opinion, mixed with the topsoil they had brought, it would make a most fertile ground for planting. One practical test of the soil quality was to see what happened to Giles' poplar and cottonwood cuttings. He had marked a line forty to fifty yards in from the shore, traversing as much of the sediment as possible, and dug in topsoil, compost and manure. Then he put down his cuttings and, like an expectant father, paced around day after day waiting to see if his saplings would take or not.

All the time there was the disturbing presence of the French observation post, newly established on the cliff-top above them. At night, the campfires were a glowing reminder of their house arrest, and the soldiers made themselves as conspicuous and intimidating as possible.

One day, on an impulse, Pilot and Bartoli climbed up to the outpost, where they were coldly received by the officer in charge and shown little hospitality. "Why don't you move your camp down to the basin out of the wind?" Pilot invited, sensing that the exposed position couldn't be making their lives all that comfortable. The French Lieutenant said he would put it to his commander and let them know in due course. "If you *do* move down," Pilot explained before departing, "You'll be expected, as temporary residents of Nillin, to do your full share of work."

Nothing more was heard from the French outpost.

France had banned flights to Eydos from her territories, so once a week a helicopter would arrive from Jersey with personal mail and any items that had been requested by the work parties. Most of the letters Pilot received were requests from people to come out and join him and his crew. Some had been heartening messages of support, including a 14-page letter from his mother, who was now living back in Penzance, having divorced the snake. Sally and Hilda had written to say how proud they were of him and how they had always known he would do well, etcetera, etcetera. A postcard from Jenny had also found its way to Eydos. It was a photograph of Ayres Rock, on top of which she had doodled a barge with half a jumbo jet on its deck. *Hope you're enjoying 'Australia'*, she had written. *Exhibition a success and there's proper food on my table. Good luck with whatever it is you're doing there and whomever you're doing it with. Missing you, Jen.* In the caption she had crossed out Ayres Rock and replaced it with its Aboriginal name, Uluru. Pilot had felt a momentary stab of guilt at never having contacted his former lover, but the demands of his own rocky outcrop had soon buried it, along with the postcard.

Already, the physical demands of life on the island and Pilot's growing feeling of responsibility were taking their toll. As far as knowing what to do next, his resolve and initiative had evaporated – like the actor who forgets his lines, or the author who writes himself into a corner in the plot and doesn't know how to get out. To the question of how to keep his island healthy in a decomposing world, Pilot had no answer as yet. What troubled him most was the possibility that his acedia might never leave him.

After six days in the spiritual wilderness, Pilot decided that a taste of the physical wilderness might act as a mental elixir. He climbed to the cliff-top, taking with him no food or water and little in the way of warm clothing, hoping that the deprivation might shock some sense into him. He followed the coast for six miles before hunger turned him around and brought him back to the bluff overlooking Nillin. Peering down at the prefabs in various stages of assembly below, he thought how ugly they all looked and how gruesome a scar the settlers had already made on the land. Then he raised his gaze towards the French encampment on the far rim of the basin. The sight reminded him of the tinker's yard near Long Rock with its axles, pallets and endless metal drums and plastic sacks fighting for the eyes' attention. In comparison to France's scar, Nillin's didn't seem so bad. This gross defilement of a young virgin signalled the end of Pilot's inertia. It was time to send their unwelcome guests home. With a sense of renewed purpose, he inflated himself to his full height and stomped back to Nillin. But it wasn't just his ire that was growing, and he needed to share his reawakening libido in secret with his new paramour.

He headed straight for the western rim where she and four other crew were planting cottonwoods. He infiltrated the group, picked up a spare shovel and began digging in topsoil and sediment with an energy he hadn't had for weeks. Every so often he would stop and look across at her. This time, she was on her hands and knees, patting the earth down around a newly planted sapling. Her pert, rounded buttocks, thinly veiled by pale blue shorts, swished invitingly to and fro and he could feel the life force pumping into his loins. At the end of the planting session, he walked up to her, looked around to see if anyone was watching, kissed her hot neck and whispered, "Are you up for some play?"

She smiled and pressed her palm against his zipper. "I see *you* are."

"Usual place?"

"You go there now. I will wait ten minutes."

No sooner had she closed the door to the tool store than Pilot was on her, and she on him. Lips and tongues locked in carnal combat as the pair urgently removed eachother's clothes, desperate to get to grips with their desire. When only her panties remained, he teasingly slowed the pace. Gripping the waistband with each hand, he gradually pulled down, lowering his head as he did so until he was facing her tangled triangle. He savoured the view for a moment, then buried his face in her lush black growth, still damp from hours of hard labour, while above him, her sighs of pleasure were like songbirds in the forest canopy…

In the ground floor flat of the ten-storey apartment block at the corner of Andrey Bartenev street, a strange thing had happened. All seven occupants of the apartment – an elderly woman, her son, his wife and their four children – had died in unison during the night, erased forever from the Siberian smokepit they called home.

Norilsk, a centre for nickel smelting and the northernmost city in the world, is also one of the most polluted. But it wasn't the strontium-90, caesium-137, carbon oxides, sulfur dioxide, phenols, or hydrogen sulfide that had killed the Yatchiks. Nor was it the nickel, copper, cobalt, lead and selenium particulates in the air. A far more lethal killer had risen from its lair far beneath the earth to pull the family to its invisible bosom...

For millennia, the permafrost over which Norilsk was built had provided a solid cap to the vast reservoirs of methane below. But continuous warming of the Earth's atmosphere had gradually thawed the permafrost and 'dislodged the manhole cover' to the point where, on this particular night, 10,000 tons of methane gas was able to vent uninvited into the homes and buildings of Norilsk.

Methane displaces oxygen in enclosed spaces, with asphyxia occurring if the oxygen concentration drops below 10-15%. The point at which the risk of asphyxiation became a fatal reality for the Yatchiks was reached just after midnight. Increased breathing and pulse rates, impaired muscular coordination, emotional upset, nausea and vomiting were followed quickly by loss of consciousness, respiratory collapse and death.

Before they realized that it was safer to breathe the poisonous air outside than the odourless axphyxiant seeping up through the floors of their flats and houses, 14,000 of Norilsk's 100,000 inhabitants had joined the Yatchik family laid out on the acid grass of the City's football stadium.

What had pierced Norilsk that day was just the tip of the iceberg. Over the following ten months a further 40 gigatonnes of methane would be released into the atmosphere through this particular breach of the permafrost. With a potency as a greenhouse gas over a hundred times greater than carbon dioxide, methane on this scale was the last thing the planet needed... and there were over 1,300 gigatonnes more *where that came from.*

One of Vaalon's spies in Paris had heard from reliable sources that France was planning to send mineral and oil exploration parties to Eydos within weeks. Len Wenlight had informed Pilot that the British were merely riding in France's slipstream – that the moment that country made more definite moves to exploit the island, Britain would let the world's condemnation fall on France first and then slip in through the back door. France had one paw on the juicy bone, while the other hungry dogs were just looking for some way to snatch it off her. The United Nations efforts to remove the French from the island had stalled, and world opinion was like water off a duck's back to Gallic pride. Eydos would have to beat the dog herself, but to do that, she needed a stick. Finding one was the main topic of conversation after every meal.

Work on Nillin's harbour was still in the planning stage and had been wallowing there for much longer than it should have. Sergio Carpecchio, the expedition's marine engineer, and Mirko Soldo, who could do things with stone, concrete and explosives one wouldn't have thought possible, couldn't have been worse suited to work with each other. Two factors in the men's make-up in particular had flown under Vaalon's radar. Not only were they from opposite sides of the Adriatic – Venice and Dubrovnik respectively – but in personality they were from opposite sides of the universe. The Italian was closed, scheming and reptilian, the Croat open, merry and bear-like – on the surface anyway. For centuries Venice and Ragusa, as Dubrovnik was formerly known, had been bitter trade rivals, and this malignant past still flowed in the veins of both men. Soldo could trace his ancestors back to 14th century Ragusa, and Carpecchio, his Venetian forbears to the 15th century. Much to Pilot's exasperation, it was this historic stain that was as much to blame for their disagreements as their differing personalities. That evening he went to visit them in the hut by the water in which they had been vainly trying to agree a plan.

Even as he came in, they were arguing. "YOU ARE DANGER-MAN," Soldo was shouting. "TWO FATHOMS IS CRAZY. WE NEED FOUR." When he saw Pilot standing in the doorway, the big man's demeanour changed in an instant. He laughed, put his hand round his employer's shoulder and pulled him into the hut. Pilot came straight to the point.

"Mirko, Sergio… Two barge-loads of topsoil from Cork will be arriving in December. Where the hell are they supposed to dock?" O'Penny's barges weren't due until the middle of January, but enough time had been wasted, and if the harbour could be finished in two months, so much the better. What really decided them was Pilot telling the men, in Carpecchio's case for the second time, that he would tear up their contracts if they didn't reach a compromise by dusk.

As Pilot was passing the communications building, he was grabbed by Jim McConie. "They're rioting in Paris, Lonnie."

"Who is?"

"The students. *Students of France for an Independent Eydos… Down with French Imperialism* … that sort of thing.

The water cannon have been out and people are being hurt. The Government is beginning to fragment on the issue, according to Mr. Vaalon's spies in Quai d'Orsay, and they think something will happen soon."

Something did. The following evening in a Paris hospital, a twenty-year-old philosophy student lay comatose on a life support machine, his skull having been fractured by a riot policeman's baton that morning in the wake of unprecedented student demonstrations. By lunchtime, the students had been joined at the barricades by members of all five French trade union confederations and 20,000 activists from the *new* Paris Commune. Unbeknown to all but a few, these developments had been the final straw for the Government of France. It would only be a matter of days before they threw in the towel and recognized Eydos for what it was: Independent; Nonaligned; and, heaven help them, Non-French.

XII

The French occupation of Eydos ended on October first. In Paris, the following statement was issued:

> 'Eight weeks after the accidental grounding of fourteen barges on that part of the French continental shelf known as Ile de Bonne Fortune, and having guarded and succored the unfortunate castaways over that period, the French Home Guard have today withdrawn to the mainland, their guardianship having been successfully concluded. The castaway leader, L. Pilot, has been informed that the French Government will be granting protectorate status to the island as soon as talks are fruitfully adjourned.'

The 'talks' were what the envoy from Paris flew in to see Pilot about. Without ceremony, he put forward the price of French withdrawal as follows:

1) A deep water submarine base to be established in a fjord some fourteen kilometers northwest of Nillin.
2) A military airfield, location as yet unspecified.
3) An exclusive mineral and oil exploration agreement between France and the island's representatives.

4) A trawler port and fish processing plant to be sited at another fjord to the far northwest of the island.
5) The establishment of a chain of scientific research stations on Ile de Bonne Fortune
6) Sites for two nuclear waste burial grounds.

"It would cost us less to let them stay," Pilot said to Mara and Bradingbrooke when the envoy had gone.

"*Protectorate* status," Mara said. "The Gauls' gall."

Unreasonable though the demands were, at least France was being open and honest about her aspirations, Pilot thought. The same couldn't be said of Britain. According to a deep-throat source close to Austin Palmer, a nuclear submarine of the Royal Navy was at that moment charting the northern-most reaches of the island as a first step towards establishing a secret base there.

Respect was something Pilot felt would have to be taught to his near neighbours as soon as he had the power to do so. Where this power would come from, he didn't know. Everything depended on how the settlement developed during Phase One. Power, or rather, immunity, would only come through a successful transition to self-sufficiency and non-dependence. The first harvests would be crucial. On that matter, it had been decided to keep all cultivation to the existing sediment pits, as the soil and compost had only to be dug into the sediment, as opposed to laying an entirely new soil base over the bare rock. The total acreage afforded by the pits was more than adequate for the colony's needs. Already, Jane Lavery's planting programme was taking root, and the hydroponic grow tents were bulging with Moringa leaves. And Giles's poplar cuttings had taken well to the soil-sediment mix, much to everybody's relief.

Down at the harbour, a sea wall had been built twenty metres out from, and parallel to, the shoreline to provide the necessary depth at quayside. The space in between was being filled with rock, courtesy of Soldo's cordite. Haulage of goods from the convoy had temporarily ceased in preference to haulage of rubble for the landfill operation.

From a home affairs point of view, Pilot had reason to feel confident. The real worry lay in the island's foreign relations – in what to do about French and British self-interest. In the end, it had been decided to invite the French Foreign Minister to Nillin for the 'Protectorate' talks, rather than hold them in Paris. An open protest regarding Britain's provocative, secret submarine incursions was also to be written and beamed up to the iPatch satellite as soon as possible.

A dozen or so early risers were already breakfasting in the mess hall when Dr. Dahl came in from his customary dawn patrol with news of trespassers on the basin rim. Three or four curious crew went out to have a look.

"What the fuck is that?" Budd said.

Jane Lavery tried to make sense of the vision. "It's Mary the Holy Mother herself," she said. In the distance, a figure silhouetted by the lightening sky behind it stood at the top of the cliff, arms outstretched, robes flapping in the wind. Budd went off to rouse Pilot, while Giles, Lavery, Billy and Horvat set off for the basin road.

Budd and Pilot caught up with them just before they reached the escarpment rim. Twenty metres further on, their strange visitor stood motionless, arms outstretched, feet apart and head thrown back to the heavens. Every now and then it would give a jerky shudder that began at its torso and rippled outwards to its fingertips, which would whiplash, as if their owner had just received ten thousand volts, then fall still again.

Around this central figure, golden-robed men and women sat cross-legged with their hands on their knees and their eyes closed. All wore the same expression of blind expectancy, like so many newly hatched sparrows.

Pilot wasted no time in walking up to their lime-green-robed leader and tapping it on the shoulder. When it turned around, it was no Virgin Mary.

"What are you doing here?" Pilot asked.

By way of an answer, the man clapped his hands as a signal for his followers to stand at ease. They immediately relaxed their stiff poses and began chatting amongst themselves in recognizable American accents.

'Lime-green' looked to be about thirty. He had long, straight hair to the small of his back and a walrus moustache over a receding chin covered in black stubble like a burnt-off bracken field. He opened his arms theatrically and embraced Pilot.

"Man, are we glad to see you. I just can't believe my eyes. The Archangel Himself. All the waiting ... all the praying ... it's like –"

"What do you want? What are you *doing* here?"

Lime-green clapped again. In unison, his followers rose up and began mingling with Pilot's crew, hugging everyone in sight.

Pilot glanced at Dubi Horvat and rolled his eyes. He had never seen an unhealthier group of people. Lime-green had barely enough flesh on him to cover his bones, and the others exhibited similar emaciation and a general lack of light in their eyes. It was revealed they had eaten hardly anything since leaving Idaho two weeks earlier. They'd flown to Brest, via Paris, and then chartered a helicopter, which had dropped them some 30 miles to the north. They had wandered in the wilderness of the shelf for ten days, carrying nothing but their money belts and a blind conviction that Lonnie Pilot was the 'Seraphic Prodigy' for whom their cult had been waiting five years.

Back in the newly erected mess hall, as the Disciples gorged their way through a week's supply of food in one sitting, Pilot and Giles huddled in a corner trying to devise a way of getting the forty-seven intruders off the island.

"We could send for the chopper and make them work for their keep 'til they're evacuated," Giles said. "They're from my neck of the woods. Let me have a word with them." He went over to talk to Lime-green, who said his name was Clarence Drance.

"Drance?" Giles asked, the name sparking a connection. "Your old man didn't work at Bonner Mill, did he?"

"You're from Bonner?"

"Missoula."

"Well if that don't beat all," Drance mumbled, his mouth crammed with bread and corned beef hash. "You *bet* Dad worked at Bonner Mill. Left his frickin' arm there."

"Yeah, I remember."

"Never worked again. Me and my brother Delaney moved out to Spokane after that and started the Disciples. When folks started victimizing us, we headed for the hills near Coeur d'Alene. And now we're here, where we belong."

Giles looked around the tables at the lost, hungry, hapless faces and felt 20% pity, 80% repugnance. "What's your religion all about?" he asked.

The eyes set deep in Drance's hairy face softened. "Basically, we're angel worshippers. Delaney and me realized that the angels are the purest of mortals. Don't let the wings fool you to thinking they're not human like you or me. The wings were invented by Italian painters. For two thousand years the angels have been living at the right hand of God, picking up on His ways, perfecting their society and cultivating their bloodline direct from the angel Gabriel."

"Is Delaney with you?" Giles asked.

"No. Bank of America in Seattle. He couldn't cut our self-deprivation."

Giles was looking at Drance as if he were a dead dog on a beach. Drance took another large mouthful and chewed and swallowed before continuing. "What does anybody know about what goes on up there, anyway? A lot of it's just commonsense. It doesn't take a genius to know that our lives down here are just getting shitier and shitier. The angels in their pure state know they got the power to help – the power to release us from our earthly chains. We believe in the Second Coming all right, but it wasn't to be Jesus this time, but an angel. It's taken over two thousand years for them to produce the Seraphic Prodigy for his mission on Earth. That's why we're here. To offer ourselves unto his service."

"You think Lonnie Pilot is an angel?" Giles said, looking Clarence Drance square in the eyes. "The Second Coming?"

"Sure as I'm here and you're there."

"Hold your horses, Clarence. Let me just say one thing to you – and I want you to listen to me as if you're the young Clarence Drance of Bonner, Montana, and not a Disciple of the Serawhatever. Will you do that?"

"It's all the same to me, man. I haven't changed. It's just, I didn't know the Truth then, that's all."

Giles sat back and adopted the down-home grin he always used in tricky situations. "Clarence, what if Lonnie Pilot *isn't* your angel-messiah? What if all this here's got nothing to do with angels, devils, God, religion *or*

Charlton Heston? Have you ever stopped to think you might have jumped the gun? Come to the wrong landing site? The real Seraphic Prodigy would have given you a sign for sure. Look over there at Lonnie Pilot. He's already got enough problems to sink a battleship. That was before *you* arrived. Clarence, we just don't have time for your kind of self-indulgence here. We can't afford to give you and your Disciples a free meal ticket on Eydos. A helicopter's coming here in a couple of days, and I want you and your friends to be inside it when it leaves."

Unbeknown to both men, Pilot had been listening to the latter part of the exchange and was now walking towards them. "I'm sorry when anyone's beliefs are shattered, but I'm no angel, full stop," Pilot said. "If I were you I'd go back to Idaho and wait some more."

Drance, for all his woolly ideas and self-deception, when having the carpet pulled from under his feet so convincingly, had no answer to it. He knew he was a fraud, but such was his instinct for self-preservation that his only thought at that moment was how to extract himself without loss of face with the only people in the world to whom he mattered – his forty-six adherents. He stared at his bony fingers for a moment, fighting back tears, then put his forehead down over his clasped hands to hide his distress from his followers.

"Shit," he blustered. "Holy shit. What am I going to tell *them*?"

Pilot looked at Giles, who shrugged.

"You could try telling them you were wrong," Pilot said without softness.

Drance continued sitting with head on hands. His followers, thinking he was deep in prayer, did likewise. Feeling like intruders, Pilot and his tree surgeon took themselves and their compatriots out of the building, leaving the mess hall in sole possession of the Disciples and their compromised leader.

When Pilot and Giles had gone, Drance climbed up on the table as if it were a pulpit and addressed his congregation. "People," he began, "I have something to tell you. I've just had holy words with the Seraphic Prodigy himself in which he conferred his blessings upon us all and thanked us for our prompt attendance. More importantly, he has entrusted us with a mission. To take his word back to the States and to let the Satan-worshippers there know what we have witnessed today. Now, I hope you all understand what I'm telling you. The Archangel has given us the entire continent of North America to convert in his name. If we succeed, he has promised to extend our parish to Central and South America. There can be but one more reward after that, you guys ... the WORLD. They're flying us out on our own chopper next week. Now, WADDAYA SAY?"

Out on deck, Lonnie Pilot could hear the cheering and clapping below and wondered what on earth Drance had said to his motley crew to so enthuse them.

Over the next two days, The Disciples of the Seraphic Prodigy worked like convicts in the sediment pits, helping to dig in soil and compost. They ate like horses, though, and after the third day, once they had been fattened at the expense of Eydos' larder, they began making adverse comments about the food – how there was no fresh fruit, for instance, and how all the vegetables came out of cans, apart from the Moringa leaves, which tasted awful.

At the last supper on the eve of their departure, the Disciples sat down to plates of sediment burgers. Clarence was the only one to laugh at the joke. But then, he was the only one of the forty-seven with a grain of intelligence.

When the antique helicopter carried away its heavy load the following afternoon, everyone on the ground breathed a sigh of relief, not least of all Josiah Billy, whose stormy affair with one of the Disciples was beginning to get out of hand.

That night, a Force Ten gale hit Eydos and blew ten weeks' hard work straight off the shelf.

XIII

The short, sharp shock given Nillin by the gales in the night had left very little of substance standing in the settlement. Most of the buildings had only one or two walls remaining, not always in the perpendicular. Ninety percent of Harvey Giles's poplar and cottonwood cuttings had been uprooted, along with most of the three hundred saplings that had already been put in the earth.

The communication system's solar power mast had survived and the satellite dish had been found undamaged in the angle between a collapsed wall and the sunken roof. McConie had recovered and repositioned it in time for his eight o'clock watch. When Pilot appeared, the man gave him his seat in front of a laptop. All messages were sent and received in encrypted form and Vaalon's decoded greeting was waiting at the top of the screen. 'McConie has already reported no causalities of the human kind, but what of your other works?' it read.

Pilot typed a short damage report, as far as he and Serman had assessed it, then went out to help clean up. The sky was beginning to reappear behind the storm's retreating skirts and the added light was imparting new energy to the work parties, which at that moment were trying to reassemble one of the less badly damaged buildings in which to store the settler's personal effects. Digging through the rubble of the mess hall, someone managed to root out the tea urn, a camping gas burner that worked and a tea caddy that was still dry inside. The milk was only an hour out of the sheep, milking stopping for no man nor Act of God, and within half an hour the entire company was assembled for the morning tea break.

As they sipped their Assam, rotor blades were heard shredding the air to the south. Over a hundred grimy faces turned and watched as the ponderous helicopter landed. It was the media. Eydos was news, the gales were news, and the two together were big news.

Aaron Serman, assigned by Pilot to deal with them, led the reporters on a short inspection tour, feeding them the same damage report they'd given Vaalon. No casualties. Much damage. Everything under control. Thank you for coming, but please go now so we can get on with our clearing up.

"I need to see Lonnie," Austin Palmer said. Serman led him to a small tent on the far side of the settlement.

"The Admiralty have issued a response to your open protest about Britain's submarine incursions," Palmer said, handing Pilot an envelope. "It'll be appearing in all tomorrow's news outlets. The gist of it is that they think you'd be better off back home on benefits than in the Bay of Biscay playing diplomacy."

In the cloudless, windless conditions that came in behind the storm, the Nillinites worked with humour, energy and resolve to put their city back together again. Half the uprooted poplars had been recovered, some from as far as a mile away, and replanted. They also redesigned the layout of the settlement, locating all the buildings in the lee of the western basin wall to provide an extra measure of protection from future storms. Most of Jane Lavery's outdoor planting had been destroyed, so new seeds for winter crops were being sown. While her associates did this, Lavery applied herself to the problem of how to make Moringa leaves more palatable. All but one of her hydroponic grow tanks had miraculously survived the storm.

Two weeks after the gale, the adjutant for the Admiral of the British Atlantic Fleet opened a letter, postmarked Stoke Newington, cast a seasoned eye over it and passed it to his superior, pretending he hadn't read it, discretion being one of the prerequisites of his post.

The Admiral was alone in his office when he unfolded the inoffensive-looking sheet of writing paper.

> *There's still time for you to save a most distinguished naval career from running aground on the shoals of scandal and dishonour by performing one last act of courage. Use your influence to withdraw the nuclear submarine, Gauntlet, from the territorial waters of Eydos immediately and to ensure that no such incursions take place in the future.*
>
> ** The Inverness Hotel. January 1999.*
> ** Timmy Vernon and Rocki Augenblau.*
> ** Account with Corporate Investors Trust, Cayman Islands, in the name of your deceased cousin.*
>
> *For your connections with the above-mentioned to be made public would be a personal tragedy. We will be watching the situation with interest.*
>
> *--EDE*
> *Englanders for the Defense of Eydos.*

EDE, a sub group of *Law and Freedom without Violence*, a 300-strong band of well-connected white collar anarchists based in North London, was the first of many secret supporters of Eydos that were to germinate within months of the island's appearance and remain working in the shadows, unknown even to Forrest Vaalon and Lonnie Pilot.

The Admiral stared at the letter for a long time, hoping the tiny writing carrying the huge threat would disappear.

The argument put forward by the Admiral of the British Atlantic Fleet for the recall of *Gauntlet* from her current mission was that: 1) the climate of world opinion had shown itself to be strongly protective towards the settlers of Eydos against the major powers who made up her immediate neighbours; and 2) it was only a matter of time before the allegations and protests being made by the island about submarine incursions were substantiated by independent sources. How they knew the submarine was there in the first place was a greater worry and required immediate investigation.

Two prominent officials at the Ministry of Defense, both of whom had received letters from EDE containing compromising information personal to themselves, gave the Admiral unreserved support in his argument. Indeed, without it he wouldn't have carried the day.

Thirty-eight year old Victor Bosse, considered by many to be a potential future French Foreign Minister, had been given the brief of devising the exploitation of Ile de Bonne Fortune back in September. At first he had considered the assignment an annoying detour from his one-way climb to the top and an obvious snub from the incumbent Foreign Minister, who made no secret of disliking him. But as media attention focused more and more on the island and its strange settlers, Bosse came to view it as a golden opportunity for self-elevation. His authorship of the demands being placed on Eydos in return for her 'independence' had won him great favour among the French old guard, who had never recovered from Waterloo, and members of France's nationalist faction which grew stronger the harder world opinion fell on their country.

Eydos' invitation to the French Foreign Office to hold the talks on the island had been passed to Bosse, the Foreign Minister himself not wishing to get involved. Seeing the publicity potential, Bosse had accepted against the advice of the Ministry, which thought Pilot should prostrate himself in Paris instead. An aide was sent to Nillin to work out the details of the visit, while Bosse organized the PR army, whose job would be to package his first major international triumph for world consumption.

The settlers couldn't believe it when the envoy arrived with Bosse's official acceptance, but were put out by its terms. Pilot listened intently as Odile Bartoli translated.

"Monsieur Bosse and his entourage of military, scientific and commercial advisers will arrive by helicopter on the morning of 21 October to collect Lonnie Pilot and his party (no more than three nominated aides will be accommodated on the flight) before taking off again to visit the sites listed in the itinerary. The helicopter will then return to your campsite for the official signing of agreements. The Independence Ceremony will take place six months after the completion of the naval base."

'*Campsite*?' Pilot had a whispered consultation with Bradingbrooke and Mara before responding. "Tell Monsieur Bosse that we look forward to his visit to Eydos. As a sign of goodwill, we will waive visa requirements for him and his party on the day." When Bartoli had finished translating, Pilot shook hands with the sour-faced envoy and accompanied him to his helicopter.

Back in his room later, Pilot opened a letter he'd received from Stratospherix, the hot air balloon company he'd been in negotiations with since late July. Inside was the paperwork and invoice for the purchase of three hot air balloons.

In Storeroom 12, Pilot counted out the cash, put it in a briefcase and walked it over to Odile's cabin. She was to take the mail helicopter to St. Helier and from there, travel to France on a false passport to complete the deal. Delivery of the balloons to Eydos had already been organized.

Seventy kilometers east of Paris is the town of Sezanne, home of 'Stratospherix Entreprise de Fabrication de Montgolfière'. Within twenty-four hours of her touchdown, Bartoli was sitting in their offices concluding the paperwork with the Company's Director, a member of the hippy-gentry with a Porsche and a slick black pony-tail down to his waist.

A black Mercedes left the Adriatic highway and began climbing the narrow hair-pin road up to Bosanka. When it arrived at the derelict restaurant overlooking the walled city of Dubrovnik, three cars were already there. The driver of the Mercedes, a shaven-headed man in an expensive suit over an open shirt, got out of the car and entered the building, where seven men in similar tie-less attire greeted him with bearhugs and handshakes. Spread out on the table were open briefcases, a couple of laptops, various folders of different colours and the all important bottles and shot glasses. Cigarette smoke hung from the ceiling in blue undulating layers.

Mercedes-man called the meeting to order, raised a glass of raki and threw it down his throat as the others did likewise. For thirty minutes, he enthralled the room with his inspiring monologue, occasionally calling on a cohort to pull a document from one of the files and pass it around the table. He then gave the floor to a large man with a Bluto beard, who placed a brushed aluminium photographer's case on the table. He opened it with a flourish and withdrew a hand-drawn map and a laptop, which he powered up. There were twelve pie slice shapes randomly spaced on the map, each with a red letter at its apex, and twelve video files on the laptop. As he pointed to each pie slice, he clicked the corresponding video and began running his finger along the curved edge of the slice as if it were the camera panning the landscape. Every now and then he would pause the video and draw a small circle on the map, inside of which he wrote a number relating to a list each man had been given. When he had finished his virtual tour, he opened a photo file, clicked the first jpeg and selected 'slideshow'... an attractive woman holding a shovel; four people pulling a heavily laden wagon; a self-portrait of Bluto-beard himself, standing at the water's edge; pegs and rope delineating a large square area at the base of a cliff; six people sitting on the ground eating something rice-like with their fingers. He paused the slideshow on this image and stabbed the third man from the left with his heavily-calloused forefinger. "Da je Lonnie Pilot."

Two crew spending their day off exploring the heights above Nillin were the first to see the balloons as they floated in low from the west. Their first thought was that they were witnessing some kind of bizarre invasion or primitive bombing mission. They watched slack-jawed as the three shining spheres, riding the Atlantic winds with terrifying speed, closed on the cliff-face on a direct collision course.

A quarter of a mile short of impact, first one balloon, then the other two, burst into flame. As their gas burners super-heated the air in the canopies above, they rose up and stepped gracefully over the headland. Immediately, the burners were shut off and the balloons began a feathery descent into the basin, their forward progress slowed by the lack of wind in the lee of the headland. Below them, figures scurried round trying to anticipate the balloons' landing points.

Fifteen minutes later, all three were safely down just short of the base of the far cliff. Because of the prevailing westerly winds, Leon Bonappe, the Director of Stratospherix, had sailed to the Atlantic side of the island, inflated the balloons on the deck of their freighter, and flown in to Nillin from the west.

Four hours later, Pilot and Bonappe stood side by side at the quay watching the freighter approach the dock. "How long can you stay, Leon?" Pilot asked.

"We were planning to sail tonight," Bonappe said in perfect English, "as soon as the gas canisters, fans, generators, fuel and other paraphernalia have been offloaded." Pilot had other plans for the man, though, and it didn't take him long to persuade Bonappe to stay on as their guest until the mail helicopter could drop him in Jersey. Pilot wanted information on air space legalities relating to hot air balloons and any other specialist knowledge that could be squeezed from the man. He also needed extra tuition in operating his new acquisitions, which were Rolls Royces in comparison with the mopeds he had flown during his course in Bath. The two other balloonists elected to go back with the ship, so a bed was found for Bonappe in one of the new geodesic domes that were gradually replacing the prefabs. Seventy of these 'domehomes' had been purchased from a company in Finland. Not only were they easy to construct, but they were light, airy, robust against the wind, warm in winter and cool in summer. They also looked good.

At dinner that evening, Bonappe acquainted Pilot with the mapping software for western Europe that had been part of the delivery, showing the prevailing winds at different altitudes and at different times of the year. "With direct links into the Comtrac V weather satellite and ground stations, we can program our flights with metre by metre accuracy," Bonappe explained. "Me? I'd rather fly by eye and inner ear."

The next few days passed quickly for Pilot and they managed to complete six half-mile practice flights. Bonappe was more than happy to impart his knowledge pro bono, as he considered the experience of being part of this 'entreprise curieuse' more than sufficient recompense. For Pilot, he preferred spending the time with his head in the clouds, rather than fretting about his looming confrontation with France.

XIV

It was the eve of Bosse's visit. The night was cold and dry, with a needle-sharp wind whipping Nillin on its unprotected north side.

In spite of the cold – perhaps even in search of its numbing anesthetic – Pilot paced the quay in clouds of worry. What perplexed him most was finding a suitable spanner to throw into the mighty French Imperialist machine, seeing as his greatest ally, world opinion, was having no effect. He was also fretting about how France would react when he said no to all their proposed footholds. A dart of cold air pierced his clothing and sent chills across his body. What am I doing here? he wondered, tightening his collar.

He was awakened by Dr. Dahl at seven, and half an hour later was sitting down to breakfast with his three nominated aides. The French helicopters weren't due until half past nine, so the four of them sipped coffee and watched the finishing touches being made to a twenty foot high pyre of wreckage donated by the storm.

"THEY'RE COMING," someone shouted in response to the flags being waved from the lookout atop the basin rim. Minutes later, five mammoth helicopters crested the escarpment and hovered at an altitude of 300 metres. One of the machines detached itself from the herd and descended. Pilot felt his innards give way, but knew that if he betrayed any sign of nervousness to their guests, his job would be made more difficult. Just a few feet from touchdown, a lone French officer leapt out and strutted up to Pilot's party. "I am Major Domaigne," he announced without warmth. "If you would care to follow me ..."

He led them into the mouth of the whale, closed them in and pressed a button on the bulkhead to signal the pilot. The rotors increased their stroke, along with their decibel output, and within seconds the machine was back with the herd. Major Domaigne then ushered the party through another door and into the main cabin where Pilot counted two men in military uniform, a dozen or so in sober suits, a few women, a film crew and a rather self-possessed figure he took to be Victor Bosse. The man had an air of command about him, but of the kind won through foul means rather than fair. Between his sensible shoes and haircut he wore the plain grey uniform of government, but there was something in his eyes that gave away his true nature. Pilot's dislike of the man was instant. Lost in thought, Pilot didn't notice that he'd been introduced to the entourage by Major Domaigne and was now expected to say something.

Instead, Mara stepped forward as per Pilot's earlier instructions. "Welcome to Eydos," she said. "I'm Eydos Press Secretary Macushla Mara, and this is Deputy Leader Henry Bradingbrooke. We are honoured to have you as our guests. Odile Bartoli is here to ensure the accuracy of your translations. And, of course, you know this man." Pilot nodded presidentially, but remained silent.

A thin man with a pencil moustache translated into French, leaving out the reference to translation checking, and ushered them to their seats.

"Monsieur Bosse is delighted to meet you all," Pencil-moustache said, "and conveys to you the paternal greetings of the French People. Our first stop will be the site of the proposed airfield – Site A on your map." Mara was handed a map of the island on which all the locations mentioned in the French proposals had been marked. She held it up for Pilot, who stared hard at it, allowing his eye muscles to relax and his vision to fall out of focus. He sank into a kind of self-induced half trance, which allowed him the minimum conscious contact with his surroundings and the maximum concentration to rehearse his speech, co-penned by Mara, for later.

At the first stop, he was only vaguely aware of a slight bump as the helicopter set down; of stepping out on to the rock; of shaking hands with Bosse for the benefit of the many photographers and video cameramen; and of then setting off for the next halt.

"Cet homme est un imbécile," Bosse remarked as an aside to one of his aides. The French Circus was proceeding like clockwork. The weather was fine, the filming going perfectly and there was triumph in the eyes of all present.

At half past one, the French helicopters appeared again over Nillin and were soon standing in company with a lone British machine, still warm after its flight from Dorset.

A distressed Major Domaigne came running up to Mara. "Qui sont ces gens? Who are they," he demanded. "What are they doing here?"

"They're a crew from the BBC's *News Briefing* programme," Mara said. "We invited them to cover today's ceremony. Do you have a problem with that?"

Major Domaigne wasn't happy. He and the other members of the Delegation cursed at the intrusion into their private show and looked suspiciously at the cameras and other equipment being unloaded from the gatecrashers. Their attention was diverted by Aaron Serman, who began ushering everyone into the conference marquee.

The TF1 and BBC satellite dishes were positioned outside the tent and cables were run under the canvas walls to where their respective crews were setting up camera tripods and microphones in front of a makeshift podium. Austin Palmer, the *News Briefing* presenter, nodded discreetly at Pilot and then began talking to camera. Ten metres away, the French presenter was doing the same. There was one important difference that would prove to be pivotal. *News Briefing* was going out live, whereas the French broadcast was on a 16-second delay, so ordered by Major Domaigne in the event of any unforeseen problems occurring.

Eventually it came time for the official business to start. The envoy who had visited the island previously stood before the table and made a short, sycophantic speech similar to that a chat-show host would make introducing his Star Guest, in this instance, the man who had 'conceived and secured the future of Ile de Bonne Fortune, Monsieur Victor Bosse of the Foreign Ministry'.

The man arose in mock humility, his eyes to the ground. He raised a hand and the orchestrated applause of every pair of Gallic hands not at that moment operating a camera or holding a directional microphone, stopped. He made a cursory bow towards Pilot and began speaking, without notes, straight from the heart of his ambition. Bartoli typed the English translation of his words into a software program which automatically ran them underneath the picture being transmitted live to the English speaking world beyond and to the monitor in front of Pilot.

Bosse spoke for two minutes without pause about the unexpected gift they had received from Nature and France's duty to share it with the world. He outlined the island's importance to Nato and its enormous potential as a safe burying ground for France's prodigious nuclear waste.

"I think we're superfluous to this part of the show," Pilot whispered to Mara.

Towards the end of his oration, Bosse was all but levitating. "Au nom du Président et du Ministère des Affaires Etrangères et de moi-même, Victor Bosse, je vous présente le Protectorat Français l'Ile de Bonne Fortune." Before Bosse had even finished speaking, his stooges were on their feet clapping. Pencil-moustache leaned across the table and informed Pilot that the signing of the agreements would be taking place next.

Anyone looking closely would have noticed the blood rise under the Cornishman's tanned skin until his entire face was an angry crimson. He rose out of his chair, cleared his throat, looked towards the BBC camera and began to speak, pausing after every sentence to allow Pencil-moustache time to interpret.

"Before I start," Pilot said, "I want to thank the French Government for organising our tour of Eydos this morning." He knew that the next few minutes would either make or break Eydos' credibility and was a little surprised at feeling so calm and composed.

"I'm relieved you managed to visit our capital, Monsieur Bosse, because it gives me the chance to clear up the misconceptions you've brought with you.

"This island, Eydos, is part of the European continental shelf that extends off the west coast of France. We all agree on that point. International law rules that Eydos lies outside French territorial waters, whether you call it three, twelve or fifty miles. You claim that the continental shelf is a natural extension of mainland France and that Eydos is therefore French territory within your Exclusive Economic Zone. It follows that New Guinea is part of Australia… Sri Lanka belongs to

India… Taiwan belongs to China… half of Japan could be claimed by Russia and the other half by Korea… and Trinidad is part of Venezuela. What else ... The British Isles. They'd be yours, too. International relations would hit melt-down. All politicians would be dismissed and replaced by geologists appointed to draw up the new borders."

At these words, Major Domaigne, who understood English and didn't have to wait for the translation, signaled a temporary halt to the TVI broadcast.

"Reprenez le tournage," Bosse commanded, overriding Domaigne. At this stage he didn't see Pilot as a threat, and still had on his side the advantage of what he felt to be superior intellect, education and standing.

Pilot ignored the commotion around him and looked consolingly towards his opponents. "I *am* prepared to concede one important point," he said, brushing the ceiling of over-confidence with his head. "And that's to admit that up until August fourth of this year, Eydos *was* French soil. For millions of years, this stretch of rock was covered by a vast blanket of sediment laid down over centuries as run-off from the rivers of mainland France. Unfortunately, when the shelf was surfacing, it shed the only real physical link it ever had with your country – the sediment I just mentioned." He was distracted by a movement to his left and glimpsed Mara mouthing the word 'no' with a *what the fuck are you saying* look in her eyes. He had deviated from the speech she had worked so hard to help craft and she was livid. Then it suddenly hit him – the sediment in the pits. French earth mixed with their own. He erased Mara's concern with an infinitesimal shake of his head. He'd already stupidly opened himself up to be shot down and his only salvation now was that no Frenchman would connect the dots before he finished his day's work.

The French delegation began to shift in their seats. So agitated had they become that the BBC sound recordist had to rebalance his microphones in order to pick up Pilot's next words – words designed to deflect from the subject of sediment as quickly as possible.

"When this virgin island came out of its muddy cocoon and broke the surface, the human race defaced it immediately. Our rusting barges southeast of here aren't a pretty sight, and this place isn't much better. Nillin is ugly now, but our aim is to bring aesthetic values into our building works – as you can see, we've already made a start – and to keep our human footprint as small as possible. Quite the opposite of what our neighbour here is suggesting. What France, among others, would like to see done to this island bears no comparison to the slight blemish we've made. Its scars would never heal.

"But we're not here to burn Victor Bosse. He has made his desires known far more honestly and openly than my former homeland, Britain."

Bosse had heard enough and stood quickly, shaking his head from side to side. Mistaking Pilot's seeming fairness towards his own country's intentions in relation to Britain's as a sign of weakness, he made a faux pas of majestic proportions.

"My young friend is an idealist," Bosse began. "Were he a realist, he would know that the survival of the human race depends upon the taming and training of the wild animal we would call Nature – the subjugation of her natural resources to the service of Man. Ile de Bonne Fortune has been sent, not only to the people of France, but to the people of the entire European Union as a sign that our efforts over the past century have been rightly placed and totally justifiable – a reward for all our labours and those of our fathers and grandfathers."

Bartoli was doing her best to keep up with Bosse's monologue, the English translation of which Pilot was reading on the monitor before him. It was sufficient to give him the general course of the man's drift.

"I can sympathise with the sensitivities of these people," Bosse continued, "but in a hard world, with hard decisions and hard consequences, it's the blacksmith, not the poet, who survives."

My words exactly, Pilot thought.

"I will ask Monsieur Pilot once more..." Bosse raised an undulating hand towards Pencil-moustache like a conductor bringing in the horn section, denoting he wanted his words translated *fortissimo*. "I invite you, Monsieur Pilot, to sign the agreements before you without recourse to further vain protest. Before you answer, I make this promise that your signature will secure a much more lenient view by my government towards the matter of reparations, which –"

"Reparations?" Pilot interrupted, sensing a possible opening to Bosse's glass jaw.

"Yes, reparations. Half a million Neuros to the families of *each* French citizen killed by the tidal waves you have openly admitted foreknowledge of, and two *billion* Neuros for the material damage they caused to our coastal towns and cities."

Pilot read the translation, head bowed, hand on chin. Then, his smart phone signaled 'message'. He read it quickly, positioned himself as near as possible to the microphone and said, "We would like to take a short recess to discuss this unexpected demand and will reconvene in an hour." With that, he began walking towards the communications building, signaling Mara and Bradingbrooke to accompany him.

Victor Bosse relaxed in a chair and crossed his legs, certain that he had just landed the knockout blow. Others in his party were not looking so confident.

"Is Mr. Vaalon online yet?" Pilot asked McConie, who pointed at the monitor by way of reply. Pilot read the decrypted message still marching across the top of the screen. 'We're watching the live broadcast and I've got Fridrik Geirsson and three lawyers on conference call with me,' Vaalon wrote. 'You're doing well, Lonnie, but we wanted to make sure you didn't miss this last trick.'

For the next ten minutes, the men communicated through instant encryption and decoding as if in an internet chatroom. Occasionally, Pilot would scribble a word or phrase in his notebook.

'Under international law, you are under no obligation to pay France or anyone else money for damage caused by the waves from your island,' Vaalon concluded. 'But for reasons which we will now explain, a payment of some kind is recommended.' His last entry contained a six digit number which raised both Pilot's and Serman's eyebrows.

'Time for the coup de grâce,' Pilot wrote in closing before sending Serman off to Storeroom 12 with a large bag.

"Thank you for waiting," Pilot said on re-entering the marquee. He ran his gaze over the French delegation and stopped at his nemesis. "I have *this* to say to you, Monsieur Bosse. Eydos will not yield a centimetre of its surface to France or to any other country you care to mention. I won't say this again and would be grateful if you all left us alone now to get on with our work before winter sets in."

Bosse looked sadly at his adversary and picked up a thin file, which he held like a spear above his shoulder. The file was in fact empty, this particular gambit having sprung into Bosse's devious but incautious mind only minutes before.

"Monsieur Pilot. We come to the serious matter of the reparations which my country demands for the families of her murdered citizens and damage to our coasts caused by the seas as this island came out of the Bay of Biscay. It isn't an unreasonable demand. Indeed, if the *true* damages were ever to be made known to you, it is most generous. The amount in full is four billion Neuros. But my government recognizes that such a vast amount is far beyond the means or the potential of your people to pay." Victor Bosse was being swept to his doom on the waves of his own oration. "Ceding this island to France by signing the document in this folder will release you from your debt. What's more, it will ensure resident status for each and every one of you on Ile de Bonne Fortune within the borders we will be drawing."

With an expression that could only be likened to a cat that is just about to bite the head off a field mouse, Bosse waggled the empty file at Pilot. "This is the best outcome your group could ever hope for, Monsieur Pilot. Take it."

After the final words of Bartoli's translation had dropped off the screen, Pilot stood up again. "At last, Mr. Bosse, you have admitted to the world that Eydos is ours. For, how can we cede territory to France which is *not*? I'm glad we've settled that point. As for reparations, under international law, Eydos is not responsible for collateral damage resulting from a natural geophysical event. Having said that, in our capacity as a friendly, concerned neighbour, we are today able to offer France an emergency aid package totaling $101,000 cash in seven different currencies." Pilot raised a finger and Serman handed the bag of notes to Bosse's nearest aide.

Pilot didn't have to see Austin Palmer's grin to know he had served an ace. There were no more points to be won in this particular game and Victor Bosse had no answer to his gaunt opponent. That he had shot himself in the foot was now obvious even to Bosse. Only one word left his mouth. To the French TV crew he made a sign with the flat of his hand as if he were slashing some unseen foe with a sabre. "ARRÊTEZ," he shouted at them. "ARRÊTEZ."

"You haven't heard the last of this, Pilot," Domaigne hissed just before boarding his helicopter. "Vous êtes mort. J'y veillerai personellement."

Far away in the east, a bank of angry black storm clouds was brewing and it was into this that the retreating French delegation flew, leaving their emergency aid package on a table in the marquee.

Shortly after dusk, the bonfire was lit and at its height sent flames a hundred feet into the air. Pilot stayed by the fire for most of the night, mesmerized by its dancing light and magnetized by its warmth. The flaming debris to him symbolized the end of French interest in Eydos. But there was caution in this thought also, because he well knew that beyond their shores much larger fires were raging out of control.

Having done enough thinking in one day to last a year, Pilot walked back to his prefab, had a wash and slid naked next to the warm body already in the sleeping bag. Instantly, power over his person was transferred from his secondary to his primary brain – from rational thought to lawless passion.

"I THINK IT IS TIDAL WAVE," Dubi Horvat screamed through the ecstacy of a multiple orgasm a short time later.

XV

No one on Eydos had ever experienced a winter so cold, bleak or depressing as the one they had just weathered. February had been a particularly negative month during which the inmates of Nillin had begun to resemble the bleak landscape they inhabited – mere abbreviations of the high-spirited personalities that had come ashore the previous August. Most of them accepted their low ebb as being an annual malady to be endured, reasoning that their dormant core would be awakened with the first signs of spring. If they had known, they could have drawn a parallel with the billions of windborne spores that were establishing bridgeheads the length and breadth of the island. These were taking hold, not just in the rare patches and pockets of trapped sediment, but in the very fabric of the rock itself which, if studied microscopically, would have revealed a texture ideal for the germination of lichen. These organisms were also just waiting for a change in the weather.

During the winter, outdoor projects at Nillin had slowed to a crawl. For most of the island's inhabitants it had begun to dawn on them for the first time *where* they were. They felt detached from the world they had left, yet unconnected to the one they had come to.

Mail deliveries had been reduced to one a month and were a highlight everyone looked forward to. One diplomatic note from the United States was especially noteworthy and caused much laughter when Macushla Mara read it out over dinner. It boiled down to being an offer of professional expertise designed, in The State Department's own words, 'to pull your brave new world alongside the free nations of the earth... to help you locate, realise and equitably husband the natural resources of Eydos to the benefit of all mankind ... and, as a token of welcome to you, the idealists of Eydos, we offer associate membership of the Atlantic Alliance ...' etc. etc.

After putting it to the vote, Lonnie Pilot had replied diplomatically, but with economy, 'We appreciate your encouraging words, but we are not in a position to join the Atlantic Alliance, even as associate members. As for the husbandry of our natural resources, we feel the best future for them remains in the ground.'

"Cocky sons-of-bitches," the Under Secretary of State mumbled three thousand miles away when he read the reply.

Like Londoners exiting their bomb shelters after a heavy visitation by the Luftwaffe, the Nillinites stepped, squinting, from their domes into the first warm rays of the March sun. After the tensions of their initial three months on Eydos, culminating in their annihilation of Victor Bosse, the islanders had every excuse to let their hair down, but they all knew that true relaxation was only possible under the umbrella of a wider ignorance. They understood the world too well and believed that the French retreat from the fray was just that – a retreat. The prevailing fear was that France would regroup and launch another sortie within the decade.

Wiser heads than Victor Bosse's had decided that only when the world stopped laughing at France could that country once again cast a covetous eye on Ile de Bonne Fortune. They believed that French interest in the island would be better served by affecting disinterest. All those who had bungled since the island's ascension had been purged. In the aftermath of Bosse's undoing, the former 'One to Watch' of French politics had been transferred to their embassy in Sofia as assistant to the cultural attaché there and was no longer being watched. Major Domaigne's recorded promise to personally see Pilot dead, a threat heard by a television and internet audience in the hundreds of millions, had earned him demotion, public humiliation and a sumptuous dinner at the home of a retired French general – son of a veteran of the Algerian troubles – where much was discussed and agreed over a fine Courvoisier L'or.

In demanding reparation from Eydos, the French, via their bungling representative Bosse, had conceded the settlers' sovereignty over the island. But one didn't have to be a student of history to know that treaties or truths agreed to in the world of men only stood until the first group who wanted to, muscled in and overturned them. There was no such thing as an absolute victory or an absolute defeat. And there was certainly no room for complacency. No one on the island would have ever expected that the next assault would come from within.

Adolf Eichmann, Radovan Karadzic and Saddam Hussein had all been run to ground and brought to justice – an end which international fugitive, Henry Bradingbrooke, had no intention replicating. So, a few days after the second cistern had been completed, he and Pilot visited Mirko Soldo in his workshop with sketches for a new project Bradingbrooke had conceived to help keep the hounds at bay.

Always the jovial host, Soldo insisted that his two guests join him in a drink before getting down to business.

"I suspect this can unblock drains," Bradingbrooke gasped after downing a fiery first mouthful of the clear liquid Soldo offered him. "What is it?"

"Raki. From home. My family have been growing grapes and making wine and raki for generations."

"I like it," Pilot said, sipping his slowly. "Where's home, Mirko?"

"The Konavle valley, south of Dubrovnik."

"Are your parents still alive?"

Soldo looked at his boss as if he were crazy. "Alive? No Soldo male has expired before the age of 90 for seven generations… apart from my grandfather. The Kordas, on my mother's side, also have industrial-strength genes. My grandfather only died because he was murdered."

"Who killed him?" As soon as he'd asked the question, Bradingbrooke withdrew it. "I'm sorry, Mirko, it's none of my –"

"He was shot in 1944 by his next-door neighbour," Soldo said, "a Chetnik. My father was five years old when it happened, but young memories burn brightest and in 1958 he got his revenge. Patient man."

"Your father killed him?"

"Executed him for his crime, yes. Twenty years after that, a new Soldo was born."

"You," Bradingbrooke and Pilot said in unison.

"The one and only Mirko." Soldo refilled the glasses. "To answer your original question, my parents still work the vineyard like teenagers. And you two? Are *your* parents still living?"

"My mother's alive and well in Wiltshire," Bradingbrooke said.

"What about yours, Lonnie?"

Pilot hesitated before answering. "My mother breathes the air, yes."

The longer the three talked, the more Pilot warmed to Soldo. The next hour slipped through their tongues like honey.

"Have you ever been married, Mirko?" Bradingbrooke slurred.

"I have never been *un*-married. My fourth wife, who is soon to be my fourth *ex*-wife, is the sister of my future fifth wife, if all goes to plan." Soldo winked at his two drinking companions. "She's very beautiful."

"Your future fifth?" Pilot asked.

"No, no, no. Your girlfriend with the spade."

Time to stop the small talk, Pilot thought. "We have a new project for you, Mirko," he said, rolling out the drawings.

Aaron Serman was making the trip with Pilot on the strength of his grandmother having a summer home near East Hampton. For it was in that very house, usually closed up until June, that the meetings were to take place.

Two tête-à-têtes had been arranged for Lonnie Pilot's three days on Long Island. The first was to be the next step in a bonding, so far by letter only, between Pilot and Senator Paul Dasching of Wyoming. Dasching, at thirty two, the second youngest senator in U.S. history, was also proving to be the greenest, in the *environmental*, not *inexperienced* meaning. He was known for his outspoken criticisms of American over-consumption and lack of awareness – outspoken for a man in public office, that is. Nonetheless, he was still a politician and knew that the people in your pocket were as important as the words in your mouth, if not more so. He was forever forging links, therefore, with those whom he felt might be of use to him. Pilot had impressed him from the outset and within a month of the landing, Dasching had fired off a letter of introduction, written so as not to incriminate him should the letter be intercepted. It was signed P. Ginschad, with a P.O. Box number address in Washington. It took some detective work on Pilot's part to figure out who it was from. When Pilot invited 'Mr. Ginschad' to visit Eydos, the Senator had declined, feeling that for him to be seen on that controversial rock shelf in the Bay of Biscay before he had properly assessed Pilot's credentials would be too great a risk to his own. So they had agreed to meet in secret at the Serman retreat at Sag Harbour instead.

For his part, Pilot wanted to meet Paul Dasching for his value as a provider of useful intelligence. He also wanted to meet Charles Williams. As Dasching represented the moderate voice of environmentalism and sustainability in the States, so Williams represented its primal scream. He'd been in correspondence with Pilot too – but openly – and would also be making the trip to Sag Harbour the day after Dasching. So, Lonnie Pilot was travelling all the way to the New World – though not as new as his own he had to remind himself – to spend time with a cowboy and a subversive.

The outward journey went like clockwork – mail helicopter to Jersey, short haul to London City Airport, tube to Heathrow and long haul to JFK on false passports. From there, they'd taken a cab to Queens where they picked up the Hampton Jitney bus to Sag Harbour, reaching the Serman house just before midnight. They were cutting it fine, because Pilot's first meeting was scheduled for 11am the following morning.

Right on time, the sound of car wheels could be heard surfing the slush of the Serman driveway. Within seconds, Pilot was at the window watching a lone sedan pull up outside. Visible a hundred yards beyond it, through the entrance of the estate, was a second car, engine idling, exhaust like steam from a locomotive in the cold morning air.

Two figures emerged from the first car and reached the front door just as Serman opened it. Standing in the doorway was a large man with a thin neck and wire spectacles. A small, oriental man was beside him.

"Good morning. I'm Joe Conrad, Paul Dasching's Press Secretary."

"Aaron Serman, Lonnie Pilot's… uh… Ambassador to the United States." They shook hands and Serman ushered both men into the study.

"Do you mind if Mr. Tsuchida here has a look around the house before the Senator comes in? Paul insists on total confidentiality in his meetings. No reflection on your integrity," Conrad lied, "but there are opponents of ours who would love to hear what's said here today." He gave a hearty 'we're all in this together' laugh, but the bonhomie, like his suntan, was manufactured. Conrad waited for Tsuchida to finish his inspection, then walked out to wave in the second car.

Paul Dasching, when he eventually entered the house with his secretary and driver, was the picture of New-Frontier-Thrust-with-Glamour. He smiled Pilot's name more than spoke it. "Welcome to America, Lonnie. It's a pleasure to meet you." He shook Pilot's hand firmly, but not gluily, and removed his parka to reveal a red lumberjack shirt beneath. Dasching ate life whole and was no grazer. "Lonnie," he said without preamble, "I don't know what the hell we're going to do about this country of mine." He spoke the words like a King. "I'm not talking about shit creek, or anything half as simple. If it was as easy as making paddles, it wouldn't be such an insoluble problem." He turned to the window and stabbed his forefinger at imaginary points beyond the glass. "They won't even let me make the goddam paddles.

It's almost impossible to be a successful politician *and* be true to the planet. And that puts me in a tricky position, Lonnie. I'm about as far upfront as I dare go on the political-environmental battlefront without outrunning my lines of supply – the people who pay my campaign bills and the people who vote for me."

Serman handed the Senator a mug of coffee, which only shut him up for a sip.

"The U.S. electorate isn't ready for people like me to be seen talking to people like you," Dasching continued. "Likewise, for you to maintain your stance of neutrality, *you* can't be seen talking with *me*. It's a dire situation when the job of saving the world has to be conducted in *secret*.

"By the way, I know you're seeing POCS tomorrow, and that's another group of people I can't be linked with, even through once-removed association. Williams is dangerous in my view, so be careful. Involvement with him, if it ever got out, could damage your cause irreparably."

"How did you know I was meeting Williams?" Pilot asked, speaking for the first time.

"It's my job to know these things. It won't leave this room, don't worry. It's not even that I disagree with their views – just their methods. Even so, they'll extend the fight into areas I won't, because they don't give a damn what people think of them. No one in POCS will be running for President term after next." This was a reference to Dasching's own ambitions which he never tried to keep secret.

How many other people know I'm meeting Williams? Pilot thought, beginning to feel the early flushes of fear.

"All you need on Eydos is the time to build up your influence," Dasching said. "There's areas nobody else will be able to touch, and I can see that's where *you're* headed. That's why I wanted to meet you. I also wanted to make it clear to you, in case you think I've been pulling too many punches, that if I'm going to stay on course and attain the power I need to start changing things around here, then I've got to be careful, Lonnie. American's don't like it if their gas goes up one *cent*, let alone if we did what was really called for. Do you mind if we sit over there?" He pointed to a pair of comfortable armchairs. It was a sign for some serious talking.

"I'd like to give you an overview of the main problems as I see them, and what can be done ... what *has* to be done to solve them ..."

Dasching's overview was overlong, and fell well short of the mark, by Pilot's criteria. The longer it had gone on, the more depressed Pilot had become. On the one hand, it was encouraging to find someone of potential power who was capable of seeing far enough up the road to realise it was leading the wrong way, but disappointing to see him then alter course by only a few degrees.

During the two and a half hours their meeting lasted, Pilot spoke for less than ten minutes in total, and then just to clarify some of Dasching's statements. The young Senator, for his part, didn't think this in any way an unfair division of the floor.

At half past one, Dasching's voluptuous secretary had started making little scissors signs with her long, sexy fingers, and, five minutes later, the entire senatorial entourage had disappeared west.

At one o'clock the following afternoon, a compact rental car pulled into the drive. No train of aides and security men for Charles Williams. He came in on his own and plopped himself and his attitude in the most comfortable chair he could find.

Williams took after his black mother in looks, albeit a shade lighter, but had his father's green eyes. It was a striking combination that held Pilot immediately, as it did everyone.

Charles Williams was a political troublemaker. It was in his blood. His grandfather had been a 'Weatherman', one of that band of underground militants from the University of Michigan who had terrorized America in the 60s and 70s. In forming POCS, Prisoners of a Consumer Society, Williams was carrying on the family tradition of opposition.

"So, you're him," Williams said, beginning to wonder why he had agreed to meet with Lonnie Pilot. "What do you want to talk about?"

"Prisoners of a Consumer Society," Pilot said. "Who are they, what do they represent, how did you find them?"

"O.K. It's a list of prisoners' names and addresses. Not a membership roster or anything like that. They're not members of POCS in literal terms, only figurative. This might surprise you, but we've got agents in almost every major US city working with the homeless, the unemployed, the sick – in other words, people who have fallen off the gravy train and are finding it hard just to stay alive. Add the radical green, the marginalized left and the plain anarchical, and you've got a pretty sizeable recruiting base. I was thinking of hitting them all with a mail-shot," Williams joked without smiling. "Free Molotov Cocktails." Anyone who knew Williams well knew that he never smiled.

"There's forty or fifty million prisoners *at least* out there." Williams' eyes were burning with the same fire his grandfather's had shown when he planted an incendiary bomb outside a Philadelphia police station in 1969. "An army of fifty million, each unaware of the others' existence, but all with the potential to rise up together. All we have to do is push a button they all respond to and *blam*. Our very own Arab Spring."

The more fervent Williams became, the more uneasy Pilot felt.

"What sort of button are you thinking of pushing?"

Williams froze like an elk hearing a hunter's footstep and squinted at Pilot. He never wore his glasses when in conversation. "I think you and I will have to get to know each other better before I tell you *that*," he answered. Pilot withdrew that particular feeler and asked another question.

"Would a Prisoner of a Consumer Society consider blowing himself out of prison?" Pilot asked. "Because I'm not a believer in the overnight revolution myself. I see it lasting a few hundred years."

"Impossible," Williams snapped. "You can't keep a revolutionary ideal alive across such a long time span. It's hard enough to keep it going a few years. Even my dad and his dad got tired trying. Look, ideas, ideals, motivations… they're like a morning mist that soon gets burnt off by the sun. Everything is constantly on the move. Things get superceded by new things every second. For one thing to remain on the surface and visible for more than a few months is impossible. If you're in prison, you don't want to *die* there. You want to escape *now*. You people are free out there in the Bay of Biscay. I envy you. But over here we're *suffering*."

Pilot didn't like the inference, although he could understand the sentiment behind it. "It's all the same, Charles. Cleveland, Nillin, Mexico City. Our suffering isn't any less acute than yours or the other POCS'. But a bloody revolution wouldn't work in this case. Its effects wouldn't last more than a few years or decades, then we'd all find ourselves back in prison again."

Williams was both angry and disappointed at Pilot's words. "In spite of what you say, man, it's easier day by day to live in an open prison like yours than in the solitary confinement most of us in the real world have to endure."

Pilot thought the point eloquently expressed and felt Williams deserved a better explanation. "The revolution, when it comes, won't – can't – be *us* against *them.* It has to be us *with* them against *ourselves.* And by ourselves, I mean human nature."

"What kind of crap is *that*?" Williams spat, being not quite so generous in return. "Judas Priest."

Pilot said nothing and instead tried to imagine what Williams was thinking of him – that Lonnie Pilot was a dud and hadn't been worth the drive to Sag Harbour. For his part, and in terms of the support they might have been able to give him when he was ready to act, Pilot felt neither Charles Williams nor Senator Paul Dasching had been worth the trek to Sag Harbour either.

"I don't think you people can help us," Williams said, softening slightly. "I really don't."

Pilot just looked at him sadly. For some reason the only thing that was going through his mind was a scene from 'Dumbo'. It was the part where the locomotive pulling the circus cars is trying to climb a very steep hill. As he painfully nears the top, his steamy voice strains, "I think I can… I think I can… I ... think ... I ... can… I .... think....... I …….can…….. I……………" and, as he crests the top of the hill and starts racing down the other side, he whoops, "I... knew... I... could… I knew I could … I KNEW I COULD." Eydos would have to pull the train on its own. There would be no political support from Dasching, even if he were to reach a position to give it. And the kind of things POCS had in mind, Pilot could do without. He had almost forgotten his own words from the Eydos Declaration of the previous August – 'we have left everything behind'. To remain impartial, Eydos could not afford to have links to *anyone*, and with sudden realization, Pilot knew that he had very nearly sunk his island.

The next morning, Pilot and Serman, faces covered with scarves, caught the Hampton Jitney bus back to New York. They got off at Grand Central Station, called Forrest Vaalon's office, spoke a few coded sentences, and hung up. Ten minutes later they were picked up in the Nissan by Vaalon's new PA and driven to the empty apartment of a major art collector.

"It was too dangerous to take you to the house," Vaalon said, meeting them at the door with a coldness uncharacteristic of the man. "It's been beseiged by photographers since December. Ludwig – this is his apartment – is in Europe, so we have the place to ourselves." The look of disdain on Vaalon's face did not bode well, Pilot sensed.

Vaalon came straight to the point. "What on Earth were you thinking of in meeting with those people?" he said. Pilot had never heard such disgust in his mentor's voice and it shamed him. "Nonaligned. Nonaligned. That's the word we use. You've been sloppy, Lonnie. Tell me, did you put your little initiative to the vote before you went?"

Pilot paused. "Yes and no. I decribed it as a fact-finding mission, but didn't mention the meetings. Only Mara and Bradingbrooke argued against my making the trip, for the very reason you mentioned. I should have listened to them. The moment Dasching, and then Williams, walked out the door, I knew I'd cocked up. Mea culpa."

Serman squirmed in his chair as the silence in the room grew thicker. "Apology accepted," Vaalon said eventually. "We have another more immediate problem to address."

"What's that?" Pilot asked.

"It's called Mirko Soldo."

XVI

Vaalon led Pilot and Serman into Ludwig's study. "This could take a while. Sit down." He poured three small glasses of brandy and made himself comfortable in a leather wingback armchair. "First of all, it's my turn to say mea culpa. I owe you an apology for inadvertently appointing a traitor as one of your specialists. Our vetting in this case was lamentable. Mirko Soldo began arousing our suspicions around November when he made two trips to Dubrovnik in as many weeks. On his third visitation in December, I put some of my people on his tail. They followed him up to a small house in Bosanka, overlooking the City, where some sort of meeting was taking place. We got the licence numbers of the three cars parked outside and were unnerved when we traced the drivers."

Pilot couldn't begin to guess where this was heading.

"One was a rental in the name of the CEO of the Flamanville Nuclear Power Plant in France. One belongs to Stanko Jerić, a Croat with underworld connections a mile deep. And the third is owned by Dragan Dragić, head of a not so secret nationalist group called The Knights of Blasius, and by *nationalist*, I don't mean Croatia, but the City-Republic of Ragusa." Pilot and Serman looked at each other blankly. "I'll tell you all about Ragusa in a minute. The following day, we managed to photograph the contents of Dragić's briefcase. But first, some background." Vaalon adjusted his posture in advance of the history lesson.

"The site of Dubrovnik – Ragusium – was first settled by the Illyrians about two and a half thousand years ago. It began as an insignificant encampment on an inhospitable shelf of rock, not unlike Nillin I should imagine.

"Centuries later, they were joined ten miles to the south by a Roman settlement – Epidaurum, where Cavtat is today. Epidaurum thrived and soon eclipsed Regusium as the power in that area. When the Roman Empire began coming apart at the seams, rule of Epidaurum passed to Byzantium. The city thrived further until the Slavs swept down from northern Europe. In the process of taking the entire Dalmatian coast, they sacked and destroyed Epidaurum. The survivors fled to Ragusium.

"The refugees were traders and seafarers, and breathed new life into the city. By the Thirteenth Century they had made it a major trading force in the Adriatic. This was about the time that Venice was emerging as a power. Control of the Adriatic was essential for the Venetians to achieve dominance, and Ragusium was a thorn it took them a long time to remove. Excuse me a moment."

On his return from the bathroom, Vaalon picked up where he'd left off. "During their spell under the wing of Venice, the Ragusans built up their city's defenses to a level where they were impregnable – be it from land or sea – and it was only a matter of time before they acquired the confidence and the strength to extract themselves from Venetian domination. At the beginning of the Fifteenth Century, Ragusa declared herself a republic.

"She was in the right place at the right time to do so. The young city-state became an important staging post between the caravan routes of the East and the major ports of the West, trading with the world of Islam, while maintaining good relations with the Pope, who more or less ran the show on the other side. It was a juggling act that made Ragusa and her leaders very rich indeed. Ragusan ships were trading everywhere – Portugal, England, Flanders. Their tiny republic had become a leading maritime force with consulates and influence all over the Mediterranean and beyond. They picked the wrong horse, though, when they agreed to support the Spanish against Elizabeth the First and lost an enormous number of ships in the Armada." Vaalon pulled his aged frame up and ambled towards the kitchen. "We'll continue this after you've tried some of Ludwig's kopi luwak."

"Kopi what?" Pilot asked.

"Kopi luwak. The most expensive coffee in the world."

After they'd finished their cups of money, Vaalon resumed his lesson. "The discovery of America, or rather, the discovery of its gold and silver, had a disastrous effect on the value of money back in Europe. It fell like a stone, sending prices up and making less and less cash available for investment in shipbuilding, seafaring and so on. Merchant shipping declined throughout Europe, but was felt more in Ragusa, because they had no other resources to fall back on. Seeing the writing on the wall, the inhabitants withdrew from trading, invested their money in banks and started living off the interest.

"That was the beginning of the end, and in 1667 an earthquake destroyed the city and killed half the population. If it hadn't been for her money in foreign banks, Ragusa would have died there and then. The place never regained its health and became easy prey for, first, Napoleon, then the Austro-Hungarians. Today, Dubrovnik, which is the Croatian name for the city, is little more than a tourist curiosity – a town with a colourful past, but very little present and no future. International trade, if you can call it that, is what people can pick up in Dubrovnik's tourist shops. Dragić and Soldo see modern day Dubrovnik as the Epidaurum of a thousand years ago and its hordes of German entrepreneurs and propertry developers as the invading Slavs. Nillin is the logical refuge for the survivors of Ragusa/Dubrovnik – a *New Ragusium* in which to rekindle the Byzantine-Ragusan culture. Saint Balsius was the protector saint adopted by Ragusa. *Blasius* is also the codename Dragan Dragić uses in the secret brotherhood of New Ragusans he founded and leads. Soldo's codename is *Buvina*, after Andrija Buvina, a 13th century Croatian sculptor and builder. Theirs is an organization not without funds and connections, and it is deadly serious in its intentions."

"Which are –?"

"In modern parlance, a coup is planned. I'm sure you've already guessed as much. The *Knights of Blasius*, as they call themselves, have set a time within the next four months for their takeover of the island in the name of Byzantium and old Ragusa. In Eydos, The Knights of Blasius see a golden opportunity which, under your policies, they feel will be lost."

Vaalon consulted one of the photographed documents on the table.

"Dragić and Soldo aim to base their *Novi Ragusa* on the old Republic's specialty of trade and banking, coupled with Dubrovnik's current pursuit of tourism. They will milk the invading hordes for all they're worth. As with old Ragusa, banking will be new Ragusa's lifejacket, but with a difference. The Knights' version will be more like a laundry than a bank.

"The Knights' blueprint also calls for the largest gambling and entertainment resort in the world," Vaalon continued. "I've seen the plans for it right here in New York. The contractor for both the resort and the international airport to service it is based three blocks from here – a major Mafia-controlled developer. One of my operatives visited their offices with a camera one night and returned with some very interesting pictures. The Las Vegas valley was just a desert before Bugsy Siegel had his dream, and the Knights want to breathe life onto the barren rock of Eydos in the same way, fashioning a powerhouse of hedonism and exploitation the likes of which have never been seen before."

Pilot was staring at the floor, shaking his head more in disappointment with his friend Mirko Soldo than in the Knights' evil intentions.

"To the world's shipping community, the Knights plan to offer not only an alternative flag of convenience to those of Panama and Liberia, but also an alternative insurance to that of Lloyds of London. That's not all. The world's largest oil refinery and storage depot will be sited eighty miles north of Nillin, with a pipeline direct to France. Then there's nuclear waste disposal. The highest bidder will gain the right to bury theirs on Eydos alongside that of the French nuclear industry, which has been given priority."

"How do Soldo and Dragić plan getting around *us*?" Pilot asked, more in anger than angst.

"We don't know that yet. We tracked Dragić to the estate of a retired French general in the Ardêche and are trying to gain access to the property as we speak. Dragić left there with your old friend Major Domaigne. It looks as if they're putting together a mercenary army."

"Do we know when all this is likely to happen?" Pilot asked.

"No. But I think you have at least a month."

"As little as that?" Pilot was finding it difficult to marshall his thoughts. "What if they succeed in taking Eydos?"

"Whatever world opinion might say in your favour, Britain and France will do nothing to help you retake at. They'll be gaining plenty from the change of management. Your only immediate ally seems to be Ireland, but I doubt if they have the power to help you."

Pilot winced. "So, France gets exactly what they always wanted without any guilt being attached to them by the outside world." He was shocked by the conniving nature of the plan. "What are we going to do about it, Forrest?"

"Split the problem down the middle. You deal with Soldo and I'll see what spanners I can throw into his arrangements with the contractors here. Surveillance on Dragić and the French general will continue and I'll let you know of any developments there. What passports did you use on your journey here?"

"Both of us were Canadian," Pilot said.

Vaalon leaned over and pulled two passsports from his attaché case. "Best not to use the same ones on the return trip." He handed a Dutch passport to Serman and an Irish one to Pilot, each with their respective photos and spurious stamps from fabricated trips. "Better get some sleep. You're flying out in the morning."

Pilot opened his new passport and smiled. "Ollie Bolling. You remembered."

At Newark Airport, Pilot found an abandoned copy of People magazine on a seat and began to read it while waiting for their flight to be called. He was soon engrossed in an article about the nine Americans on Eydos – the six 'crew' and the three specialists, arborist Harvey Giles, geologist Bart Maryburg and nutritionist/agronomist, Dr. Steven Schwartzman. The latter, according to the article, had earned the nickname 'Weedmaster' amongst the settlers because of his cultivation on the island of a variety of plants, which he maintained provided an important and unappreciated source of proteins and vitamins. Three acres of valuable sediment pit had been put aside for growing flax, barley and 'Doctor Steve's weeds'. 'The islanders can hardly wait for the first harvest,' the article sneered, 'when the barley and linseed from the flax will be mixed with pale persicaria, black bindweed, gold of pleasure, fat hen, kemp nettle, wild pansy, corn spurrey and other exotic-sounding plants to produce a kind of hippy porridge that Colonel Sanders would do well to keep out of Kentucky.'

When he'd finished reading, Pilot handed the magazine to Serman. "There's a profile of you in here, Aaron. I didn't know you played the cello."

The flight from Newark went smoothly enough, but Pilot's false identity had fooled no one at Dublin Airport. Upon opening Ollie Bolling's passport, the officer looked straight through the holder's excellent disguise and said matter-of-factly, "Will you come this way please, Mr. Pilot?" In the VIP lounge where they were taken, 'Ollie Bolling' was told that the President's car was waiting to drive his party to Phoenix Park.

When they reached Áras an Uachtaráin, the official residence of the Irish President, they were led directly to his private study for informal talks. The Prime Minister and half the Cabinet were there, all wishing to meet Eydos' wind-blown leader. After his miscalculation in meeting Dasching and Williams, Pilot was coy to the point of frigidity. As a result, his hosts knew as little about him at the end of the meeting as they did at the beginning. A naval patrol vessel was placed at his disposal for his return to Nillin, along with a promise. Whatever assistance was within the power of the Irish Government to render, would be given gratis and without strings. To prove their sincerity, the President informed Pilot of the proposal one of his ministers had received the day before from a Croat named Dragić, offering Ireland strategic concessions and a partnership in a new Atlantic oil refinery in return for her support for a group of 'enlightened individuals' wishing to establish a commercial base on Eydos.

"We've asked Dragić for more details and will forward our intelligence to you as and when we receive it," the President promised.

Aaron Serman had spent most of the two-day voyage wringing his insides out over the rail. Now, he had nothing more to give. It had been a rough haul from Dun Laoghaire and both he and Pilot were exhausted.

It wasn't policy at Nillin to post guards or stand watches. If they were invaded, they were invaded and there'd be nothing they could do about it, so the Irish patrol boat was able to tie up at the quay, deposit her two passengers and cast off again unbeknown to anyone.

Exhausted though they were, Pilot and Serman headed, not for bed, but for the mess hall and some breakfast.

With two bowls of porridge inside him, Pilot was beginning to revive. "Anything interesting happen while I was away?" he asked Bradingbrooke who had joined him.

"We acquired our first asylum seeker, Lonnie," the Baronet said, pointing out a man sitting at a far table. "He's French. Gilbert Cafard. We were waiting for you to get back before deciding what to do with him."

Pilot stood up and walked over to the Frenchman's table. "Where are you from, Gilbert?" he asked.

"I am French."

"*Where* in France?"

"The Ardêche."

Pilot returned to his table. "He's a spy, Henry."

"A spy for whom?"

Pilot finished his coffee and proceeded to tell Bradingbrooke about the Knights of Blasius, Dragan Dragić, the French general from the Ardêche and Soldo's complicity.

"Mirko's involved?"

"Up to his beard. Not sure yet how to handle this, but for the moment, we'd better keep it within the Pentad."

Bradingbrooke stared down at the table, spinning his spoon. "Have you ever heard of Agent Zigzag, Lonnie? Eddie Chapman, the World War Two double agent? If Cafard *is* a spy, we should work on him. Try to turn him like they did Chapman. He seems vulnerable and a bit wobbly."

"Vulnerable and wobbly…" Pilot let the idea settle, then lit up. "I know just the person to turn him," he said. "She could convert the Pope to Islam. I'll talk to her. What's Soldo been up to while I've been away?"

"Hard to say. He's had three visits from a lady who flies here in a private helicopter, stays a few hours with him, then leaves. We call her 'Oilslick'. Head soaked in Brylcreem, make-up like gloss paint. A human Jessica Rabbit. Mirko says she's just a rich German heiress who fancies him."

"My guess is that she's his fifth wife-to-be," Pilot said. "I also think she's more than just a sexy caricature."

Bradingbrooke thought for minute. "A cliché with a brain?"

"A female Knight of Blasius."

Pilot spent the evening in Odile Bartoli's room discussing the tactics for molding Cafard into a double agent. "Expose. Befriend. Turn." Bartoli was a psychology graduate with psychiatric training. She had worked with troubled children for many years, and over dinner with Cafard that evening, had clearly detected a childlike vulnerability in the young Frenchman.

"He's a tormented soul, Lonnie," she said. "If I can get inside him and work with his demons –"

"I'll leave it with you, Odile. I'm going to bed." Ten minutes later, Pilot was dead to the world – both his and Mirko Soldo's.

The next morning, Bartoli poured two mugs of coffee, took them to Cafard's room and knocked on his door. "Gilbert, we know who you are," she said. "Let me in." No response. "Does the word Blasius mean anything to you?" Still no response. "Gilbert. We know who you are. But is that who you *want* to be?"

"What do you mean?" Cafard said, opening the door cautiously.

"Your heart isn't in this, is it? You're better than that. May I come in?" He stepped to one side, then closed the door behind her.

When Pilot saw Bartoli and Cafard enter the mess hall to join the others for lunch he noticed tears in Cafard's eyes and compassion in Bartoli's. It looked like things were going well.

Later that afternoon, Bartoli found Pilot working at one of the sediment pits and pulled him to one side.

"Agent Zigzag is ours," she said. "And he is very cute. When I exposed him as a spy, he was mortified. He couldn't give me one good reason why he was doing what he was doing. He's a lost soul – a rudderless ship grateful to be towed by anyone who throws him a line. I told him that if he co-operated we were prepared to throw him a *better* one than the Knights'. I told him about us – why we had come here, what we were all about and why the planned invasion should never be allowed to happen." Bartoli took on a mothering expression. "Gilbert has never before felt valued, Lonnie, anywhere or at any time in his life. He's just a petty thief from Privas. He has promised to work with us and will do anything we ask. I'm one hundred percent sure of that."

At four in the morning, McConie woke Pilot with an urgent message from one of Vaalon's spies in the Hague. When he'd finished reading it, Pilot dressed and sprinted to Bradingbrooke's hut. "Wakey, wakey, Henry," he said, poking the man's shoulder. "They're coming to get you."

Bradingbrooke, half asleep, gathered up a few essentials, donned his head torch and sloped off to the cauliflower patch with Pilot, who was already wearing his. Between the third and fourth rows, they located the stone that marked the entry to the bunker, brushed away some soil and lifted the hatch on the *Hussein-asylum.* Fifteen rungs down the ladder chimney, Bradingbrooke entered the ten-square-metre cell that Soldo had recently finished building and flopped onto its canvas cot. Above, Pilot lowered the hatch, brushed the soil back over it with his foot and went back to his cabin to await their visitors.

Three white helicopters with UN markings set down an hour later and disgorged troops of various nationalities united only by their common blue berets. The Belgian Colonel in charge approached Pilot, introduced himself and stated the reason for their presence. A lawyer from the Cour Internationale dé Justice emerged from the shadows and began reading the charges laid against Henry Bradingbrooke, Bart., relating to *the negligent genocide perpetrated eighth August, last, with the full knowledge and complicity of the defendant.* "Mr. Pilot," the man said solemnly, "lead the Colonel here to Mr. Bradingbrooke, if you please."

"That, I cannot do," Pilot said, handing over a piece of paper. "This is the print-out of a message we received from Henry Bradingbrooke an hour ago."

The lawyer took the sheet and read the loaded message.

Éxito. Arrived Quito undetected. Henry.

The lawyer handed the message to the Colonel, who didn't believe a word of it. "Find him," he ordered his second-in-command as the first rays of dawn began to project above the western rim. "I want every dome and shed turned upside down."

Three hours later, the hunt for Bradingbrooke was called off. The UN visitation ended to the cacophony of rotor blades screaming in frustration as the heavy helicopters reluctantly took their leave. On the 'all clear' rap on his hatch, like a Viet Cong soldier emerging from his tunnel to finish his coffee after a multi-million dollar B52 bombing raid, Sir Henry Bradingbrooke exited the Hussein-asylum, inhaled the delicious Atlantic air and headed to the mess hall for a late breakfast.

From that moment on, because the exact number of islanders on Eydos was known to the outside world, one person *always* had to remain in their cabin out of the watchful eyes of the spy satellites in permanent orbit above them and the camera drones, fashioned to resemble seagulls, that occasionally flew over Nillin to count bodies and otherwise spy on the islanders. Meanwhile, bogus messages from Henry Bradingbrooke continued to be sent weekly by one of Vaalon's agents in Quito. The accepted intelligence in The Hague was that their prey had joined the growing colony of international whistle-blowers and political fugitives enjoying their freedom in extradition-free Ecuador.

A message from Vaalon two days later also involved a charge of murder. Not against Bradingbrooke, but against Mirko Soldo. 'Five years ago he was running a multi-million-Neuro con, smuggling counterfeit BMW car parts made in China into Stuttgart,' the note read. 'One of his partners, a German, wanted a bigger slice of the cake, so Mirko killed him. There's a warrant for his arrest in Germany. Thought it could be of use to you. Latest intelligence suggests you only have until April, so a solution to Buvina will have to be found quickly. – Forrest.'

A brainstorming session with the Pentad had yielded no obvious answer to the problem of how to deal with Mirko Soldo and the Knights of Blasius. Pilot had wanted to confront the man face to face and reason with him. The others were dead against it, saying that it was Soldo, together with Dragić, who had cooked up the coup in the first place and had justified its necessity. "To reason things out, you both have to speak the same language," Macushla Mara said. "You don't."

"The second he thinks you're on to him, Soldo will blow the whistle and the Knights will be on this place like girls on a boyband," Bradingbrooke added.

As the sun crested the escarpment and rose into a cloudless sky, Pilot's disposition was anything but sunny.

Quite the opposite. The cause of his ill humour had left their dome in the middle of the night and not returned. It was the third argument they'd had that week, and the 7th that month. Pilot was finding Dubi Horvat's moodiness increasingly difficult to bear. He had his own mood swings, but they were hidden and harmless, whereas hers were overt, hazardous and impossible to handle. Like the balloon he'd be flying in a moment, Pilot's relationship with Dubi had become directionless. More than that, it was diverting attention away from important concerns and wasting valuable energy. For Pilot, Dubi's last performance was the final straw.

He exited his cabin, zipped up his flying suit and headed for the balloon pad. Two flights had been scheduled for that morning to take advantage of the gentle southwesterly surface breeze the forecast had promised. Provided it held true and they stayed below a certain altitude, they were in for an interesting ride of at least twenty-five miles before they ran out of land. Three wagons had already been sent northeast to take position along the balloons' projected course – two to carry the baskets and canopies back, the third to haul the camping equipment needed for the overnight stops.

When Pilot arrived at the pad, Rebecca Schein was already there with Bart Maryburg and Jane Lavery. The latter's tall, slim figure was so swathed in clothing against the cold that, with her copper hair extended in the breeze, she looked like an Olympic torch. She, Maryburg and Schein were to ride with Pilot in *Blitzen*. Leon Bonappe's brother, Philipe, had taken temporary residence on the island as their instructor, and would carry three further passengers in *Donner*.

"Pressurise the tanks to 125psi," Bonappe instructed the ground crew.

All of this hot air would lead eventually to a working balloon route between Eydos and the mainland, Pilot hoped. Philipe had gone so far as to prepare a feasibility study, based on his brother Leon's wind maps, and had even drawn up a series of possible routes. But without the favour of the countries he hoped to land in – and no time had been available to curry this – Pilot was powerless to fly beyond the borders of their own coast.

The noise of the fans as they began the initial inflation of the canopies was deafening. When the canopies had reached the appropriate level of inflation, the gas burners were fired to heat the air within. As the two baskets, which had been lying on their sides, began to move to the perpendicular, the excitement of the passengers rose accordingly. The late March air smelt spring-like and full of promise – a powerful, emotive aroma that was beginning to intoxicate everyone on the island.

When everything looked stable, the signal was given for the passengers to enter their baskets. Pilot felt he would never become desensitised to the thrill of balloon travel, but there was something else this time that was adding to his arousal. He caught Jane's eye and, to his surprise, felt a warm rush of blood in his chest as she returned his searching gaze with one of her own. It was that special moment when two people's eyes meet at the frontispiece of their story, and neither wanted to look away. It was Pilot who cut off the current. He had a balloon to fly, after all, but a connection had been made and the sky wasn't the limit.

To the cheers of the many onlookers, first *Donner* and then *Blitzen* left the ground. Their ascent began in the vertical, but as they cleared the protective windbreak of the canyon rim, they were swept north and east towards the rising sun by more than the light breeze the Comtrac

V weather satellite had predicted. The jolt to the basket caused by the sudden injection of lateral acceleration forced a stifled scream from Lavery and it would be several more minutes before she could raise herself from the floor of the basket and peer down at the rolling grey rock below. "It looks like the sea has been turned to stone through some ancient Celtic curse," Pilot whispered in her ear.

"Poetic, Lonnie. It looks like rock to me. How strong are these cables?" Lavery reached up and touched one of the steel stays connecting the basket to the skirt.

"Strong enough. Look back there, Jane." Pilot pointed towards the last few domes of Nillin as they disappeared behind the receding basin rim and then studied her profile. Her hair was blowing everywhere and he reached over to guide it away from her face, brushing her freckled cheek with the back of his hand as he did so. She inclined her head slightly to reveal wide brown eyes framed by smile lines. He smiled back.

Pilot had cut out his burner almost immediately after take-off, and several minutes later *Blitzen* stabilised at around three hundred feet. Bonappe in *Donner* was still climbing and thereby ran the risk of reaching the prevailing westerlies higher up and being swept on to France.

The gap between the two balloons soon grew to half a mile and even from that distance Pilot could see that *Donner's* burner was still at full blast, sending the balloon higher still.

"Is that us, or them?" Lavery said.

Pilot followed her line of sight to a large shadow chasing them across the ground.

"Us. Donner's the smaller one behind."

"But they're ahead of us." In seconds, Jane figured out that it was Bonappe's greater altitude that placed his shadow behind theirs. "Nevermind. I get it."

"It's like orbiting the moon," Maryburg said to no one in particular. Below them, only occasional sediment-filled depressions relieved the bland sameness of the landscape. Maryburg wasn't alone in finding the island's topography oppressive. But, according to their botanist, it wasn't a scene that would endure for much longer. Citing what had happened on Surtsey, the volcanic island that had emerged off Iceland in 1963, he predicted that Eydos would likewise be green within a year, even without the benefit of fertile volcanic ash. As if to reinforce the theory, the fliers could detect a musty, fungal aroma in the air. Even so, the vision of their silver sliver of an island one day wearing a furry green fleece was difficult to imagine.

For the next two and a half hours, the balloonists talked about a future none could see. But in the valley of the blind, the one-eyed Jack is King, and Lonnie Pilot, alone of all of them, could at least see the corners ahead, even if he were unable as yet to see around them. Jane Lavery, for her part, was beginning to see their rangy, silver-flecked pilot in a brand new light, and she liked what she saw.

Bonappe had timed his run to perfection. From his initial climb to two and a half thousand feet, he had cruised the fifty miles with no further application of heat and was now, through deft use of the deflation port, coming down for a landing barely a mile short of the gently lapping waves of the shallow northeast coast. There was no chance of the wagon reaching them in time for the ground crew to assist *Donner*, but Bonappe was a master of landings and fired the burner with perfect timing – just long enough to arrest the descent without reversing it – and set his basket down with the lightest touch. Within seconds, he was pulling the cord to collapse *Donner's* canopy.

Half a mile to the south, the wagon pulled by Nirpal Banda and seven other volunteers found itself directly below the descending *Blitzen*. So close were they that the trailing line Pilot had thrown out nearly parted the Indian's hair. He made a grab for it, but missed. "Drop your traces. Run for the rope," Banda shouted to his fellow huskies as he sprinted after the elusive line. "Slow down, Lonnie."

"It doesn't work that way," Pilot called back from the basket above. "We'll come down eventually."

Before a further exchange could be made, the man from Mumbai leapt gazelle-like into the air, grabbed the line with one hand and, while making a half turn in mid-air, threw his other hand around to join it on the rope.

"Hold his legs," Pilot shouted to the other runners below. He pulled the deflation line to speed their descent, but before anyone could reach Banda's thrashing legs, a gust of wind kicked in underneath the balloon, pitching it upwards and forwards.

In the confusion, no one saw two crew drop their traces on the third wagon, which was downwind from Pilot's balloon, position themselves along *Blitzen's* line of flight and grab hold of the Indian's legs as he passed them. The sudden braking action nearly pitched Pilot over the side.

Seconds later, with the weight of the three men pulling it down, the basket crashed to the ground, impacting one corner of the compartment and causing Lavery to faint. Pilot was beside her in seconds, caressing her face and gently squeezing her hand. She came to quickly. Pilot watched her eyes dart around the basket and finally land on his hand, which was still holding hers.

She clasped it tight and the fear in her face melted away. "That was quite a whallop," she said.

"Can you stand up?" Pilot raised her to her feet and helped her out of the basket. Four layers of clothing did nothing to dampen the electricity flowing between her body and his hands. He walked her to the wagon and sat down next to her; put his arm around her waist; placed her head on his shoulder; inhaled her hair…

At five o'clock, with the light failing and the caravan having covered ten of the thirty miles back to Nillin, a halt was called for the night. Tents were erected on a suitable sheltered sediment pit and dinner prepared for twenty-four.

Late that night, with the camp sleeping, Pilot left his tent and crept to the third one from the left. She had left her flap unzipped…

Two days later Lonnie Pilot was lying awake in Nillin's dawning light carrying out a post mortem on his relationship with Dubi Horvat. The physical side of it had been blissful, but the language barrier, though unable to stop her acid rantings, had prevented a deeper connection. Conflicts with outsiders he could handle. He didn't want to sleep with them. With Jane the bond was all-encompassing, and if he weren't mistaken this time, promised calmer sailing ahead. The sound of the helicopter's arrival ten minutes earlier had gone unnoticed. A rap at the door pulled Pilot from his thoughts.

Leidar Dahl poked his head around the door. "Austin Palmer came in with the mail and wants a word with you, Lonnie." Pulling on a wool jumper and windbreaker, Pilot followed the Norwegian out of the cabin and into the crisp morning air to greet Palmer.

"Lonnie. Good to see you." They shook hands. "I'll be flying back in a minute, so I haven't much time. I've got a proposition to make to you." Before Palmer could begin, Josiah Billy appeared from around the corner.

"We're ready, Lonnie."

"Thanks, Josiah – I won't be long. What's your proposition, Austin?"

"It concerns the Fishing Wars. We're running a News Briefing Special in light of the latest sinkings and I'd like to have you on as part of the wider debate about over-fishing, stock depletions, pollution of the seas and so on. We've got representatives from all the EU countries, plus Iceland and Norway, and we'd like to have you, too."

"But we don't fish."

"Doesn't matter. I know you've got things to say and this would be a great vehicle for you. We'd record in London next Monday for a Tuesday airing. It can only strengthen your posi – "

"The short answer is *no.* I think it would be approaching the problems from the wrong side – locking the doors of empty stables. The problem wasn't the bullet in Abraham Lincoln's head, it was the intent in John Wilkes Booth's. Until the intent of the world's fishing industries changes, the problem of continuing stock depletions will worsen."

"That's exactly the kind of thing you should be out there saying," Palmer said. "You've got the advantage of having no vested interest. You're independent in the true sense of the word and can be impartial. So, anything *you* say, people will listen to in a different spirit altogether."

Pilot shrugged. "You're giving us more credence than we've got at the moment, Austin. Do you really believe the world's going to listen to what people like us think about their fishing feuds or their population problems or their chemical waste? This is a long-term project and we might not be able to even get into first gear for another five or ten years. Until then, we have to be involved by being uninvolved. As soon as an outsider gets caught up in specific issues, it's impossible for him to be fair to everyone. If we get up on a pulpit now, well short of our critical mass, we'll become as impotent as all the thousands of voices already out there. They're fine, saying all the right things, but they're powerless. It's a frustrating problem, but the pulpit we're building will be unlike any that's gone before. It'll take as long as it takes."

"You've just torn up the winning lottery ticket," Palmer said, still trying to change Pilot's mind.

"Look at it as a rollover," Pilot answered. "Just think what it'll be worth in five or ten years' time."

As Austin Palmer flew out of Nillin surrounded by empty mail sacks, final preparations were being made for the second of seven planned balloon outings over the island. Since the last trip, the weather had been unfavourable for any useful ballooning, but the day before, perfect conditions and a moderate westerly wind had been guaranteed for forty-eight hours at least. So, wagons had been sent off towards the projected landing site and a draw made for the twelve places aboard the balloons.

This time, all three were to be used. Pilot would fly *Rudolf*, Bonnape would fly *Donner* and Jack Highbell the slightly damaged *Blitzen*.

Pilot changed into his flying clothes, then led Highbell and Bonappe to the balloon pad where the winners of the draw were waiting. The three inflation fans were at maximum blow. *Rudolf* was already three-quarters spherical. The other two balloons were lying on the pad like giant quivering parathas. When the burners were lit to complete the inflation, Pilot took rookie balloonist Highbell aside for a few last-minute instructions.

It was a beautiful sight to behold – three magnificent egg-shaped envelopes, shimmering like satin in the sunlight, their gay colours set off to perfection by the somber grey-green rock all around them. As lift-off approached, the passengers readied themselves beside their respective baskets, which were now nearly upright.

"AU REVOIR," Bonappe shouted over the blast of Donner's burners. As he and his four passengers floated away, those on the ground gave a rousing cheer.

A minute later, *Rudolf* took to the air.

The temperature differential in *Blitzen*, whose burner had been at work for much longer, was so great that five extra crew were required to hold her down. The strain on their arms and shoulders as they pushed down on the basket's rim was visible in their faces.

"EVERYBODY IN," Highbell shouted above the rush of the gas. "WE'RE TAKING OFF IN TEN SECONDS." When all Blitzen's passengers were aboard, he raised his arm to signal.

"What are they waiting for?" Bart Maryburg mumbled. "WHAT THE –" The shocked surprise in Maryburg's cry was shared by most, but not all, of those present as the strange scene unfolded before them.

Three of Blitzen's passengers vaulted over the rim to the ground four feet below, closely followed by their pilot, Jack Highbell. Simultaneous with his feet hitting the rock, the ground crew let go of their hold. With nothing left to restrain her, the richly-coloured *Blitzen* flew off like a startled pheasant and was level with *Rudolf* in seconds. As it shot past his own basket, Pilot flicked the switch on his megaphone. "FOLLOW THE INSTRUCTIONS IN THE GREEN RUCKSACK AND YOU'LL BE OKAY."

Mirko Soldo, cowering on Blitzen's floor, heard Pilot's amplified voice under the roar of his burners, but the words didn't register. He pulled himself up to peer over the edge of the basket, then lowered himself back down again, fearful that any sudden movement might snap the lines attaching his basket to the collar above. The image printed on his mind in that split-second peek made him feel nauseous – Pilot's balloon, far away below and getting farther; the people scurrying around like beetles on the hide of an elephant; the ever-broadening horizon...

After several minutes, he had calmed down sufficiently to apply himself to the problem at hand. He looked around the basket – at the burners still at full blast; at the sundry dials, tanks and other mechanical details that oppressed him by their unfamiliarity; at the hamper containing the life jackets and inflatable raft; at the rucksack in the corner.

Remembering the disembodied voice and its simple instruction, Soldo pulled the backpack over and began to fumble with the flap. Inside, resting atop a silver foil zip suit, was a plastic wallet containing several typewritten sheets. He pulled them out in a sudden rash of ill-humour and began to read.

> *'We have worked out this procedure very carefully so as to avoid your coming down in the sea, in remote mountain areas, forests, big towns or cities. Follow our instructions* to the letter *and you will have a safe landing.* Deviate at your own peril. *All timings are calculated from your time of lift-off, so please check your watch now and write down the time.'*
>
> *Operating the Burners. In the diagram, note that the –'*

Soldo skipped over this section to the Flight Plan.

'Stage I, 0-5 hours after lift-off. Keep the burners going until you reach an altitude of 6,000 metres, then switch off. (The altimeter is the central dial at waist level.) When you have descended to 4,000 metres, put the gas on again until you've reached 6,000 metres and switch off. Repeat procedure and stay in this altitude band, 4,000-6,000 metres, for five hours. For your own safety, do not *try to land until instructed.*

Stage II, 5-7 hours after lift-off. Keep within the altitude band, 3,000-4,000 metres for—'

Soldo read on, his fears dissolving with every word. It didn't occur to him where *Blitzen* might be taking him. Fortuitously for Pilot, it wouldn't dawn on the flying stonemason that his landing point was deep inside the borders of Germany until too late. Soldo's sole preoccupation was in following the instructions and getting safely back on solid ground.

He read the notes through to the end. At the bottom of the last page, there was a postscript: *Mirko, not long ago you told me about your neighbour – a man your family had supped with, caroused with, laughed with, played with, cavorted with, sang with. He turned out to be a Chetnik – a traitor to your country. He killed your father.* Below this, a line had been scrawled in red felt-tip pen. It contained words well known to Mirko Soldo, aka Buvina, the Second Knight of Blasius and, as he began to read them, tears welled up in his eyes. Only a traitor exposed by the man he has betrayed could have experienced the dishonour Soldo felt at that moment.

The sentence was in Latin. *NON BENE PRO TOTO LIBERTAS VENDITUR AURO.* As the big man's watery eyes ranged over it once again, the motto of his beloved City Republic of Ragusa, always such a source of pride to him, seemed now to only mock him.

LIBERTY IS NOT SOLD, EVEN FOR ALL THE GOLD.

XVII

Three days after *Blitzen* had removed Mirko Soldo from the island, Gilbert Cafard arranged his own extraction by activating a simple transmitting device. To those receiving the message, it meant immediate airlifting was required from a predetermined pickup point out of sight and sound of Nillin. So as not to jeopardize any future return to the island, the story Cafard gave his French paymasters was that he had asked Pilot's permission to hike the west coast of the island, and that Pilot thought he was camping out on the cliffs somewhere.

The car was of French manufacture, naturally – a black Citroen from the Élyseé Palace car pool of 1958, religiously restored and maintained by its owner. Almost before it stopped, its back door swung open and Gilbert Cafard emerged, lifting an arm in salute towards the distinguished-looking madman standing in the shadow of the chateau in riding boots and pale pink designer jogging suit with turquoise piping.

General August Fascisse greeted his spy with a rebuke. "Why are you here? What is happening?"

Gilbert Cafard held up both hands in supplication. "Soldo is gone," he spluttered.

"GONE?" The General's neck had turned a deep crimson and was clashing with his shell suit. "*Where?*" Cafard could only point mutely up at the sky, the old officer's oppressive presence cowing him into speechlessness.

"DEAD? Soldo's dead?"

Cafard gathered himself and explained what had happened. "It was an accident. The others jumped out in time, but Mirko was too slow. If we're lucky, he'll come down somewhere in France."

"Merde. The idiot. So Pilot still knows nothing."

"He has no idea what's coming."

The pink general spun around and marched into the house, followed by Cafard.

"Colonel," Fascisse barked. "Get me Dragić." Although ex-Captain Rene Domaigne had been demoted by the French Army after the Bosse debacle, his current employer had personally elevated him to the rank of Colonel and Second-in-Command of his private army. As Domaigne dialed a Dubrovnik number, his commander simmered behind his right ear, depositing damp, hot breaths on the man's neck. When the connection was eventually made, Fascisse grabbed the receiver and explained to Blasius what had happened to Buvina. "More importantly, Dragić, how soon can your fleet sail?"

After a pause, the heavy Slavic voice came back into Fascisse's earpiece, "The *Libertas* is one day from New Orleans with a shipment of furniture. She can be at the Canaries rendezvous in eight or nine days. *Sloboda Dalmacija* can leave Gruz tomorrow. *Hrabrost* is already in the Canaries, as you know. Her crew needs only to be flown there with me. We could be ashore at Nillin within two weeks."

"Good. We have to go without Buvina. Pilot and the others will be neutralized *after* you've landed. It's risky, but I see no other way now."

At the other end of the line, Dragan Dragić afforded himself a little smile. "I will take care of Pilot myself, General."

"Good. We will land on your first night of occupation, secure the island and begin the removals as planned."

By the opposite wall of the majestic hall, under a vast tapestry commemorating Napoleon's victory at the Battle of Ulm, Gilbert Cafard was listening to every word of the General's conversation.

"It's imperative that we strike early," Fascisse continued. "Contact *Libertas* immediately and turn her around. Report back to me in two hours."

Although his role in the coup from the outset was supportive only – an associate as opposed to a full Member of the Board – General Fascisse was now beginning to act as if he were in charge, instead of merely being Dragić's junior partner.

While the General paced the marble floor, the forgotten third man in the room spoke. Gilbert Cafard had indeed learned something during his time on the island, an education which was distilling into positive action. "General Fascisse?" The voice was so diffident and weak that the old war horse didn't hear it at first. "General Fascisse?" he repeated, louder this time. "Return me to the island and I will do Soldo's work."

The General looked at his spy with momentary suspicion, then took a key from his desk drawer and walked over to the gun cabinet.

Twenty minutes later, Cafard was hustled aboard a helicopter to be dropped back on Eydos. At the same time, Stanko Jerić, on board the retired freighter *Sloboda Dalmacija*, was ordered to sail immediately to the rendezvous off Fuerteventura. Twenty-one days tied up in Gruz, the harbour of Dubrovnik, with its foul-smelling paint factory effluent, had disaffected but not demoralised the sixteen Knights of Blasius who made up the ship's company. All were keen to trade in their stale, run-down lives for the bright new future of Novi Ragusa. So, when Jerić gave the order to sail, his Knights leapt to the task with a keenness and enthusiasm that was almost manic. The fifty-two Albanians hired as mercenaries for eighty dollars a day remained ambivalent. They'd never known better working conditions *or* better wages and would have been happy to float in effluent for a further year if necessary.

The air was clear, dry and cold, kept that way by a strong north wind. Although some out-of-season Germans had already started swimming in the sea, the water temperature was still too cold to make April a popular holiday month. As a result, the supermarkets had not yet been given their annual injection of goods and the Knights had found their pre-voyage provisioning uninspiring and thin on the ground. Not that it mattered. Very soon they'd have all the choice and all the excess their hearts desired. Or so they hoped.

The following morning, Odile Bartoli was surprised to see Cafard jogging into Nillin, 'Zigzag' having been dropped several miles out of earshot of the settlers. "Get Lonnie," he panted. "It's important."

Ten minutes later, Bartoli, Pilot and The Pentad were seated around a table listening to Cafard's report. "The Knights of Blasius will form the first invasion wave by sea and will bring their ships into the harbour in about ten days time," he began. "This will be quickly followed by a four-Chinook airborne invasion by General Fascisse's mercenaries. The specialists will be flown out in onc of the helicopters and set free somewhere in the

French countryside. The other three Chinooks will fly all but five of your crew to the General's estate, where they will be confined until such time as the Knights deem it safe to release them. But before any of this happens…" Cafard hesitated, then withdrew a Glock and silencer from his jacket. "Stand over there by the wall with your hands above your heads," he said, fixing the silencer to the muzzle of the pistol and pointing it at the others. No one moved. "NOW." They did as instructed and walked slowly to the far side of the dome. Pilot was the last to comply. "Now turn around. All of you."

Cafard released the safety catch on his Glock, waited a few seconds for dramatic effect, then laughed. "I am sorry. This is a bad joke," he said, re-engaging the safety catch. "Please sit down." The group relaxed and returned to their seats, but no-one was laughing.

"For a minute there, Gilbert, I thought you'd zagged," Bradingbrooke said.

"What's 'zagged'?"

"Inside joke," Pilot said. "Carry on, Gilbert."

"When Dragić reaches the elbow of the fjord, he will activate my pager," Cafard continued. "This will be my signal to kill Lonnie Pilot, Jane Lavery, Henry Bradingbrooke, Josiah Billy and Macushla Mara. Your bodies will then be taken out to sea, weighed down and sunk."

The group was stunned by the heartless cruelty of the plan.

"This was to be Mirko Soldo's assignment," Cafard said, raising the gun in the air. "But now it is mine."

As *Sloboda Dalmacija* skirted the magnificent city walls of Dubrovnik, then the rocky southern shore of the island of Lokrum, there wasn't one non-Albanian aboard the ship who didn't feel a crusader's pride in the voyage upon which they were now embarking.

Mirko Soldo's incarceration in a Stuttgart jail awaiting trial on charges of murder and fraud had dented the shield of Blasius, but in no way had it checked his momentum. Dragan Dragić soon had the enterprise back on course. And of course, Gilbert Cafard, assassin in waiting, had made Buvina's loss so much easier to bear.

Jelena Milanović, never now to be the fifth Mrs. Soldo, was beginning to experience difficulties in her dealings with their U.S. associates, but she'd so far managed to keep them interested and actively involved in the run-up to occupation. Of prime importance to her as the invasion date approached was to discover who was sowing the seeds of doubt among their American partners. There was no doubt in Oilslick's mind that some outside party was attempting to sabotage the project. She was a shrewd woman and a skilled manipulator, as Forrest Vaalon was finding out. Every effort he made to get the Mafia strings cut was met by some clever splicing on her part. It was not only her devious politician's mind that retied the knot, but often her all-over tan and what it was all over. Half the aims and resolutions of the New Ragusa had been hatched on the FKK nudist beach of Lokrum.

By sundown, those aboard *Sloboda Dalmacija* could just make out the lavender mountains of Albania in the distance. Over a thousand miles to the west, and quite coincidentally, Lonnie Pilot was seeing Albania too – not the current one, but the reclusive 20th century Albania of Enver Hoxha. Pilot had always wondered how a regime so introverted and secretive could have existed in such close proximity to the rest of Western Europe for so long. In 1967, Hoxha had proclaimed Albania the world's first atheist state, under which all fascist, religious, warmongerish, antisocialist activity and propaganda were banned. Pilot didn't quite view Eydos as a new Albania, but one aspect of the country, as it was under Hoxha, interested him. Albania had exercised a strange, undefined power on the outside world – the power of mystery and of the unknown, fanned by people's imagination and the frustration of denied access. Before photographs had been received back on Earth from the first lunar orbiter, the Moon had enjoyed similar mystique. When their last veils had dropped, Albania and the Moon had both lost power. Pilot was determined not to let that happen to Eydos. He would build a similar inscrutability around his island and let those outside do the work. All he had to do was keep the veils intact.

When *Sloboda Dalmacija* arrived at the rendezvous twelve miles southeast of Puerto de Cabras, Dragić was already there. He'd flown into Las Palmas the week before with his crew and taken a leisurely test cruise around the islands aboard the rusty freighter *Hrabrost*, flagship of the Ragusan invasion fleet.

The third ship, *Libertas*, arrived late the following morning. She'd unloaded her shipment of furniture in New Orleans, carried a cargo of general commodities over to Jamaica and from there, five hundred kilos of skank to a rendezvous with a cabin cruiser off the Florida Keys. Before setting out to cross the Atlantic, her captain had made one last call at Savannah to pick up a very important passenger. Oilslick, in her attempts to keep alive the Mafia's involvement, had arranged for one of their men, Albert Nell, to travel with the *Libertas* as an observer. Nell was one of the new breed of mafioso trying to shed their stereotypical image of thuggish gangsterism. One way of doing this was by lengthening their Christian names and shortening their family names. So, Al Grancenello was now Albert Nell. And, rather than on the streets, Nell had received his education at Princeton.

When they reached the Canaries, a curious and somewhat bemused Nell boarded the *Hrabrost* to view the final invasion plans with Dragić and the ship's captain, Josip Bobkar. The details of the invasion didn't interest Albert Nell, because in his chosen line of business the end was always far more important than the means. If these thugs from Croatia could take possession of the island, as they claimed they could, then Global Hotel & Condo Inc., would be happy to accept a piece of it.

That night, the three Dalmatian merchantmen, carrying the coat of arms of Old Ragusa on their pennants, headed north on the 1500 mile voyage to the Bay of Biscay.

The communiqué read as follows:

> 'The island heretofore referred to as 'Ille de Bonne Fortune', or 'Eydos', being located in the Bay of Biscay off Western France, has today been liberated by the undersigned in the name of progress, friendship and European and world harmony. All but five of the island's inhabitants have been peaceably removed to a secret location, where they will be kept in comfort until such time as is deemed suitable by ourselves for their release. The whereabouts of Lonnie Pilot and four of his lieutenants are unknown. It is presumed that they have put to sea and fled. The handover was made without bloodshed or violence. Nor was there any damage to livestock, property or crops. All possessions of the former inhabitants will be

assessed and their owners reimbursed, where return of the goods is impossible. The island will henceforward be known as Zapad Dalmacija, or Western Dalmatia, and its capital, formerly Nillin, as Novi Ragusa. A further communiqué will be issued in due course.'

Signed
The Knights of Blasius.

Satisfied that the fiction of this prepared statement would be proven by subsequent events, Dragan Dragić clicked Save Draft on his email and downed a large slivovic.

It was their third night out, and the fleet had cleared Cape Finisterre to begin the final leg to Eydos. Dragić was too keyed up to sleep and was on the bridge when the island finally came into view at first light. Initially, it was just a dark cloud bank on the horizon. Eydos was still twenty miles away, and should not yet be visible, but as they drew nearer, the shape resolved itself into something more solid – a seemingly endless cliff rising over three hundred metres out of the sea.

From a quarter of a mile, the extraordinary smoothness of the cliff face, apart from the occasional turbidity ravine, became apparent. Unlike the craggy, chiseled coasts of her near neighbours, Eydos had not had hundreds of millions of years of erosion to etch character into her face.

In stark contradiction to earlier photographs of Eydos were the vivid lime greens, yellows and rusts of the 'tablecloth' covering the cliff top – colours rendered all the more powerful above the stark grey of the underlying rock. The sun behind Dragić lit the scene full on and was reflected back into the man's face by the mirror of a flat sea.

The three small ships were approaching that same part of the coast that Bradingbrooke's exploration party had reached from landward nine months before. The target wasn't far away now, but the fleet was ahead of schedule, so Bobkar cut their speed to five knots. The invaders did not want to reach the mouth of the fjord leading into Nillin before dusk, so they stole as near to the base of the cliffs as they dared so as to avoid detection by any lookouts that may have been posted at the top.

Bobkar was looking for an entrance resembling a narrow chink in a set of very tall curtains. Even using Global Positioning it was easy to miss unless you knew the coast well. The captain had been flown over the site and along their current route twice. He knew exactly where he was and was pacing himself to arrive at the entrance at sundown. From its mouth, the fjord cut into the island for half a mile to its elbow, where it turned east southeast towards Nillin. The difficulty would be in landing. The budding rows of cottonwoods and poplars along the northwest perimeter of the settlement would screen their approach, and might even allow them to tie up and come ashore undetected. The islanders were notoriously slack when it came to security.

Thanks to Soldo and the spy Cafard, every last inhabitant was known to the Knights, down to where they slept, where they were likely to be found at any given time of the day and how they were liable to react individually to invasion.

The Knights of Blasius, together with the Albanians, numbered ninety-seven, but only the Knights, and Gilbert Cafard, already in place in Nillin, carried firearms. If Cafard was successful in dispatching his five targets, the remaining inhabitants would be easily overpowered. On coming ashore, the Knights would disable the satellite dish and close down the radio to ensure no communication could be made with Pilot's backers, whoever they might be. General Fascisse and his fleet of helicopters would be standing by on the mainland for the signal. If all went well, the conspirators would have everyone off the island before dawn. Taking Eydos would be 'nema problema'.

There was considerable cloud piled low on the western horizon and as the sun slipped down behind it, all daylight was extinguished. So much the better. Bobkar had remarkable night vision and could steer his ship like a gondolier. The others needed only to follow his stern light.

As they cleared a last headland and began the final approach to the fjord, the radar operator detected something which, according to their information, shouldn't have been there. It was impossible from that distance to make a positive visual identification of the objects which could have been rocks or even small islets. Bobkar and Dragić peered at the radar screen as if willing the blips to unmask themselves. "What are they?" Dragić asked. But before Bobkar could answer, the lookout shouted that he could see lights. The two men looked at each other in alarm.

"Stop engines," Bobkar commanded.

Dragić looked as if his life's blood was seeping out of a hundred holes in his belly. "Who *are* they?"

Behind *Hrabrost*, Stanko Jerić, unaware of the strange lights up ahead, didn't notice the lead ship's gradual loss of forward motion until too late and only had time to turn *Sloboda Dalmacija* four points to starboard before hitting the larger ship a glancing blow at three knots. Bobkar had forgotten to command the ships behind him to stop engines. The captain of the *Libertas*, following far enough behind to avoid the pile-up, skirted round the outside before cutting his engines.

"What's going on?" Nell asked the captain.

He was answered by muttered curses. Through the window, distant lights were becoming brighter in the growing darkness.

"Is that Nillin?" Nell asked.

The captain ignored him and raised Dragić on the radio. *Hrabrost* and *Sloboda Dalmacija* weren't badly damaged and attention had once again turned to the dilemma now facing them. The radio speaker exploded with a superfluous command from Dragić to shut off their lights – superfluous, because the watchers inside the radar blips had been following the fleet's progress for the past five hours, lights or no lights.

"Are we going in there or not?" Albert Nell's instincts always preferred action over thought, despite his MA in Urban Studies. The captain wheeled around and told him to shut up.

"How many can you see?" It was Dragić again, marginally calmer this time. "We count two."

The captain left his bridge to make a visual check with his high-powered and highly treasured Swiss night binoculars. When he eventually came back into the wheelhouse he looked like the man who has lost the winning lottery ticket. "Four," he reported back to Dragić. "Four warships. It's a problem."

Old school Mafia don, Sandro 'Sandy' Condoso, President of Global Hotel & Condo, to name just one outpost of his vast business empire, and Jelena 'Oilslick' Milanović, the first and only female Knight of Blasius, left the lobster bar arm in arm and walked quickly towards the chauffeur-driven Cadillac badly parked on the curb a short distance away. The only place Condoso walked slowly was behind the fortified walls of his estate on the Hudson.

As they settled into the back seat, Oilslick slid her arm through her escort's and maneuvered her elbow to rest suggestively in his lap.

"As soon as Colonel Domaigne gets the signal from Dragan, he will phone me," she said. "It's nine at night on the island and our men will have already landed. You and I can drink a toast to the future while we are waiting for the call. Would you like to join me, Sandro?" The invitation was not spoken to the man – it was *breathed* on him.

"Sure," he answered, staring out of the window. Sandy Condoso had stopped trying to impress women years ago. Because of his immense power, he no longer had to, and as a result his life had become quite boring – in one respect, anyway. The female next to him was nervous and that made him even more disinterested.

"When we wake that island up, there will be no stopping us, Sandro," Milanović continued, trying to pump some life into the man. "I wish you could see what *I* see."

"What's that, kid?"

Oilslick gripped Condoso's thigh with both hands and turned the blowtorch of her words directly onto his face. "It's not just money, Sandro. It's international influence. And strategic importance – to NATO; to the United States; to France, Britain and Spain. We're not just talking about a Cayman Island or a Monte Carlo. Zapad Dalmacija is 5,000 square kilometers of opportunity – and it lies supremely, like a sleeping lion, at the gates to Europe itself. Out there waits the kind of power we have only dreamt about – and part of it can be yours if you stick with us."

If he found the word 'part' offensive, Condoso didn't show it, other than via the light grimace on his face and the way he tossed his mouth around as if he'd just eaten something rotten. He sat inscrutably for a moment before answering.

"Miss Milanović. Me and my organisation think that we got to come up with a classier name than the one you people put forward. The guy from Wichita's got to be able to pronounce the place he'll be spending his money in. It's middle America we're aiming at and you ain't gonna hit 'em with Zapid Almacha."

"Do you have a better name, Sandro?"

"New Liberty," he announced with the conviction of a god. Sandy Condoso was never required to explain or dress up the decisions he made. The island would be called New Liberty, full stop. That was the end of the matter.

Oilslick, at this stage of the game, sensing that their American partners were teetering on the verge of pulling out of the deal, was prepared to make any sacrifices necessary to save the project – over and above offering her body to all whose influence qualified. The Knights of Blasius would object vehemently to losing Zapad Dalmacija, but without the capital and the input from their American partners, there would be *no* island, *no* development, *no* power.

"New Liberty is a beautiful name, Sandro," she lied.

The instant the car pulled to a halt outside the Algonquin Hotel, a gold-braided, white-gloved doorman appeared from nowhere to help remove its contents. Jelena Milanović got out first and had to stop herself from assisting her portly companion. She stood to one side pretending not to look and reapplied her lipstick as one of Condoso's soldiers struggled to get him out of the car.

As they walked regally towards the hotel entrance, Condoso's presence towered over all around him. The fact that Oilslick was five inches taller than the man made not the slightest difference to his stature in Manhattan.

They hesitated a moment in the grand foyer in the self-conscious posture people adopt when they enter a crowded room. Condoso was looking for enemies; Milanovic, for admiring glances. Beside them, a deep and rounded Vincent Price voice cut through the classy cacophony of the Algonquin and caused them to turn.

"Miss Milanović, Mr. Condoso. I'd like a word with you, please. It's important." The odd couple looked at the tall man in puzzlement. "Let's sit over there." Oilslick stopped dead in her tracks, an expression of annoyance just discernable under her make-up. Condoso's three bodyguards, looking like badly decorated cupcakes on a plate of caviar, also stopped and were weighing up the potential threat to their boss.

"I represent Lonnie Pilot and this will only take a minute." Condoso signaled his men to stand down and followed the stranger to some rich red leather chairs set around a magnificent mahogany coffee table. "I'm here to lance a very painful boil on Lonnie Pilot's bottom, Mr. Condoso." He turned towards the man's simmering consort. "Miss Milanović, your invasion fleet is shut out of the mouth of the fjord by the Irish navy, so I wouldn't bother waiting up to hear from Dragić if I were you. We've sent a message to General Fascisse at his airfield in Brittany, telling him what I just told you. I don't think he'll be taking any independent action with half the world's press – on a tip-off from ourselves – camped by his helicopters. Mr. Condoso, rather than your celebrating with champagne on false pretenses, and then hearing this news in the morning and taking it out on Miss Milanović, I thought I'd give it to you in person now."

Intelligent people don't fight against unbeatable odds, being quick to see the futility of such action. Jelena Milanović, stripped naked in the lobby of Manhattan's foremost hotel, had just resigned. Forrest Vaalon turned towards the woman with a benevolent look in his eyes.

"From what I've heard about this man, Miss Milanović, I'm probably saving your life by killing this serpent in the egg before it gets up to your hotel room." With that, Vaalon sat back, having said what he came to say, and looked at each in turn.

Without uttering a word, and without so much as looking at either Vaalon or Oilslick, Condoso rose up on his tiny, alligator-skinned feet and marched out of the hotel, followed by his three minders.

The young woman from Dubrovnik just stared at the coffee table, powerless through the presence of the milling hotel guests, to vent her anger and frustration on the man who had just caused her ruin.

Two weeks after the abortive invasion, Mirko Soldo was still languishing in a Schweinfurt jail awaiting news from the Knights. No one had bothered to tell him. *Libertas*, *Hrabrost* and *Sloboda Dalmacija* were no longer to be found in the Bay of Biscay. The Ragusan fleet had scattered. Stanko Jerić's ship was back in the effluent of Gruz Harbour. *Libertas* was on her way to South Africa and the *Hrabrost* was once again gathering barnacles in Las Palmas.

In Whitehall and the City of London, in more than one corridor of British power, important men who had hoped to become even more inflated on the hot air of the new regime of Zapad Dalmacija, silently mourned the coup's failure, as did other men of avarice in Paris, Brussels, Bonn, Kansas City, Las Vegas, Miami and New York City.

In the Bay of Biscay, love was in the air. Dubravka Horvat had recovered from Pilot's rejection with a vengeance. She and Aaron Serman had hurdled the language barrier with their eyes closed and were inseparable. Odile Bartoli and Gilbert Cafard were already a quarter way through their unique adaptation of The Perfumed Garden. And it had only taken Lonnie Pilot and Jane Lavery one trip to move her personal effects, including a perfect specimen of an infant bonsai tree, into his dome. Other pairings had been made, leaving only a handful of unattached people on the island – some more detached than others. Henry Bradingbrooke had been dipping his toe in the water but had not yet jumped in with anyone. And, since landing in August, Macushla Mara had turned down the advances of eight crew members, including her latest suitress, Rebecca Schein, preferring for the moment to remain single and heterosexual.

On a cliff-top overlooking the entrance to the newly named Blasius Fjord, five people strolled on a shallow carpet of spongy green lichen, their hair and clothes rippling like flags in the fierce east wind.

"It's beginning to look like proper land," Jane Lavery said, picking up a clump of lichen. She held it in her open palm and it was immediately ripped away into the distance. "How on Earth does it hold on in this wind?"

"A bit like us," Macushla Mara said, composing the colours and shapes for her next knitted jumper from the inspirational rusts, greens and greys underfoot. "Still holding on against all the odds." In another sense, conditions had never been calmer in the Bay of Biscay. The wind of invasion had abated for the moment; the island's position was as secure as it ever would be; and it was time for the settlers to throw all their energy into their Big Idea before the world outran Eydos' ability to rein it in.

Lonnie Pilot's gaze was directed seaward. Beyond the horizon, an unthinkable blight was descending. Unthinkable but not unexpected. Just three hours earlier they had been watching news footage of the half-million-strong 'Poor March' on Washington. Unlike the Great March for Jobs and Freedom in 1963, this one had ended in violence. The images had stunned them all and was soon colouring their wind-blown conversation.

Henry Bradingbrooke: The bloodstains on the steps of the Lincoln Memorial ...who would have thought that could ever happen?

Josiah Billy (after Martin Luther King): *I have a dream... that one day the waves reaching our western cliffs will be red with the blood of all fifty States.*

Lavery: Not funny, Josiah.

Bradingbrooke: Poetic, though.

Billy: No. *Prophetic.*

Mara: It doesn't bode well for the Land of the Free.

Lonnie Pilot: There's no such place.

(*pause*)

Mara: Where do we go from here?

Billy: I feel sick.

Lavery: Where *do* we go from here?

Billy: To the bottom of the Bay. Put us out of our misery.

Mara: Cheer up, Josiah. It might never happen.

Billy: *What* might never happen.

Mara: It.

Billy: I've got post-traumatic stress, Macushla. I can't help it. The French… the Knights of bloody Blasius…

Lavery: Take it out on one of your pieces of wood, Joe. Carve some sonnets.

Mara: Or limericks.

(*pause*)

Mara: There once was a man named Bill-ay, Who fretted and bayed in Biscay.

(*pause*)

Lavery: His groans and his moans, Set negative tones,

Mara: And drove all his neighbours away.

Billy: I see no reason to be cheerful. None at all. Do you think they'll come back?

Bradingbrooke: Who? Your neighbours? The French? The Knights?

Billy: No. The Disciples of the Seraphic Prodigy.

Bradingbrooke: You mean Debbie Rae.

Billy: She was nice. Uncomplicated.

Mara: Ignorance is bliss.

Billy: She was nice. Uncomplicated. Unthreatening.

Mara: Yes, she was, Josiah.

Billy: She needs looking after. I hope she finds someone.

Lavery: There are eight billion people out there who need looking after. I hope *they* find someone.

(*pause*)

Lavery: I've got a new recipe to try on you.

Bradingbrooke: Let me guess. Moringo leaves on toast.

Lavery: No. On *lentils*. But you mash the leaves up with brandy and chilli peppers into a paste first before adding it to a soya roux.

Billy: Can't wait to try it, Jane.

(pause)

Billy: As soon as the first potatoes come up, I'll make us all a giant vat of pottage and we can get pissed for a month. Drown our… *my*… sorrows.

Mara: You're thinking of poteen, Josiah. Pottage is soup.

Bradingbrooke: I'm thinking of handing myself over to the International Court.

(pause)

Lavery: What did you say?

Bradingbrooke: I said I'm thinking of turning myself in. There's a stain on this place in the eyes of the world – an impurity – and it's *me*. It's time I was removed.

Mara: But everyone thinks you're in Ecuador.

Bradingbrooke: I'm *not* in Ecuador. I'm here.

Lavery: But we're the only ones who know that.

Mara: You can't just –

Bradingbrooke: I'm the only person on this island who knows what it feels like to have a price on his head. To be a wanted man.

Lavery: Yes, and we want you more than they do.

Mara: We *need* you, Henry. Don't be foolish.

Bradingbrooke: *Foolish*? This isn't a foolish decision. I've wrestled with it for months and keep arriving at the same conclusion. For the sake of our island's moral integrity and long-term credibility, it's a sacrifice that needs to be made.

Lavery: Eydos is a consensual democracy, Henry. We'd have to put it to a vote. I doubt very much if it'll pass.

Bradingbrooke: Then I'll invoke my right to leave the island without ostracism or hindrance. I'm going.

Billy: You can't do that, mate. It –

"Let him talk," Pilot interrupted. "He might have a point."

Bradingbrooke's intention to surrender himself to The Hague was heatedly debated for two weeks. Everyone except Lonnie Pilot had been against it to begin with. The worst case scenario was life in prison. That was the future Bradingbrooke would be choosing. Their need for him on the island far outweighed any 'purification' of Eydos' good name such an action might effect, they argued. Pilot took the opposite view. His stance, which many thought ruthless and cold, had not endeared him to his compatriots.

"Every cause needs a martyr," Bradingbrooke argued. "Six of us knew in advance about the catastrophic upheaval that was to come. Obviously, we can't all give ourselves up to the International Court. That would rip the heart out of Eydos. I'm the most expendable."

"What would you gain?"

"Nothing. The gain would be yours."

"But *negligent genocide*? They'll throw the book at you."

"The only people who were negligent were those who died," Pilot said. "That will be the basis of Henry's defence. We've been talking with an English barrister and he's confident Henry will get no more than a few years, if not acquittal."

"I'm willing to take my chances," Henry said, closing the matter.

The plan was to fly Bradingbrooke to St. Hellier on the mail helicopter. Using a false passport, he would then travel to The Hague by train and present himself at the doors of the *Vredespaleis*. On his day of departure, everyone gathered at the helipad to wish him well. Some were in tears. Others tried to keep the mood upbeat. Pilot was the last to say goodbye. He placed his friend in a bear hug that lasted a full minute, then stepped back and looked Bradingbrooke in the eye. Neither man said a word. Enough had been spoken on the matter, which was now out of *all* their hands.

"What do you think's going to happen to him?" someone said as the helicopter disappeared into a low cloud. "What's going to happen to *us*?"

"Henry will be just fine," Lavery said. "*We'll* be fine. Let's just carry on our work here and see what life throws our way."

What life threw their way next was going to be one of the toughest tests Pilot would face. Late one night, lying in the damp warmth of post coital bliss, Lavery took her lover's hand and placed it once again on her small, perfectly formed bosom.

"Give me twenty minutes, Janey," Pilot said, still breathless.

"No… not that, love." She took his forefinger and directed it into the soft flesh of her breast. "Feel this."

PART THREE

XVIII

Pilot had wasted no time in getting Jane to Dublin's foremost cancer hospital for a double mastectomy and the first of many courses of chemotherapy. During the eight weeks spent in Ireland for the operation and initial treatments, they stayed incognito in the very house Josiah Billy had offered up as a base for their Utopian experiment. Between treatments, the couple would return to Eydos, where Jane worked the gardens and hydroponic growing tents with as much heart as her diminishing energy levels would allow. After two years, she could do no physical activity at all, and had bravely passed control of the food production programme to her deputy, Paola Rendina.

Over the course of the illness, the bond between Lonnie and Jane deepened, though they both knew it was an oncological inevitability that their connection would soon be severed. Jane had fought the disease with humour and resolve, supported by Lonnie and her close friends, Paola and Macushla, but four years, two months, eight days, five hours and sixteen minutes since she first got the results of her biopsy, Jane Lavery took her last breath. In one sense, her partner stopped breathing at that moment, too. He had just had his 31st birthday. And he had had enough.

Lonnie Pilot was becalmed in the Bay of Biscay. Everyone knew it. His eyes remained lifeless, and the laptop which he used to fill daily with ideas and observations remained switched off. He would walk out with a tent and be gone for days, returning in no better frame of mind than when he had left. Words didn't seem to help, so, on the first anniversary of Lavery's death, one of the unattached females took it upon herself to try a physical approach to healing. "I appreciate what you're trying to do, Darrell," Pilot had told her. "I'm not ready, though. Not for that."

Eydos herself was merely treading water in a sea of increasing turbulence and instability. The more energic and committed islanders did what they could to keep the Big Idea on course, but without Pilot's leadership it had become no more than a vague notion.

No one was more worried about the situation than Forrest Vaalon. And when Serman reported that Pilot had decided to resign and cede leadership to anyone who would have it, a radical solution was called for. Vaalon immediately tracked down Jennifer Springs, now one of England's most successful artists, and commissioned her to paint the 'Eydos Landscapes'...

Pilot greeted Springs with the familiarity of a former lover, but none of the electricity. She looked more beautiful and alluring than ever, he couldn't deny it, but in the five years that had passed since their last meeting, an unbridgeable chasm had opened between them. Jenny's last three exhibitions had been sell-outs and her arc was diametrically opposed to Pilot's trough. She was looking forward and he was looking backward. They stood in silence for a while like two people trying to recognize where they'd seen the other before. "I'm sorry about the Australia thing," Pilot said, "but I couldn't tell you the – "

"The truth was out of the question. I understand, Lonnie." Jenny took both Pilot's hands in hers. "Forrest told me about Jane."

"Is that why you're here?"

"What do you mean?"

"To sex me out of my funk?"

"He's worried about you, yes. But I wouldn't have put it so crudely." Jenny looked offended. "I'm also here to paint. Forrest really *does* want six landscapes for his ranch in New Mexico."

Pilot back-tracked. "I'm sorry, Jenny."

"Don't be. I'll be very busy here, even if it's not with you."

"Of course."

"It can be therapeutic, you know."

"Painting?"

Jenny thought for a moment. "*And* painting."

Pilot helped carry Jenny's bags to her dome, wrestling with his thoughts as they walked. He needed a partner, but not just a sexual one. Six years earlier she had been the most important woman in his life, but in retrospect and in light of what had happened since, Pilot realized that his connection with Jenny had only been skin deep. He also knew that the woman who had succeeded her, and had dug so much deeper, was dead, and that life had to go on. So, why not rewind – lie down with Jenny, and see what happened? He tried to imagine the outcome, but couldn't.

Two days later, Pilot marched over to Jenny's dome after she'd returned with her easel from a morning of cliff painting and invited himself in. Without preamble, he placed his hands on her shoulders, buried his face in her neck and inhaled her familiar scent. His butterfly kisses, beginning around her ear, were soon landing on her lips. At this point, the butterfly became a ravenous animal and began devouring her mouth with single-minded abandon. Always sensitive to his lovers' signals, Pilot was encouraged by Jenny's. She was opening like a flower. Soon, they were sex-wrestling naked on her bed. Even after five years, neither had forgotten the other's preferred erogenous zones, and these were being mutually attended to like a Tai Chi progression. But there were two things missing. A deeper connection and an erection. Failing to find either during twenty minutes of feverish foreplay, Pilot flopped over on his back, sweat pouring off his body, and sighed. "I'm sorry, Jenny. This just isn't working."

For the next two months, Springs worked zealously on her landscapes, aided by an unusually long spell of fine weather. The day before she was to leave, she went to Pilot's dome to offer herself to him one more time. She had to wake him up. It was 4pm.

"Lonnie, I've done seven paintings. Forrest only asked for six, so I'd like to give you one. Will you come to my dome and choose?"

Pilot unrolled himself from bed and ran his fingers through his unruly grey mop. "Jenny, you don't have to do that." But the intensity in her eyes told him she *did*. "Thank you. I'd love one of your paintings."

When he entered her dome, seven canvasses in various states of dryness were resting against the crates Josiah Billy had made for them with material from the dismantled prefabs. It was the first time Pilot had seen the completed paintings and he was astounded by their power and technical prowess. He thought the painting of a sediment pit work party was stunning – eight figures toiling in the long shadows of dusk with the sun poised to set behind the basin rim in the distance. Next to it was an atmospheric composition of the barge site, but with no figures. He preferred paintings that had people in them. He ran his eyes over the others – superb renditions of the island in all her moods and colours. Only the seventh painting stood out as being different, in that it was more a flight of imagination than an impression of reality. "This one reminds me of *The Destruction of Pompeii and Herculaneum* by John Martin. I think I know what you're saying here."

"What goes up, must come down, Lonnie. Eydos will return to the sea one day…"

Pilot pondered the painting for another minute, its depressing weight speaking to him like a Leonard Cohen song. "I don't think Forrest will like it, so if you don't mind, I'll – "

"It's yours. I'll leave it here for you. My parting gift." There was a finality in her words.

Jenny's departure sent Pilot into an even deeper depression. As the weeks passed, he became more and more ineffectual as a leader. Eydos was rudderless and everyone knew that Lonnie Pilot's days as leader were over. But, before a vote of no confidence could be taken, he preempted it by calling a general meeting and resigning his leadership in less than a minute. In the ensuing election, a reluctant Aaron Serman was chosen as Eydos' new leader, having beaten his even more reluctant opponent, Nirpal Banda. It was a situation that didn't sit well with Forrest Vaalon. Jennifer Springs hadn't worked, and the partner he and Ruth had originally picked for Pilot seemed as disinterested in him as he in her. Forrest Vaalon made it his next mission to find out why and surprised everyone with his first ever visit to the island.

After a rousing speech over lunch, Vaalon asked if he could speak to everyone individually, "to gauge morale and get more than just a general picture of what's going on here." By the following afternoon he had canvassed everyone but Pilot, who he found moping under a cottonwood.

"Lonnie, I saved you for last," he said, shaking Pilot's hand. "The future success of this experiment is resting on what I'm going to say to you." Pilot stood up and suggested they retire to the warmth of his dome. As they walked the short distance into the settlement, Pilot wondered what revelation the man had up his sleeve. Vaalon didn't waste time on a preamble.

"The theory of arranged marriages can't be faulted," he said, "only the practice. Ruth always maintained that if the matchmakers themselves are inadequate, then you will get an inadequate match. But if they have set the right criteria, done their homework and made the correct assumptions, then that all-important affinity can be achieved. Ruth's intuition was based on collected and stored experiences that cannot be arrived at through logic or study. Thirty of the pairings that have been made on this island are as per Ruth's original blueprint, although for some of them it took one or two mistakes before they got there."

Where's this going? Pilot thought.

"The natural courting process doesn't necessarily result in a good match," Vaalon continued. "Many marriages are the product of rebound. Some marriages are the product of sexual attraction only, or don't include sexual attraction or are otherwise just partially alive. Whatever it is that makes two people compatible is only found by luck, if at all, through conventional methods." Vaalon reached into his briefcase, withdrew a faded photograph and handed it to Pilot. A woman in her early thirties was standing arm-in-arm with an athletic, dark-maned Forrest Vaalon. The fashion of the day had not disguised a timeless quality about her, nor deflected from the intensity in her eyes – the same eyes that had so captivated Robert Frank, Man Ray and Lee Miller. "I'd like to think there were never two more compatible people who ever walked the Earth together," he said.

"What *is* compatibility, Forrest?"

"That's a tough one. There's no measure for quantifying it in our society, so Ruth had to make one up. She named this measurement *climacy*. Climacy includes such areas as communication, rapport, physical attraction, chemical attraction, sexual appetite, romanticism, humour and imagination. Couples can be paired as either *sames* or *opposites*, because opposites often attract, as we know. Now, if your partnership has over 65% climacy, you've got a good chance at a successful marriage. Ruth reckoned that she and I were 85%. An arranged marriage should work adequately, but without sparkle, below 65 down to 55, although it gets more fragile as it drops. Anything below that is grounds for divorce.

"Your getting together with Jane was a surprise to me, but it was working well and heading towards great things. Jane wasn't the partner Ruth and I had planned for you, though."

He's going to introduce me to my future wife in a minute, Pilot thought with a mixture of fear and curiosity. "I think arranged marriages are just polite rape, Forrest, with both parties the victim."

"Our six candidates for leader, do you remember them?" Vaalon said, deliberately ignoring Pilot's comment.

"How could I forget? I was only your second choice."

Vaalon smiled. "I'm surprised you never asked me who the surviving four were. They've been here the whole time."

"Over the years I guessed them." Pilot scribbled four names on his pad and handed it to Vaalon.

"Correct names, but wrong order," he said. "You've got three and four transposed. You know who we're talking about, Lonnie, don't you?"

He knew damn well who she was. The only surprise would be if she felt the same about him.

Vaalon arose and put on his Astrakhan coat. "I'll be back in an hour," he said. "Spruce yourself up, Lonnie. You'll never impress her looking like that."

It was just before midnight when Vaalon returned to Pilot's dome in the company of another. "I'd like to introduce you to my Number Three," he said.

When she came through the door, her green eyes reflecting light from behind the long black curtains of her hair, Pilot's heart skipped. He'd always been drawn to Macushla, but he had also felt intimidated by her stunning beauty, quick mind, razor wit and superior formal education. He was no Adonis and it made him feel mediocre and unconfident. He could not see the attractions that others, none moreso than Macushla Mara, saw in him. Having worshipped her from afar for so long, it was as if Vaalon had just granted him permission to climb up and join Macushla on the pedestal he had built for her. Whether she would take his hand and help him up was another story.

"I told Macushla the same thing I told you," Vaalon said before walking out of earshot of the pair.

Pilot turned to face Mara. "And what was your reaction?" he asked her. "Over all the years we've been here, I've never picked up any signals that you might be interested in me as more than just a friend and colleague."

"That was my defence, Lonnie. Jane and I were extremely close, as you know. We liked the same flowers, the same music, the same literature, the same art... and the same man. She got you first, and my defence was to switch off. When Jane died, I knew I had to remain switched off until two things happened."

"Which were...?"

"First, that you put Jane's picture away – figuratively speaking. I don't think you've done that yet."

"What's the second thing?"

"That you wake Snow White from her eternal sleep." The vulnerability in Macushla's eyes surprised Pilot. "Whether you'd even want to do that, Lonnie... kiss me awake... I have no idea. You're completely unreadable and have been from the very beginning."

"That was *my* defence, Macushla. I didn't *want* to want you, because I don't do well with rejection."

Vaalon, who had been standing respectfully apart, approached them now. "Are you two willing to give Ruth her head? I honestly think she got this one right."

Mara, who had had a few flings, but nothing of note, and Pilot, who had had a few flings *and* something of note, looked at eachother in bemusement. But under their smiles – hers Mona Lisa, his Cheshire Cat – something inevitable and unstoppable was about to flower.

Vaalon departed without fanfare or farewell the following morning, leaving behind him not only a re-energised and refocused island nation, but also the final chemistry towards forming the synergy crucial to the future success of the mission.

XIX

Macushla Mara's craving of choice – Balkan Black Olives in Brine – was the only foodstuff on the island that still came out of a tin. Everything else from the convoy's original larder had long since been consumed. One or two of the other pregnant women were also finding these delectable nuggets the only satisfying taste to be had on an island dedicated almost solely to the production of whole foods. Ten years on from the convoy's landing, lentils, pulses and 'Doctor Steve's Weeds' dominated the daily menu.

Macushla popped an olive in her mouth and immediately began to feel better. Over on the other side of the room, the male half of the conception was settling down to read a survey Bart Maryburg had commissioned in the States – 'Eydos in the Awareness of the American People'. Being independently wealthy, Maryburg had paid for the poll out of his own pocket. After his contract on the island had expired, Eydos' former geologist had volunteered to act as their unofficial representative in the U.S., a position he had filled for the past eight years from a small office in Baltimore. Unlike conventional emissaries, Eydos' ambassadors had no nameplates, no titles, and were not bound by protocol. In Britain, Pilot's former doctor, whose son Lonnie had tutored, maintained the link from his surgery in Penzance. If the British Prime Minister wished to communicate with

Eydos, then an appointment to see the doctor had to be made just like anyone else. It was a procedure that infuriated Her Majesty's Government no end. Jane Lavery's mother, a retired school teacher who Pilot had gotten to know well at the safe house during Jane's treatments, represented Eydos in Ireland. 'Agent Zigzag' and Odile Bartoli, who had taken a false identity, fulfilled the same role in France. Their efforts to secure permission for balloons from Eydos to traverse French airspace had yielded nothing, though. After ten years, *Rudolf* and *Donner* had yet to venture further than Eydos' eastern coast. For his part, with The Big Idea consuming more and more of his time, Lonnie Pilot had lost all interest in hot air ballooning.

For the moment, Eydos was at relative peace with her neighbours. With far more pressing challenges requiring their energy, the UK and France had put their covetous designs on indefinite hold. The dissolution of the European Union, following on the heels of the annexation of Greece by Turkey, was the overriding concern of both countries.

Border controls everywhere were being tightened as more and more disillusioned, desperate people sought greener grass and increasingly, food to eat, elsewhere. As a result international migration had reduced to a dribble. Eydos, with no economy to tap into and no cultivatable land apart from the odd sediment pit, was not an attractive destination for most, but the threat of larger scale invasion remained. A small measure of security had been achieved on the island with the installation of early warning radar stations to detect such incursions onto her territory. The other question of how to repel unwelcome visitors once they were detected had been solved by *DAD*, the long range, solar powered *Directional Acoustic Device* developed by one of Vaalon's companies in

Virginia. DAD generated 105 decibels of sound at 7 Hz via a network of pipes to an array of open emitters deployed across the island. Seven Hz was a frequency that could penetrate armour, providing little defense to those within. The sound waves were designed to cause physical pain, breathing difficulty, vertigo, nausea, disorientation, and other systemic discomfort, but not death. Prior to activating the device, any unidentified helicopters, planes or boats would be warned over emergency radio bands of what would happen if they did not turn back. So far, DAD had not been tested against a full-scale invasion, but had proven effective against small-time interlopers trying to land on Eydos' shallow, seaweed-swathed eastern shore. Word soon spread around these disaffected people that, although the concept of Eydos sounded wonderful, the reality was excruciatingly painful.

Three months after he and Macushla Mara joined body and brain, Lonnie Pilot had regained all his drive and more, much to Aaron Serman's relief. Never happy at the helm, Serman had resigned and called a third election. Pilot ran against token opposition and had won by a unanimous count.

To enforce Pilot's motion from Year One that there be no populating of Eydos for the first five years, and to supplement their vast supply of condoms, non-hormonal intrauterine devices had been consensually fitted in all the island's females by their gynecologist. Remarkably, there had been no accidental pregnancies, and on August 4th, exactly five years after landing, the IUDs were removed from all the women who wished it. Like the Oklahoma Land Rush, billions of sperms were suddenly released to stake their claims with the newly emancipated ova.

Pilot's first motion on re-election was to limit births to one per female – to be reviewed biannually. The Pentad had pointed out to him that if a one child per couple policy were adopted, the population of Eydos would drop away generation by generation until it finally disappeared. Pilot had reassured them that there would be time in the future to bring in new people to keep the population stable, but that it was important now to introduce population 'halving' for reasons that would be made clear down the line. "If you have something up your sleeve, you have to show us now," Macushla had said. "Where's the transparency?"

"Let's just call it opaque for now," Pilot had answered. "I can't see it clearly myself, yet. I just know it's the right thing to do." To his surprise and relief, the motion carried.

The islanders had stuck to their game plan of keeping Eydos clear of the machinations, conflagrations and assassinations of the outside world, and the island had remained an enigma. To keep herself in the periphery of the world's eye, however, Eydos would periodically launch statements and observations at the iPatch satellite – utterings which would be worldwide within minutes. The words were always pointed, always relevant, but not always well received by the world's policy makers and captains of industry.

After the outbreak of civil war in the United States, and through the entire three years of the conflict, Eydos had kept her mouth shut, preferring to let events do the talking for her. The Second American Civil War, which was more of an insurgency, had begun with the simultaneous assassinations of the Vice President, two State Governors, half a dozen prominent bankers and the chief executives of four corporations. Condescendingly described by the rich as a war between 'US and Them' –

between the United States and its treacherous underclasses – CW2 had been germinating for years. The gap between rich and poor had become so wide, it had been only a matter of time before the 'Have-nots' would rise against the 'Haves' in an instantaneous explosion of violence and pent up frustration. With so much plenty around them, and such desperation in their own ranks, it required only a person with an understanding of combustion to set CW2 in motion. That person had been Charles Williams.

When Williams sealed his apartment, went underground and woke up the Prisoners of a Consumer Society through the POCS website and a brilliantly executed social media offensive, the match was touched to the dry brushwood of American inequity, injustice, greed, and self-interest. Tools were downed and guns loaded. Gated communities were attacked by the Have-nots, who were then randomly executed by sniper vigilante-mercenaries hired by the Haves. Under the cover of smoke, other scores were settled. Right-wing militants shot the heart out of the environmental movement in America, and several thousand bank officials who had overseen American mortgage foreclosures since 2008 had been run to ground and executed by their victims. With over 300 million firearms in private possession, the United States had become an open firing range – a 3.7 million-square-mile killing field. After two years, the number of dead was close to half a million, nearly the same number as in the first Civil War. When Homeland Security finally got their man, killing Charles Williams during a shoot-out in Washington DC, the insurgency had begun to deflate. Within a year it was over. Within another two years, although the scars were there for all to see, things were back to the inequitable status quo of before.

Henry Bradingbrooke's trial at The Court of International Justice had not produced the outcome everyone had expected. The legal machine had ground out its case relentlessly, giving Bradingbrooke's broken barrister a fatal heart attack in the process. The sentence passed down – 35 years' incarceration in 'The Hague Hilton', as Scheveningen Prison was still called, had been reduced to 25 years on appeal. The world had been outraged, feeling that a stern admonition was all that the polite and amiable English aristocrat deserved. Bradingbrooke himself had taken the fall with stoicism. Mission accomplished. A purefied Eydos had her martyr. For Lonnie Pilot, in terms personal loss, Bradingbrooke's sentence was second only to Jane's death.

In the corner of his eye, Pilot could see Macushla at work on her laptop, so he directed his attention to Maryburg's survey, curious as to its conclusions. Between the covers were five hundred spiral-bound pages of data and a separate report of just a few pages – Maryburg's own summary of the findings. And it was this that Pilot turned to first. Like a playwright opening the reviews after his production's first night, he began to read.

Baltimore, November 19

Lonnie,

These results were generated through a stratified sample modeled after the most recent US Census. In measuring your support in the States, the most significant factors were age, socio-economic group and, to a lesser extent, gender. We can write off the majority of those in groups D and E and those without further education beyond high school. The reasons they will never be supporters of Eydos is because they're too engaged in mere survival to look beyond their own four walls. Some of them thought Eydos was a cleaning fluid.

The majority of your support comes from the over 70s and the under 35s. Maybe it's only when we stand at the doors at either end of our lives – the Entrance and the Exit – that we're able to visualize a saner, more serene world. In between, self-interest rules.

Your real enemies are males in the age group 45-59. They hold the key executive posts in business, government and education, but because they're not quite at the top yet, they still have hunger and that's what makes them such a destructive bunch. They live down in the engine room of the world and can't see what's happening on the surface. Nothing will change until they change. Remember, these men were Charles Williams' prime targets during CW2, and leaving a stable world for future generations is the last thing on their minds.

When you cross the fence to the females in the same age band, it gets interesting. There are two camps. The first doesn't want to rock the boat, or jeopardise the lifestyle they've become accustomed to, and can be written off. The second group supports your ideals, but individual comments suggest it's more a reaction against their menfolk, who they can see losing interest not only in them, sexually and emotionally, but in everything else outside their husbands' single-minded march to personal success.

Men in the 60-69 sub-band are still active in their jobs or otherwise sewn into the financial cloth of the country and are too busy feathering their nests to think philanthropically. They dismiss you outright, being too set in their ways and too self-confident to be swayed by a small cadre of free thinkers on the other side of the Atlantic. The females in this band are likewise indifferent and don't even want to mother you.

Your detracters see you as socialists and communists. But those people I've labeled 'the Thinkers' – the core of your present and future support – see you as independent, non-partisan, apolitical and smart. Eydos is giving them a platform on which to practice what was only talked about in isolation before. What's important is that you've avoided being fashionable and have eschewed social media and self-publicity. That's been key to your longevity and growing influence. Also, you're still here after ten years against all the odds and they like that. It makes them feel secure when making their own sorties against the system. The sociological model you're providing is beginning to flower nicely, at least in America.

You can plant *anything* in the fertile soil of the Western mentality, Pilot thought. That's half the trouble. It's fertile, but shallow. We need deeper roots if we're going to stay put there and take hold in more rudimentary societies.

The knock on the door had gone unnoticed, and when a small vial containing a horrible-looking green-black liquid appeared under Pilot's nose, he jumped.

"Taste this, Lonnie," Rebecca Schein said. For several months she and some of the others had been working in the kitchens devising sauces and flavourings capable of improving the taste of the food. Pilot sniffed the mouth of the vial, then took a small sip of the mixture inside.

"What's in it?"

"Mustard seed, wild garlic, basil, parsley and the brine from the black olives. Oh, and halite from the new salt beds. What do you think?"

"I love it." Pilot wiped his mouth with his sleeve and wondered what Eydos' supporters among the woolly-knicker-brigades would think if they knew how much he and the others hated the food they were forced to eat in the name of self-sufficiency. With the tang of garlic still teasing his taste buds, he said goodbye to Schein and went back to Maryburg's report.

> Awareness of you is well over 60% among your contemporaries. Most people's idealism has evaporated by their thirties, but you've managed to keep it stoked up for a lot of them. Apart from the old stand-by flirtations with basic environmental and social issues, they're beginning to seek out and attack the hidden sources of what they perceive as the rot around them. They don't approach them through organized pressure groups, but are challenging their friends and associates as unaffiliated individuals. That way, nobody gets called a subversive, a terrorist or an anarchist, and the catalysts of change stay out of public scrutiny, just like you hoped they would.
>
> To wrap this up, Lonnie, I know it's just a sample of 10,000 people out of 400 million, but when

> looked at from a distance, the results are encouraging. The questions now are: How can you continue to inspire your current supporters *and* win new ones; and, What can you do to fashion the trends we're seeing into something longer-lasting? Our Thinkers *want* you to have influence in the world, even if you haven't got it yet. To me, that's as good as having it. I sense that in Western Europe, Japan and the Antipodes, the trend is the same. There are some chinks of light beginning to appear in India and China, but the Middle East doesn't figure in the equation owing to religious and cultural interpretations. And there's too much strife in Africa for any meeting of minds there. The important point is that, in the U.S. at least, you've crossed over into the realms of possibility.
>
> – Bart

Pilot set the report down and pondered over what he had just read. Macushla had yet to cross into the realms of possibility as far as her own baby was concerned, being only two months pregnant. It was an interesting parallel. A baby born prematurely, although viable, would have difficulty surviving, and if it did, could possibly have inherent long-term defects. Conversely, although his own plan for Phase Two had its framework in place, the details in the blueprint had been changing with world events for the past ten years. He couldn't give birth to his Big Idea now even if he wanted to.

If his Great Aunts' maxim was, 'Anything for a simple life', Pilot's was, 'Nothing *without* a simple life'. The stage on which he now played out the role of leader of the world's smallest nation was providing him at last with an environment and a simplicity conducive to clear thinking and creativity: the womb-like comfort of their geodesic dome; the solar heating orb dispensing warmth like a stout grandmother; his partner spinning schemes with him at all hours; and best of all, unhurried sexual marathons under diffused moonlight to the music of wind chimes.

XX

In a penthouse apartment in São Paolo's plushest apartment building, Diogo was slaughtering the last of the family's pigs in the bathtub. Blood spattered the gold taps and lay in sticky pools at the bottom of the bath. Mains water to wash it down had disappeared a few days after the power required to fill the building's water tanks was lost, and the water in the plastic containers they'd hauled up 37 liftless floors was too precious to waste on cleaning. A makeshift barbeque pit in the kitchen sink, using splinters from a smashed up antique armoire, was being tended by Diogo's wife. None of the windows in the penthouse was designed to be opened, so they'd had to break one. With the building's ventilation system dead, the smoke from the fire rolled across the ceiling and over the powerless extractor fan and smoke detector towards the opening like a grey undulating sea. In the dining room, thirteen Rosenthal dinner plates had been set in preparation for the feast to come. The couple's seven children played happily in a back bedroom the size of a squash court, while their three surviving grandparents took in the magnificent views of São Paolo from the living room, coughing occasionally when the smoke dropped too low.

Forty miles to the east, the owners of the apartment, Brazil's top eye surgeon and her husband, were climbing into their Cessna TT at São José dos Campos airport for their planned breakout to Argentina, unaware that the plane's fuel had been siphoned out that morning by an enterprising teenager and sold to another pilot whose tank he had emptied the night before. So far, this little scam had netted him a small fortune in jewelry and expensive handbags –

Brazilian currency having become worthless. His stash would soon be augmented by the eye surgeon's diamond wedding ring…

The situation in Brazil was as would be expected in any fragile society whose structure suddenly collapses. Having relied almost entirely on packaged foods which were suddenly nowhere to be found, and with international food aid falling woefully short of their needs because of shortages elsewhere, Brazilians in their thousands, faced with the ultimate inconvenience of starvation, had been leaving the cities and towns in a vain search for land on which to grow food. Those who hadn't been part of the initial surge north into Central America and Mexico before those countries had secured their borders, now found themselves imprisoned by ocean to the east and the troops of Brazil's continental neighbours to the west, north and south.

The middle and upper classes had taken flight. In their attempts to reach the US and Europe, and with no commercial flights out, many well-heeled refugees had taken to their private planes and luxury yachts, often with inadequate supplies and non-existent navigational skills. It had followed that many of these wealthy Brazilian Boat People had been swept down by the prevailing current into the South Atlantic Gyre and a languishing death through cold and thirst. The last known sighting of the President of Brazil himself had been at Rio's most exclusive marina.

The rot had begun to set in years before with the cancellation of the Olympic Games due to global instability. This event had landed the knock-out blow on Brazil's fragile glass jaw. Her collapse – not just on paper, which happened to countries all the time, but in real and tragic terms – had been no surprise to Lonnie Pilot. He had followed the news knowingly as 220 million people had been thrown back in time a thousand years – a far bloodier version of what had already taken place in Greece, Italy, Spain and Portugal. Only the millions of shanty town and slum dwellers were experiencing a happy upturn in their standard of living. Many from the favelas now occupied the empty hotels and luxury apartment blocks of Rio de Janeiro and São Paolo, albeit without utilities. But that was nothing new for them. Dysentery and cholera were rife. That was nothing new either.

The outside world had been conspicuous by its absence during the disastrous chain of events in Brazil. While this much-respected member of the Country Club jigged and foamed in the throes of a fatal fit, the other members could only look on in mute horror.

The citizens of Eydos, by contrast, were seeing it as another arrow for their quiver…

XXI

Steven Schwartzman, like Harvey Giles, had decided to settle on the island after his contract had expired. But, unlike Giles, who had brought his long-time lover to the island to work as a physiotherapist, there was no woman in Schwartzman's life, just his plants, foremost among them Jane Lavery's bonsai tree, which he had adopted and lovingly nurtured over the years. Lately, he'd been experimenting with new varieties of edible flora, aided by the recent installation of three vast greenhouses to replace the island's weather-beaten polytunnels. (The greenhouses had been donated by Clarence Drance, former Disciple of the Seraphic Prodigy, who had derived material salvation in California from a chain of cycle-through juice bars.)

One entire greenhouse, plus half the other, was given over to Paola Rendina and her team of gardeners, with a small section reserved for the horticultural education of the island's children. Doctor Steve was allowed free rein to potter about in the remaining half. He was well aware of Rebecca Schein's sauce experiments, but as for people not liking the taste of his plants, Schwartzman considered it more of a challenge than an insult and he was determined to come up with something novel and nutritious which could be eaten without being smothered in sauce first.

The answer lay in kelp, laver and, most of all, rock tripe, a strange lichen that had begun growing in dense mats over the rocks and was nourishing if not tasty – something like licorice-flavored tapioca pudding. To improve the palatability of these abundant natural food sources, the Doctor had begun cultivating samphire, coriander, wild basil, corn mint, fenugreek, lovage, parsley and sand leek, a relative of garlic.

Before the arrival of the greenhouses, only lentils and other leguminous plants had been grown with any success outdoors and in the hoophouses, but now everyone looked forward to regular harvests of Rendina's aubergines, peppers, marrows, tomatoes, spinach, French beans, and lettuce. The third greenhouse was a living, hydroponic memorial to Jane Lavery, with Moringo oleifera leaves being harvested by the bushel-load.

In other areas things were also coming together. Ten crew had been apprenticed to a retired fisherman from Newlyn, who had spent two months teaching them how and where to fish. The boat Pilot had purchased from him was a traditional Newlyn trawler with a difference – it carried no nets. Pilot had no intentions of joining in the gang rape of the North Atlantic. All their fish would be caught by handlines. It was a time-consuming process, owing to decimated fish stocks off Nillin. As a result, every single line-caught fish was given reverential treatment when it reached the kitchen.

The fish and the newly arrived herd of goats were bringing welcomed variety to the Nillin menu. As was the case with the male lambs, which could not be milked, the male kids also posed a dilemma. The solution was considered cruel by many. But it did furnish the settlers with a different tasting source of protein. Only a few people knew the identity of the volunteer who had come forward to take on the unpopular job of dispatching the young animals – a task she performed with skill, speed and compassion.

Then there were the orchards. For three years, Harvey Giles had been struggling with the problem of how to make fruit trees grow on the island. From his early experiments he had determined which varieties did and did not like living in sediment and had then instituted a massive grafting project. Large pockets of deep, rich sediment had been discovered in sheltered areas sixteen miles southeast of Nillin and it was in these that the orchards had been planted – apple mainly, but also some plum, pear and peach stocks. They had their first fruit harvests after three years. After ten years, the orchards were well-established and productive enough to allow Eydos to cancel its apple imports from the Duchy of Cornwall.

The island's face was filling out daily, due mainly to the achievements of the lichen spores, grass pollens and other wind-borne immigrants. Ten years and eight months after emerging from the sea, less than a quarter of the shelf remained in its original grey and barren bleakness.

The other great natural gift to the island – its wind – was being harnessed by a new form of generator developed by one of Forrest Vaalon's companies. Instead of a machine of the windmill variety, this one, set atop the basin rim above Nillin, comprised an intake duct fifty metres across by eighteen inches high. Inside, over a thousand small propellers generated electricity at any wind speed over three knots. Being so low to the ground, the Wide Mouth Generator was visually unobtrusive, was far less prone to wind damage than blades on towers, and supplied more than enough power for the settlement's meager needs.

There was, however, one conventional wind turbine on the island, and this was being used with good effect at the barge landing site. The reason it had been erected there was to provide electricity for some very important visitors. The idea to turn the convoy into a 'sponge' with which to soak up knowledge and information of particular relevance to the Big Idea had been Macushla Mara's. "When it comes time to act, we can't afford to come across as ill-informed tree-huggers with no grasp of reality and no real understanding of the issues," she had argued. "And the best way to get inside the human machine is to talk to it… without giving too much away, of course."

Work parties had spent nearly a year preparing the site for its first guests. A large table with seating for twenty-four had been built inside *Bimbo's Kraal* and skylights installed in the deck above it; *King Solomon* was now a comfortable library containing books in sixteen languages; a cloister had been fashioned around the inner three barges of the middle row; flowers had been planted in cavities and crevices throughout the wreckage where none were growing wild already; and the canteen and messroom had been spruced up to two-star hotel standard.

Because of the angle at which *Ptolemy* was lying, it had been necessary to adjust her bunks and table tops to the horizontal, and this task, followed by the redecoration of all the cabins, had taken four months. A separate suite comprising bedroom, study, bathroom and kitchenette had been built in *Fort Lowell* to accommodate a person whose identity the crew knew, but were forbidden to reveal to outsiders.

Twenty people – identified by Forrest Vaalon as being in the vanguard of their respective fields of finance, medicine, climate change studies, industry, ecology, demographics, information technology and policy-making – were scheduled at monthly intervals to come to the island for two or three days to have their brains harvested through 'friendly inquisition', as Mara called it.

The first to arrive was a high-ranking Japanese executive from Toyota. Pilot wanted to know how malleable the motor industry was to change, what the main blocks to change were, and how these could be overcome. Although unable to speak for the other automotive giants, Mr. Takada was able to impart valuable information, only some of which was encouraging. *All* information was welcomed, though. After fifteen meetings, the islanders – individually and in their respective task groups – had received an education money can't buy, or in this case, through Forrest Vaalon's bottomless pockets, *did* buy.

Lonnie Pilot coasted gently downhill on his mountain bike, its flywheel storing energy with every rotation. As he approached the convoy for his third meeting with a high-ranking officer from the World Bank, he marveled at a sight which never failed to impress him. So ugly on the one hand and yet strangely beautiful and powerful on the other. Fourteen massive, rusting barge carcasses rose up before him and exuded a comforting stillness and steadfastness from their dead weight. Colourful strips of wild flowers seemed to tape the rusting hulls of the barges to the grey-green rock on which they rested. Over the years, billions upon billions of nutrient-laden particles – the dead skin shed by continental Europe, Africa and the Americas – had been carried on the wind to their current resting place at the base of each exposed barge side. There they had rested until the time came for the sleeping seeds within to awaken and throw back their covers.

On his arrival, Pilot went straight to Ptolemy's galley for some water. He was early and had three hours to kill before his meeting with the banker, but he had someone else with whom to kill them. Pilot finished his drink, climbed the ladder to *Fort Lowell's* deck, knocked on the door of the wheelhouse and went in…

Pilot knew that something was amiss when Serman met him at the top of the escarpment above Nillin with a face like death. "What's up, Aaron?"

"Josiah's dead." The words ripped through Pilot like bullets. Three seconds earlier, he had been brimming with purpose and hope, the rub-off from his productive meetings at the convoy. Now, all he could see were multiple images of Josiah Billy framed in black.

"How did… what happened?"

"He jumped off the cliff at the fjord entrance. Budd and Highbell were fishing just off shore and saw him drop," Serman said. "We haven't found his body yet. He left a couple of notes – one for us and one for Paola – plus this verse carved in wood, which we found at the top of the cliff." Serman handed over a large canvas sack, along with the note, which Pilot read first.

> *I'm sorry it's come to this. Suicide is a selfish act, especially among such a small and close band as we are. You're great people and I was proud to include myself as one of you. This voyage we're on is an impossible one, though. That's how I see it. We're going down with the rest of humanity sure as eggs is eggs and there's nothing we can do about it. I've wrestled for years trying to hold on to hope, but outside events keep ripping it out of my hands. That's the reality. It'll soon be over. I'm leaving the losing game early by way of the coward's exit. That in itself takes courage, right?*

Pilot folded the note and handed it back to Serman. "How's Paola taking it?"

"I don't know. Macushla's with her."

Pilot walked his bike into Nillin with the canvas bag under his arm and went straight to Josiah and Paola's dome. Inside, Billy's distraught partner was lying on her back staring at the ceiling, her eyes red-rimmed from crying. She clutched his four-page letter in her hand, but no length of explanation could have lessened her anguish. Macushla was sitting in a chair next to the bed, her hands folded over her belly. Pilot went over and hugged her, then stooped down and kissed Paola on the forehead. No words were necessary. He sat down next to his partner and placed his hands over hers. When Rendina at last closed her eyes and fell into a shallow sleep, Pilot whispered, "I had no idea Josiah was so near the edge."

"No one did. Not even Paola."

"He never talked to her about it?"

"That's what she told me."

Pilot remembered something he'd read in Billy's file – that he had attempted suicide once before after being dropped from the Ireland rugby squad – a flaw in his character that had now come back to bite them all. Then Pilot picked up the canvas bag containing Josiah's final poem, took out a length of weathered driftwood and held it up so that he and Macushla could both read it at the same time. It was short but potent.

When the Earth was flat we had a fear
Of falling off the edge.
Now the earth is round we've lost that fear,
And all hope of staying on.

XXII

May Day, as celebrated by the inhabitants of Eydos, didn't have the pagan or political connotations as elsewhere. The date was used instead as a collective birthday and was the second most important day in the island's calendar after August 4th. For Lonnie Pilot it also marked the anniversary of his meeting with Forrest Vaalon – in this case, eleven years.

Normally, it would have been a day of merrymaking, but Josiah Billy's suicide had thrown a blanket of melancholy over Nillin that was difficult to kick off. To lift the somber mood, Rebecca Schein suggested a moonlit bike race to the convoy and back in Billy's memory. Everyone but Paola Rendina, whose initial shock at the loss of her partner had been replaced by anger at his selfishness, thought this a great idea. Twenty years earlier, Schein's mother had killed herself with champagne and tramadol. But in the time since, Rebecca had reasoned that her mother's inner anguish must have far outweighed all other considerations, including the feelings of her teenage daughter. Schein had long ago forgiven her mother and took that same reasoning to Rendina's dome. It worked. Twenty minutes later, Paola wheeled her bike out to join the others. Only the women in the latter stages of pregnancy and those with young children (Eydos now had seven youngsters ranging in age from two months to four years) were missing from the start of the 'Tour d'Eydos'.

The first stage to the barges, being all downhill and with a strong following breeze, lulled everyone into a false sense of achievement, in marked contrast to the return leg, which presented not only the incline to fight against, but also a westerly wind gusting to 30mph.

Nirpal Banda won the race, but there was no one at the finish to cheer him home. Pilot himself, on coming in fifth from last, downed the remainder of a flagon of cider and went home, knowing Macushla would still be up. Three hours of painful uphill peddling had been a physical reminder to him of what lay ahead vis-á-vis their Big Idea and he needed to talk to her. Not about the speech they'd been painstakingly crafting for the past six months, but about how they were going to operationalize the concept.

For five years, the islanders had been applying their imagination and energy to analyzing global threats and concocting cures. They viewed each situation from afar, like Martians. But then, they were the nearest thing the Earth had to aliens. It certainly made for some novel thinking. Task groups had been formed around each issue – working independently, mostly, but in concert if two or more of the 'cancers' overlapped. One overriding peril seemed to engulf them all, and this forum Pilot led personally. Crew were encouraged to move from group to group to ensure that lines of thought would always be fresh, wide and inventive. As with any proposal, there had to be some kind of editorial shaping and polishing and this was exercised by Pilot, Mara and Serman. The final word on everything, however, was Lonnie Pilot's. The fact that Eydos had still not set out its stall in the outside world was because he felt they weren't yet ready. Ultimately, the Big Idea would be viewed as a preposterous intrusion if it were presented half-baked, so it was still in the oven.

Pilot's immediate problem was how to remove the tension that was beginning to grip him like angina. He lay fully dressed next to his partner for a long time, not wanting to wake her, but knowing that the tension in his body would soon permeate her sleep. It didn't take long.

"What are you thinking, Lonnie?" Mara asked.

It took him a few seconds to realize he was being spoken to. "Ah… I'm glad you're awake," he said. "What am I thinking… I was thinking about thought… about the thinking *processs*."

"And?"

"Here's the question. How do a billion cells in Person One's brain link together to write a poem… a billion cells in Person Two's split an atom… and a billion cells in Person Three's kill hitchhikers?"

"Or hurl themselves off a cliff," Macushla said.

Pilot stood up and peeled off his cycling shorts. "Speaking of cliffs, how do we get the brain cells of nine billion people to follow the same line of thought as ours and pull away in unison from the edge of *their* cliff?"

Macushla helped Lonnie pull his T-shirt up and over his head. "First of all, I don't think you need all nine billion," she said. "There are leaders and followers. All we need to do is convert the leaders, and the rest will follow."

"Hmmm. Mrs. Normal raises her ugly head again."

"Mrs. Who?"

"Normal." The eleven-year-old image of Jane Lavery sitting across from him in *Ptolemy's* messroom flitted across Pilot's mind's eye. "Normal isn't always good, Cush, it's what *usually happens*. We don't want leaders and followers. *Everybody* needs to be enfranchised in their own salvation and liberation. There's a blanket of fear and apprehension descending on the entire world and it'll take *all* of us to throw it back."

"But in that world there's a natural hierarchy of leaders and followers. Always has been, always will be."

Pilot helped his partner out of her nightdress, laid her on her side with her back to him, placed his arm over her and began stroking her seven-month-old bump and ripening breasts.

"When the human world reaches the edge of the precipice," Mara said, "the first person to come along with an understanding of leverage and a strong enough stick can either send the boulder crashing, or maneuver it back from the rim, depending on their own particular leaning. The right idea, the right appeal to mass emotions, the right promises – these are the strong sticks. Understanding leverage is knowing when to use them. The magic moment isn't a long one, but the impact can be long-lasting, and either constructive or destructive. Spartacus, Lenin, Mao, Hitler, McCarthy, Gorbachev, Bin Laden, Chuan Wa, Williams, Tomashvili – they all knew when to exert leverage."

Pilot moved his hand to the base of Macushla's skull and traced her vertebrae lightly with his fingertips, up and down, going lower and lower with each stroke. "The magic moment isn't far away now," he whispered, stopping at her tailbone. He knew that she knew where his hand was going to go next, and seconds later her wetness confirmed it. He moved his head downwards and she automatically pulled her knees towards her chest. His fingertips passed her tailbone and continued south, quickly replaced by his lips and his tongue as he expertly began leading her on a short but thrill-packed journey to completion. When she could bear no more pleasure, Macushla pulled Pilot's face from between her legs and waited for the tremors to die down. After a short rest, she shifted her position, rolled her lover over, kissed his chest and began moving her head slowly down his torso…

When Lonnie was spent, and before he could get his breath back, Macushla did what she did after every blow job. Talk. "Those electric maps you get in town squares that light up the route between where you are and where you want to go when you push a button… that's the brain at work," she said. "One single route linking centillions of brain cells lights up and the connection becomes the thought. If you then want to express this thought to someone else, you have to get all those bits of information down to the speech warehouse and pack them into boxes. The boxes are words and sentences, but because they're too small to accommodate the full thought, half the idea gets left on the floor. That's why saying something is never as rich and complete as the original thought."

Macushla's words were like falling leaves and took several seconds to settle on Pilot's consciousness. "Some of the cleverest people are the least articulate," he said eventually, taking his partner's hand and gently placing it over his testicles. He relaxed into the feeling and was about to power down his brain again when another notion appeared from nowhere. "Do you believe there's such a thing as extra sensory perception?" he asked. "I think that if we practiced more we could master mind-reading. All the basic emotions, like fear, hunger, greed, amusement, lust and contentment have chemical and electrical fingerprints. They're the same whether you're an antelope, a squirrel or a human. Identifying these thoughtprints, or emotionprints is just a case of having a developed sixth sense – of having the ability to interpret the information the other five senses are collecting. There's nothing mysterious about – "

Pilot stopped abruptly, sensing he was alone in the room. He leaned over Macushla and listened to her soft, rhythmic breathing. She'd been asleep for the past two minutes, dashing any ideas he may have had for a second helping of the only activity that was capable of disengaging his overactive brain.

Franz Barta arrived in Nillin for the latest in a series of meetings Pilot had been having with the man to realign the island's financial affairs. Vaalon's slice of wealth invested in Eydos' name had always posed a dilemma. Pilot considered it dirty because of its connections, direct or indirect, with the very industries and businesses that, like plaque, were causing the world's slow decay. So, with the consensual agreement of his cohorts, he had decided to sell the holdings and funnel the capital into projects considered clean and worthy of patronage, for example, the Wide Mouth Generator.

Barta had been given the job of processing these projects and had already submitted a hundred and ninety-three to Eydos. Of these, forty-six groups and individuals, whose ideas the islanders felt deserved risk capital, were given immediate support. As the last item on his agenda, Barta presented a new application for venture capital from a man in Australia who had a proposition for harnessing energy via the heat in the Earth's mantle – *Pyrogeneration*, he called it.

"Good luck to him. We'll study it later and let you know. One more thing, Franz." Pilot handed Barta a map of the world with half a dozen circles drawn on it at various latitudes. "We need you to find six serviceable office blocks in these locations and ready them for occupation. The particulars of what goes in them will follow."

"That I can do." Barta put the map in his briefcase and walked to the helipad with Pilot. When the helicopter had disappeared from sight, Pilot took *Pyrogeneration* back to his dome, imagining the Australian scientist hard at work in his laboratory with a saucepan of porridge, a pancake and some spam simmering over a Bunsen burner.

XXIII

Pilot awoke late, quickly donned track suit and trainers and arrived at the satellite dish for his match with Kerry Jackson just before eight. His opponent had not yet arrived, so Pilot set down his basket of tennis balls and began to practice.

The dish, a giant of its type, had been airlifted onto the island unsolicited by a communications baron who saw it as a possible lever into the minds of the islanders. The dish had been accompanied by 40 HD receivers and all the other cabling and connections required to drown Eydos in soap operas and reality TV shows. The natives, unimpressed by these beads, had voted to return everything but the satellite dish, which was locked at a 45 degree downward angle. Rackets and balls completed the equipment needed to play 'satellite tennis'. Jackson was currently at the top of the ladder and Pilot had been looking forward to the game for weeks, having worked his way up from twentieth to second. The sky was cloudy, the air not too hot, and there wasn't a breath of wind. Perfect conditions.

"Nice day for it," Jackson said, tardily timing his appearance in true champion style.

Pilot's first serve landed just outside the circular court, drawn to three times the diameter of the satellite dish standing at the edge of the circle. Fault. His second serve landed at about 4 o'clock on the 'clock' and two inches in from the line. Jackson's scrambled return bounced weakly off the dish into the centre of the court, allowing Pilot time to pick his spot on the dish and deliver a point-winning smash.

Fifteen minutes later, the score stood at twenty-thirteen to Jackson (the first player to reach 30 points won). Pilot gradually clawed his way back to within a point of his opponent at twenty-six to twenty-five, but at that score the game ended, never to be resumed.

The sheep sensed it a split second before Pilot and Jackson did – an infinitesimal vibrato rising from deep below the surface of the island. At first it merely tickled the players' soles, but soon grew in intensity and pitch to a level that struck terror into their souls.

"EARTHQUAKE," someone behind them shouted. Throughout Nillin, the residents were abandoning their domes in favour of open territory, erroneously so, as the domes' geodesic structure could withstand the most severe seismic activity. Those who knew this simply preferred to see, as well as feel, what was happening around them.

Pilot dropped his racket and sprinted towards his dome, reaching it just as Macushla was exiting, carrying their two month old daughter, Pandora, in her arms. The ground was shaking so violently, it was impossible to stand, so they found a soft patch of moss and sat down. Each was lost in their own worst thoughts and no words were exchanged. Pandora gurgled at her mother's breast, unaware of the drama unfolding around her. Eventually, Pilot grounded himself, took Mara's hand in his and gave it a reassuring squeeze. He peered beyond the cottonwood wall of the harbour, trying to catch a glipse of the water level to see if it was rising, but his view of the shoreline was blocked. The tremors were becoming more violent and Pilot could see panicked looks on those faces around him not already thrust between knees in 'crash position'. A particularly brutal tremor pulled Macushla's nipple from Pandora's mouth and sent Pilot's heart rate to 180.

A loud crash heralded the demise of the satellite tennis dish, followed by another as their communications mast hit the ground, fatally crushing Jim McConie under its metal skeleton.

"ARE WE SINKING?" someone shouted.

"WE'VE SUNK FIVE OR SIX FEET AND ARE STILL SINKING," Aaron Serman called from his position higher up.

Dubi Horvat, who had been manning the communications dome with McConie and was as yet unaware of her colleague's death, crawled up to Pilot with the first few words of a transmission from the IGP. Pilot took the printout and tried to steady his hand, which was being violently shaken by the earthquake. 'EMERGENCY,' he read. 'BATTEN DOWN THE HATCHES, YOU'RE IN FOR A –', and that was it.

"We lost our connection when the mast went down," Horvat explained.

Some of the other mothers were sobbing into their babies' necks, certain that the cold Atlantic would soon be swallowing them whole. It felt as though they were riding a derailed train over cobblestones – next stop, the bottom of the Bay of Biscay.

For fifteen minutes, the fledgling island of Eydos shivered in its cold bath, the humanity on its skin counting and treasuring every second it remained above sea level. After a particularly bone-jarring seizure deep within the rock, Pilot locked eyes with Macushla's to fix what he was sure would be his last vision on Earth. There was one final, awful, back-breaking jolt and then it was all over…

In the IGP building in London, six scientists were hunched over a computer monitor watching readings being transmitted by the IGP research ship *Pima Verde* 200 miles west of Nillin. Five thousand miles away in his ranch in Taos, New Mexico, Forrest Vaalon was instantly in the room with them via speakerphone. 'Why didn't we see this coming, Geoff?' the disembodied voice asked one of the geologists.

The man in the firing line could only stand mutely staring at the screen.

"The anomaly was too small to pick up through general monitoring, Mr. Vaalon," one of his colleagues said. "But now that we know it's there, we've been able to lock on and follow it."

'What *is* it?'

"A localized extrusion on the dorsal plane of the pyrocoagulum," the man said. "About a mile long by two hundred metres wide… with a mean height of fifteen metres. Half an hour ago it impacted with the crust about seven miles north of Nillin. At the point of initial impact it read… hang on." The man double-clicked one of the measurement bars and with his left arrow took the readings back thirty minutes. "Six point three magnitude."

"Is Eydos still there?" Vaalon asked.

"We'll get back to you on that, Sir," the voice in London said.

Although they couldn't see it, Forrest Vaalon was the picture of despair – a broken man in a broken world. He closed his eyes and pressed his hands over his temples. Could it all be ending here – a hundred men, women and children washed into oblivion at *his* instigation – his life's work nullified by a geological hangnail snagged on the sheet under their island? The mental anguish had awakened the angry tumour inside him and he swallowed a pill to relieve the sharp pain assaulting his gut. Before the medication could take effect, a signal from his laptop indicated an encrypted message coming in from Eydos. He jerked upright, typed in the decryption code and waited anxiously for the communication to appear. Seconds later it burst onto his screen and Vaalon's anguish fell away like a bath towel.

In his message, Pilot reported the loss of Jim McConie, the seven injured – two serious, the intense level of fear and panic still pervading, and the hasty re-erection of the communication mast. *What's the prognosis, Forrest? We need one FAST.* At the same time, London got back to Vaalon with news that the tremors were receding and that the transponder installed five years earlier on the headland above Nillin showed a reading only 2.49 metres lower than it had been at the start of the day. The important thing was that the reading had stabilized.

Immediately, Vaalon shot back a reply to Pilot, repeating what he had just been told from London and reassuring Lonnie that, to the best of their knowledge, the worst was over. 'You don't have to stay, though,' he concluded. 'We can fly everyone out now with Jim's body.'

'Yes,' Pilot fired back without hesitation. There was a pause, then a qualifying transmission settled across Vaalon's screen. 'By *yes*, I mean, YES, I *do* have to stay.' Anyone else who wants to go, can.'

When Pilot, Mara and Pandora returned home later, Jennifer Spring's *The Destruction of Eydos* was still hanging defiantly from the cross struts of the dome.

Three months after Eydos' brush with drowning, three 'lifepods' ordered from The Antigua and Barbuda Salvage Company arrived on the island. Unlike the open-topped lifeboats of old, these were watertight fiberglass modules with a hatch similar to a submarine's. There was a forty person capacity for each pod – more than enough to accommodate all the settlers and any other people who might be on the island in the event of an emergency evacuation. These particular lifepods had once served the Carribbean cruise ship, *Sargassso Sunrise*, now lying at the bottom of the sea off Tortuga, and had proved their effectiveness by saving the lives of over a thousand of that unfortunate ship's passengers. Lonnie Pilot had acquired three of them for $10,000 each. An open space in the middle of Nillin was designated for their deployment and metal rings sunk in the rock to secure them with quick release knots. In front of the three lifepods, engraved into the moss in one metre high letters, were the words, 'EMERGENCY EXIT'.

Work on the new harbour wall, which had to be raised three metres in line with the raised sea level, was going well, as was the blasting to produce the hardcore required as landfill behind the wall. What the earthquake had created was a new deep water harbour capable now of receiving much larger vessels. This fact had given Pilot an idea, which he jotted down and put with the hundreds of others that were beginning to collect inside the admin dome.

Early morning milking had just finished when the 'djum-djum-djum' of an approaching helicopter was heard in the distance. Pilot watched with curiosity as the machine set down and a single figure stepped onto the rock. As he watched his old friend approach, he noticed that Fridrik Geirsson had barely aged in eleven years. The hair was still predominantly blond as opposed to his own, which was now more salt than pepper. But the closer Geirsson got, the sicker Pilot felt. With that sinking sensation associated with falling from a great height, and with an overwhelming sense of dread, Pilot began preparing himself for the news he could see etched on Geirsson's face.

"We didn't want to tell you by radio," Geirsson said.

"When did he die?"

"Yesterday afternoon. It was expected and it was peaceful."

Invisible black curtains were already being drawn across Pilot's face.

"This is for you, Lonnie," Geirsson said, handing over an envelope.

Pilot led Geirsson to a table at the far end of the mess hall, opened the envelope and unfolded a letter of several pages. As the words leapt athletically off the page onto Pilot's retinas, Forrest Vaalon seemed far from deceased.

'*Dear Lonnie,*

The fact I didn't get a chance to speak to you in person from the proverbial death-bed is to be regretted. We don't choose the time or manner of our natural deaths, so this letter will have to do, sad though it is for me not to have seen you one last time.

Paradoxically, and at no disrespect to myself, with my death the integrity of Eydos has been purified. There are few modern day capitalists greater than I was and, although I used my wealth as a means to an end, that doesn't excuse the fact that for the past fifty or sixty years I've played a leading roll in bringing your '*boulder*' *to the edge of the cliff.*

I'm sure the reality of my position didn't go unnoticed by you. In mitigation, I've always tried to maintain some *integrity in my business dealings and in this respect my hands are clean. My feet, however, are filthy. I've walked through the effluent of free enterprise up to my thighs and this marks me out as a vandal of epic proportion. So be it. You alone know the reason. The effluent will never rise above your ankles, because of what* Ruth *and I have done. And because of us, little* Pandora *will, with luck, never even see it, let alone set foot in it.*

There's truth in the adage 'you have to speculate to accumulate'. *What I've done is extend it a step further.* You have to accumulate to eradicate. *My accumulations in this world have allowed you to eradicate their necessity in yours, which was the plan all along. Over our three generations – ours, yours, your childrens' – the initial task will have been completed. Something will have been eradicated from the world, even if only in your small part of it.*

You, Lonnie, are a child of both worlds. Born in mine and fed on it; replanted in yours. But your very knowledge of my *world ensures you'll never be totally free of it. Not so your children. What they do with their lives and what you do with the rest of yours is out of my control. There's no reason to think your children will be born 'special'. They'll be exceptional only in that they'll have been born into the rarefied atmosphere of Eydos. That's all you can count on as being certain, but it's enough.*

I edit this letter every month to take in new thoughts and to keep abreast of breaking news. I have an overpowering feeling that this month the envelope will be sealed once and for all.

I could ramble on for pages and probably would if I didn't feel so tired. In closing I must tell you again how inspired I find your initial ideas for Phase Two. I've been giving a lot of thought over the past few months to your Big Idea as you call it, and you're correct. The time to push is almost here. Sooner than we expected or would have hoped, but here nonetheless. As for my part in it, there's nothing further I can do here. Knowing the framework is in place –

in your mind anyway – makes it easier for me to take my leave. There's nothing to be lost now by hesitating.'

There was a laboured signature at the bottom of the page, followed by a P.S.:

One last thing. To ensure the works you propose are not hindered by lack of finance, I have set up The Ruth and Forrest Vaalon Trust, currently valued at $9 billion, to help oil your wheels. As of today Forrest Vaalon, personally, is penniless, and it feels good.

Pilot sat quietly for a time, then slipped the letter into its envelope and looked back over what little of the island was still visible in front of a thick fog rolling in from the east.

As he lay in bed with Macushla and Pandora that night in their dome, Pilot was feeling a strange combination of sadness and elation – the two emotions perfectly in balance. The past was lying in a coffin in Manhattan; the future, in large boxes of notes, print-outs and flash drives in the admin dome.

XXIV

Associated Press. – Phoenix, Arizona, Tuesday, February 7th, 1830 MDT.
Over a hundred hospital admissions this morning have been attributed to an atmospheric inversion, which created a blanket of noxious air over central Phoenix late yesterday afternoon. Residents – especially the old, infirm and young – have been advised to stay indoors until the air quality returns to safe levels…

CNN – Phoenix, Arizona, Wednesday, February 8th, 1500 MDT.
'BAD AIR' IN ARIZONA KILLS SEVEN. The cocktail of carbon monoxide and other lethal gases which has been trapped over metropolitan Phoenix since Monday has now killed seven people, hospital authorities report. Dozens more are being treated for serious respiratory difficulties. Meteorologists say there is no sign of the atmospheric inversion abating for at least a week and are recommending evacuation to outlying areas, where the air remains good.

BBC NEWS – Phoenix, Arizona, Thursday, February 9th, 0730 MDT.
POISON AIR DEATH TOLL 'OFF THE CHARTS' – PRESIDENT DECLARES STATE OF EMERGENCY. A sudden and deadly deterioration of breathable air in Phoenix 'killed several thousand people overnight', an observer on the ground has reported. Nothing

of this magnitude has been seen since 200 people were asphyxiated by traffic fumes in Bangkok three years ago. A shortage of breathing apparatus for emergency workers is making rescue of the sick and retrieval of the dead extremely difficult. Although some people have left the city, it is thought that many thousands still remain. 'Our citizens have been so debilitated by the lack of breathable air that they cannot even panic,' Governor Lopez stated at 0530 Mountain Time. 'The situation here is critical and we need immediate assistance.' Washington responded in the past hour with a Federal Declaration of a State of Emergency in Phoenix.

The Walter Wexler Blog – Wednesday, February 15th.
Think of a hundred Twin Towers and you'll get an idea of the final massive loss of life that occurred in Phoenix last week. 'Atmospheric inversion', my ass. Those people killed themselves with their own cars. Just look at the numbers. The carbon monoxide blanket woven from their own exhaust fumes measured a massive 300ppm at its most concentrated. There was no way out of the city for those poor people – even on foot. TWO HUNDRED AND EIGHTY-FOUR THOUSAND, FOUR HUNDRED AND SEVENTY-EIGHT. *I'll give you that figure again in numerals – 284,478. That's 20% of the population of Phoenix, snuffed out in a few painful breaths. I don't want to say I told you so, but didn't I warn about this kind of disaster happening in our country three years ago? I told you so. It was only a matter of time before the isobars, temperature, wind, or in this case, lack of it, and our own deadly emissions, got together and conspired to kill us all in the perfect storm…*

Round the refectory table, Lonnie Pilot, Len Wenlight and Macushla Mara, nursing fourteen-month-old Pandora, were eating North Ronaldsay sheep yogurt and talking about the horrific events in Arizona they'd been following on the internet for the past week. Wenlight was there in his capacity as the island's 'embedded journalist of choice'. He'd been trying in vain to glean details of Eydos' proposals for the forthcoming conference, but Pilot continually stonewalled him.

Never had there been more call for an Earth Summit. In the twelve years since Eydos had risen from the sea, the globe's human cancer had progressed from 'critical' to one stage below inoperable. Population had grown by 1.7 billion, putting unbearable pressure on the world's vital organs. This, in spite of the H7N7 Equine-1 flu pandemic having killed 50 million people when it crossed over to humans two years previously. Through all this global upheaval, the doctor-politicians of the Earth's A&E ward remained inactive – frozen like rabbits in the headlights.

All but one. If there was one politician who commanded universal respect among her peers and the world at large, it was the Secretary General of the United Nations, Lim Lin Hok. To call her a 'politician' was a slur on her character. She was outspoken but always fair; single-minded, but flexible when necessary; and had brokered three international peace deals in the past twelve months alone. That she had been corresponding with Lonnie Pilot through encrypted messaging for two years and knew more about the Eydos package than anyone off-island, was the world's best-kept secret.

The idea to hold the summit on Eydos had been Pilot's, but Lim had presented it to the world as hers. "Nillin is as neutral a meeting place as we will ever find," she had argued. "Holding the Conference on Eydos will allow us to view our problems and broker our solutions from a unique and unprecedented perspective – an out-of-body experience through which we will all benefit."

On a flat area of the basin just outside Nillin, a vast geodesic structure a hundred and fifty metres in diameter and fifty metres high had been built. Inside, seating for four thousand people had been installed. Scattered around the 'Mother Dome', as it was called, were smaller 'baby domes' for private meetings, catering, communications, medical facilities, generators, chemical toilets etc.

In just under a month, three idle cruise ships would be slipping into Nillin's new deep water harbour to deliver delegations from every country on earth to 'the shrinking island with the growing credibility' – cruise guests by night, delegates by day. Top of the agenda of the emergency congress were the crippling economic blood clots, social hemorrhaging and environmental heart attacks the world had been suffering throughout most of the participants' lifetimes and before.

After years of ever-widening drought, Australia had virtually run out of all fresh water, its entire population huddled around only two or three locations in the Southeast. Before the rains finally came to give temporary respite, a number of Australians out of desperation had decided to abandon ship and sail uninvited to water-rich New Zealand. Four hundred of these antipodean water migrants had died in their yachts and cruisers, either from thirst or by drowning. The situation down under was dire – the deaths, a stark warning of worse to come.

Los Angeles was having severe water shortages of her own, caused mainly by the antics of pressure group CWC – Colorado Water for Coloradans. CWC militants had blown up pipelines and disabled numerous pumping stations crucial for the extraction and delivery of *their* H20 to California. The National Guard had been mobilized in both states to ensure the residents of Beverly Hills did not go thirsty.

As for Phoenix, only a small percentage of the hundreds of thousands of citizens evacuated to cleaner mountain air had felt confident enough to return to their city. Five other conurbations on three continents had only just escaped similar loss of all breathable air during the four months leading up to Phoenix, a tragedy that had been waiting to happen and cared not where it received its cue.

The celebrated cure for AIDS had merely taken the brakes off Africa's unsustainable population growth. More babies were being born than were starving to death. Irreversible shortages of water had led to states of war between no less than eight African nations. The bloodiest of these conflicts – between South Africa and Angola over possession of the Namibian aquafir, Ohangwena II – made the Colorado-California water war seem like a bun fight.

By contrast, in India over a million people a month were crossing the divide from poverty into full consumerhood. The extra demand on resources and energy on the sub-continent was breaking the world's back, as was the ever-widening rift between rich and poor.

Global warming was running away from all measures to curb it. The Maldives, Marshall Islands, Tuvalu and Vanuatu had all been lost to rising sea levels, as had low-lying coastal regions in Bangladesh, India, China and Vietnam. Compounding the problem was the insufficient land at higher elevations to support displaced coastal populations. The crisis facing the Philippines, Indonesia and seven other nations was the incursion of saltwater into their fresh water aquifers. Even Eydos had lost 5% of its landmass, all from its eastern coastline, and Nillin harbour was two feet deeper than it had been after the earthquake.

Subtropical dry zones had been pushed up into the American southwest and southern Europe, and down into southern Australia, making those regions increasingly susceptible to prolonged and intense droughts. La Niña and el Niño didn't know if they were coming or going. And arctic warming had caused the polar Jetstream to meander north-south, causing more temperature extremes in Europe, Canada and the northern States of the US. The vagaries of global warming had brought with it global *cooling*. The Gulf Stream and North Atlantic Drift had shifted to a more southerly course, leaving Eydos, Ireland, The United Kingdom and much of northern Europe under temperatures more in keeping with their high latitudes. It was already being likened to the Little Ice Age of the sixteenth to the nineteenth centuries.

In the ever-widening tornado belt of the American interior, 'Thornadoes', as the media dubbed them, were wreaking havoc. The worst of the half dozen thornadoes that had hammered the United States – Storm #817 – had laid a winding, nine hundred mile long by two mile wide highway of devastation from Lubbock, Texas, to Madison, Wisconsin, well north of normal tornado patterns. A wind speed of 329 miles an hour, the highest ever recorded on Earth, had been logged 50 miles east of Kansas City. If Storm #817 hadn't veered westwards just short of Chicago, the death toll of sixty thousand could conceivably have been six *hundred* thousand. The insurance industry was in meltdown, unable to keep up with claims or meet payouts.

Further south, the phenomenon known as 'Marine Plastic Massing' had closed the Panama Canal from the west. A floating plastic island, one hundred and fifty miles across and an eighth of a mile deep in places, had lodged itself within the bowl of the Gulf of Panama, effectively 'plugging' the canal. Consisting of an amalgam of flotsam and jetsam from the Japanese tsunami of 2010 and the California-Oregon tsunami of 2016, the plastic island was proving impossible to move or break up. There was even talk of digging a *new* Panama Canal through it – a proposal opposed by religious groups who felt that the hundreds of thousands of Japanese and American corpses encased within it should be left in peace.

Also on the agenda for the conference was the on-going rot of corporate Earth. After Eastern Europe's wholesale turn towards the capitalist West in the late eighties and early nineties, the people there had found they were *still* facing in the wrong direction. Unemployment, economic chaos and, more importantly, disillusion, was the rule, not the exception. People in Minsk, Tbilisi and Bucharest had begun to starve to death. The 'dirty bomb' detonated outside the Kremlin, killing fifteen thousand on the spot and fatally irradiating a further forty thousand, was the worst in a growing spate of rogue attacks using weapons of mass destruction. The glut of small arms and munitions in circulation worldwide had rendered law enforcement impotent in many countries. Tombstone-style gunfights, using real bullets, were taking place hourly in the streets of Mexico City, Naples and Marseille.

Those that the Eastern Bloc had turned to with such high hopes – The United States and Europe in particular – were having a problem of their own. The medical community called it Societal Disintegration Anxiety Syndrome. SDAS was what happened when you rocked all those things that made Westerners feel secure – their jobs, their financial institutions, their hopes and prospects, the very fabric of their lives. Those with a sense of humour remaining likened it, in America anyway, to 'Linus without his blanket'.

Just three months earlier, the digital data collapse everyone predicted *would* happen *did* happen. On reaching nine zettabytes of data – a billion terabytes of information for every person alive on Earth, the world's information ocean simply froze over. The 'machine' of online selling, stock trading, banking and social networking had edged beyond human capacities to control and oversee its automated processes. Dirty data entering the 'ocean' had triggered system failures across the globe, bringing trade and communication to a standstill. People couldn't fix the problem because they no longer understood the colossal tangle of interconnected software that had caused it. What's more, digital currency, which had all but replaced physical money in more advanced countries, had also been frozen within the silicon chips that housed it. Paper dollars, euros, pounds, rupees, yuan and yen were being printed by the billions in an attempt to unblock trade. And retailing, which had been operating almost entirely in cyberspace was being returned to the street – to the flea markets, bazaars and market stalls of its birth. It was back to zero for millions of businesses and their billions of employees.

People were looking to their leaders for answers, but they weren't getting any. Unemployment and hopelessness were drying up fragile societies like brushwood, ignitable by the smallest spark. In Northern Ireland this had resulted in the highest single-day death toll in the Province's history, as Protestant and Catholic gunmen once again took to the streets. Across Europe and the US, suicide had quadrupled, as had rape. The upper class crimes of company fraud and embezzlement had reached unprecedented levels. This, coupled with an almost ten-fold increase in murder, armed robbery and petty theft, had served to capsize and drown the West's judicial systems, entrenching SDAS still deeper into the psyche of its citizens.

Infant capitalism, suckling the teats of cheap labour, had been passed first to the BRICS – Brazil, Russia, India and China, then to the MINTS – Mexico, Indonesia, Nigeria and Turkey, and then to the PIPES – Pakistan, Iran, the Philippines and Ethiopia. The cradle of capitalism had at last fallen from the tree and now lay in a billion pieces on the ground. Nowhere was this more visible than in Great Britain where four major conurbations seethed under martial law and smoldered in the ashes of the worst rioting ever experienced in a temperate zone country.

And the baby? No capitalist nation had ever thought to ask itself what it would do when the markets for its products and services either choked or dried up. With world trade log-jammed by overproduction and paralyzed by the data crash, the capitalist sun had reached its nadir.

All these events had served to shift the centre of gravity of Pilot's symbolic boulder to that very position of imbalance he'd been waiting for, but hadn't expected quite so soon. The stick Eydos had fashioned to lever the boulder away from the edge was ready and waiting to be placed in position.

With the Summit less than four weeks away, Pilot was edgy. Everyone was doing what they could to calm him down, including Pandora, who was the picture of placidity and contentment at her mother's breast.

Len Wenlight, who'd been sitting quietly in a corner, could contain himself no longer. "We're fucked, guys," he said. "Hog-tied. Trousers down. Fucked. You'd think every acid-dead tree, every failed harvest and skin cancer, every inch of new desert and every teenage heroin death would count towards prising our grip from the time bomb. Instead, we just seem to clutch it tighter. Our technological advances are like double-edged swords. GM crops that can grow in sand, new ways of squeezing oil out of a stone… they just lure us into a false sense of security where we think we can carry on reproducing until the cows come home."

"They came home 250 years ago, Len," Pilot said. "We have a few ideas about that."

"*Eydosians for the Defense of the Earth*," Wenlight said.

"What?"

"E-D-E. Eydosians for the Defense of the Earth. Twelve years ago I set up another E-D-E – Englanders for the Defense of Eydos. You never knew this, Lonnie, but it was EDE who persuaded the Royal Navy to withdraw her sneaky submarines from your waters."

Pilot's jaw dropped. "I'll be damned, Len. How did you manage to – "

"These ideas you've got," Wenlight interrupted, "they'd better be good. If you put rancid carrots in the shop, no one's going to buy them."

"You would if they were the last carrots on Earth. Anyway, it's not a carrot we'll be offering… more like an emetic. Everyone thinks you have to *reward* people to make them do what you want them to do. The seal claps, he gets a fish. Our inborn optimism makes us think that everything will turn out all right. Politicians throw us the fish that feed this optimism, with the result that nobody does anything to make sure things *will* be all right. Next day they're worse than ever.

"When the teeming billions hit the bottom, as they're beginning to now, and they're lying there in each other's filth looking up at their leaders for more fish, it's the brave man who'll stand there and give them nothing – who will actually *take things away*. We're the only group that can be trusted not to give people what they want.

What they want is fish – comfort and security. Nothing too radical."

Wenlight was getting frustrated. "So, what *are* you going to give them?"

Pilot spooned himself another bowl of yogurt while his friend waited for a reply. It came from Mara instead.

"What we put down on the table isn't going to be what people want. Not at first. They might see the sense in it eventually." Macushla handed Pilot his daughter across the table, which meant it was burping time.

"We haven't arrived at this point blind," Mara continued. "There are a lot of interests at stake, and we've brain-stormed them all; consulted all the top minds. Our conclusions and solutions are sound. Now, we need to convince *everyone* that the only interest of any real and lasting importance is that of the planet. We're not going to turn around nine billion people just like that, but they can turn *themselves* around with a little persuasion and a sound premise."

"*Persuasion*?" Wenlight said. "Do you people really think you're ready for this?" The baby burped and was handed, smiling, back to her mother.

"Not as ready as we would have hoped," Pilot said. "And there's another problem."

"Namely?"

"How to get our voice heard beyond the borders of the developed nations. In those places where deprivation is the norm, people's lives never rise above their basic daily needs and, because of that, the influence this island can wield is limited to only a small fraction of the planet – to those people with the time and opportunity to think, talk, read. I thought we'd have more time, you know, to build up our credibility and widen our audience. But it's all happening so fast, our audience is actually *shrinking* as more people are thrown into subsistence, or mere survival living. We've got to go straight in there and deliver our package next month, credibility or no credibility." He threw in Maryburg's premature baby analogy, then shut the door on further discussion.

"I'll just have to wait till then, will I? No special preview for friends?"

"Sorry, Len. We've only got one bullet in our gun, so… no practice."

Just then, Leidar Dahl entered with news of a meteor shower taking place overhead. Thirty seconds later, the room was empty.

As he peered up at the hundreds of meteors rushing like sperms in search of an egg – and likewise dying in the process – Pilot wondered what chance *their* little meteor had of getting through and impregnating the world.

XXV

Neptune Rising, *Galene* and *Nereides*, three superficially opulent cruise ships rusting under their new paintwork, rose and fell gracefully at their berths in Nillin harbour, their vast multi-storey superstructures all but blocking the view of the fiord. Eydos hadn't seen so much activity since the French invasion twelve years earlier. Even so, compared to previous environmental congresses in Stockholm, Nairobi, Rio de Janeiro, Kyoto, Johannesburg, Rio again, Abu Dhabi, Honolulu and Shanghai, the Eydos Summit was a mere foothill, austerity being the order of the day. The island had set limits on the number of delegates, scientists and support staff each country could send, and the journalists had been capped at two hundred. The quotas were not flexible and the organisers, supported by a hundred displaced Maldivian stewards, had turned away forty Russians and over a hundred Chinese whose names were not on the list.

The parties of both Eire and Iceland, comprising just 22 people between them, stepped ashore just after the 130-strong American delegation had debarked from the cruise ship *Neptune*. On entering the vast dome, the occasional delegate would look up and read Josiah Billy's wood-carved suicide poem hanging above the entrance, but most did not even notice it.

Returning from his morning jog above the fjord, Pilot was ambushed by a horde of reporters eager to embroider the rumour going around that Eydos was planning to drop a bomb on the Conference. The questions came at him from all angles, overlapping each other and making understanding impossible. Some of the words smelt of alcohol, Pilot noticed. Aaron Serman forced a passage between Associated Press and the Cable News Network and led Pilot into the Mother Dome to meet the Secretary General of the United Nations and Chair of the Eydos Summit, Lim Lin Hok.

"Welcome to Nillin, Secretary General," Pilot said for the cameras. "We meet at last," he whispered just for her.

As host nation, the Eydos delegation of Lonnie Pilot, Macushla Mara and Aaron Serman occupied the front seats on the far left. The other countries were then arranged alphabetically, with the delegates from Afghanistan just a few feet from Pilot's right shoulder. In front of them all on a raised stage was the speaker's podium, behind which, on another platform, was a long table where the Chair, the Secretary, the Executive Secretary, the Deputy Executive Secretary and four other United Nations officers were seated.

At the appointed hour, Lim Lin Hok rose from her seat, stepped down to the lectern and opened the Conference with a spirited ten-minute speech welcoming the scientists, economists and delegates, praising the 193 countries in attendance, and urging everyone present not to leave the words and rhetoric behind when they left Eydos. "In every preceding Earth summit to this one, nothing was ventured, and nothing was gained," she said in conclusion. "And look where it has landed us. This time, I urge you all, for Mankind's sake, to make that giant leap of faith required to wrest us from the fire." They'd heard words like this before, but something in their delivery made the delegates feel chastened before the Conference had even begun.

Days One and Two featured men of science explaining precisely what was happening to the Earth. Rising temperatures, rising sea levels, failed harvests, drug-resistant viruses… facts and figures flew about the dome like so many startled bats, causing great commotion but never settling on anyone.

Lonnie Pilot tried to take the information in, but felt that data of such breadth and depth was counter-productive and had the adverse effect of dampening the fear and emotion necessary to germinate action. In a whispered aside to Aaron Serman, he likened it to being attacked by a grizzly bear and responding by measuring the animal's paws and counting its teeth.

The whole of Day Three and the morning session of Day Four saw speeches from the delegates of Indonesia, Colombia, Estonia, Egypt, Finland, Greece, South Korea, Kenya, Chile, Haiti, Germany, Chad, Portugal, Papua New Guinea and Japan, the order having been drawn by lots.

With the afternoon of Day Four free, delegates used the time to network and hold smaller meetings in the baby domes. Members of the Eydos delegation attended them all, but said nothing. Day Five was given over to crisis management workshops in which Pilot noted much hot air, but very little in the way of crisis management. Eydos was conspicuous by its lack of involvement in the workshops, too. The other delegations were becoming disturbed by the island's deadweight at the meetings, having expected more. But 'more' was just waiting.

The President of the United States had decided to remain at home, much to everyone's disgust, so at the mid-day adjournment of the sixth and penultimate day of the Summit, Pilot collared the head of the U.S. delegation, hoping to have a quick word with the high-flying Senator he had met with such hopefulness eleven years earlier at Sag Harbour. Paul Dasching, who'd lost some hair and gained some pounds, was to be the first speaker of the afternoon session. "I have to go, Lonnie. Sorry. Some last minute material to run through with my people. Great to see you again. We've got a terrific package to announce. Talk to you later, okay?" The truth of it was that Paul Dasching felt compromised in Pilot's company and couldn't get away fast enough.

"Someone said you're going to dunk our heads in shit later," one of the reporters called out. Pilot ignored the comment, left the Mother Dome quickly and melted into a crowd taking advantage of the refreshing breeze outside. The remainder of the adjournment he spent with Macushla in their dome, expending nervous energy at five times his normal rate as he fought to control his nerves. Lonnie Pilot, as the first and only speaker on the final day, would soon know whether their wingless jumbo jet would fly or not.

"...and as an indication of the gravity and urgency with which the United States views the global crises facing us all, the President yesterday directed, under the new emergency powers granted the Chief Executive, that industrial emissions in the U.S. be reduced by *THIRTY per cent* – this new target to be achieved *within the next two years.* Moreover, two billion dollars in federal funds are to be directed into the development, manufacture and implementation of the new General Electric CLAIR Inner City Air Purification System, the first units to be in operation in Phoenix within eighteen months."

The remainder of Paul Dasching's 'great package' Pilot found to be hopelessly short of the mark. Purifying poisoned air without eradicating the poison was suicidally lame. That the most powerful nation on earth remained, at governmental and business levels at least, the most intransigent, worried him and weighed against the success of his own proposals. Great innovations were being created in the States by individual Americans, but had become stuck in the mud of under-funding and executive disinterest.

Dasching's address, when he had finished, was received with enthusiastic applause from the US delegation, a rather more tempered response from the Europeans and Japanese and total silence from the remainder of the delegates. Pilot could feel his spirits rise through this audible expression of dissatisfaction.

Following the USA, delegates from Italy, Russia, Denmark, Namibia, Australia, Vietnam and Pakistan each had their moment on the podium. Like a broken record of past summits, the speeches only sent the listeners lower on the scale of impotence and disenfranchisement. As the Spanish Environment Minister, the final speaker of the day, shuffled his papers in preparation, Pilot's mind began to fast forward. The plan was this: a quiet dinner in their dome; a final run-through of his speech with Macushla; late night sex; seven hours of undisturbed sleep (hopefully); early morning sex, followed by breakfast… then it would be *their* turn at the lectern.

A ripple of unenthusiastic applause signified the end of the Spaniard's speech. Ten minutes later, Pilot and Mara were back in their dome steaming Moringa leaves to accompany their goat stew.

His build-up had gone like clockwork, apart from the seven hours' sleep. A twenty minute doze was all that Pilot's nerves had afforded him. The sex had been fast and furious and had done the trick of pinning his butterflies. Now, as he walked arm in arm with Macushla to the Mother Dome, Lonnie Pilot was the picture of calm resolve.

As he took his seat in the front row, Pilot couldn't understand why it was so noisy in the auditorium. Every clunking headphone, scraping chair, every 'good morning', 'bon jour' and 'buenas dias' seemed to amplify off the roof straight into his inner ear. The white noise was deafening. His sharpened state of mind had had the effect of heightening all his senses, including the one he had not quite put his finger on yet – the one that was now telling him that every eye in the building was on him. Waves of expectation were breaking on shores of distrust. He could feel it. It'll be a good day's work if I can get through to even *ten percent* of them, he thought.

Like four thousand starlings landing in the trees, the delegates took their places and settled. Once the hubbub had subsided, Lim Lin Hok arose and took her place on the podium. Pilot's heart began to pound with the same purposefulness that had carried him to victory over Victor Bosse twelve years before.

The Secretary General spoke slowly, but with supreme authority. "Why are all of us here?" she began. "What brings us to this seemingly empty strip of rock in the Bay of Biscay?" She raised an elegant hand and pointed to the far wall of the auditorium. "Beyond this womb-like dome, our world lies in tatters. Try as we might, we have been unable to do the first thing to arrest our decay. Is it because we have not tried hard enough? Is it because our resolve is gone? Why is that? An inability or reluctance to admit the problems exist? Vested interest? Self interest? Short-term thinking? Indecision? We conspire against ourselves to ensure that we remain in our downward spiral. Faster and faster we fall." She paused for dramatic effect. "The ground is nearer than anyone thinks, or *wants* to think. But there is still time to pull ourselves out of our death dive. I believe that. Lonnie Pilot believes that." As Lim took a sip of water, Macushla reached over and squeezed her partner's hand.

"People have said that Eydos is a cult of personality and that their leader is a modern day Stalin, Mao, Castro, or Waheed. I can tell you now that Lonnie Pilot will be standing down as the leader of Eydos directly after this conference. In the next hour, therefore, I urge you to view Eydos as a cult of *concept*, not of personality. It could be the most important hour in this planet's history. Eydos is linked to no religion, no political dogma, no country or government… Unlike the rest of us, she is without chains. Unlike the rest of ours, her message is without conditions and impediments. In my country…" she turned to her right and beckoned Pilot forward, "…we do not shoot the messenger."

Pilot made his way to the platform in four-foot strides and took the steps two at a time. Settling in behind the lectern, he was oblivious to the sights and sounds encased in the Mother Dome with him. The respectful but reserved applause that had accompanied him from his seat had stopped, signifying that the owners of the hands now expected something in return.

Pilot stared hard at the microphone straining its neck towards his mouth, then faced out across the tiered hall. Myriad faces shimmered like sequins amongst the predominant greys and blues beloved of self-important males as he gradually brought the picture into focus.

Pilot nodded at Mara and Serman, then fished the vast pool of humanity for clues as to the state of mind of his audience. What he sensed more than anything was an overriding feeling of expectation from those he scanned – the expectation that Lonnie Pilot was about to fall flat on his face.

He stood in rigid concentration for a while, shifted his weight from left leg to right, and tried to recall his opening line. By this time, some of the delegates had begun exchanging whispered judgments with each other, and those commentators who hadn't previously written off Eydos' 'accidental tourists', were now inclining towards that position. The all-important opening to his speech was still eluding him, and the harder he tried to catch it, the further away it drifted. All he needed were the first few words and the rest would follow like magician's handkerchiefs. He glanced over at Macushla who was forming a letter 'D' with her hands. They'd set out a number of hand prompts for just this type of situation, but he hadn't expected to need one so soon. D denoted Decision. He was ready. To everyone below it seemed as if he had just been waiting for the proper level of attention before beginning. The delay did him no harm.

"There is no question as to the decision we have to make at this crucial point in our evolution," Pilot began. "The answer is so simple, most intelligent people will have already logically considered it. Yet it is so monumentally frightening that they will have just as easily – but without logic – dismissed it.

"My own progression towards this point started with the notion of reversing time. How much more constructive and fulfilling our lives would be if we could lead a two-lap existence, where we run forward until reaching what our bodies somehow instinctively know is the half-way mark. At this point, instead of running the second lap as before, we make a complete about turn and run the first lap in reverse – righting the wrongs of our past decision-making, seen with the advantage of hindsight as having been the *wrong* decisions; repairing the people and the places we have insulted, hurt, defaced, defiled, damaged or destroyed; and tidying up on the second lap the debris we created on the first one.

"When you, the individual, arrive back at your birth, which now occupies the same point in time as your death, you will be able to look back and say with honesty that you feel no guilt. You won't have to seek forgiveness from God or anyone else because a second, *reverse* lap would have allowed you to make good the damage in *actual* terms. Forgiveness is a concept invented to paper over our lack of awareness at the time of our misdemeanors."

A delegate from the Ukraine stopped breathing and died at this point, but it had nothing whatever to do with Pilot's speech. The man's colleagues wouldn't even notice his demise for another hour. A heavy drinker, he had, they thought, merely fallen asleep.

"There's a kind of physical reversal of time in people with Alzheimer's Disease," Pilot continued. "For them, the end of the first lap is the onset of the disease and the second lap consists of peeling away memory layers in reverse chronological order until all that is left of the individual are their earliest memories from childhood and then infancy. The next stop is birth, which for them is also death.

"These people get nearer to time reversal than the rest of us. No one can physically walk through the past doing those things I just said, but a *collective* form of the same process *is* possible." Pilot counted to ten in his head to give the translators time to catch up.

"If you treat all of humanity as one person, grant them a lifespan of five hundred years, and call today the half-way mark, then our subject will have been born in the late Eighteenth Century – roughly the beginning of the Industrial Revolution.

"We'll make this person male, because the motivating force of this first lap has been very much male in its nature. He has been charging forward since birth with blind invention – incredibly intelligent on the one hand and grossly insensitive, arrogant and irresponsible on the other. Now that he has reached our imaginary mid-way line, we're calling to him to turn around and go back."

Pilot shook his head, conceding the tallness of this order.

"That is the nature of the problem. How do you stop nine billion stampeding people, turn them all around and march them off in the opposite direction when all they know is forward? How do you convince them that the way ahead is *behind* them?

"That is the job that faces us now. If you want to give this job a name, *Dismantlement* is as good a word as any. Abbau… Demontere… Ontmanteling… Avtackla… Smatellamento… Demontowac… Demantelement."

Pilot had been speaking with exaggerated slowness from the beginning of his address to allow time for translation, but the word 'dismantlement' he had translated himself.

"The job specification of Dismantlement is simple: to achieve the same population level, and comparable quality of air and water, green space, forestation and wilderness by the twenty-third Century as we had in the eighteenth. We're now at the point of *must return* – the beginning of the longest revolution in human history." Lethal silence filled the Mother Dome like radon.

"We cannot determine the shape of our island by walking around its coastline," Pilot continued, borrowing Vaalon's words of twelve years earlier. "So bear with me while we fly over it at altitude.

"Returning to our global person, as well as turning him around, we need to change his sex. For the next two hundred and fifty years, a *female* order must supercede the male one which has dominated through history, otherwise Dismantlement – synonymous with protection, care, nurturing and sensitivity – won't be possible. Benevolence and compassion flows in the hormones of both sexes and we must bring them to the fore. With the correct disposition and a clear vision, we will be able to dismantle the machines and practices that are killing us. Illustrations…

"The arms industry. The black flashdrives in your information packs contain the roadmap and timetable for a global disarmament programme designed to dismantle the arms industry down to the last bullet and the last arms dealer within forty years." The opposing poles of the human magnet before him – positive/negative, applause/silence in equal strengths – gave Pilot cause for satisfaction. That so many seemed emotionally in favour of killing the arms industry surprised him. He wasn't confident his next target would be as well received.

"Globalization. We propose the deglobalization of world trade and the dismantlement of the multinationals. The red flash drives contain a detailed blueprint for restructuring multinational companies into groups of smaller, more ethical and more accountable entities. Twenty of the most eminent thinkers in the corporate world have lent their expertise to the authorship of not just attainable multinational company dismantlement, but of a further dozen sensitive dismantlement issues covering commerce, business and industry. Differing cultural and national mores have been recognized and accommodated across all of these proposals, and the word *profit* has been redefined.

"Urbanization. We propose a gradual disurbanization of the world's cities. How? The average life of a New York skyscraper is thirty or forty years. Replace every other building with an open space for parks, squares and allotments, put a ceiling of four storeys on all rebuilding, and by 2260 Manhattan could be the same pleasant town it was in 1760, but with all the technological advances we enjoy today. This is the template for all cities. Dismantlement will create a new balance.

"Remember, we're talking about a timescale of two hundred and fifty years, so it's not going to be as disruptive as it may appear. Dismantlement can happen gradually. But it has to happen *consensually.*"

Pilot paused to allow the translators time to catch up.

"The current Dismantlement map includes all the developed nations as a matter of course. Depending on which Dismantlement we're talking about, additional countries may be added to this list.

"Those nations listed under each Dismantlement should, if they all act together, effect the desired changes on those countries currently outside their influence, and therefore not yet prospects for inclusion on the Dismantlement map. They will quickly see the stark choice before them – dismantle like the rest or suffer." Pilot glanced down at Aaron Serman, sitting sphinx-like and unreadable in the front row. Next to him, Macushla was following the bullet points in the folder on her lap like a theatre prompt, ready to cue when necessary. Apart from the shaky beginning, her partner was doing well.

"Dismantlement starts at the top," Pilot continued. "Like tearing down a building, it has to be done one brick at a time, because it is a building we still occupy. The top countries, the top people in government, commerce and industry – that's where Dismantlement begins. The workers have had their revolutions, now it is the turn of the managers. The reason it has to start with them is simple. The underdeveloped countries will only consider halting their own mindless charge towards the seemingly gold-paved streets of globalization if they see the developed countries ripping up those very same streets and walking back to join them halfway."

The vacant expressions before him showed Pilot that he had hit a brick wall. He decided to go off-piste. It was Mara's job to return him to the script after he'd made his point. "To those of you at the top looking down, your fears are understandable. Today, you are at the peak of your game, the peak of your competitiveness, drive and potential. By your way of thinking, there is no stopping you… But there *is*. The foundations are crumbling beneath your feet." Pilot chose a particularly corpulent corporate type at whom to aim his next words.

"Imagine being told that you have cancer. The worst news you could possibly hear. The good news is that it's operable, and your chances of survival are good if you take your medication as instructed. It isn't Eydos telling you of your condition, it's the Earth. Turn your considerable skills towards self-healing and the world will heal with you… and your great-great-grandchildren will stand a chance of being born."

Austin Palmer winced. Len Wenlight clenched his fist. Lim Lin Hok nodded imperceptibly.

"Industrial and commercial Dismantlement will be the task of the developed nations," Pilot said, returning to message, "but its positive effects will be felt everywhere. It is a daunting task, but one which has had the benefit of much preliminary work already.

"Today, on Eydos, we are officially opening *The Office of Dismantlement* – The O.D.. OD is an acronym in

English of where we as a civilization stand on the balance sheet and the medical chart. We are *overdrawn* on our account with the planet and we have *overdosed* on our indulgent borrowings. I'm sorry if this play on words does not translate into your language. The basic truth remains. Our destiny is to die in poverty – very soon, at our current rate of spending.

"Most of you came here believing this congress would be a waste of time – that vested interests and politics would ensure that nothing was agreed and that nothing would be achieved from it, like a football match without a referee. This time, it's different. Because this time there's an independent arbiter." He looked over his shoulder at the Secretary General, who was nodding her head in affirmation for all to see.

"There was only one place The Office of Dismantlement could be located to overcome the massive barrier of global lethargy and partisanship which threatens our survival. Only one place that has *everyone's* interests at heart. And when I say everyone, I'm drawing a line from you straight through to your descendants in the twenty-third and twenty-fourth centuries. To make sense of Dismantlement, you have to look way beyond your own lifetime.

"One of the most important jobs of The O.D. will be to keep the various Dismantlement programmes on the boil. Collective human concentration has no staying power. To keep the resolve of our global person alive for *two and a half centuries* is going to take some doing, especially when our circumstances begin to improve. Dismantlement stops *only when the job is finished*."

Pilot took several gulps of water from his glass, wiped his mouth with the back of his hand, then looked up at the vast curved ceiling, glowing with the transluscence of white jade.

"Let me describe The Office of Dismantlement to you. One room – the cockpit of a jumbo jet fuselage atop the grounded ocean-going barge *Ptolemy*. It has no desk, no phone, no filing cabinet, no computer. The Office of Dismantlement is not a place of work. It's a symbol. A reminder that the principles of Dismantlement are lodged at the only truly neutral point to be found on the planet. They will remain there until the job is finished.

"The actual work of Dismantlement will take place elsewhere – in office blocks, government ministries, factories, laboratories… in people's attitudes… in their conjugal beds."

'S-N-O-W-B-A-L-L-I-N-H-E-L-L', CNN's Chief Correspondent typed in large caps on his tablet, not in spite, but in sympathy.

"In six administrative centres – Lucerne, Switzerland; Niigata, Japan; Cambridge, Massachusetts; Lima, Peru; Wellington, New Zealand; and Mumbai, India – we are providing facilities for the study, research and strategic planning of Dismantlement. These places will be both University and Ministry. We will be recruiting professionals from the sciences, academia, economics, industry and other crucial disciplines to administer and coordinate the work of these six centres – people to define the terms of Dismantlement within specific regions… to determine the priorities for change… to draw up the timetables for change… and to anticipate the knock-on effects of Dismantlement from one area to another.

"These six centres, working strictly to the Dismantlement blueprint drawn up on Eydos, will set the parameters for action which individual governments should then, with the much vaster intellectual and economic resources at their disposal, put into practice. We on Eydos are lucky in that we are already where the rest of you could be in 250 years' time. Our job is to ensure that you all get there too."

On a signal from her partner, Macushla lifted an object covered in a colourful patch of dacron cut from one of the mothballed hot air balloons and approached the stage. Pilot moved to the edge of the platform to take it from her, then returned to the podium.

"The planet Earth is out of control, thanks entirely to her dominant species, homo sapiens," he said, positioning the object on the lectern. "Today, we have a choice. Let the garden grow wild by letting human nature take its course, or use our brain power – that most remarkable, yet most misused of tools – to exert control over where we are heading and avoid needless suffering in the future." Pilot removed the dacron and raised Jane's bonsai tree above his head. "With Dismantlement we are attempting to shape our destiny by controlling our expansion and keeping it within the bounds of our growing tray, the Earth. As in the art of bonsai, we do this through cutting, pruning, wiring and careful tending. Dismantlement is all about containing ourselves without losing our shape… about restricting our outward growth without curbing our inner development. This tree will live in The O.D. on board *Ptolemy* as a living symbol of the skills we have to learn and apply over the next two hundred and fifty years." He placed the bonsai tree on the stage in front of the podium, catching Macushla's reassuring eye for a millisecond, then returned to his position behind it.

"Effective and fair Dismantlement can only be achieved through consensus, as I said before. And the mechanical intricacies can be mastered only by people fluent in those fields included in the Dismantlement agenda. For example, the motor industry can only be dismantled by the motor industry itself, and the –"

A hoot of derision sounded from somewhere within the US delegation. A US Congressman of twenty-six years' service to his State, Country and Self, was finding Pilot's words tantamount to blasphemy. He was not an environmentalist at heart and had manipulated his appointment to the Congressional Committee on Environmental Projections not through altruism, but as a way of heading off any Federal controls that might curb the interests of his select friends in commerce and industry.

"When we say dismantle the motor industry, we don't mean they should stop making vehicles," Pilot said, throwing his words in the general direction of the heckler. "Your blue flashdrives contain a number of novel concepts in transportation solutions, co-authored by some of the motor industry's most creative and innovative strategists during visits to Eydos. *Road trains*, for example. Through the introduction of road trains, powered by a new breed of hybrid engine adding human muscle power to the mix through hand and foot pedals, there will be better transport efficiency, greatly reduced emissions, no traffic jams – not to mention their impact on obesity."

"The fat guys will just let the healthy ones do all the work," Reuters said to Associated Press. "Lonnie Pilot has no understanding of human nature."

"Yeah, but the fat guys'll die first," AP replied.

"Another idea currently in development is the *Mus*," Pilot continued, "an inner city muscle-powered bus driven by as few as fifteen medium-fit passengers out of a seating capacity of forty-five. Any shortfall in the power generated through the pedals is made up by the vehicle's battery. The Mus has a top speed of fifteen miles an hour and will operate on any incline under one in twelve, even when pulling its trailer of light-weight bicycles. The same technology is being used for the Domestic Energy Table, or DET, around which families can sit and have quality time together as they charge their home generator through pedals under the table. The family stays healthy, enjoys valuable together-time and makes electricity all at the same time. Half an hour around the DET generates enough power to run their lights and computers for a day." Pilot stole a quick glance behind him and drew strength from Lim's eyes. Above her, the giant video screen displayed a moving image of someone who looked just like Lonnie Pilot.

"The brain power and financial resources that *could* be thrown at our problems are enormous, and our projects are only scratching the surface," he said. "Dismantlement isn't all about the salvation and restoration of Homo Sapiens, though. It's about returning wild animals to their original status by restoring their wildness… by dismantling the zoo and creating mega-reserves – not of tens or hundreds of square miles, but of *thousands* of square miles. And not in the world's most remote countries and places, but right in the middle of the most developed ones. Once the borders of these mega-reserves are drawn, the gradual removal of the human footprint can begin. As the land demands of humans decrease as a result of the most important single Dismantlement, which I will come to shortly, our presence within the mega-reserves will shrink correspondingly."

Pilot looked across at Mara, who was signing the letters E and X. He had almost forgotten. "As I said before, all of these proposed dismantlements have to be adopted by global consensus. The O.D. is not a Dictatorship. The O.D. is an *Exemplarship*." Pilot allowed time for the word 'Exemplarship' to be translated, which was no mean feat. "The Greek word eîdos is defined as *the distinctive expression of the cognitive or intellectual character of a culture or a social group.* The character and culture of Eydos can act as the model, or *exemplar* of change."

Pilot shook out his legs the way footballers do during national anthems, but less obviously. He'd been standing for quite some time. No one was prepared for Pilot's next bombshell.

"Now we arrive at the most important Dismantlement of all. If we succeed with this one, then everything else will follow like a Jacob's ladder. But… IT IS THE SINGLE MOST DIFFICULT TASK WE FACE.

"We've cured cancer and AIDS. Now we have to treat that most threatening of conditions, *pregnancy*." There was a collective intake of breath which Pilot sensed immediately. He was ready for it. "While respecting the gift of pregnancy and the wonder of new life, we have to begin *rationing* it to protect those very lives we are creating. Only by halving our rate of regeneration can future life be safeguarded. The gradual, systematic dismantlement of the human population is the most important Dismantlement of all." Pilot waited for the hubbub invoked by his words to die down.

Please," he said pushing down with his hands to signal silence. "The old concept of zero population growth is not radical enough to achieve what we believe to be the optimum global population of nine hundred million by the year 2275. That's a reduction of *ninety percent* off today's number."

Four thousand people in the Mother Dome were stunned to silence.

"The human world is like a business that has grown too big and has failed to adapt to market changes. 'Go Forth and Multiply' was written when the global population was less than 230 million. We are grossly over-manned and have to make large-scale redundancies if we are going to stay afloat. I use these market economy analogies to illustrate the point because, for many people out there, it's a language they can easily understand.

"Before we explain how to make these cuts, let me tell you why they are necessary. Most of you sitting here already know, but for many watching this live on their computers, TVs and phones, it would be a serious omission on our part to speak as if all the problems are universally understood, because they are not.

"Let us take this auditorium as being the Earth. It has four thousand seats and, as you can all see, today we're full. It took around a hundred and fifty thousand years, from modern Man's supposed beginnings up to the year 5000 B.C. to fill just the first eight *seats* of our four thousand seat auditorium. By the time of Christ, this had doubled to sixteen seats. Fifteen centuries later, when Columbus landed in America, 200 seats, or the first *two rows only* of these forty rows, were occupied. By the time of the American Revolution, just three hundred years after Columbus, this had doubled to four rows. By the beginning of the 20th century there were still only six rows occupied. Six hundred seats out of four thousand." Pilot turned to the Chair and extended his hand. "Within Lim Lin Hok's lifetime, the population has doubled *twice* – to two thousand seats, now to four thousand. That's every last seat in this hall. In just twenty years' time there will be *two* people occupying every seat… in thirty years, *four*… in thirty-five years, *eight*. Not only is the auditorium full as of today, but it was really only built to house four hundred people comfortably at most. Each person needs at least ten seats – four to stretch out on at night and the other six for their possessions, work, gardens, recreation etcetera. Occupying all available seats does not worry us here today, because we have somewhere else to go afterwards. But if this dome were the earth, there *is* nowhere else."

Pilot's mind went blank at this point and he signalled Macushla to turn the light back on. She slid her finger slowly across her throat. Extermination. It had been one of *her* ideas.

"Sticking with the seats analogy, although it has taken us over *a hundred and fifty thousand years* to fill the auditorium, it is sobering to think that we are never more than *fifty years* away from emptying it completely. And before I get back to the finer points of Population Dismantlement, I will tell you how the human race can be quickly and efficiently eradicated from the Earth."

'You've gone too far now, Lonnie Pilot,' Austin Palmer thought. Len Wenlight merely clung to a blind hope that Pilot wasn't about to hang himself.

"If, starting today, we had the wherewithal to begin administering a potent sterilization agent worldwide, and no antidote were discovered for at least fifty years, then, when the last of today's female babies reaches menopause, the human race in its entirety will be doomed. Another fifty years after that, with no way to reproduce its kind, homo sapiens will have disappeared forever from the Earth. We will have achieved *total* dismantlement of the population from nine billion to zero in just a few generations.

"Now I will explain *how* this can be done. Three years ago, we secretly commissioned a sympathetic research chemist in Cheshire to develop a chemical agent that would make any male who ingested it irrevocably sterile."

"DISONORARE SU LEI," an Italian delegate shouted above the uproar Pilot's pronouncement had triggered. Seconds later, it entered Pilot's earpiece as 'Shame on you.'

"No," he said after the noise had died down. "There is no shame in issuing a warning. If we, for a modest investment, could develop the chemistry to cause irreversible sterilization, then so could others. More important and ominous is the fact that a delivery system also exists.

"The way global distribution is structured today, we would be able to reach three-quarters of the Earth's population just through normal commercial channels. Our tasteless, colourless chemical agent added to a popular soft drink at its worldwide bottling plants would sterilize sixty to seventy percent of this number within twelve months. We have identified fifty other routes, from chewing gum to chicken nuggets, that would account for the rest. It can even be absorbed through the skin through shower gels, deodorants and after shave. The remaining billion or so males outside this net – most of them in Asia and Africa – could be targeted by other means like crop spraying and doctoring the drinking water.

"A small country, a medium-sized corporation, or just a well-organized group of fanatics with the intent, chemistry, strategy and finance, could sterilize ninety percent of the world's males within two years, and the remainder within five. And that would be it – apart from whatever life could be produced in the laboratory."

A blanket of silence fell over the delegates. This was *not* what they had expected of Eydos, but Pilot saw no reason to hold back. "There are enough radical groups out there, harbouring enough diabolical purpose, to make the scenario I've just described a reality," he continued, Charles Williams' wrathful stare still strong in his memory. "And the odds of it happening will shorten as more and more people fight for less and less of everything."

"CHANTAJE," a Costa Rican delegate cried, echoing a second later in Pilot's earpiece as, 'Blackmail.'

"This is not blackmail," Pilot shot back at his heckler. "It's a warning that if we do not *voluntarily* reduce our numbers starting today, someone else will institute a programme of *malevolent* population dismantlement tomorrow, with the danger that they'll take it all the way. Failure on our part to act will increase human suffering to dimensions most of us cannot comprehend." Pilot felt it was time to head to quieter waters, if there were any.

"The population-resources issue falls into two halves – one developed, one undeveloped," he said. "Both sides are killing the world in different ways. The industrialized, consumption-based developed nations are eating the planet alive. For good measure, we're poisoning it at the same time, accounting for over two-thirds of the greenhouse gases and most of the poisons in the sea.

"The undeveloped third world, on the other hand, although barely making a scratch on the surface in terms of its consumption of resources, is suffocating the Earth through sheer numbers. Because they outnumber the rich by ten to one, some will argue that Population Dismantlement across the board would be unfair to developed countries. The answer to that is that one rich man does as much damage to the Earth as ten poor men." Pilot waited for the scattered applause from the delegations of Burundi, Liberia, Haiti, Ethiopia and Burkina Faso to die down before resuming.

"Some developed countries have already reached zero population growth, resulting in an inverse pyramid. The broad base at the top represents older people and the narrower part, those of childbearing age and younger. So, in these countries, more people will be taken off the top than will be added to the bottom, with the obvious result that the populations of the developed countries will fall faster than the populations of the third world, where the ratio of young to old is about equal. This creates the worrying disparity that it would largely be the educated people in the developed countries who would be dismantling their populations. With their numbers steadily halving, in contrast to the doubling, trebling and quadrupling of the uneducated, distracted poor, it wouldn't take long for reason and commitment towards a better future to be drowned by their exact opposites. One way to correct this would be to link foreign aid to population reduction. Other possible solutions to this problem are detailed in the purple flashdrives. Put your collective minds to this disparity and balance can be achieved."

Loud silence assaulted Pilot's ears. He expected nothing less.

"It is implausible that countries will be able to depopulate mandatorily, and that's why Population Dismantlement has to be *consensual* – a life practice woven *into* our culture the way smoking was tweezed *out* of it. Today, all but seven countries have eradicated smoking completely within their borders. With the same perserverence, we can reach the stage where the single child family is the socially accepted norm. Over our two hundred and fifty year Dismantlement period, those people who stop at one child will be hailed as heroes by their peers and revered forever by future generations for their sacrifice."

Pilot's intuitive mind could sense opposing opinions shooting around the auditorium like laser beams.

"We are here – Eydos is here – to simplify an easy job that has been made difficult by the mass of opposing positions on the subject of birth control. There are people looking at it through the eyes of religion, through the eyes of civil rights, market interests and nationalism. A common Population Dismantlement policy, drawn up by a party whose interests lie indelibly *outside* those I have just mentioned, will cut through all these differences. It will neither favour nor disfavour personal, religious or political beliefs, economic systems or national interests. It is the only guarantee we've got that what has to be done, *will* be done."

There was loud, albeit scattered applause at these words, but Pilot was eager to carry on, sensing that he did not have long before emotional overload took him down.

"Vested interest has no role in population or any other form of Dismantlement," he shouted above the ruction. He shifted from one foot to the other in an attempt to relieve his back, which he could feel tightening at the base of his spine.

"Let us go back to the mid 1700s and the birth of our global man. There were nine hundred million people alive then. As I said earlier, that's just four rows of our forty row auditorium, and a much more manageable number in every respect. Anything more than a billion people in the world is unsustainable by natural means. Our huge numbers today depend on intensive farming, genetic modification and chemical fertilization to keep them alive. To get back below a billion mouths to feed by the end of our second lap two hundred and fifty years from now will, in theory anyway, be easy to accomplish.

"If every single female during this period has only one child, we will be very near our target by the year 2275. Through this natural shrinkage, or generational halving, the world would shed a city the size of Shanghai – 20 to 30 million people – *every year*. When we reach our target two and a half centuries from now, the single child can be replaced by a two-child norm to maintain the population at around the nine hundred million mark. Cousins, uncles and aunts – absent for 250 years – would once again exist. If we ever get there, we will have achieved the greatest Dismantlement of all. Future historians will look back and document the courageous step we took from this conference and thank us for their existence."

Pilot paused for a moment, not for dramatic effect, but because he could sense trouble ahead.

"How will halving be accomplished on our second lap? How will single births be encouraged worldwide? We will no doubt be told it is impossible. The Chinese method was not consensual. It was imposed. We are not so naïve as to think Population Dismantlement is going to be easy to put in place. Couples will resist the single child ideal as an infringement of their rights. Big Business will fight it for reducing their markets. In a perfect world there would be *no* opposition to Population Dismantlement. We are all in the same boat, and the stability and smoother sailing that will come through having fewer people in it will benefit everyone. Our proposals may sound draconian, but not when you place them next to the alternative." He looked across at Macushla and smiled for a millisecond.

"We have done some work on the mechanics of the problem. One of our projects has been the development of a device, quite different from the intra-fallopian inserts our women here used up until last year, that can be implanted inside the female to render her eggs latent for as long as it is in place." He raised his hands to forestall the storm he could feel breaking. "Before I go any further, I need to state our reasons for selecting the female and not the male to carry this responsibility. Our own women asked for and participated in the development of this appliance, reasoning that it is far easier to implant such a device into the mother at the time her first child is born than to similarly treat the father, who may not even still be in the picture by the time of the birth. It is also our belief that the female will be more accepting of the overall aims of Dismantlement than will the male, especially as it relates to her progeny. No mother will ever be *forced* to have the device implanted. She can opt out if she so wishes."

In an attempt to get this sensitive subject behind him, Pilot quickened his rate of speech and cut out his long pauses. "Obstetricians will be trained in the simple surgical procedure for inserting our tiny device, which, I might add, is safer, more effective and more tamper-proof than any existing contraceptive. It is as good as permanent, but, in extenuating circumstances later on, such as the death of the single child, it can be removed until a second, healthy child is delivered. We have been testing a prototype of the device for two years on our own women, including my partner, whose idea it was in the first place.

"Females will support the programme for different reasons. Some will do so through altruism and a genuine belief that it is right. Others will have to be offered financial and other incentives. The orange-coloured flashdrives in your packs contain details of a variety of such incentives tailored to different socio-economic groups, geographies, religions, political structures. With the *PSA* Incentive, for example – *Pregnancy Set-Aside* – countries will pay a levy based on their rate of population growth into a central fund. The money in this fund will be used to make payments to new mothers on insertion of the device – similar to agricultural set-aside, where farmers are paid *not* to grow crops. Countries will encourage population control amongst their citizens to reduce their levies, and mothers who agree to be fitted after the birth of their first child will bank a sizable sum of money." There was a wave of white noise from the delegates which Pilot rode like a seasoned surfer as it swept over the stage. He took a step back and announced that he was handing over to the President of Ireland, who had some relevant points to make on the issue of Population Dismantlement. From the wings, a man with a rust-red Asterix moustache strode forward to scattered applause from a congress half bemused and half enthused. Pilot shook hands with him, then returned to his seat.

"My fellow delegates, don't look so shocked," President Traill began. "I sympathise with you. The ideas emanating from Eydos *are* shocking. It seems as though they want to take away all those things that make us human beings – ambition, expectation, competitiveness, libido… What are we supposed to do, trapped inside the only bodies we know? What is a society trapped inside *its* body of jobs, economies, religions and social mores supposed to do when faced with the apocalyptic vision that, to stay within it, means certain degeneration and eventual death? What Eydos is really proposing is that we *redirect* our societal body towards a different goal.

"As Madame Lim said, you don't kill the messenger for bringing bad news. In fact, Lonnie Pilot is only telling us what we know already in our heads and hearts. Nor do you kill the doctor because you don't like the taste of the medicine he's prescribed. As George Bernard Shaw said, 'People are always blaming their circumstances for what they are. The people who get on in this world are the people who get up and look for the circumstances they *want*, and if they cannot find them, *make* them.' Dismantlement will allow us to create a world that we would all rather live in than this one.

"My fellow delegates, I don't claim to speak on behalf of the Irish people, who had no prior knowledge of this initiative put forward by our friends in the Bay of Biscay, nor of my decision to support it. However, it is my duty as Head of State to serve the interests of the people of Eire to the best of my ability. We have been watching Eydos closely since its first days above the water. Lonnie Pilot has always had our ear, and vice versa. Our concord, however, has never been the incestuous one of worldly alliances with their mutual back scratchings, favours granted and favours exacted. For Ireland's part, we've always known that any solution to the human condition would never come from the existing cast of players, but would have to come from the outside … from a free state.

"The Saorstat Eireann, or Irish Free State, wasn't every Irishman's answer to the questions of the day over a century ago. Nevertheless, there was no doubt the State needed freeing. Just as we need freeing today. From ourselves. Eydos was *born* free. And it's on this wind-blown rock shelf that our hopes now lie.

"I've heard it said that Eydos represents only those people living in the developed, educated, privileged countries either side of the North Atlantic. Well now, that's not surprising when you consider that the majority of those who settled this island were from Western Europe and the United States. Also hardly surprising when you consider where most of the rot in our world was born. Dismantlement must begin in these countries, so the authors of Dismantlement might as well speak their language. *Everyone* will benefit from Dismantlement, even if they never fully understand the word, let alone hear it spoken." President Traill turned to make brief eye contact with Lim, then slowly panned the auditorium.

"There's no conspiracy afoot here and no outside paymaster. That's why my first job on returning to Dublin will be to bring Dismantlement to the Oireachtas, our national parliament. As an advocate for Population Dismantlement first and foremost, I will stake my Presidency on its passage."

"I don't know whether to praise our President or certify him insane," an Irish journalist whispered to the woman next to him.

"If I were you, I'd start writing his obituary," she answered.

President Traill stuffed his notes in his pocket and turned to shake hands with another moustachioed man who had joined him on the podium from the wings – a man whose own mother, Gabriella Lucia Laurenço Barreiras, would not have recognized him. His fifteen months on the grounded ocean-going barge, *Fort Lowell*, had served him well.

"I am Doctor Carlos Laurenço, President of Brazil," he announced slowly in Portuguese whilst removing the white wig he had been wearing since leaving Rio de Janeiro two years previously. There was an audible intake of many breaths from the audience, and the born-again President stood silent to allow the shockwaves from his surprise reincarnation to pass over the hall.

"What, my friends, am I President *of*?" he said eventually, almost in tears. "I am President of a country broken by excesses of every kind. I am the head on the fleshless skeleton of a man who has eaten himself to death." Laurenco's speech was slow, the clauses separated by enormous gaps – a translator's prayer.

"I, myself, am a criminal of epic proportions."

(Three seconds)

"In that respect, I do not differ so much from the leaders of your own nations."

(Four seconds)

"We rape and pillage as one... stealing from our own children... from our own planet... and defecating in its emptied jewel boxes. We Brazilians were unfortunate in that we got caught.

"How long, I wonder, can the rest of you remain at large with the truth closing in all around you?" His doleful brown eyes seemed to probe those of each delegate over what seemed like an age.

"You are banging on the gates of hell now with increasing persistence, in spite of all the signs – the heat behind the door; the smoke seeping through the cracks; the smell of burning flesh. One day it will open for all of you as it has done already in Sao Paolo, Rio de Janeiro, Phoenix and a thousand other places. I have been through those gates. Therefore I am qualified and duty-bound to give you this admonition.

(Five seconds)

"*Turn around*, as our friend says. Start the dismantlement process *now*. If the first tentative steps of Dismantlement had been applied in Brazil ten years ago, even five, my country would be on the long road to recovery today.

"It *is* a long road back. A Long March that will span twenty generations. Those twenty generations will go down in history as *the people who saved the human race from itself*. We must use the time we have left to turn this massive machine of ours around and begin that march. And we must empower those willing to go in the right direction to help those who are not.

(Seven seconds)

"The questions you have to ask yourselves today, and then take back to your respective governments, are,

"Do we admit that these problems exist?

"If so, do we accept that we need to meet them with drastic action?

"If yes, do we believe that Dismantlement is the answer?

"If yes, do we accept the premise that only a guide of the cleanest, purest impartiality can steer us down the road of Dismantlement fairly and logically?

"If so, are we willing to place our future survival in the hands of The O.D.?

"Finally, do we have faith in the Exemplarship of Eydos, or are we to continue stumbling in the dark – aimless and disunited – until circumstances take us down?" The final five words, spoken as the man moved away from the podium, were delivered in a kind of mournful song.

The atmosphere in the hall was electric, and Lim Lin Hok, not wishing to lose a single watt, moved quickly to the lectern. Even though the conference was being broadcast live to an audience of billions, five journalists were making for the exits and their satellite video phones, having decided that Carlos Laurenço's return from the dead, and not The O.D., was the biggest news story of the day and deserved their personal commentary.

The Chair of the Eydos Summit stood patiently at the lectern waiting for the thunder around her to subside. When the dome eventually fell silent, she began to speak in the calm, measured tones for which she was famous. "So, what is to be done? Protocol says we should debate Dismantlement, but logic says debate would merely suffocate this baby at birth, as it did to any proposal of weight in Kyoto, Rio and all the other summits before. To consider the spirit – not the details, but the *spirit* of Dismantlement you need no data, and no time for rumination. Dismantlement is not something that can be argued or watered down. Its basic premise is incontrovertible. Nor can Dismantlement be put into a simple draft or protocol. To do so would take years we don't have. The established code of summits such as this has proved to be impotent, so, as Chair, I am changing it. A simple Yes or No to the premise put forward by Eydos is all we need today. *Agree in principle* to the 250 year task of dismantling and rebuilding our world… or don't. If the vote today is Yes, then tomorrow you can take it home for ratification by your respective governments. The day after that, we can start working on the details and writing the policies that will turn us around and lead us away from the precipice."

The die-hard debaters in the audience and the sticklers for protocol were finding Lim's dictatorial stance and unashamed partiality hard to swallow. Others, more aware of what lay beyond and ahead, were thinking, why the hell not? Lim raised her hands to dampen the din. "Let me quote from a religious book. Which book and which religion is of no consequence. A wise word is a wise word. It said, 'Pay attention to your thoughts, because they become words. Pay attention to your words, because they become actions. Pay attention to your actions, because they become habits. Pay attention to your habits, because they become your character. Pay attention to your character, because it is your *fate*.'

"The problems we all face together are bigger than people, bigger than political parties and bigger than countries. So are the solutions. As Conference Chair I cannot in all good conscience remain impartial on this matter. I urge you to give your unqualified support to The Office of Dismantlement. Take consensus home with you and let the work begin. Vote *now*."

For this conference, each delegation had Yay and Nay buttons connected wirelessly to a control box mounted on the wall of the dome six feet above the floor. Out of this box, two calibrated LED tubes, one red, one green, rose in an arc to a point just short of the top of the dome. Over the previous six days, the system had responded perfectly to the motions thrown at it. A small number of countries always knew which way they would vote on any given issue. The rest would wait and see how the votes were going before casting their own. As a result, there would be two surges. The first would show a bias low down towards either red or green, followed a few seconds later by the dominant colour surging towards the top of the dome. A third button would allow a country to clear the vote it had just cast and change it, so, in the ten minutes allowed before vote casting was locked, there would often be oscillation between the red and green LEDs. Such was the case now.

Ten seconds after Lim's call for the vote, the green tube was on two and the red tube on eight… then five… then eight again. The green tube went up to five, then dropped back to three. With over 180 countries yet to vote, the weight of unexpressed confusion in the dome was taking its toll on Pilot, whose skin had taken on a ghostly pallor. Macushla Mara looked worriedly at her partner as the Secretary General called him up to the stage to stand beside her.

Pilot walked over and took position next to Lim, who was a full head shorter. He peered towards the press gallery looking for a friendly face and caught Austin Palmer's eye. Palmer winked at him and then began tapping feverishly on his tablet. Hoping to glean some kind of reaction from the sea of delegates washing against the cliff of the stage, Pilot could just make out the United States delegation at the far back. Only Paul Dasching was transmitting positivity in the way he was standing and holding court, voting box in hand, finger on button. But which button? As a potential Presidential candidate, would he ever be able to back Dismantlement and cast a Yay vote? Soon, Dasching was looking as worried as the rest of them. The voting process itself was taking on the appearance of red and green yo-yos dancing in the lower reaches of the tubes.

Pilot transferred his gaze from the red and green undulating tubes to the Eydos delegation in the front row. Macushla's face gave little away, but her eyes were sparkling. At the corners of her mouth, he detected the faintest smile. Lim and Pilot stood like ramrods, staring defiantly and challengingly at the delegates below them. Their afternoon's work was finished and there was nothing more they could do.

The Conference effectively ended at this point.

At ten minutes to six on that strange Friday afternoon, the world turned over…

Everything happened simultaneously. The full three hundred and sixty degrees of the horizon fell away as Pilot's dais rose up on a vast plateau of emotion. *I think it is tidal wave.* Dubravka Horvat's words, spoken over a decade before, popped up in his mind from nowhere. Arrayed before him, a centillion brain cells in four thousand skulls were agitating like molecules over a flame, but it wasn't a vocalized reaction. The hall itself was strangely quiet – the hell, all in Lonnie Pilot's head.

The upward acceleration lasted for twenty seconds. Pilot's stomach told him when he had reached the peak of positivity in the auditorium and told him again, a few seconds later, that the plateau was collapsing beneath him and that he was now dropping at a frightening speed, without support, straight down towards a trough of negativity.

Midway through his fall, he found himself looking *up* at the delegates in favour of Dismantlement and *down* at those against. What he was experiencing was the solidification of world opinion into two separate camps. It was futile for him to have expected it to be any other way. The human race had always been a double sided coin. North–south, yin–yang, hot–cold, sensitive–thick, enlightened–lights out, haves–have-nots. These opposing walls of knotted resolve seemed to be heading towards each other with irresistible force, swallowing up any smaller waves of indecision standing in their path. The two were merging to create a maelstrom of vacillation. Fastening his attention on some cheering Danish delegates swirling at the top of the whirlpool, he followed it round and watched it disappear inside the funnel.

A split second later, another wave hit him with a ferocity that nearly rendered him unconscious. Mental exhaustion had weakened him to the point that he could no longer keep the gates closed against the onslaught of information coming his way. The 'noise' was deafening and, for the second time in his life, Pilot felt fear.

To everyone else present, however, the sea was flat calm. Silence hung over the auditorium like a wet blanket. To these people, Dismantlement was far too significant and consequential to demean with applause, far too logical and sensible to dismiss with boos, yet far too large and terrifying to embrace with conviction. What Pilot alone was experiencing was the utter violence of their indecision. What he also knew was that Dismantlement would never fly with *these* people. The final vote was locked at just ten votes cast out of a possible 193 – Ireland, Israel, Iceland, Bhutan and Tonga in the green tube; Russia, Saudi Arabia, Zimbabwe, Brunei and North Korea in the red. What of the others? The delegates of the Eydos Summit, representing a global constituency of nine billion people, just looked vacuously at one another like airline passengers whose cabin roof has been ripped off at twelve thousand feet.

Lonnie Pilot, meanwhile, the man who had blown their cover, could only stand helpless as row upon row of stampeding horses bore down on the soft and vulnerable inner sanctums of his mind…

There was no way anyone at the Eydos Summit could have known what was happening beyond the Mother Dome. In the TV lounge of Scheveningen Prison, Henry Bradingbrooke watched the broadcast with lines of concern etched in his brow. He couldn't tell if they had won or had lost. No-one could. But underneath this doubt, a seed of hope had been sown by Pilot's and Lim's empassioned presentations, aided by those of a serving- and an ex-president. And it had germinated in front of computer, television and smartphone screens throughout the world. A billion people – two-thirds of the live global audience – were creating the beginnings of their own wave. A wave of immense, but as yet untapped power coursing freely and strongly in the direction of Jane Lavery's bonsai tree. Whatever arguments against The O.D. their representatives might bring home from Eydos would be inconsequential in the face of this human tsunami. Control of their, and civilization's destiny would be wrested from the hands of the weak and the blinkered and passed to those of the strong and the visionary.

Possibly.

And possibly, the human world would run with its one last chance at survival.

XXVI

The southwesterly wind, heavy with tropical heat, even at this early hour, collided headlong with a massive cold front pushing down from Scandinavia and threw darkly menacing cumulus clouds up into a four mile high iron curtain, bisecting the island length-wise. Innocently caught between the two worlds of darkness and light, Eydos lay in the Bay of Biscay like a quarter moon. In the Nillin basin, all was calm and bright. The six hundred foot basin rim shut out the gales on the one side and hid all but the upper reaches of the growing cloud bank on the other. Thickets of gorse thrashed in the wind atop the rim, while the grasses in its lee stood motionless.

It was the start of another summer's day in the Bay of Biscay, a day already being noisily celebrated by hundreds of thousands of seabirds bivouacked on the ledges and in the crevices of the island's vast western wall. Whitecaps bucked along the entire length of this coast while what seemed like whitecaps, but were in actuality patches of guano, climbed up the cliffs from the sea below.

A musty fragrance filled the air, seasoned by the ever-present salt spray and soured by occasional pockets of guano fumes rising off a cliff face still warm from the day before.

In the water at the entrance to Blasius Fjord, a family of seals bobbed around in the angry waves, looking out to sea, waiting…

Things were not as the seals liked them. The fish they would normally have breakfasted on were nowhere to be found. Added to which was the unusual tickling sensation attacking the sensitive skin around their ear holes, and the pressure on their bellies normally associated only with deep swims. To creatures programmed from birth by the natural signals of their surroundings, the messages they were now receiving just served to confuse. And so they waited. In the circumstances it was the only thing they could do.

Action, albeit no answer, was not long in coming.

At an unseen, unheard signal, half a million nesting seabirds threw themselves off the cliff and into flight as if the entire island had just been electrified. At the exact same moment the seals dived under the surface like a team of synchronized swimmers, only to arise some moments later in disarray and more befuddled than ever.

A lone mollusk, attached for the past four months to a point on the rock just a few metres under the waterline, could sense through its primitive nervous system a slight change in its condition. The mollusk had no way of knowing what that change was – that the waterline was now nearly a meter *below* it.

Inside Mirko Soldo's cistern, lightly illuminated through a crack in the roof, tiny waves reflected in miniature what was happening in the sea beyond and forced a lone water-boatman to row frantically for its life. There was no haven for this insect, however, and it was buffeted first one way, then another, then another – tossed between waves formed not from any lateral force, but from one directly below. For several minutes the water-boatman weathered the storm in ignorance, but with great skill. Then, as suddenly as the disturbance had begun, it subsided.

Half a mile away, a white butterfly slalomed along a row of cottonwoods and eventually alighted on a honeysuckle flower. The honeysuckle was the most common bush now in these parts and, for several weeks every year during flowering, gave the island a distinct creamy glow. This day, the honeysuckle flowers were probably at the height of their beauty.

It seemed only fitting that Eydos should be buried in her best clothes.

The butterfly took to the air again, fluttered about for several seconds, then landed on another flower. As the insect's legs came into contact with the flower's sepals, Lonnie Pilot's 'spam' exploded.

With a shockwave that felled dead trees as far away as Brittany, half a million cubic miles of igneous rock figuratively rolled over in bed, first rising twenty to thirty metres, then dropping between two hundred and a thousand metres, pulling the blanket of the Atlantic Ocean over its shoulders as it did so. Blasius Fjord, once a turbidity canyon, and soon to be one again, simultaneously opened at the seams on the upward movement, then ground closed again on the downward.

The mollusk was ripped from its home on the rock and sucked down to a fatal depth by the sinking island, as were thousands of seals, field mice, wild sheep and fledgling gannets.

The white butterfly, its entire world pulled from under its legs, flew in circles for the rest of its life before waltzing dead into the boiling sea below.

Three hundred and eight years after her birth, Eydos returned once again to her resting place under the sea. Seven minutes was all it took.

Lonnie Pilot and Macushla Mara were long gone. And the outside world bore no resemblance to the one they had left. Civilization had achieved what destiny had prescribed it from the fashioning of the very first tool.

Among the flotsam and jetsam, the feathers and the broken branches left by the island, five ancient flatdeck barges, one with a partial aircraft fuselage on its deck, tossed heavily for several minutes before sinking – their rusted, holed hulls unable to repel the churning seas around them.

Several miles to the southwest, three egg-shaped lifepods in various states of deterioration were also fighting the maelstrom's attempts to suck them down. Then, forty minutes after the epileptic sea had flattened, something else happened… The wheel on the hatch of one of the pods began to rotate slowly anticlockwise.

Acknowledgements

Many thanks to my wife, Melinda, and Diane Johnstone *(writersbestfriend.com)* for their constructive criticism and encouragement; to Jo Harrison *(ebook-formatting.co.uk)* for her formatting skills and advice; and to T.J. Miles and Ryan Ashcroft *(loveyourcovers.com)* for the cover artwork.

About the Author

Chris James was born in Manhattan and lived in Tucson, Arizona, and Chicago before moving to England at the age of 18. He has worked as an advertising copywriter, newspaper cartoonist, environmental activist, animator and award-winning filmmaker (YouTube Channel: *chrisjames60)*. He's married and lives in Penzance, Cornwall.

Website: *chrisjamesbooks.com*

Blog: *chrisjameswriterartist.tumblr.com*

6934794R00218

Printed in Great Britain
by Amazon.co.uk, Ltd.,
Marston Gate.